haunts

haunts

Reliquaries of
the Dead

Edited by
Stephen Jones

Ulysses Press

For full copyright information see pages vii–viii

Published in the United States by
ULYSSES PRESS
P.O. Box 3440
Berkeley, CA 94703
www.ulyssespress.com

ISBN 978-1-56975-984-4
Library of Congress Control Number 2011926024

Printed in the United States by Bang Printing

10 9 8 7 6 5 4 3 2 1

Acquisitions Editor: Keith Riegert
Managing Editor: Claire Chun
Copyeditor: Barbara Schultz
Editorial and production: Abigail Reser, Judith Metzener
Cover design: what!design @ whatweb.com
Cover artwork: classic chair in room © Anterovium/fotolia;
    girl © Ivan Bliznetsov/fotolia.com
Interior artwork: girl © Ivan Bliznetsov/fotolia.com;
    skulls © bukhavets/istockphoto.com

Distributed by Publishers Group West

For
RICHARD DALBY
—who knows this stuff
better than anyone else!

Contents

Acknowledgments

Special thanks to Keith Riegert and the staff of Ulysses Press, Linda Smith, Katie Grimm, Susan Ramer, Jerad Walters, James R. Wagner and, as always, Dorothy Lumley and all the contributors, for giving this book a ghost of a chance . . .

Introduction
The Restless Dead

SOMETIMES THE DEAD are restless. Sometimes they come back.

Ghosts, phantoms, revenants, lost souls—call them what you will—but sometimes the dead are anchored to our world by something that will not let their essence pass over until their needs have been fulfilled.

Sometimes, when life is gone, and before the spirit moves across to whatever lies beyond, *something* lingers on . . .

—in a person . . .

—in a specific location or structure . . .

—in a piece of clothing . . .

—maybe in an item as small or insignificant as a pen . . .

—perhaps even a human heart . . .

—or even a sliver of bone.

The twenty-five ghostly contributions to this anthology range from the classic "A Warning to the Curious" by M. R. James—who practically invented the "cursed reliquary" story—through some of my favorite supernatural stories about haunted people and places from the past four decades, to ten original tales about the restless dead that were especially written for this book by some of the most talented authors working in the genre today.

Sometimes the dead want answers, or have unfinished business this side of the veil. Their spirits cannot rest until they have accomplished what they failed to achieve while they were still alive.

Sometimes these needs are motivated by love . . . or loss . . . or even guilt. And sometimes they are driven by much stronger emotions.

Sometimes they simply want *revenge*.

Sometimes the dead come back, and perhaps they are attracted to something as simple as a book . . .

Maybe even the very volume that you are holding in your hands right now.

And that is when you really need to be afraid . . .

—Stephen Jones
London, England
June 2011

The Revenant

RICHARD L. TIERNEY

RICHARD L. TIERNEY lives in his house, "The Hermitage," in Mason City, Iowa. He has a degree in entomology from Iowa State University and worked with the U.S. Forestry Service for many years. An editor, poet, and critic, his seminal essay, "The Derleth Mythos," is considered a cornerstone of modern Lovecraftian criticism.

A great admirer of the writings of Robert E. Howard, Tierney edited *Tigers of the Sea* and *Hawks of Outremer* for publisher Donald M. Grant, completing a few unfinished tales in the process.

His novels include *The Winds of Zar*, the Bran Mak Morn pastiche *For the Witch of the Mists* (with David C. Smith), *The House of the Toad*, *The Scroll of Thoth: Simon Magus and the Great Old Ones*, *The Gardens of Lucullus* (with Glenn Rahman), *The Drums of Chaos*, and six Red Sonja books (1981–83), also in collaboration with Smith.

Tierney's influences include Edgar Allan Poe, H. P. Lovecraft, Donald Wandrei, Robert E. Howard, and Frank Belknap Long. His poetry has been collected in *Dreams and Damnations*, *The Doom Prophet and One Other*, the Arkham House volume of *Collected Poems: Nightmares and Visions*, *The Blob That Gobbled Abdul and Other Poems and Songs*, and *Savage Menace and Other Poems of Horror*.

S. T. Joshi has described Tierney as "one of the leading weird poets of his generation."

(From the French of Charles Baudelaire)

LIKE A DARK ANGEL, feral-eyed,
I will return and softly glide
Into the silence of your room,
Wrapped in the shadows of night's gloom.

And you I'll give, my sweet delight,
Kisses cold as the moon's cold light
And chill caresses like the crawl
Of snakes around a pit's dank wall.

You'll find, when comes the livid dawn,
The vacant place I've lain upon
Where a strange cold shall bide till night.

Though some by love and tenderness
Would rule your youth and zestfulness,
Me, I would seize your soul by fright.

A Warning to the Curious

M. R. JAMES

MONTAGUE RHODES JAMES (1862–1936) was Provost of King's College, Cambridge, and Eton. Most of his ghost stories were occasional pieces, written for friends or college magazines, and were collected in *Ghost Stories of an Antiquary* (1904), *More Ghost Stories of an Antiquary* (1911), *A Thin Ghost and Others* (1919), and *A Warning to the Curious and Other Ghost Stories* (1925).

Widely regarded as one of the finest authors of supernatural fiction in the English language, James is credited as the originator of the "antiquarian ghost story," replacing the Gothic horrors of the previous century with more contemporary settings for his subtle hauntings.

Many of his stories were originally written as Christmas entertainments and were read aloud by the author to selected gatherings of friends.

"A Warning to the Curious" has twice been adapted for television—first in 1972 for a BBC dramatization starring Peter Vaughn and Clive Swift, and then again in 2000 for the same network's *Ghost Stories for Christmas*, in which Christopher Lee portrayed the author. More recently, actor Alex Jennings read the story on BBC Radio 3 in June 2011.

According to James, the ghost story should "put the reader into the position of saying to himself: 'If I'm not careful, something of this kind may happen to me!' Two ingredients most valuable in the concocting of a ghost story are, to me, the atmosphere and the nicely managed crescendo . . . Let us, then, be introduced to the actors in a placid way; let us see them going about their ordinary business, undisturbed by forebodings, pleased with their surroundings; and into this calm environment let the ominous thing put out its head, unobtrusively at first, and then more insistently, until it holds the stage.

"Another requisite, in my opinion, is that the ghost should be malevolent or odious: amiable and helpful apparitions are all very well in fairy tales or in local legends, but I have no use for them in a fictitious ghost story."

The classic tale that follows could stand as the prototype for every "cursed object" story that has appeared since it was first published in *The London Mercury* in 1925 . . .

THE PLACE ON THE EAST COAST which the reader is asked to consider is Seaburgh. It is not very different now from what I remember it to have been when I was a child. Marshes intersected by dykes to the south, recalling the early chapters of *Great Expectations*; flat fields to the north, merging into heath; heath, fir woods, and, above all, gorse, inland. A long seafront and a street: behind that a spacious church of flint, with a broad, solid western tower and a peal of six bells. How well I remember their sound on a hot Sunday in August, as our party went slowly up the white, dusty slope of road towards them, for the church stands at the top of a short, steep incline. They rang with a flat clacking sort of sound on those hot days, but when the air was softer they were mellower too. The railway ran down to its little terminus farther along the same road. There was a gay white windmill just before you came to the station, and another down near the shingle at the south end the town, and yet others on higher ground to the north. There were cottages of bright red brick with slate roofs . . . but why do I encumber you with these commonplace details? The fact is that they come crowding to the point of the pencil when it begins to write of Seaburgh. I should like to be sure that I had allowed the right ones to get onto the paper. But I forgot. I have not quite done with the word-painting business yet.

Walk away from the sea and the town, pass the station, and turn up the road on the right. It is a sandy road, parallel with the railway, and if you follow it, it climbs to somewhat higher ground. On your left (you are now going northward) is heath, on your right (the side towards the sea) is a belt of old firs, wind-beaten, thick at the top, with the slope that old seaside trees have; seen on the skyline from the train they would tell you in an instant, if you did not know it, that you were approaching a windy coast. Well, at the top of my little hill, a line of these firs strikes out and runs towards the sea, for there is a ridge that goes that way; and the ridge ends in a rather well defined mound commanding the level fields of rough grass, and a little knot of fir trees crowns it. And here you may sit on a hot spring day, very well content to look at blue sea, white windmills, red cottages, bright green grass, church tower, and distant martello tower on the south.

As I have said, I began to know Seaburgh as a child; but a gap of a good many years separates my early knowledge from that which is more recent. Still it keeps its place in my affections, and any tales of it that I pick up have an interest for me. One such tale is this: it came to me in a place very remote from Seaburgh, and quite accidentally, from a man whom I had been able to oblige—enough in his opinion to justify his making me his confidant to this extent.

I know all that country more or less (he said). I used to go to Seaburgh pretty regularly for golf in the spring. I generally put up at The Bear, with a friend—Henry Long it was, you knew him perhaps—("Slightly," I said) and we used to take a sitting room and be very happy there. Since he died I haven't cared to go there. And I don't know that I should anyhow after the particular thing that happened on our last visit.

It was in April 19—, we were there, and by some chance we were almost the only people in the hotel. So the ordinary public rooms were practically empty, and we were the more surprised when, after dinner, our sitting-room door opened, and a young man put his head in. We were aware of this young man. He was rather a rabbity anemic subject—light hair and light eyes—but not unpleasing. So when he said: "I beg your pardon, is this a private room?" we did not growl and say: "Yes, it is," but Long said, or I did—no matter which: "Please come in." "Oh, may I?" he said, and seemed relieved. Of course it was obvious that he wanted company; and as he was a reasonable kind of person—not the sort to bestow his whole family history on you—we urged him to make himself at home. "I dare say you find the other rooms rather bleak," I said. Yes, he did: but it was really too good of us, and so on. That being got over, he made some pretence of reading a book. Long was playing Patience, I was writing. It became plain to me after a few minutes that this visitor of ours was in rather a state of fidgets or nerves, which communicated itself to me, and so I put away my writing and turned to engaging him in talk.

After some remarks, which I forget, he became rather confidential. "You'll think it very odd of me" (this was the sort of way he began), "but the fact is I've had something of a shock." Well, I recommended a drink of some cheering kind, and we had it. The waiter coming in made an interruption (and I thought our young man seemed very jumpy when the door opened), but after a while he got back to his woes again. There was nobody he knew in the place, and he did happen to know who we both were (it turned out there was some common acquaintance in town), and really he did want a word of advice, if we didn't mind. Of course, we both said: "By all means," or "Not at all," and Long put away his cards. And we settled down to hear what his difficulty was.

"It began," he said, "more than a week ago, when I bicycled over to Froston, only about five or six miles, to see the church; I'm very much interested in architecture, "and it's got one of those pretty porches with niches and shields. I took a photograph of it, and then an old man who was tidying up in the churchyard came and asked if I'd care to look into the church. I said yes, and he produced a key and let me in. There wasn't much inside, but I told him it was a nice little church, and he kept it very clean, 'but,' I said, 'the porch is the best part of it.' We were just outside the porch then, and he said, 'Ah, yes, that is a nice porch; and do you know, sir, what's the meanin' of that coat of arms there?'

"It was the one with the three crowns, and though I'm not much of a herald, I was able to say yes, I thought it was the old arms of the kingdom of East Anglia.

"'That's right, sir,' he said, 'and do you know the meanin' of them three crowns that's on it?'

"I said I'd no doubt it was known, but I couldn't recollect to have heard it myself.

"'Well, then,' he said, 'for all you're a scholared, I can tell you something you don't know. Them's the three 'oly crowns what was buried in the ground nearby the coast to keep the Germans from landing—ah, I can see you don't believe that. But I tell you, if it hadn't have been for one of them 'oly crowns bein' there still, them Germans would a landed here time and again, they would. Landed with their ships, and killed man, woman, and child in their beds. Now then, that's the truth what I'm telling you, that is; and if you don't believe me, you ast the rector. There he comes: you ast him, I says.'

"I looked 'round, and there was the rector, a nice-looking old man, coming up the path; and before I could begin assuring my old man, who was getting quite excited, that I didn't disbelieve him, the rector struck in, and said: 'What's all this about, John? Good day to you, sir. Have you been looking at our little church?'

"So then there was a little talk which allowed the old man to calm down, and then the rector asked him again what was the matter.

"'Oh,' he said, 'it warn't nothink, only I was telling this gentleman he'd ought to ast you about them 'oly crowns.'

"'Ah, yes, to be sure,' said the rector, 'that's a very curious matter, isn't it? But I don't know whether the gentleman is interested in our old stories, eh?'

"'Oh, he'll be interested fast enough,' says the old man, 'he'll put his confidence in what you tells him, sir; why, you known William Ager yourself, father and son too.'

"Then I put in a word to say how much I should like to hear all about it, and before many minutes I was walking up the village street with the rector, who had one or two words to say to parishioners, and then to the rectory, where he took me into his study. He had made out, on the way, that I really was capable of taking an intelligent interest in a piece of folklore, and not quite the ordinary tripper. So he was very willing to talk, and it is rather surprising to me that the particular legend he told me has not made its way into print before. His account of it was this: 'There has always been a belief in these parts in the three holy crowns. The old people say they were buried in different places near the coast to keep off the Danes or the French or the Germans. And they say that one of the three was dug up a long time ago, and another has disappeared by the encroaching of the sea, and one's still left doing its work, keeping off invaders. Well, now, if you have read the ordinary guides and histories of this county, you will remember perhaps that in 1687 a crown, which was said to be the crown of Redwald, King of the East Angles, was dug up at Rendlesham, and alas! alas! melted down before it was even properly described or drawn. Well, Rendlesham isn't on the coast, but it isn't so very far inland, and it's on a very important line of access. And I believe that is the crown which the people mean when they say that one has been dug up. Then on the south you don't want me to tell you where there was a Saxon royal palace which is now under the sea, eh? Well, there was the second crown, I take it. And up beyond these two, they say, lies the third.'

"'Do they say where it is?' of course I asked.

"He said, 'Yes, indeed, they do, but they don't tell,' and his manner did not encourage me to put the obvious question. Instead of that I waited a moment, and said: 'What did the old man mean when he said you knew William Ager, as if that had something to do with the crowns?'

"'To be sure,' he said, 'now that's another curious story. These Agers—it's a very old name in these parts, but I can't find that they were ever people of quality or big owners—these Agers say, or said, that their branch of the family were the guardians of the last crown. A certain old Nathaniel Ager was the first one I knew—I was born and brought up quite near here—and he, I believe, camped out at the place during the whole of the war of 1870. William, his son, did the same, I know, during the South African War. And young William, *his* son, who has only died fairly recently, took lodgings at the cottage nearest the spot, and I've no doubt hastened his end, for he was a consumptive, by exposure and night watching. And he was the last of that branch. It was a dreadful grief to him to think that he was the last, but he could do nothing, the only relations at all near to him were in the colonies. I wrote letters for him to them imploring them to come over on business very important to the family, but there has been no answer. So the last of the holy crowns, if it's there, has no guardian now.'

"That was what the rector told me, and you can fancy how interesting I found it. The only thing I could think of when I left him was how to hit upon the spot where the crown was supposed to be. I wish I'd left it alone.

"But there was a sort of fate in it, for as I bicycled back past the churchyard wall my eye caught a fairly new gravestone, and on it was the name of William Ager. Of course, I got off and read it. It said OF THIS PARISH, DIED AT SEABURGH, 19—, AGED 28. There it was, you see. A little judicious questioning in the right place, and I should at least find the cottage nearest the spot. Only I didn't quite know what was the right place to begin my questioning. Again there was fate: it took me to the curiosity shop down that way—you know—and I turned over some old books, and, if you please, one was a prayer book of 1740 odd, in a rather handsome binding—I'll just go and get it, it's in my room."

He left us in a state of some surprise, but we had hardly time to exchange any remarks when he was back, panting, and handed us the book opened at the flyleaf, on which was, in a straggly hand:

> Nathaniel Ager is my name and England is my
>   nation,
> Seaburgh is my dwelling place and Christ is my
>   Salvation,
> When I am dead and in my Grave, and all my
>   bones are rotton,
> I hope the lord will think on me when I am quite
>   forgotton.

This poem was dated 1754, and there were many more entries of Agers, Nathaniel, Frederick, William, and so on, ending with William, 19—.

"You see," he said, "anybody would call it the greatest bit of luck. I did, but I don't now. Of course I asked the shop man about William Ager, and of course he happened to remember that he lodged in a cottage in the North Field and died there. This was just chalking the road for me. I knew which the cottage must be: there is only one sizable one about there. The next thing was to scrape some sort of acquaintance with the people, and I took a walk that way at once. A dog did the business for me: he made at me so fiercely that they had to run out and beat him off, and then naturally begged my pardon, and we got into talk. I had only to bring up Ager's name, and pretend I knew, or thought I knew something of him, and then the woman said how sad it was him dying so young, and she was sure it came of him spending the night out of doors in the cold weather. Then I had to say: 'Did he go out on the sea at night?' and she said: 'Oh, no, it was on the hillock yonder with the trees on it.' And there I was.

"I know something about digging in these barrows: I've opened many of them in the down country. But that was with owner's leave, and in broad daylight and with men to help. I had to prospect very carefully here before I put a spade in: I couldn't trench across the mound, and with those old firs growing there I knew there would be awkward tree roots. Still the soil was very light and sandy and easy, and there was a rabbit hole or so that might be developed into a sort of tunnel. The going out and coming back at odd hours to the hotel was going to be the awkward part. When I made up my mind about the way to excavate, I told the people that I was called away for a night, and I spent it out there. I made my tunnel: I won't bore you with the details of how I supported it and filled it in when I'd done, but the main thing is that I got the crown."

Naturally we both broke out into exclamations of surprise and interest. I for one had long known about the finding of the crown at Rendlesham and had often lamented its fate. No one has ever seen an Anglo-Saxon crown—at least no one had. But our man gazed at us with a rueful eye. "Yes," he said, "and the worst of it is I don't know how to put it back."

"Put it back?" we cried out. "Why, my dear sir, you've made one of the most exciting finds ever heard of in this country. Of course, it ought to go to the Jewel House at the Tower. What's your difficulty? If you're thinking about the owner of the land, and treasure trove, and all that, we can certainly help you through. Nobody's going to make a fuss about technicalities in a case of this kind."

Probably more was said, but all he did was to put his face in his hands, and mutter: "I don't know how to put it back."

At last Long said: "You'll forgive me, I hope, if I seem impertinent, but are you *quite* sure you've got it?" I was wanting to ask much the same question myself, for of course the story did seem a lunatic's dream when one thought over it. But I hadn't quite dared to say what might hurt the poor young man's feelings. However, he took it quite calmly— really, with the calm of despair, you might say. He sat up and said: "Oh, yes, there's no doubt of that: I have it here, in my room, locked up in my bag. You can come and look at it if you like: I won't offer to bring it here."

We were not likely to let the chance slip. We went with him; his room was only a few doors off. The boots was just collecting shoes in the passage, or so we thought: afterwards we were not sure. Our visitor—his name was Paxton—was in a worse state of shivers than before, and went hurriedly into the room, and beckoned us after him, turned on the light, and shut the door carefully. Then he unlocked his kit bag and produced a bundle of clean pocket handkerchiefs in which something was wrapped, laid it on the bed, and undid it. I can now say I *have* seen an actual Anglo-Saxon crown. It was of silver— as the Rendlesham one is always said to have been—it was set with some gems, mostly antique intaglios and cameos, and was of rather plain, almost rough workmanship. In fact, it was like those you see on the coins and in the manuscripts. I found no reason to think it was later than the 9th century. I was intensely interested, of course, and I wanted to turn it over in my hands, but Paxton prevented me. "Don't *you* touch it," he said, "I'll do that." And with a sigh that was, I declare to you, dreadful to hear, he took it up and turned it about so that we could see every part of it. "Seen enough?" he said at last, and we nodded. He wrapped it up and locked it in his bag, and stood looking at us dumbly. "Come back to our room," Long said, "and tell us what the trouble is." He thanked us, and said: "Will you go first and see if— if the coast is clear?" That wasn't very intelligible, for our proceedings hadn't been, after all, very suspicious, and the hotel, as I said, was practically empty. However, we were beginning to have inklings of— we didn't know what, and anyhow nerves are infectious. So we did go, first peering out as we opened the door, and fancying (I found we both had the fancy) that a shadow, or more than a shadow—but it made no sound—passed from before us to one side as we came out into the passage. "It's all right," we whispered to Paxton—whispering seemed the proper tone—and we went, with him between us, back to our sitting room. I was preparing, when we got there, to be ecstatic about the unique interest of what we had seen, but when I looked at Paxton I saw that would be terribly out of place, and I left it to him to begin.

"What is to be done?" was his opening. Long thought it right (as he explained to me afterwards) to be obtuse, and said: "Why not find out who the owner of the land is, and inform—"

"Oh, no, no!" Paxton broke in impatiently, "I beg your pardon:

you've been very kind, but don't you see it's *got* to go back, and I daren't be there at night, and daytime's impossible. Perhaps, though, you don't see: well, then, the truth is that I've never been alone since I touched it."

I was beginning some fairly stupid comment, but Long caught my eye, and I stopped. Long said: "I think I do see, perhaps: but wouldn't it be—a relief—to tell us a little more clearly what the situation is?"

Then it all came out: Paxton looked over his shoulder and beckoned to us to come nearer to him, and began speaking in a low voice: we listened most intently, of course, and compared notes afterwards, and I wrote down our version, so I am confident I have what he told us almost word for word. He said: "It began when I was first prospecting, and put me off again and again. There was always somebody—a man—standing by one of the firs. This was in daylight, you know. He was never in front of me. I always saw him with the tail of my eye on the left or the right, and he was never there when I looked straight for him. I would lie down for quite a long time and take careful observations, and make sure there was no one, and then when I got up and began prospecting again, there he was. And he began to give me hints, besides; for wherever I put that prayer book—short of locking it up, which I did at last—when I came back to my room it was always out on my table open at the flyleaf where the names are, and one of my razors across it to keep it open. I'm sure he just can't open my bag, or something more would have happened. You see, he's light and weak, but all the same I daren't face him. Well, then, when I was making the tunnel, of course it was worse, and if I hadn't been so keen I should have dropped the whole thing and run. It was like someone scraping at my back all the time: I thought for a long time it was only soil dropping on me, but as I got nearer the—the crown, it was unmistakable. And when I actually laid it bare and got my fingers into the ring of it and pulled it out, there came a sort of cry behind me—oh, I can't tell you how desolate it was! And horribly threatening too. It spoilt all my pleasure in my find—cut it off that moment. And if I hadn't been the wretched fool I am, I should have put the thing back and left it. But I didn't. The rest of the time was just awful. I had hours to get through before I could decently come back to the hotel. First I spent time filling up my tunnel and covering my tracks, and all the while he was there trying to thwart me. Sometimes, you know, you see him, and sometimes you don't, just as he pleases, I think: he's there, but he has some power over your eyes. Well, I wasn't off the spot very long before sunrise, and then I had to get to the junction for Seaburgh, and take a train back. And though it was daylight fairly soon, I don't know if that made it much better. There were always hedges, or gorse bushes, or park fences along the road—some sort of cover, I mean—and I was never easy for a second. And then when I began to meet people going to work, they always looked behind me very strangely: it might have been that they were surprised at seeing anyone so early; but I didn't think it was only that, and I don't now: they didn't look exactly at me. And the porter at the train was like that too. And the guard held open the door after I'd got into the carriage—just as he would if there was somebody else coming, you know. Oh, you may be very sure it isn't my fancy," he said with a dull sort of laugh. Then he went on: "And even if I do get it put back, he won't forgive me: I can tell that. And I was so happy a fortnight ago." He dropped into a chair, and I believe he began to cry.

We didn't know what to say, but we felt we must come to the rescue somehow, and so—it really seemed the only thing—we said if he was so set on putting the crown back in its place, we would help him. And I must say that after what we had heard it did seem the right thing. If these horrid consequences had come on this poor man, might there not really be something in the original idea of the crown having some curious power bound up with it, to guard the coast? At least, that was my feeling, and I think it was Long's too. Our offer was very welcome to Paxton, anyhow. When could we do it? It was nearing half past ten. Could we contrive to make a late walk plausible to the hotel people that very night? We looked out of the window: there was a brilliant full moon—the paschal moon. Long undertook to tackle the boots and propitiate him. He was to say that we should not be much over the hour, and if we did find it so pleasant that we stopped out a bit longer we would see that he didn't lose by sitting up. Well, we were pretty regular customers of the hotel, and did not give much trouble, and were considered by the servants to be not under the mark in the way of tips; and so the boots *was* propitiated, and let us out onto the seafront, and remained, as we heard later, looking after us. Paxton had a large coat over his arm, under which was the wrapped-up crown.

So we were off on this strange errand before we had time to think how very much out of the way it was. I have told this part quite shortly on purpose, for it really does represent the haste with which we settled our plan and took action. "The shortest way is up the hill and through the churchyard," Paxton said, as we stood a moment before the hotel looking up and down the front. There was nobody about—nobody at all. Seaburgh out of the season is an early, quiet place. "We can't go along the dyke by the cottage, because of the dog," Paxton also said, when I pointed to what I thought a shorter way along the front and across two fields. The reason he gave was good enough. We went up the road to the church, and turned in at the churchyard gate. I confess to having thought that there might be some lying there who might be conscious of our business: but if it was so, they were also conscious that one who was on their side, so to say, had us under surveillance, and we saw no sign of them. But under observation we felt we were, as I have never felt it at another time. Specially was it so when we passed out of the churchyard into a narrow path with close, high hedges, through which we hurried as Christian did through that Valley; and so got out into open fields. Then along hedges, though I would sooner have been in the open, where I could see if anyone was visible behind me; over a gate or two, and then a swerve to the left, taking us up onto the ridge, which ended in that mound.

As we neared it, Henry Long felt, and I felt too, that there were what I can only call dim presences waiting for us, as well as a far more actual one attending us. Of Paxton's agitation all this time I can give you no adequate picture: he breathed like a hunted beast, and we could not either of us look at his face. How he would manage when we got to the very place, we had not troubled to think: he had seemed so sure that that would not be difficult. Nor was it. I never saw anything like the dash with which he flung himself at a particular spot in the side of the mound, and tore at it, so that in a very few minutes the greater part of his body was out of sight. We stood holding the coat and that bundle of handkerchiefs, and looking, very fearfully, I must admit, about us. There was nothing to be seen: a line of dark firs behind us made one skyline, more trees and the church tower half a mile off on the right, cottages and a windmill on the horizon on the left, calm sea dead in front, faint barking of a dog at a cottage on a gleaming dyke between us and it: full moon making that path we know across the sea: the eternal whisper of the Scotch firs just above us, and of the sea in front. Yet, in all this quiet, an acute, an acrid consciousness of a restrained hostility very near us, like a dog on a leash that might be let go at any moment.

Paxton pulled himself out of the hole and stretched a hand back to us. "Give it to me," he whispered, "unwrapped." We pulled off the handkerchiefs, and he took the crown. The moonlight just fell on it as he snatched it. We had not ourselves touched that bit of metal, and I have thought since that it was just as well. In another moment Paxton was out of the hole again and busy shoveling back the soil with hands that were already bleeding. He would have none of our help, though. It was much the longest part of the job to get the place to look undisturbed: yet—I don't know how—he made a wonderful success of it. At last he was satisfied and we turned back.

We were a couple of hundred yards from the hill when Long suddenly said to him: "I say, you've left your coat there. That won't do. See?" And I certainly did see it—the long dark overcoat lying where the tunnel had been. Paxton had not stopped, however: he only shook his head, and held up the coat on his arm. And when we joined him, he said, without any excitement, but as if nothing mattered any more:

"That wasn't my coat." And, indeed, when we looked back again, that dark thing was not to be seen.

Well, we got out on to the road, and came rapidly back that way. It was well before twelve when we got in, trying to put a good face on it, and saying—Long and I—what a lovely night it was for a walk. The boots was on the lookout for us, and we made remarks like that for his edification as we entered the hotel. He gave another look up and down the seafront before he locked the front door, and said: "You didn't meet many people about, I s'pose, sir?" "No, indeed, not a soul," I said; at which I remember Paxton looked oddly at me. "Only I thought I see someone turn up the station road after you gentlemen," said the boots. "Still, you was three together, and I don't suppose he meant mischief." I didn't know what to say; Long merely said, "Good night," and we went off upstairs, promising to turn off all lights, and to go to bed in a few minutes.

Back in our room, we did our very best to make Paxton take a cheerful view. "There's the crown safe back," we said; "very likely you'd have done better not to touch it" (and he heavily assented to that), "but no real harm has been done, and we shall never give this away to anyone who would be so mad as to go near it. Besides, don't you feel better yourself? I don't mind confessing," I said, "that on the way there I was very much inclined to take your view about—well, about being followed; but going back, it wasn't at all the same thing, was it?" No, it wouldn't do: "You've nothing to trouble yourselves about," he said, "but I'm not forgiven. I've got to pay for that miserable sacrilege still. I know what you are going to say. The Church might help. Yes, but it's the body that has to suffer. It's true I'm not feeling that he's waiting outside for me just now. But—" Then he stopped. Then he turned to thanking us, and we put him off as soon as we could. And naturally we pressed him to use our sitting room next day, and said we should be glad to go out with him. Or did he play golf, perhaps? Yes, he did, but he didn't think he should care about that tomorrow. Well, we recommended him to get up late and sit in our room in the morning while we were playing, and we would have a walk later in the day. He was very submissive and piano about it all: ready to do just what we thought best, but clearly quite certain in his own mind that what was coming could not be averted or palliated. You'll wonder why we didn't insist on accompanying him to his home and seeing him safe into the care of brothers or someone. The fact was he had nobody. He had had a flat in town, but lately he had made up his mind to settle for a time in Sweden, and he had dismantled his flat and shipped off his belongings, and was whiling away a fortnight or three weeks before he made a start. Anyhow, we didn't see what we could do better than sleep on it—or not sleep very much, as was my case—and see what we felt like tomorrow morning.

We felt very different, Long and I, on as beautiful an April morning as you could desire; and Paxton also looked very different when we saw him at breakfast. "The first approach to a decent night I seem ever to have had," was what he said. But he was going to do as we had settled: stay in probably all the morning, and come out with us later. We went to the links; we met some other men and played with them in the morning, and had lunch there rather early, so as not to be late back. All the same, the snares of death overtook him.

Whether it could have been prevented, I don't know. I think he would have been got at somehow, do what we might. Anyhow, this is what happened.

We went straight up to our room. Paxton was there, reading quite peaceably. "Ready to come out shortly?" said Long. "Say in half an hour's time?" "Certainly," he said: and I said we would change first, and perhaps have baths, and call for him in half an hour. I had my bath first, and went and lay down on my bed, and slept for about ten minutes. We came out of our rooms at the same time, and went together to the sitting room. Paxton wasn't there—only his book. Nor was he in his room, nor in the downstairs rooms. We shouted for him. A servant came out and said: "Why, I thought you gentlemen was gone out already, and so did the other gentleman. He heard you a-calling from the path there, and run out in a hurry, and I looked out of the coffee-room window, but I didn't see you. 'Owever, he run off down the beach that way."

Without a word we ran that way too—it was the opposite direction to that of last night's expedition. It wasn't quite four o'clock, and the day was fair, though not so fair as it had been, so that was really no reason, you'd say, for anxiety: with people about, surely a man couldn't come to much harm.

But something in our look as we ran out must have struck the servant, for she came out on the steps, and pointed, and said, "Yes, that's the way he went." We ran on as far as the top of the shingle bank, and there pulled up. There was a choice of ways: past the houses on the seafront, or along the sand at the bottom of the beach, which, the tide being now out, was fairly broad. Or of course we might keep along the shingle between these two tracks and have some view of both of them; only that was heavy going. We chose the sand, for that was the loneliest, and someone *might* come to harm there without being seen from the public path.

Long said he saw Paxton some distance ahead, running and waving his stick, as if he wanted to signal to people who were on ahead of him. I couldn't be sure: one of these sea mists was coming up very quickly from the south. There was someone, that's all I could say. And there were tracks on the sand as of someone running who wore shoes; and there were other tracks made before those—for the shoes sometimes trod in them and interfered with them—of someone not in shoes. Oh, of course, it's only my word you've got to take for all this: Long's dead, we'd no time or means to make sketches or take casts, and the next tide washed everything away. All we could do was to notice these marks as we hurried on. But there they were over and over again, and we had no doubt whatever that what we saw was the track of a bare foot, and one that showed more bones than flesh.

The notion of Paxton running after—after anything like this, and supposing it to be the friends he was looking for, was very dreadful to us. You can guess what we fancied: how the thing he was following might stop suddenly and turn round on him, and what sort of face it would show, half-seen at first in the mist—which all the while was getting thicker and thicker. And as I ran on wondering how the poor wretch could have been lured into mistaking that other thing for us, I remembered his saying, "He has some power over your eyes." And then I wondered what the end would be, for I had no hope now that the end could be averted, and—well, there is no need to tell all the dismal and horrid thoughts that flitted through my head as we ran on into the mist. It was uncanny, too, that the sun should still be bright in the sky and we could see nothing. We could only tell that we were now past the houses and had reached that gap there is between them and the old martello tower. When you are past the tower, you know, there is nothing but shingle for a long way—not a house, not a human creature, just that spit of land, or rather shingle, with the river on your right and the sea on your left.

But just before that, just by the martello tower, you remember there is the old battery, close to the sea. I believe there are only a few blocks of concrete left now: the rest has all been washed away, but at this time there was a lot more, though the place was a ruin. Well, when we got there, we clambered to the top as quick as we could to take breath and look over the shingle in front if by chance the mist would let us see anything. But a moment's rest we must have. We had run a mile at least. Nothing whatever was visible ahead of us, and we were just turning by common consent to get down and run hopelessly on, when we heard what I can only call a laugh: and if you can understand what I mean by a breathless, a lungless laugh, you have it: but I don't suppose you can. It came from below, and swerved away into the mist. That was enough. We bent over the wall. Paxton was there at the bottom.

You don't need to be told that he was dead. His tracks showed that he had run along the side of the battery, had turned sharp round the corner of it, and, small doubt of it, must have dashed straight into the open arms of someone who was waiting there. His mouth was full of sand and stones, and his teeth and jaws were broken to bits. I only glanced once at his face.

At the same moment, just as we were scrambling down from the battery to get to the body, we heard a shout, and saw a man running down the bank of the martello tower. He was the caretaker stationed there, and his keen old eyes had managed to descry through the mist that something was wrong. He had seen Paxton fall, and had seen us a moment after, running up—fortunate this, for otherwise we could hardly have escaped suspicion of being concerned in the dreadful business. Had he, we asked, caught sight of anybody attacking our friend? He could not be sure.

We sent him off for help, and stayed by the dead man till they came with the stretcher. It was then that we traced out how he had come, on the narrow fringe of sand under the battery wall. The rest was shingle, and it was hopelessly impossible to tell whither the other had gone.

What were we to say at the inquest? It was a duty, we felt, not to give up, there and then, the secret of the crown, to be published in every paper. I don't know how much you would have told; but what we did agree upon was this: to say that we had only made acquaintance with Paxton the day before, and that he had told us he was under some apprehension of danger at the hands of a man called William Ager. Also that we had seen some other tracks besides Paxton's when we followed him along the beach. But of course by that time everything was gone from the sands.

No one had any knowledge, fortunately, of any William Ager living in the district. The evidence of the man at the martello tower freed us from all suspicion. All that could be done was to return a verdict of willful murder by some person or persons unknown.

Paxton was so totally without connections that all the inquiries that were subsequently made ended in a dead end. And I have never been at Seaburgh, or even near it, since.

The Door

R. CHETWYND-HAYES

RONALD CHETWYND-HAYES (1919–2001) was born in Isleworth, West London. Known as "Britain's Prince of Chill," in 1989 he was presented with Life Achievement Awards by both the Horror Writers Association and the British Fantasy Society.

Chetwynd-Hayes's first book was *The Man from the Bomb*, a science fiction novel published in 1959 by Badger Books. His subsequent novels include *The Dark Man* (aka *And Love Survived*), *The Brats*, *The Partaker: A Novel of Fantasy*, *The King's Ghost*, *The Curse of the Snake God*, *Kepple*, *The Psychic Detective*, and *World of the Impossible*, while his short fiction has been collected in *The Unbidden, Cold Terror, The Elemental, Terror by Night, The Night Ghouls, The Monster Club, A Quiver of Ghosts, Tales from the Dark Lands, The House of Dracula, Dracula's Children, Shudders and Shivers, The Vampire Stories of R. Chetwynd-Hayes* (aka *Looking for Something to Suck*), *Phantoms and Fiends*, and *Frights and Fancies*, among other titles.

In 1976, Chetwynd-Hayes ghost-edited and wrote almost all of the material in the one-shot magazine *Ghoul*. He also edited the anthologies *Cornish Tales of Terror, Scottish Tales of Terror* (as Angus Campbell), *Welsh Tales of Terror, Tales of Terror from Outer Space, Gaslight Tales of Terror, Doomed to the Night, Great Ghost Stories* and *Tales to Freeze the Blood: More Great Ghost Stories* (both with Stephen Jones), along with twelve volumes of *The Fontana Book of Great Ghost Stories*, and six volumes of the Armada Monster Book series for children.

The author of two movie novelizations, *Dominique* and *The Awakening* (the latter based on Bram Stoker's *The Jewel of Seven Stars*), Chetwynd-Hayes's own stories have been adapted for radio, TV, and film, including *The Monster Club*, in which the author was portrayed by veteran actor John Carradine.

"The Door" was one of five of the author's stories used in the 1973 portmanteau film *From Beyond the Grave*, which featured Ian Ogilvy and Jack Watson. "It was a lovely idea," Chetwynd-Hayes recalled. "The dialogue was all mine, and Lesley Anne Down made a very attractive appearance."

"WHY A DOOR?" Rosemary asked. "I mean to say, the house has a full complement of perfectly satisfactory doors."

William continued to run his hands over his latest acquisition, his eyes alight with that glow of pure pleasure that is peculiar to the ardent collector.

"I liked it," he explained, "besides it is very old. Three hundred years, if a day."

"But it doesn't match the paintwork or anything," Rosemary protested, "and it's so heavy."

She was right, of course. The door was massive; made of solid walnut, fully four feet wide and seven feet high, the panels embossed with an intricate pattern that seemed to grow more complicated the longer it was examined. It had a great tarnished brass knob on the left side, and four butt hinges on the right.

"What are you going to do with it?" Rosemary asked after a while. "Hang it on the wall?"

"Don't be so silly." William tapped the panels with his knuckles. "I'm going to put it to its proper use. You know that cupboard in my study? Well, it's dead center in the wall opposite my desk; I'll get the builders to take away the old door, enlarge the aperture, and hang this one in its place."

"A great thing like that as a cupboard door!" Rosemary gasped.

"Then," William went on, "I'll hang a large 16th-century print on either side, a couple of crossed swords over the top, and the result should be pretty impressive."

"Like a museum," Rosemary observed.

"It will inspire me," William nodded slowly, and Rosemary, with a woman's inconsistency thought he looked very sweet. "It must be

French polished of course, and the lock burnished and then lacquered."

"Where did you find it?" Rosemary asked.

"At Murray's. You know, the demolition people. Old Murray said it came from a 16th-century manor house he knocked down last year. I can't wait to see the door in position, can you?"

"No," Rosemary said doubtfully, "no, I can hardly wait."

The builders made an awful mess, as she knew they would, but when the job was finished, and of course the study had to be completely redecorated, the effect was certainly very impressive. The entire wall was covered with red wallpaper, and in the exact center was the door, now resplendent with polish, the brass knob and hinges gleaming like gold, giving the impression that behind must lie a gracious drawing room instead of an eighteen-inches-deep stationery cupboard. On either side hung a Rembrandt print, each one housed in a magnificent gilt frame, and over the door were two crossed sabers with shining brass hilts. William sat behind his desk, his face wearing the look of a man well satisfied with the world and all it contained.

"Wonderful," he breathed, "absolutely marvelous."

"Well, as long as you're satisfied." Rosemary frowned, and puckered her lips into an expression of faint distaste. "Frankly I'm not certain I like it."

"What!" William scowled his displeasure. He liked people to share his enthusiasm. "What's wrong with it?"

"It looks very nice and original," Rosemary admitted, "but somehow . . ." she paused . . . "it's rather creepy."

"What utter rot."

"Yes, I suppose it must sound that way, but I can't help wondering what lies behind."

"What lies . . .!" William stared at his wife with growing amazement. "You know what lies behind, an ordinary stationery cupboard."

"Yes, I know, and you don't have to shout at me. I keep telling myself it is only a door and behind is a shallow cupboard lined with shelves, but I can't really believe it. I mean, cupboards don't have grand doors like that, they have cheap ply-paneled ones covered with layers and layers of old paint, and they're sort of humble. If they could talk, they'd say: 'I'm a cupboard door, and I don't pretend to be anything else.' But that thing . . ." She jerked her head in the direction of the large door. "That wouldn't say anything. Just stare at you and wait to be opened by a butler."

"What an imagination," William pointed to his typewriter, "you ought to be doing my job. But you're right. I never thought about it. A door must take on the character of the room it guards, in the same way a face assumes the character of the brain behind it. Now . . ." He got up, walked round the desk, and moved over to the great gleaming door. "What kind of room do you suppose this once guarded?"

"A big one," Rosemary said with conviction, "yes, I'd say a big room."

"A reasonable deduction," William nodded, "large door, large room. What else?"

"I think it must have been a beautiful room. Sinister maybe, cold, but beautiful. A big expanse of carpet, a great fireplace, high blue walls, a big window with an old-world garden beyond . . . blue velvet chairs. I think it would have been a room like that."

"Could well be," William nodded again, "a large drawing room that hardly changed with the years. There again, it might have been a picture gallery—anything. Tell you what, I'll ring up Murray and find out what he can tell me."

"A big room," Rosemary murmured, more to herself than to her husband, "I'm certain it was a large drawing room. Certain."

"Good morning, Mr. Seaton, what can I do for you?"

"About that door I bought," William pressed the telephone receiver closer to his ear, "I wondered if you could tell me something about the house from where it came."

"The house?" Murray sounded a little impatient. "Clavering Grange you mean. An old place down in Kent. The last owner, Sir

James Sinclair, died recently and the chap who inherited—Hackett was his name—had no use for it, falling to pieces it was, so he sold the lot to a building contractor. We had the job of clearing the site. Why do you ask?"

"Oh, my wife and I wondered what sort of room went with such a fine door. I suppose you wouldn't know?"

Murray chuckled. "Matter of fact I do. It came from the blue drawing-room. A great barn of a place with a ruddy great fireplace. Very grand in its day I'm sure, but was a bit of a mess when we came to drive our bulldozer through it. You know, damp, the paper peeling from the walls. Can't tell you much else."

"Well, thanks anyway. My wife was right, she thought it was a large drawing room, and strangely enough, she guessed it was blue."

"You don't say? What do you know about that? Must be psychic or something."

"Probably something," William laughed. "Well, thanks again. "Bye."

"So," William spoke aloud, "we have established a blue drawing-room should be behind you, but there isn't, is there? Only a horrible little cupboard, so you had better get used to your reduced circumstances, and be mighty grateful you didn't finish up as firewood."

The door ignored him.

William often worked late into the night, finding the peace and quiet of the small hours conducive to creative thinking. Usually there was a feeling of serene contentment when he settled down in his old chair, heard the muted roar of a passing car, and let his brain churn out a steady flow of dialogue. But once the door was installed he found his attention was apt to wander to it, or rather to what had once lain behind it. The blue room. Grand old country houses seemed to go in for that kind of thing. Blue rooms, red rooms, yellow rooms. Presumably if one had a lot of rooms, it was as good a way as any to identify one from the other. Also, decorating must be greatly simplified. Blue walls, blue hangings, carpet, upholstery—William chuckled to himself—there was really no limit. Why not have blue flowers just outside the great window, or perhaps a little blue creeper that completely surrounded the window and in fact gently tapped the glass panes on a windy night. He must get old Jem to cut it back.

William sat upright, dropped his pen, and frowned. Who the blazes was old Jem? It was all very well having a powerful, cultivated imagination, but he must keep it under control. But still . . . He stared at the door thoughtfully; there was a certain rather eerie satisfaction in creating an imaginary world for the door to guard. William lay back in his chair and half closed his eyes. First of all the room; it must be reconstructed properly. You open the door, walk onto a thick, extremely beautiful, blue carpet, clearly made to measure, for it stretches from wainscoting to wainscoting, and in front of that great fireplace with its roaring log fire, is a dark blue rug. So much for the floor, now the furniture. Situated some six feet back from the fireplace is a settee, at least so William supposed it to be, for it had a high back and a round arm on each side, would seat possibly four people at one time, and was covered with blue brocade. Six matching chairs were placed around the room, and William sank down onto one. It was very comfortable. He examined the walls. Blue of course, but the covering appeared to be some kind of material, embossed with dark blue flowers, and there were several pictures in blue velvet-edged frames. Indeed this is a blue room. Or it was. Funny this obsession for blue. What kind of man had he been . . . or was? There was a portrait of him over the mantelpiece, painted when he was a young man; his face still clean, not yet scarred by lines of debauchery and evil, but the eyes . . . By God and all his saints, the eyes . . .

William got up and walked towards the fireplace; he could feel the heat of the fire; a log settled and sent a shower of sparks rocketing up the chimney. An oval face with the dark beauty of a fallen angel, long, black hair that curled down to his shoulders, lace collar, blue velvet doublet, the epitome of a Restoration gentleman. The dark, terrible eyes watched him, and William pulled his gaze away, then walked to the window. The garden was a place of beauty, close-clipped lawns, islands of flowers, trees beyond, farther still, blue-crested hills.

He turned and went over to the great desk; a quill-pen grew out of an ink-horn, a blue velvet-covered book lay upon the desk and his hand went down to open it, when . . .

Footsteps outside, just beyond the windows, slow, halting steps, punctuated by an occasional dragging sound, like a lame old man who is trying to overcome his handicap; drawing nearer, and the room was becoming colder. William shivered, then overcome by an unreasoning fear darted towards the door. He opened it, went out, closed it carefully behind him, then went over and sat down behind his desk.

He opened his eyes.

Five minutes passed. William got up, moved very slowly towards the door, turned the brass knob, then pulled. A cupboard, eighteen inches deep, filled with shelves on which nestled stacks of typing paper, carbons, ribbons, the familiar materials of his trade. He shut the door, then opened it again, finally closed it with a bang before returning to his desk.

He sat there for some time, then suddenly was seized by a fit of shivering that made his body shake like a dead leaf beaten by the wind. Gradually the spasm passed, leaving him weak, drenched with perspiration, but strangely at peace, like a man who has recently recovered from a brief, but serious illness. A dream, an illusion, or perhaps a rebellion on the part of an overworked imagination. What did it matter? It had been an experience, an exercise of the mind, and no writer worthy of his ink should be afraid of a journey into the unknown.

He watched the door for the rest of the night, and the door stared right back at him. Once he thought the handle began to turn, and he waited with breathless expectancy, but it must have been an illusion caused by his overstrained eyes, for the door remained closed.

The door became an obsession. His work was neglected, a bewildered agent telephoned at regular intervals, muttering dark threats about deadlines, broken contracts, and William tried to flog his brain back to its former production line, but to no avail. The door was always there, and with it the memory of a room; a study in blue, an anteroom to another age. "Next time," he told himself, "I will go out through the great window, and walk across the garden and rediscover yesterday."

He sat by the hour with closed eyes trying to re-create the dream, willing himself back into that armchair, gazing up at the portrait over the mantelpiece, but the 20th century remained obstinately present, and several times he fell asleep. Rosemary was becoming worried.

"What's the matter? Are you ill?"

"No," he barked the denial, his irritation growing each time the gentle inquiry was made. "Leave me alone. How am I to work?"

"But you're not working," she persisted, "neither are you eating. William, this must stop."

"What?"

"You and that damned door." She glared at the door. "I do not pretend to understand, but ever since that lump of old wood came into this house, you haven't been the same man. It scares me. William, have it taken out, let's burn it in the boiler."

He laughed harshly and experienced a pang of fear at her suggestion, and saw the startled expression on Rosemary's face.

"Don't worry so much. The truth is I've run dry, writers do occasionally. It's happened before and the old brain has always started ticking over once it was good and ready. But it makes me a bit irritable."

"That's all right," she brightened up at once, "I don't mind you being a bit testy, but you're getting so thin. Are you sure that nothing else is bothering you?"

For a mad moment he toyed with the idea of telling her about the room, the dream, then instantly discarded it. She would not understand or believe, so he kissed her gently and said, "Absolutely nothing."

"Then pack it in for a bit," she pleaded, "and let me cook you a decent meal. One you will eat."

It was suddenly very important she be pacified, her mind be put at rest.

"All right. I'll give you a hand."

He helped her in the kitchen, was surprised to hear himself making small talk, while all the time his mind, his very soul hungered for the blue room and the fear that lurked in the garden. For that was the truth, and the realization burst upon him like a blast of light. The terror inspired by approaching footsteps, the heart-stopping, exciting horror of wondering what would come in through the great French windows, the craving for a new experience, even if fulfillment meant madness or worse.

They ate in the kitchen, two young, beautiful people, as modem as Carnaby Street. He tall, lean, dark; she petite, blonde, blue-eyed. His dark, clever eyes watched her, and he smiled often.

That night they retired to bed early, and long after Rosemary had fallen asleep he lay thinking about the room behind the door.

"It does not exist," he told himself, "maybe it did long ago, but not now. A bulldozer flattened the house, and only the blue room door remains. A flat piece of polished wood."

There was comfort in that thought, and presently sleep closed his eyes with soft fingers, and for a while he was at rest.

The room had not altered, the log fire still spluttered, the chairs were in the same position as on his last visit, and the blue journal lay upon the desk. William found he was dressed in his pajamas and his feet were bare.

"I must have sleepwalked," he whispered, "but now I am wide awake. This is not a dream."

He walked over to the door, opened it and stared into the gloom; a few yards away the outline of his desk shimmered softly, the door of his study was open, beyond was darkness. William closed the door, crossed the blue carpet and flattened his nose against the French windows. Back in his own world it was night, out in the garden it was sunset; long shadows lay across the smooth lawn, the trees were giant sentinels rearing up against the evening sky, and although it all looked beautiful and peaceful, there was something eerie about the scene. Suddenly William knew why. Nothing moved. There were no birds, the leaves did not stir, the flowers stood upright; it was as though he were looking at a three-dimensional picture.

He shivered, then turned and walked over to the desk. The blue journal lay waiting, and he fingered the soft velvet cover before sitting down, then with a strange reluctance opened the book. Crisp parchment, about fifty pages he estimated, bound together; the first one was blank, serving as a fly-leaf. He turned it slowly, then read the clear, beautiful copperplate inscription:

AN EXPERIMENT IN DARKNESS

BY

SIR MICHAEL SINCLAIR, BART.

of the county of Kent, Lord of the Manor of Clavering,
written in this the twenty-second year of the reign of his
gracious majesty, King Charles the Second.

It took a great effort of will to turn the title page, for the room seemed suddenly to have become very cold, and the dying sun sent its last shafts of light through the window, making the shadows scurry like so many disturbed mice. But he had to read on; the page went over with a disturbingly loud crackling sound.

PART 1.

INSTRUCTIONS AS TO THE ENTRAPMENT OF
THE UNBORN.

Having kept myself aloof from the troubles of the preceding reign, I have devoted these many years to the pursuit of that knowledge which fools call evil, and from which, even those men that are dubbed wise, cover their faces, even as the night hides from the rising sun.

To say that the knowledge I have confined to these pages is the unadulterated fruit of my own labors would not be true for I have been helped by the old masters, such as Astaste and his *Book of Forbidden Knowledge*, Conrad von Leininstein with his invaluable *Transformation of Living Matter Through Quickening Time*, and many others. But I have gone beyond them, have made myself as a seething-pot, created an essence of bubbling truth such as no man has yet conceived.

Men avert their eyes rather than meet my glance, for I wear my knowledge about me like a cloak; they whisper about me in corners, and there is much talk of witchcraft, and were I not who I am, I might fear the stake.

I prepared me the room after many years and the expense of much blood, and the damnation of my soul should the Black One whose name must never be uttered ever assume power over me. I brought me slaves from the Africas; young persons whose disappearance would never be commented upon; although their screams have doubtless been heard, but such is the reputation of this house, the fools merely cross themselves and take to their heels. It was necessary to kill their body with a painful slowness, and draw off their soul or life essence while the blue room and all pertaining to it was imprinted upon their dying gaze. Thus did I make a *karma* or ghost room, kept alive by the life essence of those who had been sacrificed to it. But even as the body needs food, the earth needs fertilizing, so the room from time to time, must be fed. Many of the Africans have a poor lasting quality, the power fades and my soul trembles lest *He* be able to enter. Therefore, I prepared me the door, seeping it in blood that was still warm, and making it into a trap that will function for a brief spell in the time that has yet to come. I pray that this be not destroyed in the centuries yet unborn, for without it will I be unable to acquire that which is needful, and be lost for all eternity.

The unborn must come in when the time is ripe, and should he be of the right mixture, then shall he give

of his body and soul that I and the room may continue
to be; or I will go forth beyond the door and find me a
woman of his kind, which would be better, for a woman
have a more lasting quality . . .

William slammed the book closed and looked about him with
sudden fear. A sound had disturbed him and for a moment he could not
be sure what it had been. Then it came again—a slow, halting footstep,
just beyond the French windows. William seemed to be frozen to his
chair; he wanted to get up and run back to the safety of his own world;
at the same time, there was an irritating curiosity to know who—what,
would shortly come in through the window.

Suddenly the overhead chandelier lit up; every one of its candles
took on a yellow spear-shaped light, and beyond the window it was
night, a black impregnable wall of darkness. But the slow, faltering
footsteps continued to draw nearer, and it seemed as though the room
shivered with fear at the approach of its dread master, for the coldness
grew more intense, and William whimpered like a terrified puppy.

The French windows opened and slowly a black figure emerged
from the darkness and limped into the room. The scarlet-doublet was
rotten with age, the blue velvet had long since lost its plume, the knee
breeches were threadbare, the black boots cracked and down-at-heel,
and He—It—had no face. Just an oval-shaped expanse of dead-white
skin surrounded by a mass of bedraggled white hair.

William screamed once, a long, drawn out shriek, then he was on
his feet and racing for the door. He pulled it open, crossed the dark
study in a fear-mad rush, barked his shins on a chair, then tore out into
the hall, and up the stairs, to finally collapse on the landing where he
lay panting and trembling like a hunted animal.

Slowly he recovered, fought back the terror, mastered his shaking
limbs, and marshaled his thoughts. He crawled forward and peered
down through the banisters to the dark hall below. He could see the
pale oblong that marked his study doorway. The door was still open.
Then another more terrible thought exploded and sent slivers of fear

across his brain. *The door was open.* What had he read in the blue-covered book?

"Therefore I prepared me the door . . . making it into a trap that will function for a brief spell . . . or I will go forth beyond the door and find me a woman of his kind, which would be better, for a woman have a more lasting quality."

Rosemary! If Sir Michael was beyond the door, then he might be but a few feet away, hidden by the darkness, peering down at William with that face that was not a face, perhaps even moving silently towards the bedroom where Rosemary lay asleep.

William got to his feet, stretched out a hand and groped wildly for the light switch. He found it, pressed, and the sudden light blasted the darkness, shattered it into splinters, sent the shadows racing for protecting corners, forced imagination to face reality. The landing was empty; the familiar cold linoleum, the white painted doors, the brown banisters, the stairs . . . William peered down into the hall. The landing light did not extend to more than halfway down the stairs, the hall was still in total darkness. It took great courage to descend the stairs, and a great effort of will to press the hall switch. Light, like truth, is all-revealing; the hall table was in its proper place, the carpet he and Rosemary had chosen with such care covered the floor, two prints still hung on the green-papered walls, and all doors were closed, save the one leading to his study; and standing in the opening was something extra—a bedraggled, nightmare figure with no face. Almost no face, for since William had seen it last, it had acquired a mouth. Two thin lines that opened.

"Thank you," the voice came as a harsh, vibrant whisper, "thank you very much."

For the first time in his life William fainted.

Rosemary was crying. Sitting by his bed sobbing, but when she saw his eyes were open, a smile lit up her face, the sun peeping through the rain clouds.

"Oh, William, you're awake. Thank goodness, when I found you down on the hall floor, I thought . . . Do you feel better now? The doctor said you have a slight concussion. Hit your head when you fell."

He felt very weak, and his head hurt, a dull ache. There was also a nagging fear at the back of his mind, trying to remind him of something he wanted to forget.

"I feel fine," he said, "great, simply great. What happened?"

"I don't know," Rosemary was wiping her eyes, "I guess you must have walked in your sleep, and fell downstairs. I did not find you until this morning, and you lay so still . . ."

She began to cry again and he wanted to comfort her, but the nagging fear was coming out into the open, making him remember, causing him to shiver.

"You must leave this house," he tried to sit upright, "He is looking for someone—a woman who has . . ." he giggled inanely, ". . . who has a lasting quality."

"Oh, no," Rosemary had both hands clutched to her mouth, staring at him with fear-filled eyes, "your poor head."

"I'm not mad," William clutched her arm, "please believe me. He— It, I don't know, but there is a room behind the door, and He made it—kept it alive and himself by the life essence—soul's blood, of living people. I know the door is a trap, is only active for a little while at certain periods, and *now* happens to be one of them. I don't know why sometimes I can go through, and at others I cannot, but it is so. But the point is, He—Sir Michael—has come through. He is on this side of the door. He wants a woman he can take back—make part of the room—take to pieces, tear soul from body, but you won't die, you won't be so lucky."

Rosemary ran from the room, raced down the stairs, and he heard the telephone receiver being removed; she was telephoning the doctor, convinced beyond all doubt he was mad.

Perhaps he was, or at the very best a victim of a walking hallucination. He was suddenly very confused. He had lived off his imagination for years—it could have rebelled, manufactured a sleepwalking nightmare. After all his first "visit" had begun by him mentally building up the room item by item.

He pretended to be asleep when Rosemary returned.

The doctor said: "Run-down," remarked sagely on the effects of overwork, strain, advised rest, wrote out a prescription, and then departed. William felt almost happy after his visit, quite willing to accept the certainty that his experience had been nothing more than a vivid and unpleasant dream. He would rest, stay in bed, then in a few days he and Rosemary would go away for a long holiday, and during their absence a builder could remove the door. That was the sensible solution.

"Sorry if I scared you," he told Rosemary, "but I had such a horrible nightmare—a sort of two-part dream, and it seemed so real. We'll go away when I feel fit."

She was delighted; chatted happily about where they should go, spent as much time as possible by his bedside, and left all the doors open when she went downstairs, so she could hear should he call out. The day passed and as the shadows of night darkened the windows, a faint chill of returning fear began to haunt his mind. Rosemary turned on the lights, drew the curtains, smiled at him, but there was an expression of unease in her eyes, and it was then he knew his hard-won peace of mind was merely self-deception.

"Anything wrong?" He tried to make the question sound casual.

"No," she straightened the counterpane, "no, nothing."

"Tell me," he whispered, fearful lest the very walls were listening, "please, tell me."

She averted her head.

"It's nothing, only silliness on my part. But—that door—it won't remain shut. Every time I close it, the handle turns, and it opens."

"Then I was right, it was not a dream."

"Nonsense," she was pushing him back onto the pillows, "the door is shrinking, the warm air is making it contract, that must be the answer. It must be."

"Did . . . did you see anything beyond the door?"

"Only the cupboard shelves, but . . ."

She paused, and he did not want her to go on, tried to blot out her voice, but the words came to him, like echoes from yesteryear.

"I keep thinking there is someone else in the house."

He shook his head: "No . . . no . . ."

"I know it's pure imagination, but . . . I thought I saw a face looking down at me over the banisters."

"Rosemary," he took her hand, "don't say anything more, just do as I say. Go downstairs, get the car out of the garage and wait for me. I'll pack a bag and will be with you in a few minutes."

"But . . ." Her eyes were wide open, glazed with fear, and she made a faint protest when he clambered out of bed.

"Please do as I say. Now."

She ran from the room and William was reaching for his clothes when he had a glimpse of a figure gliding across the open doorway. For a moment he stood petrified, then he shouted once: "Rosemary!"

"What's the matter?" Her voice, hoarse with fear, came up from the hall. "What . . ."

Her scream seared his brain like a hot knife and he raced for the landing, ran down the stairs, then stood in the hall, calling our her name, trying to master his fear, the weakness in his legs.

"William . . .!"

The scream came from his study and for a moment he surrendered to the paralyzing terror, stood trembling like a statue on the brink of unnatural life, then with a great effort of will he moved forward, staggered rather than ran through the doorway and took in the scene with one all-embracing glance.

He—It—Sir Michael, was complete, rejuvenated by the life force of the girl that lay limp in his arms. The face was now lit by a pair of dark terrible eyes, the nose was arched, cruel, the lips parted in a triumphant smile, the long hair only slightly flecked with grey, but his clothes were still ragged, old, besmirched with grave mire.

The door was open but the room beyond was slightly out of focus, the walls had a shimmering quality, the chandelier candles were spluttering, making light dance with shadow; a chair suddenly lost one leg and it fell over onto the floor.

He watched William, eyes glistening with sardonic amusement, and made no attempt to intervene as the young man edged round the walls towards the door. When William stood in the open doorway, with the blue room behind him, the thin lips parted again, and the harsh voice spoke:

"I must thank you again. The woman may have a more lasting quality, but two bodies and souls were always better than one."

He moved forward, and Rosemary, now mercifully unconscious, lay in his arms, her head flung back so that her long hair brushed the desk-top as they passed.

"The door," William's brain screamed, "destroy the door."

He would have given twenty years of his life for an axe. Then he remembered the crossed sabers hanging just above the doorframe. He reached up and gripped the brass hilts, jerked and they came away, then he spun round to face the approaching figure.

Sir Michael chuckled as he slowly shook his head.

"Never. You will only harm the lady."

William swung the saber in his right hand sideways; struck the door with a resounding crash, and instantly Sir Michael flinched, fell back a few paces as though the blade had been aimed at him.

"No-o-o." The protest was a cry of pain; William struck again, and red fluid began to seep out of the door panel, and something crashed in the room behind. Then in a fear-inspired frenzy, William slashed wildly at the door, and was dimly aware that Sir Michael had dropped Rosemary, was reeling around the study, jerking as each blow fell, emitting harsh animal-like cries, his eyes black pools of pain-racked hate.

The door shivered, then split; one half, now splintered, soggy, crashed to the floor; William swung his right-hand saber and struck at the hinges, the door frame, and did not cease until the brickwork lay bare.

Sir Michael disintegrated. The face dissolved into an oval featureless mask, the hair turned white, then seemed to melt into a white powder, the entire body collapsed and became an untidy heap of rags and white bones. In a few minutes these too faded away and William was left staring at a dirty patch of carpet.

He had one last fleeting glimpse of the blue room. The walls and ceiling appeared to fall in, turn into a mass of swirling blue-mist; he saw a great jumble effaces; Negroes with frizzy hair and large, black eyes, young fair-haired girls, children, even animals. Then the shelves of his stationery cupboard came into being—typing paper, ribbons, carbon paper, all merged into their proper place, and William turned his attention to Rosemary, who was stirring uneasily.

He gathered her up into his arms.

The splintered remains of the door lay all around, crumbling, rotten with age.

Hand to Mouth

REGGIE OLIVER

REGGIE OLIVER has been a professional playwright, actor, and theater director since 1975. His biography of Stella Gibbons, *Out of the Woodshed*, was published by Bloomsbury in 1998.

Besides plays, his publications include four volumes of horror stories, with a fifth collection, *Mrs. Midnight*, due from Tartarus Press. An omnibus edition of his stories, entitled *Dramas from the Depths,* has been published by Centipede Press as part of its Masters of the Weird Tale series.

The author's novel, *The Dracula Papers I—The Scholar's Tale,* the first in a projected series of four, was published in January 2011—the same time as his farce, *Once Bitten*, was a Christmas season sold-out hit at the Orange Tree Theatre in Richmond, West London.

As Oliver recalls: "On a boat trip up the Dordogne last year I was intrigued by the sight of a château on a bend in the river near Beynac. The guide on board told us that it was owned by an American, but seemed reluctant to offer further information except that it was inaccessible to the public and not often lived in. It is these little mysteries that stimulate the imagination.

"Then I was reading a book about the famous 'Blood Countess,' Elizabeth Báthory. It appears that when the late Ingrid Pitt was making a film about her called *Countess Dracula*, she wanted to add a certain detail to her performance to make it more authentic, but the producers forbade it on the grounds that it was 'too horrific' (for a *horror* film?).

"In honor of her, that detail is present in my account of the legend."

MY COUSIN JUSTIN is one of the undeserving rich. You won't want to know the details, but I'll just say he is something very high up in Grippmann-Savage, the international merchant bank, and his bonuses alone amount to several million a year. That is how a couple of years back he could afford, on a whim, to buy a Château in the Dordogne. He told me all about it when we lunched together at his London club, Brummell's, that September. He was paying, of course. I am a frequently unemployed actor, and the nearest I usually get to a meal out is my local Indian for a takeaway. Unlike my cousin, I lead a hand-to-mouth existence.

I knew that this was not going to be a purely social lunch. Justin does not give away expensive food, even to his relations, for nothing. In a way, that is what I like about my cousin: you know exactly where you are with him. Everything he does is for his own convenience or financial benefit and he makes no secret of it. A hypocrite he is not.

I arrived at Brummell's punctually to find Cousin Justin waiting for me in the bar. He shook my hand and said: "We won't bother with a drink beforehand. Let's go straight into the dining room, shall we?"

Once we had sat down at our table Justin immediately began to choose what we were going to eat. For formality's sake I was handed a menu, but I was not even asked what I might like. From the waiter he ordered mulligatawny soup for both of us, followed by roast beef from the trolley; then he had a long consultation with the wine steward before finally settling on a decanter of the club claret. When this was done he gave a little sigh of satisfaction and smiled in my direction as if he had just done me an enormous favor.

"Now then, Cousin James, are you in any sort of gainful employment at the moment, or are you, as you say, 'resting'?"

People like my cousin Justin are under the illusion that we actors say we are "resting" when we are out of work. No actor in my experience has ever used that expression. I told Justin that I had just finished a thirteen-week tour of a successful farce; I went on to tell him about the company, and the theaters we had been to, but Justin did not even pretend to be interested. He actually waved at a passing high court judge as I was talking to him. Finally he interrupted me.

"Yes, yes . . . But what I mean is, are you likely to be working this winter?"

"Well, I don't know. I suppose I might get a pantomime at Christmas."

Justin looked shocked. "Pantomime! Pantomime? You mean being the back legs of a cow or something?"

"Usually, I do the villains. Like Abanazer in *Aladdin*, or—"

"No. Listen! I've got a proper job for you. Or the nearest thing to a proper job you'll ever do."

At that moment the waiter arrived with our soup and for a few brief seconds I was excited. Perhaps Cousin Justin had invested heavily in a movie and was going to use his influence to get me a part in it. Then he spoke again and the illusion was shattered.

"You know I've just bought this château in the Dordogne?"

I nodded. As it happens I did know—my sister had told me—but it was typical of his arrogance that he should assume I kept myself informed of his doings.

"It's called the Château de Bressac. Incredible place. On a bend of the Dordogne a few miles upstream of Beynac. Fantastic possibilities. Well, obviously, I can't get down there and do anything about it until next spring, and the builders won't be in until then anyway, because it's pretty run-down. Naturally I wanted someone to keep an eye on the place until then. You know: not just look in on it twice a day, but actually live there. See it doesn't get broken into. Well, I tried the locals but they wouldn't play ball. You know what locals are like." I nodded as if I too believed that "locals" belonged to a universal and predictable human category. "The long and the short of it is that no one down there is actually prepared to live in the place and look after it over the winter months, so that was when I had my brain wave. I thought of you. I'll pay you, of course, but your tasks won't be exactly onerous. Just a bit of light dusting and general maintenance, I should imagine.

There's an old *deux chevaux* down there that you can use, so you will be able to get about a bit. Not too much obviously, because your job is to be there and house sit. Château sit, I should say!" He laughed a good deal at his little joke and I politely joined in the mirth. "It could be a golden opportunity for you. You could—I don't know—read, write, study something useful like accounting, brush up your French. Well?"

By mid-October it was clear there was going to be no pantomime for me that year, so I agreed.

I got a cheap flight to Bergerac and splashed out on a taxi to Beynac. There I was picked up in the *deux chevaux* by a Monsieur Bobelet, whom Justin had retained to keep an eye on the château grounds. Gaston Bobelet owned the farm that adjoined the château. He was one of those taciturn, permanently unshaven French rustics who seem to harbor a grudge against the world in general and foreigners in particular. His wife, whom I met later, was bright-eyed, almost completely spherical, and charming. She complimented me on my French and gave me a delicious cassoulet to eat on my first night at the château.

I had arrived in fine weather. It was the end of October and Southern France was enjoying an Indian summer. As we drove towards the château along the banks of the Dordogne, I couldn't help feeling exhilarated.

The grounds of the château are surrounded by a high brick wall, except for the northern side where it is bounded by the river. There is only one entrance and that is through a gate of exquisite 18th-century wrought iron work, now badly rusted. From there, there is a long, straight drive through a park dotted with some fine old trees. To my right as Gaston took me down the drive in the *deux chevaux*, I could just see through a belt of poplars and willows the broad stream of the Dordogne glittering in the afternoon sun.

The château itself was a tall, irregular construction built mostly in the 16th century but with later additions. There were numerous turrets topped by conical slate roofs that gleamed dully like pewter in candlelight. It was not exactly a beautiful building, but it was imposing and picturesque, and, yes, I suppose its ancient grandeur gave it a sort of romantic beauty.

Madame Bobelet was waiting on the drive before the front door. She was far less taciturn than her husband, but she seemed nevertheless in a hurry to be done with her task. She showed me the main areas of the château and the bedroom on the first floor that she had made up for me to occupy. There was no electricity: lighting was by oil, candle, or gas bottles, which also provided heat for the stove and a primitive boiler for hot water.

Madame Bobelet was extremely conscientious in providing me with practical information about my new home, but I noticed that when I asked her more general questions about the place and its former inhabitants she brushed them aside. Through the kitchen window, as she was showing me the stove, I caught sight of Gaston, pacing about on the drive, puffing at the soggy end of a *Gauloise*. Suddenly, Madame Bobelet finished her recitation, wished me a *bonne aprésmidi*, and a *bon appetit* (with regard to the cassoulet) and darted out of the kitchen door to join her husband.

I watched them as they walked down the straight drive to the château gates, leaving me with the *deux chevaux*, my evening meal, and the vast unknown spaces of the Château de Bressac.

My first action when I was alone was to switch on my mobile phone. I could get no signal at all in the château, so I walked out into the grounds. It took me some time before I found a spot that gave me a reasonable connection. It was quite a distance from the château and on the very banks of the Dordogne among the willows. I called Justin.

"Yes?"

I told him that I had arrived safely.

"Right. Well, you won't need to call me again. If you come across any problems, you and the Bobelets can sort it out between you. That's what you're there for, isn't it?"

Feeling that I needed to extract some sort of human response from him I said: "It's a beautiful place."

"Well of course it is! I know that!"

He was offended, I suppose, because he thought I was subtly accusing him of being a philistine. After that there seemed no point in pursuing the conversation so I rang off. Apart from the distant ripple of water, there was no sound. High above in the cloudless blue air, a pale bird of prey with long slow wing beats circled. It was a short-toed eagle, quite common in those parts, though not usually so late in the year. I was proud of myself for having identified it and would have liked to share the moment with someone.

For the first ten days the weather continued fine, and I settled into a routine of shopping, cooking, and reading. I visited the Bobelets once in their farmhouse to return the cassoulet dish, and though Madame was very civil, it was made quite plain to me that they were both very busy people who had no time to spare talking to the indolent Englishman from the château.

I tried to be, as far as possible, a diligent caretaker and inspect every part of the building. It was an extraordinarily rambling structure with rooms of all different sizes organized in no particular order with numerous corridors and staircases. Nearly all the rooms were dusty, shuttered and void of furniture, apart from those great dark coffin-like armoires that the French go in for. I tried, for my own amusement really, to make a plan of the place for each of its three main floors, but it baffled me. Not even the tape measure I bought in Beynac for the purpose was any help. I couldn't make sense of it.

There seemed to be parts inside the château that were inaccessible. I remembered the story of Glamis Castle, where there was said to be a secret room in which a monster was kept. One day the guests at a Glamis house party decided to hang a towel or cloth from every window they could find. If there was a window which was unmarked, then that was the monster's window. I can't remember what was the result of the experiment, but I decided to do something similar with the château. I walked round it from the outside counting all the windows, then did the same from within. They more or less added up to the same total. Perhaps, I thought, the hidden parts of the building were internal and windowless.

One thing I did notice was that at the back of the château on the southwest corner it looked as if there had once been a large octagonal tower of some kind which had either fallen down or had been destroyed. Against one outer wall I could see the remains of a fireplace and an overmantel clinging to it. Farther up there was a series of stone steps, which spiraled up into the château and were lost in darkness. I tried to look for that staircase from the inside, but without success.

Let me state categorically that I don't believe I have a psychic bone in my body; nevertheless, there was something I didn't like about the Château de Bressac. It was not that there was some sort of atmosphere of evil or menace about it, at least as far as I could tell; in fact, there seemed to be no atmosphere at all. That, I suppose, was what I didn't like. The place felt empty, not just physically but in some other way, too. And it was silent, especially at night. With any normal old building, you expect the odd creak or click, but this one was a tomb.

I discovered that there is a terrible thing about silence, especially the silence inside a building. Your ears become supersensitive. You find yourself tensed up, waiting for a noise to happen, but of course it doesn't, so you remain tense. I thought music might help. I had an MP3 player with earphones, but when I had it on in the château I caught myself not listening to the music at all, but somehow listening *through* it to see if there was any sound to be heard in the spaces beyond.

It was worse at night. For some reason the shutters of my bedroom window were jammed shut and no amount of shoving and banging could dislodge them. So, once I had extinguished my lamp or candle— no electricity, remember—I was left in complete darkness and silence. It was like being in a void. I wondered if death was like this. Only a tiny thread of pale light through a gap at the bottom of one of the shutters told me when it was morning.

In spite of this, the first ten days passed fairly easily; then the weather broke. I can remember it exactly. It was eleven fifteen at night according to my watch, and I was reading in bed by candlelight when suddenly there was a low roaring sound. I started violently. The rain had begun—a downpour in fact. I took my candle and went downstairs. Through the long windows in the hall I could see beyond the glass a vast, darkly glistening curtain of rain. There was a flash and the château's park was leprously illuminated for a moment by a thunderbolt, like a great crack of light in a black wall. I counted slowly up to three before the thunder rumbled.

The innards of the building were still noiseless, but we were now encased in sound, the rustle of rain, the groan of thunder. I began to walk upstairs to my bedroom. As I reached the first floor I did think I heard something else—something from inside but far off. It was such a tiny noise that I might have imagined it, but it was very distinct. It sounded like the cry of a baby, the senseless, angry yell of a newborn child pitched unwillingly into the world. It might have lasted a second, if that, then it was gone. I stood still for a long time waiting for the noise to repeat itself, but it didn't.

When I was in bed again I put my candle on the bedside table, but I did not blow it out. I let it burn down into its socket while I lay awake listening, but all I heard was rain and thunder.

For a few nights after that I kept a candle or a night-light on in my bedroom until at last I was ready to tell myself not to be a fool. The weather was getting colder. As well as the rain there was wind, which sometimes penetrated into the château, catching you unawares with cold blasts and occasionally slamming doors shut. There was a great fireplace in the main salon of the castle with a huge hooded overmantel in the French style, on which was carved a heraldic escutcheon, presumably of the Bressac family. I lit a fire in this and ate my supper in front of it every night. It was the crackling of the fire as much as its heat and light that comforted me.

One night, about a week after the thunderstorm, I had sat long in front of the fire, finishing a bottle of the local wine. I was drinking a lot more wine these days because it was plentiful and cheap. I hoped vaguely I was not becoming an alcoholic, but, to be honest, I did not much care if I was. It was nearly midnight, the bottle was empty, and I had no more excuses for not going to bed, so I took my candle and stumbled upstairs. I managed to undress and put on a nightshirt, but when I accidentally knocked over my candle and it went out, I was drunk enough not to care. I got into bed and fell asleep almost immediately.

Some time later—how long I don't know—I was awake, or half-awake, or at least somehow aware of myself and my surroundings. I found that my cheek was rested against something rounded and firm and soft. It was not like my pillow: it yielded, but yielded less and it was very cold. Then the thing that touched me began to move restlessly as if alive. I pulled myself violently away from it and sat up in bed, letting out a stupid, involuntary, childish yelp.

I tried to find an explanation for my experience, but none came to me. I did not know what it was, but I knew exactly what it had felt like: a baby's belly, a baby's bottom perhaps, but a dead baby.

I felt around in the dark for the candle until I remembered that in my drunken carelessness I had left the matches downstairs.

On the nights following, I once more kept a light on in the bedroom and barely slept. When I did, I sometimes felt again that touch of soft, cold flesh against me, but more distantly and through the veil of dreams. I tried vainly to remember what the dreams were, because I thought they might be telling me something, but they never did. In the evenings before going upstairs I sometimes got through more than one bottle of wine.

One night I had gone to bed particularly drunk and, after a few hours of drugged sleep, I found myself suddenly, horribly awake. I had a headache from the wine, and the blood was thumping in my temples, but that was not what was making me sweat. It was the thing that was touching me again.

This time it felt like a hand, soft and cold. It was small—a baby's hand, it must have been. For a moment it played with my chin and then began to reach towards my mouth. Then tiny but perfectly formed little fingers were trying to force their way between my lips. The silky little digits were inexorable, insistent. I wanted to pull them away but my arms wouldn't move from my sides. I was both awake and somehow paralyzed. I might have prevented the thing from reaching farther if I had bitten down on it, but that idea revolted me beyond words. The hand had reached inside my mouth, now numb with the cold, and was stretching out towards my throat. I could feel the fingers flickering inside me, tickling the roof of my mouth and the soft palate. They reached the back of my tongue. Then I began to choke. That convulsive movement jerked me up and into full consciousness. I was awake, alive, gasping for air in a cold black room.

I held my breath, waiting for something to break the silence, but nothing did. It was a windless night. I was entombed in silence and alone. Now, once more, I had to find something to explain what I had experienced. Of course it had been a dream, but what had caused such a vivid one? Had I unconsciously put my own hand into my mouth? Was that it? I tried it out, but I wasn't convinced. My fingers were far too big, and they were warm, comparatively speaking. Had it been some sort of animal? But what?

The following morning I decided I must do something about all this. It was time to see if there was any explanation to be found in the history of the château. Of course, if there wasn't, that would be something of a relief—or would it? I couldn't decide.

I drove into Beynac and represented myself at the municipal library in the *Mairie* as a scholar wishing to study the history of the district. I was shown to a rather dingy little room full of books that looked as if they had been haphazardly gathered together. There were large official-looking tomes full of maps and facsimile documents, huddled against town guides, biographies of local worthies, manuals on wine making, boat building, and other local trades.

Most of the guidebooks and local histories had little or nothing to say about the Château de Bressac. The most I could find out from a work in English was a passing mention in a book called *Rambles in the Dordogne*:

> From the river you may see the Château de Bressac, home to the Counts of Bressac until the French Revolution. Since then, this imposing structure has passed through many hands and has never been occupied by one family for any great length of time. It is now believed to be more or less derelict. Permission to view the château and grounds is, to my certain knowledge, never granted.

Finally, on a dusty shelf behind some bound volumes of old local newspapers, I discovered a work that looked as if it had what I was searching for. *Légendes et histoires de Beynac et ses environs* by Henri Fauvinard had been published in 1876 and did not appear to have been much consulted since that date. In it there was a chapter entitled "The noble house of Bressac," which gave the history of the Counts of Bressac who had inhabited the château since the 16th century. Until the mid-18th century, the family seems to have enjoyed a fairly uneventful run of aristocratic prosperity, then things began to get interesting. Here is a rough translation of the relevant passage:

> In the year 1763 Count Etienne de Bressac, then in his sixty-sixth year, married for a second time. He had been married as a young man, but his wife had died early and without issue. Since then, he had pursued a life of reckless and untrammeled libertinage, until it was borne in on him that unless he soon produced a legitimate heir, the great name of Bressac might perish with him. So the count took a young bride of seventeen from the princely Italian house of Bartori. Why he chose this young woman

from a foreign land is something of a mystery, but he had traveled much in Italy and had formed (it was said) strange ties with this ancient but ill-famed noble family.

The Principessa Eleonora Bartori was a young girl of quite exceptional beauty: her skin was white, and her hair, which she did not powder as was then the fashion, was jet-black. Many remarked on the redness of her lips and the purity of her complexion. The old count duly married her and she bore him a son, Armand, who was the delight of his old age. But as the count grew older, increasingly his countess seemed to rule over him, demanding that a great suite of rooms in the château be put at her exclusive disposal, and that none should be allowed to enter it, not even the count, except by her permission.

Her servants there were slaves, bought from the East, mostly blackamoors and all, save for one eunuch who was her personal steward, were dumb, their tongues having been cut out at the roots in the Eastern fashion.

So the count grew older but still would not die, and she, miraculously it seemed, remained the most beautiful woman for miles around. Her black hair showed not a thread of silver and her skin seemed, if anything, whiter and smoother, and her lips redder. Though many disliked the power she wielded and the strangeness of her personal retinue, no one could find anything against her. With the count in his dotage and she still young and beautiful, it might be thought that she would take some young lover to herself, but she had no favorites, and this in itself was counted against her.

There were at that time many poor families in the village of Bressac and the surrounding district. When one of their children disappeared without trace, no great notice was taken of it at first, but this began to happen with more frequency. It was observed, moreover, that the children who disappeared were generally young girls who had received their first communion, and were about to reach puberty.

In 1784 the old count died and Armand, his son, succeeded to the title, but his mother was still countess and her influence was as great as when she had been the count's consort. There were those in the neighborhood who tried to set Count Armand against the dowager countess in order to destroy her power, but in vain. They began to call her "The Old Countess" as a kind of insult, even though she seemed as young and as fresh as ever.

Finally a friend of the young count, the Marquis d'Elboef, saw that the only way to depose this woman's influence was by means of another woman: Count Armand must marry, but he seemed in no hurry to do so. Suitable candidates were sought out and put forward, but each time the Old Countess's machinations and the young count's indifference dissipated the scheme. During this time it was noticed that Count Armand would spend many hours in the countess's apartments.

A family named Duplessis moved into the district: a husband and wife and their eighteen-year-old daughter, Louise. The father was a baron, and the family of Duplessis was a very wealthy one, having inherited estates from their great great-uncle Cardinal Richelieu.

Soon after their arrival, the Marquis d'Elboef held a great ball at his château in Montpeyroux and invited all the noble families for miles around, but his true purpose was to bring Louise Duplessis and Count Armand together, so breaking the hold that his mother had on the young man. It is said by some that the Marquis had conceived a great hatred for the dowager countess because of some wrong she had done him, but no one could say what it was.

Whatever the truth of this was, the Marquis' plan succeeded and a match was made between Louise Duplessis and the young Count Armand. The moment had come and the countess saw no way of opposing the marriage without prejudice to her own position, so she bowed to the inevitable and even showed enthusiasm for it.

Nevertheless, she did not travel to Bergerac with Count Armand to see him united to Louise in the cathedral there. She remained in the château, saying that she was preparing it for the arrival of a new countess. During that time two more children, both girls, went missing from the nearby village of Bressac.

And so Count Armand returned to the château from his wedding trip with his bride, pleasant enough to look at, with brown curls and blue eyes, but no match for the beauty of the countess. She stood at the gate of the château to meet the young pair in a dress of scarlet satin, her ebon hair elaborately coifed and held in place by a tortoiseshell comb studded with diamonds and emeralds. She greeted her daughter-in-law effusively, and for some months all seemed well, but during that time Louise began to show the strength of her character. She had none of the charm and skill of her mother-in-law, but she had a kind of resolute stubbornness, and her position as Count Armand's wife was inviolable. The count, torn this way and that, seemed to have no will of his own. Meanwhile, Louise began to forge firm alliances with the servants and workers on the estate, as well as with her wealthier neighbors.

The dowager countess, isolated, made as much use as she could of her formidable allure. Whenever she emerged from her apartments all eyes, including those of her son, were upon her.

That winter a young servant girl at the château called Berthe disappeared. This might not have aroused much interest had it not been for the fact that Countess Louise had taken a great liking to the girl. Being dogged and stubborn by nature, Louise instituted a thorough search of the château, much to the disgust of the countess, who regarded all this fuss over the disappearance of a mere servant as undignified and a waste of time.

It was when Louise ordered a search to be made in the dowager countess's apartments that the last battle was joined. The dowager countess seemed to prevail at first and Count Armand ordered that no one should enter her apartments without permission. But Louise was not to be rebuffed. She insisted that where the search was concerned, nobody should be shown favor. Her persistence began to wear the count down.

Then one day it was Louise who could not be found. Like Berthe she had vanished.

The scene in the great salon of the château that day was strange indeed. Count Armand sat alone by the fire, silent, gnawing his fingers, servants and retainers at a discreet distance. It was clear that he knew more than anyone there what had become of his wife. The silence intensified, and with it the count's torment. At last he summoned his steward and four footmen to go with him to the dowager countess's apartments.

There was a fierce struggle at the entrance to the rooms. The dumb slaves of the Old Countess fought with their bare hands until the steward pointed his blunderbuss at them. Every room was searched, and then they came to a door behind which a low murmuring could be heard like a chant.

Here Count Armand hesitated for, although he had been in his mother's apartments many times, this was the one door that had always been barred to him. A kind of superstitious dread held him back. But the steward— who was my grandfather and I had it from him—turned the handle and opened the door.

The room was a bathhouse done up in the Turkish style. There was a great tessellated basin set into the floor, and around it stood the Nubian eunuchs in attendance with precious vases of ointment to hand. The chief eunuch in ceremonial robes stood at one end of the bath muttering an incantation. In the bath itself stood the countess, quite naked.

Never, said my grandfather, had she looked more lovely—at least for one brief moment. Her slender figure seemed rounder and fuller than usual; her pale skin was rosy from the heated water, and her lips were red. Then they noticed the little splashes of scarlet on her body, and that the gently steaming water around her feet was incarnadined. Above her was suspended, by an elaborate system of ropes and steel hoops, the white, drained corpse of Berthe the servant girl, her throat slashed, the wound no longer red but grey. At that moment the countess was enjoying the last drops of her infernal shower bath. And in the corner, the poor naked body of the young Countess Louise—plump and pleasing, but no match for her mother-in-law—was being trussed up to provide a further supply of blood.

The learned reader may be aware that in some mystery religions of the East, particularly that of Cybele, the Mountain Mother, it was customary to be thus showered in the blood of bulls or goats as a rite of initiation, but it was only the blackest of sects which believed that the blood of virgins and young children would restore youth and preserve beauty. The dowager countess had been initiated into one of these hellish cults in her native Italy and, either through the release of dark power or from more natural causes, her looks had been preserved.

Countess Louise was at once set free. The dowager countess's unholy crew were taken away to be handed over to the jurisdiction of the local magistrate. As for the dowager countess herself, even as she was, naked and dabbled with her innocent victim's blood, she threw herself screaming at Count Armand's feet and begged for mercy. The speech she made was the most terrible that my grandfather can ever recall hearing, for in it she confessed to the slaughter of many of the district's missing children. Why she incriminated herself it is hard to say, unless she wanted, pitiless and inhuman as she was, to relieve her conscience. But one phrase, repeated over and over again, remained in the minds of everyone present: "Remember the child! Remember the child!"

Count Armand ordered that she be given a week's supply of food and drink and then, even as she was, shut up in that awful bathhouse with one candle, and all entrances to the place sealed. It was a fearful sentence, her agony being prolonged because Count Armand did not want to be immediately or directly responsible for her death.

Those who were appointed to lock the entrances to her tomb remembered that she never ceased to scream out for her son and to repeat that phrase: "Remember the child!"

Two weeks went by, at the end of which Count Armand could endure it no longer. He ordered that the bathhouse be broken into. This was done, and there the Old Countess was found, dead—not from starvation, but from choking. The shock of her incarceration had brought on a pregnancy already sufficiently advanced, and she had given birth to a child—whether boy or girl I have been unable to ascertain. In the terrible pangs of her hunger, she had begun to devour the wretched infant. A tiny hand that had she tried to swallow whole had become lodged in her throat, and she had choked herself to death. The baby's head remained intact, and those who saw its features swore that only her own son Armand could have been the father. Of the countess's hair not a strand retained its natural blackness—it was all as white as the moon.

So the countess's apartments were sealed up. The main entrance was bricked over and, as I understand, only one secret entrance remained. Where this was situated only the count knew.

As for Louise, she never spoke to Count Armand again, but she gave birth to a son and soon after, died. Count Armand lived on for a short while until the Revolution came. During this, he and his young son perished by the guillotine. No collateral heirs could be found to succeed to the title or estates, and so expired the noble house of Bressac.

> It is said, of course, that the dowager's apartments
> in the Château are haunted, and the countess's screams
> echo still in that empty bathhouse, but who has ever
> been in there to prove it?

I drove back to the château with reckless speed. Something like
madness had taken hold of me, a madness that compelled me to see
this through to the end. It was about 5:00 p.m. when I returned, and
still light. The sun was setting in blood behind the trees. As I entered
the hall, I picked up the big old electric torch that the Bobelets had left
me. I switched it on and off a couple of times. The batteries appeared
to be young.

As I was driving back, a plan had formed in my mind. I had decided
that I knew where the hidden entrance to the countess's apartments
might be. In my walks about the château I had come across a room
on the first floor that was oddly shaped, like a right-angled triangle.
It might have been the corner of a much bigger room, and it had
running almost the length of its longest wall a huge fireplace with an
elaborately carved overmantel, quite out of proportion to the size of
the chamber. The carving in alabaster on the overmantel was badly
damaged, but I noticed that it included a heraldic shield. The insignia
carved on it were the arms of Bressac, as on the fireplace downstairs,
but quartered with them on the shield was another armorial image:
that of an eagle in full flight carrying a baby in its talons. I guessed
that this could be the heraldic device of the Bartori family, and that
the strangely situated fireplace might mark the entrance to the Old
Countess's secret apartments.

It may have taken me an hour—perhaps longer—to find that
three of the carved alabaster bosses on the overmantel, when turned
anticlockwise, released some system of counterweights that allowed
part of the wall of the fireplace's inglenook to slide back. A short
dark passage with a flight of steps leading upwards at the end of it
was revealed.

Putting a handy broken chair in the way of the stone door to prevent it from accidentally sliding shut, I switched on my torch and entered. At that moment I was too possessed with finishing and resolving what I had set out to find to think of the consequences.

I began to climb the steps. The masonry here was smooth and of the highest quality; its surface so polished that it dimly reflected the light of my torch. At the top of the steps I found a wooden door with a great ring handle of iron, richly wrought. I half-hoped the door would be locked and that my researches would end there. But I turned the ring and, after an initial protest, the latch rose easily on the other side. Rust had not corrupted: it was all too dry.

Beyond the door there was a series of small interconnecting chambers. The thing of which I was most immediately aware was an overpowering odor. The place reeked of decay and disintegration. As I looked around I saw the visible evidence of it. I was in a sort of lobby or anteroom, lavishly furnished. A Levantine Turkish rug was on the floor, its rich colors misted over with dust. Great hangings drooped in tatters from the walls. I was startled by a terrible scrabbling noise, only to find it was mice gouging a little city for themselves out of a divan.

I went into the second room, and there in the center was a great bed. It was roofed with a vast canopy of grey velvet dripping with golden thread. Moths and other creatures had gnawed great holes in its draperies, so it looked as if the bed was enmeshed in the web of a gigantic spider. Sheets and pillows were on the bed, the clothes slightly rumpled. If it wasn't for the dust you might have thought that someone had just got out of it.

The next room was a dining room, and even thicker with dust. The table was made of various marbles in the Italian *pietra dura* style; its surface, still visible under the grime, a dazzling patterned mosaic of color.

Silver plates and jugs, much tarnished, stood on the table. Cobwebs festooned the epergnes and candelabra. At one end of the room was a magnificent cupboard, made from all kinds of wood, with rustic scenes fashioned out of gilt and tortoiseshell on the doors. The doors opened up to reveal the miniature façade of a house in the Palladian style with pillars and pilasters, rusticated masonry on the lower range and a wonderfully carved pediment depicting Neptune in his chariot drawn by sea horses and surrounded by conch-blowing Tritons. All this was in ivory, gilded here and there, with the windows made from the finest Venetian glass. The doors all opened to reveal spaces for keepsakes or old letters. Sections of the building could be pulled out as drawers by means of tiny golden knobs, and these drawers were filled with jewels of every kind, some loose, others made up into ornaments, and a hoard of gold and silver coins. I drew back from the sight, half afraid I might be tempted to steal them. I had a feeling that they were protected from theft by more than my own scruples.

Above the cupboard was a picture in a gilded wooden frame. It was the half-length of a woman in a powder-blue dress from about 1770. She was seated and leaning back idly on her left elbow, the hand caressing her cheek, one finger coquettishly playing over her lips as she stared out from the picture directly at the spectator. I was reminded of Boucher's famous portrait of Madame de Pompadour, except that this was the work of a competent journeyman and not a master. The face was white, the hair jet-black and shining like polished ebony, the lips red and perfectly formed, while in the green eyes the painter had captured an expression of malign suspicion. They seemed to glitter in the torchlight and fix me with a particular gaze, as if she were alive.

At the end of this suite of rooms was a door of wood, braced and ornamented with ironwork in the Arabic style. It had a great iron catch that lifted easily enough. On smooth, uncreaking hinges the door swung outwards towards me. I stepped into the next room, which was vast, with a coldness about it quite unlike the others.

I knew that I must be in the bathhouse of the Countess's apartments. I hardly had time to shine my torch over the Eastern sumptuousness of its marble and mosaic before a cold gust of wind from somewhere gave me such a shock that I dropped the torch. I saw it rolling away from me still alight. Then it disappeared, and I heard it smash against something and all light went out. It must have fallen into the bath. Then another blast of wind blew the door shut behind me.

The bang of the door was like a cannon shot, and the sound reverberated for what seemed like minutes. I knew terror then as I had never known it before—like a great marble fist thumping at my chest. Shaking and retching, I felt my way back to the door, murmuring little prayers like a child. I found the door, but it was shut fast and there was no way of opening it on my side. I tore my nails, scrabbling at the wood. I screamed and whimpered and banged until I was wet with blood and tears and perspiration. It was idiotic, I know. Nobody could possibly have heard me.

For a time—I have no idea how long—I was no better than a wild beast caught in a trap, and I only stopped shrieking finally out of exhaustion. If I had had the means to do so, I would have killed myself. I don't like to think about some of the things I screamed aloud. I was cursing a God I hardly believed in, then the next minute groveling and begging his forgiveness. The only excuse I can offer is that my terror drove me a little mad, and so perhaps did the almost palpable evil of this place. Oh yes, I felt it this time.

Once my emotions were spent, a kind of calm came to me. My senses were sharpened. I could see absolutely nothing as the place was pitch dark, but I could hear, feel, and smell with great intensity. I felt again the cold blast of wind that had taken away my torch, then blown the door shut.

Well, I thought, if there is wind in the place, there must be some aperture through which it comes. I got up and began to walk around the bathhouse, keeping close to the walls. Many times I stopped, held my breath and listened. Had I heard something other than the sound I made? Was it a quiet, breathy, almost imperceptible snicker of laughter? The walls were damp, and once or twice I touched patches of slime. My feet slid gingerly over the floor in case I should meet with some obstacle. Once I tripped against something that rattled. I fell and, stretching out my right hand to protect my fall, I touched an object hard and round which rolled away. I stretched out again to grasp the thing. It had large holes in it. Some of its surface was smooth, some of it cracked and ragged. Then further down there were two rows of smaller objects like pebbles . . . or *teeth*. My hand first recoiled from the skull in horror, but then I picked it up and hurled it away from me. It gave me an odd satisfaction to hear the thing smash like a china vase against a wall.

Twice I went around those walls. The first time I seemed to come across a door, and I became elated. But no, it was the door that had closed on me. I confirmed my fears with a second tour. Then again I wanted to scream curses at God and die. I think I was closer to madness then than I have ever been, but something in me fought against it, silently in the dark. Slowly the urge to madness weakened, then it vanished as if it had never been. It was a victory of sorts, but I felt dull and lifeless after it. I was still going to die alone and never be found.

Slowly, my lethargy and despair lifted a little. I remembered that I had not yet located the source of the breeze and began to walk about feeling for it with my hands in front of me. The impression that I received was that it came up from somewhere. But it arrived in gusts, so that I had difficulty in following it to its source. Nevertheless, my attention was so fixed on feeling and hearing this one thing that I began to track it like a hound on a scent.

It was then that my enthusiasm almost betrayed me. As I began to feel this blast of air, I stepped forward confidently and my foot met emptiness. I threw myself backwards, and so just managed to prevent myself from falling into the sunken basin of the bathhouse. My caution returned. I crawled to the edge of the basin and let myself down into it.

The draught seemed to be coming from the floor of the bath, which was dry and had no trace of water in it, but though I was walking cautiously I nearly came to grief again. There was a hole in the floor. I knelt down and felt around it.

Part of the tiled base of the bath had given way and a hollow space underneath was exposed. I reached my hand inside. As far as I could tell the base of the pool was held up by brick pillars some two feet high. Evidently it had been heated in the ancient Roman manner by hot air from a furnace underneath. I climbed down into the spaces under the basin, where there was just room enough to crawl. If there had been a furnace under there, there would have been doors from which the fire was fed. It must have been from these that the breeze was coming. It was a small hope that I would be able to get through those doors, but it was the only hope I had.

I had to clear much debris before I began my journey under the bath and through the forest of brick pillars that supported it. In the pitch dark I was always bumping my head against them. Afraid that the floor above me might collapse, I moved gingerly. It was virtually impossible to tell where the breezes were coming from because the brick pillars were diverting their flow.

It might have been an hour, or more, or less—my situation had taken away from me all sense of time—before I ran up against a wall. I could have been going in circles for a long time before I met it. I worked my way along its brick surface, feeling carefully for any kind of door or aperture. I felt every crevice of the brick for a breath of wind. At last I could hear its whistling and moaning more distinctly. My hopes rose, but also my fears. I realized that I would soon know if there was a way of escape or not. Then my hands touched a pair of rusty metal plates under which the draught was blowing. These were the oven doors of the hypocaust. Would they open inwards or outwards?

I pushed, and they made no movement. There was no way of gripping them from the inside. With all the power that was available to me in that confined space, I heaved my shoulder against the metal. For that little effort I was deluged by an invisible but choking fall of dust and plaster. Even now the whole floor could collapse on top of me and I could die. Yet I fancied that the metal door had moved a little.

After a moment's thought I decided to brace myself against one of the brick pillars and thrust with my feet against the metal doors. They grated against the stone lintel at the first shove and opened a fraction. I saw a column of dazzling moonlight ahead of me and drank in a mouthful of cold air. One more thrust with my feet, and the doors were open just as a further deluge of tiles and plaster began to rain down on me.

I scrambled out feet-first onto the floor of a narrow, vaulted passageway. The moonlight was coming in from ragged holes in the roof. It was hideously cold, but the relief warmed me. To my left was a staircase going downwards, to my right a fall of rubble and masonry. My only way was down. I took a few steps before I realized that I was on the winding stair that I had seen on the outside of the château. I stopped before the steps did and hesitated again. I faced a drop of what? Thirty or forty feet? Death was still the likeliest option.

A small hand pushed me and I fell into dark open air.

Gaston Bobelet found me the following morning lying on the gravel path at the southwest corner of the château. I was suffering from a mild concussion and a sprained ankle, but no bones had been broken so he did not see fit to take me to hospital, and for that I was grateful to him. During the rest of my term as château caretaker I spent my nights in a room at the Bobelets' farmhouse, but Justin never knew that. When I returned to England I was not summoned to meet my cousin and make a report; I simply received a check through the post for the remainder of my house sitter's salary. The following year I heard that Justin had sold the château: no reason was given.

Cousin Justin and I did not meet again until a family christening in the spring of this year. My sister had produced a male child and, not being one to pass by such an opportunity, had decided to call him Justin and invite his wealthy namesake to be the godfather.

The ceremony at her little village church went well. Little Justin received the baptismal waters without complaint. Big Justin and the other godparents, of whom I was one, stood around the font as the vicar conducted the ceremony. When this was over my sister, perhaps for the benefit of photographers, handed the baby to his richest godfather to hold. I saw a troubled look pass across Cousin Justin's face, but he did his best to show willing. Like most childless men, he is not at ease with extreme infancy.

Justin junior emitted a gurgle of delight and stretched out a soft, plump little hand to caress his godfather's cheek. When the baby touched his mouth, my Cousin Justin started violently and nearly dropped him. I saw the look on his face, and it was one of sheer terror. When our eyes met across the font I smiled and lifted my fingers to my lips, flickering them a little as I did so. Justin's normally reddish complexion was now as grey as the surrounding stone. The baby began to cry, so my sister rapidly grabbed him back from his godfather's arms.

I felt at last that I had been paid in full for my time at the Château.

To the memory of the late, great Ingrid Pitt.

Two O'Clock Session

RICHARD MATHESON

RICHARD MATHESON is a master of modern science fiction, fantasy, and horror, and Stephen King credits him with single-handedly regenerating a stagnant genre. Matheson's first published story, "Born of Man and Woman," appeared in *The Magazine of Fantasy and Science Fiction* in 1950 and was the title story of his first collection, published four years later.

His work has subsequently been collected in such volumes as *The Shores of Space*, four volumes of *Shock*, *The Collected Stories of Richard Matheson*, *Nightmare at 20,000 Feet: Horror Stories by Richard Matheson*, *Duel: Terror Stories by Richard Matheson*, *Off Beat: Uncollected Stories*, *Button Button: Uncanny Stories*, and *Steel and Other Stories*. His best-known novels include the influential *I Am Legend*, *The Shrinking Man*, *A Stir of Echoes*, *Hell House*, the World Fantasy Award–winning *Bid Time Return*, and *What Dreams May Come*, all of which have been turned into movies.

More recent titles have included a series of Westerns, plus *7 Steps to Midnight*, *Now You See It . . .*, *Camp Pleasant*, *Hunted Past Reason*, *Come Fygures Come Shadowes*, and *Other Kingdoms*.

Not only did Matheson script fourteen episodes of Rod Serling's classic *The Twilight Zone* TV series, but his produced film scripts also include *The Fall of the House of Usher*, *The Pit and the Pendulum*, *Master of the World*, *Night of the Eagle* (aka *Burn, Witch, Burn*), *Tales of Terror*, *The Raven*, *The Comedy of Terrors*, *Fanatic* (aka *Die! Die! My Darling!*), *The Devil Rides Out* (aka *The Devil's Bride*), *De Sade*, *Duel*, *Dying Room Only*, *Scream of the Wolf*, *Dracula*, *The Stranger Within*, *Trilogy of Terror*, *Dead of Night*, *Twilight Zone: The Movie*, *Jaws 3-D*, *The Dreamer of Oz*, *Twilight Zone: Rod Serling's Lost Classics*, *Trilogy of Terror II*, and the two "Kolchak" TV movies, *The Night Stalker* and *The Night Strangler*.

Matheson was awarded the World Fantasy Lifetime Achievement Award in 1984 and the World Horror Convention's Living Legend Award in 2000.

"Ray Bradbury was the icon to be emulated when I was starting as a writer," explains the author. "The opportunity to write a story for a book which was to be a tribute to Ray was not to be resisted. That is this reprinted story. I tried to make it possess the 'flavor' of a Bradbury tale.

"I hope I succeeded, at least partially. The readers will decide that."

THE BREAKTHROUGH CAME at 2:41. Until that time, Maureen had done little more than repeat the bitter litany against her parents and brother.

"I have nothing to live for," she said then. "Absolutely nothing."

Dr. Volker didn't respond, but felt a tremor of excitement in himself. He'd been waiting for this.

He gazed at the young woman lying on his office couch. She was staring at the ceiling. What was she thinking? He wondered. He didn't dare to speak. He didn't want to break in on those thoughts, whatever they might be.

At last, Maureen spoke again. "I guess you didn't hear that," she said.

"I heard," Dr. Volker replied.

"No reaction then?" she asked, an edge of hostility in her voice. "No sage comment?"

"Like what?" he asked.

"Oh, God, don't start that again," she said. "Respond with an answer, not another goddamn question."

"I'm sorry," Dr. Volker said. "I didn't mean to make you angry."

"Well, it *did* make me angry! It made me—!" Her voice broke off with a shuddering throat sound. "You don't care," she said then.

"Of course I care," he told her. "What have I ever done to make you think I don't care?"

"*I said I have nothing to live for.*" Maureen's tone was almost venomous now.

"And—?" he asked.

"What do you mean *and?*" she snapped.

"And what does that make you feel like?"

The young woman shifted restlessly on the couch, her face distorted by anger. "It makes me feel like *shit!*" she said. "Is that precise enough for you, God damn it?! I feel like *shit!* I don't want to live!"

Closer, Volker thought. A shiver of elation laced across his back. He was glad the young woman was turned away from him. He didn't want her to know how he felt.

"And—?" he said again.

"Damn it to hell!" Maureen raged. "Is that all you can say?!"

"Did *you* hear what you said?" Volker asked as calmly as he could.

"About what? About having nothing to live for? About wanting to *die?*"

"You didn't use the word *die* before," he corrected.

"Oh, big deal!" she cried. "I apologize! I said I don't want to live! Anyone else would assume from that that I want to die! But not you!"

"Why do you want to die?" Volker winced a little. He shouldn't have said that.

Maureen's silence verified his reaction. It became so still in the office that he heard the sound of traffic passing on the boulevard. He cleared his throat, hoping that he hadn't made a mistake and lost the moment.

He wanted to speak but knew that he had to wait. He stared at the young woman on the couch. Don't leave me now, he thought. Stay with it. *Please.* It's been such a long time.

The young woman sighed wearily and closed her eyes.

"Have you nothing more to say?" he asked.

Her eyes snapped open and she twisted around to glare at him. "If I said what I wanted to say, your hair would turn white," she said, almost snarling the words.

"Maureen," he said patiently.

"*What?*"

"My hair is already white."

Her laugh was a humorless bark of acknowledgment. "Yes, it is," she said. "You're old. And decrepit."

"And you're young?" he asked.

"Young and . . ." She hesitated. "Young and miserable. Young and lost. Young and empty. Young and cold, without hope. Oh, *God!*" she cried in pain. "I want to die! I want to die! I'm going to see to it!"

Dr. Volker swallowed dryly. "See to what?" he asked.

"God damn it, are you stupid or something?" she lashed out at him. "Don't you understand English?"

"Help me to understand," he said. His pulse beat had quickened now. He was so close, so close.

Silence again. Oh, dear Lord, have I lost her again? he thought. How many sessions was it going to take?

He had to risk advancing. "See to what?" he asked.

The young woman stared at the ceiling.

"See to what, Maureen?" he asked.

"Leave me alone," she told him miserably. "You're no better than the rest of them. My father. My mother. My brother."

Oh, Christ! Volker clenched his teeth. Not the goddamn litany again!

"My father raped me, did you know that?" Maureen said. "Did I tell you that? Tell you that I was only seven when it happened? Tell you that my mother did nothing about it? That my brother laughed at me when I told him? Did I tell you that?"

Volker closed his eyes. Only about a thousand times, he thought.

He forced himself to open his eyes. "Maureen, you were onto something before," he risked.

"*What do you mean?*" she demanded.

Oh, no, he thought, chilled. But he couldn't stop now. "You said you wanted to die. You said—"

The young woman twitched violently on the couch, her head rolling to the right on the pillow, eyes closed.

"No!" Volker drove a fist down on the arm of his chair.

One more failure.

When the young woman sat up, he handed her a glass of water.

Jane Winslow drank it all in one, continuous swallow, then handed back the glass. "Anything?" she asked.

"Oh . . ." He exhaled tiredly. "The usual. We're right on top of it, but she backs off. She just can't face it." He shook his head. "Poor Maureen. I'm afraid it's going to be a long, long time before she's free to move on." He sighed in frustration. "Are you ready for the next one?"

She nodded.

At three o'clock she lay back on the couch and drew in long, deep breaths. She trembled for a while, then lay still.

"Arthur?" Dr. Volker said.

Jane Winslow opened her eyes.

"How are you today?"

"How *should* I be?" Arthur said bitterly.

Dr. Volker rubbed fingers over his eyes. Helping them was difficult. My God, how difficult. He had to keep trying though. He had no choice.

"So, how's life treating you, Arthur?" he asked.

Inheritance

PAUL McAULEY

BEFORE HE BECAME a full-time writer, Paul McAuley worked as a research biologist at various universities, including Oxford and UCLA, and for six years he was a lecturer on botany at St. Andrews University.

His first novel, *Four Hundred Billion Stars,* won the Philip K. Dick Memorial Award; his fifth, *Fairyland,* won the Arthur C. Clarke and John W. Campbell Awards. His latest novels are *The Quiet War* and *Gardens of the Sun*.

He lives in North London in an early Victorian house that, so far as he knows, contains no ghosts.

"This story was written while I was living in Oxford," recalls McAuley, "and two things in it are true: the lost village with its ruined mill and burned-down manor house (although I've changed the name), and certain details about the railway accident."

THERE WAS NO DOUBT about it: he was lost.

Richard Tolley tossed the map onto the backseat, levered himself out of the rented Volkswagen, and walked back to the T-junction and looked at the signpost. Sure enough, the fingerboard pointing in the direction from which he'd just come indicated that South Heyston was a mile away, and Upper Heyston three miles.

According to his Ordnance Survey map, Steeple Heyston was situated between these two villages, but he'd now driven through both villages from east to west and back again, and had seen no trace of it.

He knew there wasn't much left of the place, but there was a church clearly marked on the map, and a river and a railroad. How had he missed it?

He'd parked the car in front of a gate in the hedgerow, so that he wouldn't block the narrow country road. He leaned against the gate now, a tall, bear-like man in a white Burberry raincoat he'd purchased in London two days ago, twisting his signet ring around and around the middle finger of his right hand as he wondered if he should give up the search and try to find his way back to Oxford.

The car, cooling, ticked behind him. A fine rain only slightly heavier than a mist hazed the cold air, the kind of rain the English called a "mizzle." That quaint way with words they had, like calling an elevator a lift, or fall autumn, or the way the peppy red Volkswagen was badged as a Golf rather than a Rabbit. Like, but not like. The way the fields, vividly green even in the middle of December, were subtly different from the New Hampshire pastures of his childhood. Softer, nature's rawness blurred by centuries of human history.

Three in the afternoon, and it was already growing dark. He would try again tomorrow, Tolley decided, and was about to get back in the car when he saw two figures leave the cover of a clump of leafless trees in the far corner of the field.

Their dog, a black-and-white collie, raced across the field ahead of them and wriggled under the gate and barked at Tolley, who held his hands out of reach of its sharp white teeth and murmured, "Good boy, good boy," afraid that it would jump up and muddy his brand new Burberry.

One of the walkers, a man, whistled sharply, but the collie didn't stop barking at Tolley until the man had clambered over the stile and clipped a lead to its collar. He was in his sixties, small and wiry and sharp-featured. A flat cap was pulled low over his springy white hair. An expensive camera was slung over the shoulder of his Norfolk jacket and a walking stick with a heavy carved head was tucked under his arm.

"Sorry about that," he said. "He's young and excitable, but he rarely takes a bite from strangers."

"Maybe you can help me," Tolley said. "I guess I'm a little lost."

"Ask away," the man said, as he turned to help the woman—Tolley assumed she was his wife—over the stile. She was a short, plump woman with glossy black hair bound back in a girlish ponytail. Heavy amber earrings, silver rings on every finger of her hands and the magenta silk scarf that peeked above the top button of her fur-collared coat gave her an exotic, gypsy-ish air.

Tolley said, "I was looking for a place called Steeple Heyston. You know it?"

"You must have missed the turn," the man said. "It's about two miles back, past South Heyston. There's a wood, and a sharp bend in the road. Steeple Heyston's off to the left of that bend, down a rough track."

"I think I remember the sharp bend."

"The track isn't signposted. No one lives there anymore, you see."

"Isn't there an old manor house, something like that? That's what I've come to see—my family on my father's side used to live there. Tolley. The name mean anything to you?"

The man and the woman shared a look.

The man said, "There's a bit of the old manor house still standing."

The woman said, "You're American, aren't you? We have a son over there, in Boston."

"Harvard University," her husband said.

"He's a professor in the Medical School," the woman said.

Tolley told them that he'd heard of Harvard, but he was from New York. The man introduced himself as Gerald Beaumont, a retired mining engineer, introduced his wife, Marjorie, and the dog, Sam. Marjorie Beaumont studied Tolley for a moment, her gaze unnervingly direct as he said that he was some sort of academic himself.

"I work in a picture library," Tolley added, slightly flustered.

"Give her another minute," her husband said, with a fond twinkle, "and she'll tell you your age, how long you've been married, and how many children you have."

"Actually, I'm divorced. Or rather, I'm getting divorced. That's kind of why I'm on holiday, to get away from all that. And take a look at the place my folks came from."

And to spend as much of his money as possible in one glorious jamboree before Rachel and her lawyer got their hands on it. How she'd started the divorce, she'd phoned him at work one day, after the latest in a series of rows about money, and told him not to come home. Which he'd done straight away, of course, to find she'd changed the locks on their apartment—strictly speaking it was *her* apartment, but they'd been living there as man and wife for two years.

He'd hammered on the door; she'd called the police; two days later a process server had handed Tolley divorce papers and a court order forbidding him to go within five hundred yards of his soon-to-be-ex-wife. That's when Tolley, who'd been couch surfing in the apartment of an increasingly grumpy workmate, had decided to take the holiday of a lifetime, and go check out his roots, the place in England his family had once owned.

After he'd told the old couple something of this (leaving out the humiliating bits about the rows, being locked out of his own home, the court order), Marjorie Beaumont asked if he knew anything about his family history. Tolley said that all he knew was that they had once owned the manor house at Steeple Heyston and a good deal of farmland around it, that his grandfather had sold up and moved to the States in the late 19th century.

"I know the manor house burned down around then," Tolley said, "but I don't know much else. I think there was some kind of scandal, but my family's papers have been lost over the years. I'm hoping to look in the local history archives and find out about what would have been my inheritance, if things had turned out different."

Marjorie Beaumont said, "It's a terribly sad place. The saddest place I know."

"Now, Marjorie," Gerald Beaumont said.

"Even people without my gifts know that Steeple Heyston is an unquiet place," his wife said. "Even you think it's haunted, dear."

"I don't know about ghosts," Gerald Beaumont said, "but it *is* a lonely place with a lot of history. The manor house and the mill burnt down, and before that there was the railway accident, of course."

Tolley said, "There was a railway accident?"

Gerald Beaumont told him that it was a very famous one that had happened over a hundred years ago, that more than forty people had been killed, that some thought it was why Steeple Heyston was haunted.

"He should hear the story properly," his wife said. "Perhaps, when you've visited Steeple Heyston, Mr. Tolley, you would like to have tea with us. I can tell you all about it then."

"I don't want to put you to any trouble," Tolley said. He was amused and charmed: the Beaumonts were like two eccentric supporting characters from that Agatha Christie detective show Rachel used to watch on *Masterpiece Theatre*.

"He doesn't want to be bothered with these old stories," Gerald Beaumont said.

"It concerns his family," Marjorie Beaumont said firmly, "and it's no trouble, is it, Gerald?"

"Of course not," her husband said, with fond patience, and told Tolley that they lived in South Heyston. "Glebe Cottage, two doors down from the pub. You can't miss it. Come and see us when you've done at Steeple Heyston, and we'll tell you what we know."

He repeated his directions to Steeple Heyston, and his wife told Tolley that he shouldn't stay there too long because it would be dark soon.

They watched as Tolley fitted himself into his rental car and awkwardly turned it in the narrow road, grinding gears because he wasn't used to the stick shift, and then the Beaumonts and their dog were dwindling between the hedgerows in the rearview mirror.

Tolley found the turning and steered the car, its springs complaining, down a rough, unsurfaced track that ended in a small turnaround with trees on one side and an unkempt hedge on the other.

He switched off the motor and clambered out into the unnerving stillness of the unpopulated countryside. There was a farm gate half-buried in the hedge, held shut by a loop of orange twine.

Beyond was a wide, rough meadow backstopped by a steep railway embankment, with a line of bare trees on one side and a small river on the other.

As Tolley unhooked the gate and stepped through, a train hurtled out of the misty gloom, the lights of its passenger cars like a string of yellow beads, dragging a dull roar behind as it dwindled away.

There had once been a narrow road or street here; there were grassy humps on either side where houses and cottages had once stood, although not a stone showed now. Tolley followed its line towards the trees and realized, as he wandered beneath them, that here were the ruins of the manor house his family had once owned.

The moment was curiously disappointing; perhaps it was because there was hardly anything left of the place. A low hummock, narrow and straight, was all that remained of a wall; a huge briar patch might have once been a rose garden; ragged shoulders of red brick fell away either side of a tall cluster of octagonal chimneys.

Tolley used his pocket Olympus to take a few photographs in the doubtful light; as he framed the last, he noticed the small church that stood a few hundred yards beyond the ruins, its square tower not much higher than the railway embankment behind it.

The hedge around its graveyard had grown tall and wild; long briers trailed from it like unkempt hair. Tolley found an iron gate, saw headstones standing in waist-high grass obviously untrimmed since spring, saw a bramble bush that had rooted in the shoulders of a headless stone angel. Yet the gravel path was free of weeds, and a hand-sized hole in one of the stained-glass windows had been patched with hardboard, suggesting that although its congregation had long since deserted it, or lay under the long grass, someone still cared for the place.

It was growing dark, the sun a bloody smear in clouds low over cold fields where mist was beginning to gather. Too dark, Tolley thought, to examine the inscriptions on gravestones or look in the church for relics of his family.

He walked back through the overgrown ruins of the manor house, and in the last of the light crossed the hummocky meadow to the little river. Where it passed beneath a steel railway bridge, the water dropped in a glassy rush over the step of a weir; on the far bank were the remains of a big, square building that had to be the mill Tolley's family had once owned.

As Tolley framed in his camera's view finder a broken wall that stood amongst a clump of leafless trees, he thought for a moment that someone was lurking in the shadows there, a man with an oddly shaped head. Or no, he seemed to be wearing a top hat.

A freight train trundled around the curve and crossed the bridge with a hollow roar, sounding a two-note horn. Tolley glanced up, then took his photograph. The figure, if that's what it had been, was gone.

He had another bad moment when he got back to the car, and saw what he thought was a face peeking up at him from the back seat: but it was only the map, lying where he'd tossed it.

All that talk about ghosts had evidently primed his jet-lagged imagination, he thought, as he drove the scant mile to South Heyston. There was a tumbledown farm, a string of pebble-dash council houses, and then a cluster of picturesque stone cottages around a tiny village green, a church steeple poking against the evening sky behind them. Glebe Cottage was next to the churchyard.

Gerald Beaumont shook Tolley's hand at the front door and ushered him into what he called the lounge, turning down, but not quite muting, the sound of a big color television that was showing some old B movie. During the strange conversation that followed, the television flickered and mumbled in its corner like some idiot child.

Seated in an overstuffed armchair, Tolley felt like a fledgling cuckoo as the Beaumonts fluttered about, plying him with hot, milky tea and cookies and small, buttery cakes.

He learned that Gerald Beaumont had worked in the Yorkshire coal mines, but had taken early retirement when many of them were closed down in the aftermath of a big strike. The Beaumonts had moved to Oxford to be near their only child and his family when he had been working at the University, but then their son had become another statistic in the Brain Drain, and had moved to America.

Tolley guessed that they were lonely, like a lot of retired folk who move from where they have lived and worked; it was as if they, not their son, were exiles in a foreign land.

When Marjorie Beaumont asked him about his impression of Steeple Heyston, Tolley told her that he hadn't seen all that much; it had gotten dark too quickly. He had forgotten until that moment the glimpse he'd had of that shadowy figure—perhaps it had been nothing more than a figment of his imagination, conjured out of twilight and Marjorie Beaumont's talk of ghosts, but now he felt a shiver, an undeniable *frisson*.

He said, "I guess I'll have to come back tomorrow. I want to take a look at that church, and take some photographs, too."

Gerald Beaumont said, "It's a good place for photography, all right. Let me show you a few I took of the place."

"He won't want to look at your snaps," Marjorie Beaumont said, as her husband rooted in the cupboard under the glass-fronted bookcase that held an *Encyclopaedia Britannica* and what looked like a complete run of *Reader's Digest* condensed novels.

"He can tell me himself if he isn't interested," Gerald Beaumont said, and pulled out a spiral-bound album and passed it to Tolley, saying that he would appreciate a professional opinion.

Tolley wiped his buttery fingers on his sweater before he took the album—he'd eaten all of the little cakes, and most of the cookies (no, they called them biscuits here)—saying, "I work in a photographic library, but I'm no photographer."

Large 8 x 10 prints, black-and-white, one to a page. The church stark against a wintry sky. Gravestones leaning this way and that, all sunlight and shadow. The brambly angel Tolley had noticed, shot from an acute angle, the sun making a halo behind it. Grassy hummocks defined by their shadows. Dead weeds bent before a lichenous stone. The ruined chimney standing stark amongst leafless trees. The ruined chimney rising out of a cloud of wild roses.

Tolley was impressed, and told Gerald Beaumont that he had definitely captured the atmosphere of the place.

"There are some things photographs can't capture," Marjorie Beaumont said. A lavender cardigan was draped over her shoulders like a matador's cape, pinned at her neck by a big Victorian brooch. The paste jewel flickered in the light of the fire that burned in the brick fireplace. "I expect you saw the railway that runs past. That's the old Oxford-to-Birmingham line, and it was about a hundred years ago that the tragedy happened."

"A hundred and six," Gerald Beaumont said.

His wife ignored him. "There was a passenger train on its way to Birmingham, and a goods train going towards Oxford. One of the wagons of the goods train jumped the tracks and pulled others across the line, and the passenger train couldn't stop in time, and crashed into them. They said that you could hear the shriek of its brakes in Oxford, that the sparks from its wheels set fire to three miles of the embankment. More than forty people died, but it's said that many of them would have been saved if the squire—I suppose he'd be your great-grandfather, Mr. Tolley—if he hadn't stopped the villagers of Steeple Heyston from helping the injured."

"He hated the railway with a passion," Gerald Beaumont said. "He'd lost a lot of money fighting and losing a legal battle against the Act of Parliament that gave it the right of way across his land. When the other passengers carried the injured away from the wreck, he told his tenants that anyone who lifted a hand to help would lose their livelihood and their home. 'Let them use their blasted railway to save themselves,' he's supposed to have said. Anyhow, it was more than two hours before a relief train arrived, and by that time many had died who might otherwise have survived."

"There's a monument to them in a corner of the churchyard, raised by public subscription," Marjorie Beaumont said. "The squire tried to prevent that, too, but the diocese council overruled him. Two bodies, a man and a woman, were never identified, and they're buried in the churchyard. They say you can see them on the anniversary of the accident, walking along the railway line, as if they're looking for something they've lost or left behind."

Tolley smiled. "Have you ever seen these ghosts?"

Marjorie Beaumont shook her head. "I wouldn't go near Steeple Heyston on that night or on any other, for that matter. Even on a hot summer's day, it's a sad, lonely place."

Gerald Beaumont said, "I'm not given to believing in ghosts and such myself, but it's true that Marjorie fainted there once, and she's never gone back."

"It's the woman, I expect," Marjorie Beaumont said softly, as if to herself. "Their ghosts are stronger."

Gerald Beaumont pretended to ignore this, saying quickly, "You didn't know about this story, Mr. Tolley?"

"Please, call me Dick. No, not a thing. My grandfather never said a word about what happened to the manor house. That he came from Steeple Heyston, I know only because my father saved grandpappy's naturalization papers. That's about all he left the family, apart from this signet ring," Tolley said, showing off the gold ring with the family crest incised into its flat surface.

His grandfather had been rich—he'd owned a large house on the Upper West Side of New York, and had never needed to work—but had squandered most of his fortune on bad business deals, and what was left had been lost in the Wall Street Crash. After the war, Tolley's father had built up a real estate business from scratch, but he'd blown every cent on horses and poker, and shot himself as his creditors were closing in. All Tolley had inherited had been the signet ring, a few family papers, and a careless attitude towards money; most of his arguments with Rachel had been about money.

"Ten years after the accident," Gerald Beaumont said, "there was a fire in the manor house. The mill burned down at the same time. The manor house and the mill were the only reasons the village existed. They weren't rebuilt, and the people in the village drifted away."

"I guess that was when my family came to the States," Tolley said.

Marjorie Beaumont got to her feet. "I'll make another pot of tea. You'll have a cup before you go."

"Traffic's bad this time of night," Gerald Beaumont said as he carefully filed away his photograph album. "If you wait thirty minutes the worst of the rush hour will be over."

"I appreciate it. I'm still not used to driving on the wrong side of the road, and your traffic circles scare me silly."

The collie, which all the while had been dozing under the murmuring television, scrambled up, looked at the door of the lounge and made a low noise that was half-whimper, half-growl. Then there was the sound of crockery smashing. Gerald Beaumont hurried out, and Tolley followed.

Marjorie Beaumont was standing in the middle of the small, brightly lit kitchen, one hand pressed against her throat. Her husband asked what the matter was, and she pointed at the window. Her hand trembled. Backed by night, the two letters traced in an ornamental script on the steamy glass, a linked *O* and *R*, were clearly visible.

"I saw it happen," Marjorie Beaumont said in a small voice. Her lavender cardigan had slipped from her shoulders and lay on the floor. Her husband put an arm around her, and she added, "I didn't ever think it would come here. I'm sorry, Mr. Tolley, but I think you ought to go."

Driving back to Oxford, the headlights of homeward-bound commuters flashing by on what still seemed like the wrong side of the road,

Tolley began to think that the Beaumonts had set him up: Marjorie Beaumont had told him her ghost story, given herself an excuse to go out of the room and write those the two letters in the steam on the kitchen window, and then deliberately dropped a cup and given that Oscar-worthy performance.

Maybe they were a couple of crazies who liked to put on a little act for strangers; maybe it was to prepare him for an offer, in exchange for a fat fee, to exorcise the place, or to conjure up the ghosts of his ancestors. In any case, Tolley resolved to have nothing more to do with them.

First thing the next morning, he found an express photographic developer that promised to process his film in three hours, then walked through a modern shopping arcade to the town's library and spent a couple of hours browsing in the local history section.

He read several accounts of the railway accident, all more or less confirming Marjorie Beaumont's confabulation, and found a book on lost villages that gave a good précis of the history of Steeple Heyston.

It was mentioned in the *Domesday Book* and had been a thriving agricultural village until the 16th century, when it had been badly hit by the plague. Tolley's ancestors had confiscated much of the surrounding land by shrewd use of the enclosure acts, and by the middle of the 19th century, Steeple Heyston had been no more than a hamlet of some forty souls, dependent upon its wool mill. Then there had been the two fires Gerald Beaumont had mentioned, arson suspected but no one arrested, and after that a swift decline. The last cottage had been demolished a few years after World War II, although it seemed that the church was still occasionally used.

Tolley couldn't find any mention of ghosts, or of why his grandfather had quit the ancestral home. He'd have to check the archives of the local newspaper, and the county records, he thought, and pocketed his notes and went out to look for some lunch.

Away from the old buildings of the university, Oxford was much like any other English market town. Laden shoppers moved past long lines waiting for double-decked buses. Street performers strummed guitars or juggled in shop doorways. At the Carfax crossroads, a Salvation Army band was playing carols beneath a huge plastic Santa Claus strung high in the cold air.

Tolley found a McDonald's and hungrily devoured a double cheeseburger with all the trimmings and washed it down with a strawberry milkshake. Looking through the plate-glass window towards the tower of Christ Church, poised like a spaceship beyond the gloomy stone pile of the town hall, he decided that he'd done enough work for one day. He spent the rest of the afternoon checking off the minor colleges he'd missed the first time around, then fought his way through the crowds to the photographic shop.

After the assistant handed him the envelope, Tolley opened it straight away. There were the half-dozen snaps he'd taken before leaving London, several of Oxford, including the picture of the four-poster bed in his hotel room that he intended to mail to his soon-to-be-ex-wife, but none of Steeple Heyston. One of the strips of developed film was cloudily blotched. Tolley showed it to the shop assistant, a teenager with streaks bleached into her hair. "It looks like you've made some kind of mistake processing this."

"I dunno, it's all done by computers and stuff. Maybe your camera's broke."

"Let me speak to your manager."

"She won't be in until the day after tomorrow," the girl said, adding, as if it explained everything, "It's Christmas, see."

After a supper of steak and kidney pie and several pints of bitter in a public house, Tolley returned to his hotel, intending to make an early night of it.

As soon as he opened the door, a dense smell of burning, thick as molasses, hit him. There was no smoke, no sign of any kind of fire, but his case and its contents, mostly underwear, lay on the floor and the quilt and sheets had been pulled from the four-poster bed.

His first thought was that the room had been burgled, but his passport and plane ticket were sitting on the night table, next to his Walkman and pile of CDs. And then he noticed the carpet under the window. Scraped into the pile were the letters O and R, linked with the same flourish as the letters in the steam on the Beaumonts' kitchen window.

Gerald Beaumont looked genuinely surprised when he opened the door and found Tolley on his doorstep.

Tolley gave the man his best smile, said, "I want some pictures of Steeple Heyston to show the folks back home, but my camera has broken and it can't be repaired here. I was passing by, and remembered your wonderful photographs, and wondered if you'd mind giving me a little help . . .?"

He'd worked up this plan over a couple of double scotches in the hotel bar last night. Either the Beaumonts were hounding him for some crazy reason, had bribed the photographic shop to ruin his film, had gained access to his hotel room and burnt some kind of stink bomb in the waste bin and traced the interlinked letters in the carpet with the heel of a shoe, all of which was more or less completely unbelievable, or there was something to the story about the ghosts of victims of an old railway accident.

He didn't believe that, either, but he wanted to return to Steeple Heyston in daylight to look around the church and satisfy himself that the figure he thought he'd seen was nothing more than a trick of shadows and twilight. It seemed to him that the best way to find out if the Beaumonts really were trying to work some trick or scam on him was to take one or both of them to Steeple Heyston, see if they rose to the bait.

He said, "I'll pay whatever it costs, of course."

"I'd be delighted," Gerald Beaumont said.

Behind him, Marjorie Beaumont came out of the lounge and said, "Surely you're not thinking of going back to Steeple Heyston, Mr. Tolley? You've already disturbed something that's best left alone."

"Stuff and nonsense," Gerald Beaumont said amiably, and winked at Tolley. "She still isn't over her little shock."

"If that had anything to do with me," Tolley said disingenuously, "you must let me know how I can make it up to you."

"We invited you here in the first place," Marjorie Beaumont said stiffly. "I suppose that it isn't your fault that you brought an unexpected guest with you."

As he drove away from the cottage, Tolley said to Gerald Beaumont, "I hope I haven't upset your wife."

"It doesn't take much sometimes. Last time she went to Steeple Heyston, a couple of years ago it was, she fainted dead away. She's always been sensitive to what she calls atmospheres."

Tolley saw an opportunity to plant his baited hook. "When I was there, I saw what looked like a man, standing in what I guess were the ruins of the old mill. At the time, I thought it was just a trick of the light, but now I'm not so sure. Maybe it was a ghost. If this place was somehow responding to me, could your wife do anything about it?"

"She's sensitive to atmospheres," Gerald Beaumont said, "and that's all there is to it. She isn't a medium, she doesn't channel spirits or any of that nonsense."

"You invited me to your home in the first place, Mr. Beaumont, and told me your ghost story. It was never my intention to upset your wife."

"Aye, well, like Marjorie said, it wasn't your fault. But if I may speak plainly, Mr. Tolley, I don't want her upset again. If you're looking for some mumbo-jumbo exorcism, I'm sure there are plenty of people who'll be more than happy to take your money. But don't think of asking Marjorie. If that's the only reason you came back to see us, you can let me out right now. I can easily walk home from here."

"I really do want some good photographs of the place," Tolley said.

Gerald Beaumont smiled. "And I'm sure you could take them yourself, but our story has made you nervous of going there alone, and I'm a daft old man who's easily flattered into helping you."

Tolley smiled too, disarmed by the man's direct manner, and admitted, "Something like that."

Gerald Beaumont said, "Miners are as superstitious as sailors, and like it or not, I suppose a bit of that rubbed off on me. I don't believe in ghosts, but some places do have an atmosphere to them. Down in the mines, there are galleries you didn't like to be alone in, old workings with a funny feel to them. Maybe places can be affected by things that have happened in them, if you follow me. That would be your ghosts, you see. That would be what Marjorie picks up."

Tolley thought of the initials scrawled in the steam on the kitchen window of the Beaumont's cottage, in the carpet in his room. It wasn't a feeling, a sense of place, that had done that. And if it hadn't been anything to do with the Beaumonts . . .

Frost lay in the hollows of the rough meadow at Steeple Heyston; a light mist floated above the river. Tolley felt a little *frisson* of anticipation when he saw the stub of wall amongst the scrubby trees on the far bank, but in the cold flat daylight it seemed quite ordinary.

He asked Gerald Beaumont to take a couple of photographs of it, waiting patiently as the older man fitted the appropriate lens to his battered old Canon and fussed with a handheld light meter.

The frost made the contours of the ground easy to read; Tolley could make out the long strips of an ancient field system beyond the ruins of the mill. Everything was quiet and still, the solitude emphasized when a long goods train trundled past.

"It's always a lonely place," Gerald Beaumont remarked, echoing Tolley's thoughts. "But it's not as bleak as this in summer. There are wild flowers all over the place, boats on the river . . . People will punt all the way up from Oxford to picnic here."

They walked across the meadow to the line of trees and the scattered remnants of the manor house. Gerald Beaumont leaned on his walking stick every other step (he had a touch of arthritis, he said, because of the damp weather) and laboriously took several photographs while Tolley huddled inside his Burberry and stamped his frozen feet.

In the churchyard, Gerald Beaumont showed Tolley the stone pyramid that commemorated the railway accident, led him under a dark green yew where two gravestones stood apart from the others, their brief inscriptions blotted by lichen.

"Those are the buggers that are causing the trouble, according to local legend. Doesn't look like much by daylight, does it?"

"Your wife said something about a woman," Tolley said.

"There's a man *and* a woman buried here. Two strangers who were killed in the accident, who were buried here because no one could identify them, no one would claim their bodies. And that's all there is to it, Mr. Tolley."

While Gerald Beaumont photographed from every angle the memorial's pyramid, Tolley tried the door of the little church. The iron handle was so stiff he thought for a moment the place was locked; then it gave, and the door creaked open.

It was colder inside the church than outside. Tolley shivered inside his Burberry, taking in the pews either side of the aisle, the plain pulpit and the draped altar beyond. Tablets were set in the rough stone walls. One listed the names of those killed in the Great War, another mentioned a Victorian incumbent of the parish, the next was marked with the same crest that was incised in Tolley's signet ring and memorialized Alfred Tolley, squire of this parish, and his wife Evangeline, both dead in the same year, 1886. The year the manor house and the paper mill had burned down.

There were other memorials to members of Tolley's family amongst the uneven flagstones of the floor; as he studied them, he thought he heard the door creak open and said, "How about a few photos of these, Mr. Beaumont?"

There was no reply. Tolley looked around, saw that he was alone, the door was closed, heard a distant, drawn-out metallic screech, smelt the same, gritty, sulphurous stench he'd encountered in his hotel room, suddenly so thick he couldn't catch his breath. His first step turned into a stagger, and then he ran, wrenching the door open, bursting out into the bleak daylight.

Gerald Beaumont was squatting on his heels near the gate in the hedgerow, preparing to photograph a headstone. Tolley walked up to him and said, as casually as he could manage, "Did you hear something just then?"

Click. Gerald Beaumont looked up from his camera, asked what he meant.

"I don't know. Like . . . no, forget it. Maybe we should quit. It's so cold I can't feel my feet."

Tolley's hands were shaking. He couldn't stop them shaking, and jammed them into the pockets of his Burberry. He thought of a tape recorder, a hidden speaker . . .

Gerald Beaumont said, "Did you see the memorials to your family in the church? I've a good flash attachment, I could take some nice pictures of them if you want."

The last thing Tolley wanted to do was to go back inside the church. "It was good of you to come all the way out here," he said, "but I have a touch of jet-lag. I should get back to my hotel, catch up on my sleep."

As he and Gerald Beaumont walked through the line of trees and crossed the wide space of rough grass beyond, Tolley felt something huge and implacable looming behind him, as in one of those dreams from which you wake bathed in cold sweat. It was all he could do not to break into a run, and as he drove off, he startled Gerald Beaumont by popping the clutch and spinning the wheels of the Volkswagen, as if he were a teenager again, burning rubber in the drive of his girlfriend's house.

As they drove back to South Heyston, Tolley thanked Gerald Beaumont for his trouble, refused the ritual offer of a cup of tea, and said that he should head straight back for Oxford.

"You'd better give me your address, Mr. Tolley. I'll make some contact prints and send them to you, and you can choose which ones you'd like done properly."

"That's very kind, Mr. Beaumont, but if you give me the film, I can get it developed in town. I'll pay you for it, of course."

"You don't owe me anything, Mr. Tolley. It's only a roll of film. I'll just pop in my darkroom and unload it. Are you sure you won't come in and have a cup of tea? Marjorie baked another batch of those butter cakes you liked so much the last time."

"If it's all the same, I think I should head straight back." Tolley felt a little calmer now. He'd take the film and take off, he thought, and never come back.

When Tolley pulled up outside the cottage, the collie dog was barking behind the gate to its small front garden. Gerald Beaumont climbed out of the car, calling to it, then suddenly pushed through the gate and gimped quickly up the path to where his wife sat on the step of the front door, knelt beside her and put his arm around her shoulders.

Tolley climbed out, walked slowly towards them, dread thumping in his heart, hardly noticing the dog that danced about in a frenzy of excitement.

Marjorie Beaumont's glossy black hair was tumbled around her face. Her hands were covered in what look like drying blood and there were white handprints on her black slacks and cardigan. She looked up at Tolley through her shroud of hair and said, "I saw him."

Gerald Beaumont, his face stiff and pinched, said "Let it lie, Mr. Tolley. Let it lie and leave us be."

"Orlando Richards," Marjorie Beaumont said, and turned into her husband's embrace and began to sob.

It was past two o'clock when Tolley arrived back in Oxford. He left the Volkswagen in the hotel's car park, found a public house in nearby Broad Street, and bought a cheese roll mummified in cling film and a pint of bitter.

He was scared and angry. Something had torn up his hotel room, had let him know its name through Marjorie Beaumont . . . what would it do next? More importantly, why did it have anything to do with him in the first place? He hadn't chosen his ancestors—why should he be blamed for what one of them did more than a hundred years ago? And besides, Marjorie Beaumont was the one who believed in ghosts, atmospheres, and all the rest of that nonsense.

Maybe she'd brought all this upon herself, Tolley thought, knowing that it was uncharitable. Maybe she'd woken whatever it was that was persecuting them both. The ghost of a man. O.R. Orlando Richards.

He finished his pint and the cheese roll, which sat in his stomach like a cannonball, found a taxi at the rank near the hotel, and asked the driver to take him to the newspaper offices.

"*Mail* or *Times*, mate?"

"Whichever is the oldest."

That turned out to be the *Oxford Times*, which occupied a seedy office block in a seedy industrial estate beyond the railroad station. Tolley's business card got him past the receptionist to a young, friendly reporter, who listened to his story about researching family history, and showed him the cubby hole where the microfilm reader was kept and introduced him to the secretary in charge of the newspaper's archives.

Finding articles about the train wreck was easy enough because Tolley knew the exact date. The news reports were prolix and soberly sensational, and those about the train wreck took up most of the next day's edition of the newspaper; but Tolley quickly spotted a reference to the body of an unknown gentleman burnt alive in the first carriage of the wrecked passenger train, a silver snuff box bearing the initials O.R. the only surviving form of identification. The police had 'believed him to be a man of some thirty years, some five feet six inches in height and of average build', and asked anyone who might know who he was to report in person to the coroner's court in Oxford, or their nearest police station.

Farther down there was a briefer mention of an unknown woman, no more than twenty years old, who had died like several others at the scene of the tragedy, her purse "containing no more than the stub for a third-class railway ticket from London to Birmingham, and eighteen pence in small coins."

Tolley had to scan a whole year's worth of microfilmed back issues to find the report about the TRAGIC FIRE AT STEEPLE HEYSTON, which had killed his great-grandfather and great-grandmother. The first fire had started in the kitchen of the manor house, and when that was burning well and when "the attention of everyone in the vicinity was occupied upon saving its inhabitants," a second fire had been set in the mill.

Tolley followed the story through succeeding editions of the newspaper. There were the death notices of Tolley's great-grandparents, from which Tolley learned that his great-grandfather had fought and won several cases brought against him by relatives of those who had died in the "railway tragedy" at Steeple Heyston. A maid claimed that the manor house had been troubled by small fires caused by falling candles, or candles flaring up unexpectedly, or fires collapsing from their grates. More prosaically, a man was arrested for setting the fires, the son of a woman who had died in the train wreck; two days later, he was found hanged in his cell.

Tolley borrowed a phone and a telephone directory. When Gerald Beaumont answered, Tolley started to tell him what he'd found, but Gerald Beaumont said, "I don't want to hear anything more about it, Mr. Tolley. Don't you think you've caused enough trouble?"

"It isn't me, it's this dead guy. Orlando Richards. He was killed in the train wreck, he was never properly buried. Maybe he possessed the guy who set those fires, but I don't think so. I don't think he wants revenge. I think he was trying to tell your wife—"

"I think you should leave Marjorie out of this, Mr. Tolley."

"I'm sorry. I forgot to ask how she was."

"Sleeping now. Our GP came round and gave her something to help her sleep."

"Do you know what happened?"

"She thought she glimpsed someone through the kitchen window, but she can't remember anything after that." Gerald Beaumont paused, then said, "She left the kitchen in a bit of a state. Wrote those two letters everywhere in tomato sauce, in flour . . . But I cleaned it all up, and she's resting now, she doesn't want to be disturbed. It's all very well for you—you can just run away back to America. We have to live with whatever it is you've disturbed."

"Me? I didn't do anything but come here."

"Aye, well," the man said truculently.

"I don't suppose by any chance you're Catholic, or you know someone who is Catholic?"

"I'm Church of England, Mr. Tolley, which in this country means you can believe in God and all the rest, or you go to church once a year for the carols, like I do. If you're thinking of arranging an exorcism, or any other kind of mumbo-jumbo, forget about it."

"Orlando Richards was never properly buried, but he made his name known to us. Perhaps all he wants—"

"Let it lie, Mr. Tolley. Maybe, when you're gone, things will calm down," Gerald Beaumont said, and cut the connection.

Tolley decided to change his room, just in case, but the desk clerk politely but firmly told him that it was impossible, the hotel was fully booked.

"Don't tell me," Tolley said. "It's Christmas."

"If you're unhappy here, sir, I could try to book you into another hotel. Or perhaps a bed-and-breakfast would suit."

"I guess I'll have to manage," Tolley said.

He had just one more night here, and then he was due to travel to London—surely he would not be followed there. Maybe Gerald Beaumont was right, maybe things would calm down after he left. If they didn't, well, it was no longer Tolley's problem. He'd tried his best, it wasn't his fault the old guy wouldn't listen.

Tolley ate a solitary dinner in the reassuringly expensive restaurant, treating himself to a bottle of Chablis that cost twice as much as the food, and a glass of fifty-year-old Cognac that cost more than the wine.

Then he moved on to the bar, where he drank several double scotches and smoked a Cuban cigar and fell into conversation with a married couple from Idaho—she had majored in architectural history, and was in her element, showing Tolley every photograph of Oxford she had taken with her brand new camera. Her husband grumbled about the six-hour journey from London to Oxford on a train that was unheated and made long unscheduled stops in the middle of nowhere; grumbled about shop assistants who were either surly or obsequious but never helpful, dribbling plumbing, the litter and graffiti in town centers . . . in short, the lack of all the comforts of any truly civilized country.

He was the living caricature of a Yank abroad, appalled by his discovery that foreign countries aren't anything at all like the good old US of A, but Tolley cheerfully agreed with everything he said and added a few stories of his own, including the anecdote about his ruined film and a tale about a crazy old couple that grew more and more difficult to tell without mentioning ghosts.

"The point is," Tolley said, when he realized that he had lost the thread, "people like to think that all Americans are stupid and rich, and I'm neither." He meant it as a joke, but it left him feeling sorry for himself, and led him to talk about the way his family had selfishly squandered its wealth and left him with nothing, and about the way he was making sure that he spent as much as possible on this trip so that all his soon-to-be-ex-wife and her lawyer would get out of him was half of an enormous credit-card bill.

His new friends, suddenly restless, declared that they had to turn in because they were headed for Stratford-upon-Avon tomorrow, and Tolley was left alone with the barman, who made a point, after he served one more double scotch, of rattling down the security grille at the other end of the bar.

It was after midnight. The noise of the key turning in the lock of the door to Tolley's room was loud in the deserted corridor, and despite the warm blanket of booze that muffled his thoughts, he had a nasty moment groping for the light switch, remembering an account, surely the world's shortest ghost story, of how someone had awoken with a start and groped for matches to light a candle—and felt something place them in his hand.

The light came on, revealing his suitcase on its stand, the four-poster bed tightly made, one corner turned back and a chocolate wrapped like a gold medallion on the plumped pillow. Even the initials scraped into the carpet pile had been erased when the maid had vacuumed the room.

Tolley looked inside the wardrobe in case a spook was hiding there, checked the lock on the window, dropped his clothes in a heap and crawled into the cool shelter of the bed. Reckless with Dutch courage, he even switched off the light.

He was woken by the shrill ring of the phone beside his bed. He groped for it without turning on the light, pressed the handset to his ear without raising his head from his pillow. Gerald Beaumont's voice said, "Tolley?"

"What's up?" The digital clock in the bedside radio told him that it was half-past-six in the morning. His teeth and tongue felt as if they had been rubbed in ashes and he knew that he was still drunk, and that he was going to pay for it pretty soon.

"I didn't want to ring you, but there's no one else I can turn to," Gerald Beaumont said. "You're involved. You *understand*. It's Marjorie. She left."

"Left?"

"Left the cottage. She was sleeping in the spare bedroom. I got up just now, and she isn't there."

Tolley sat up and switched on the bedside lamp. He was wide-awake, and his heart was beating quickly and lightly. "Call the police, Mr. Beaumont. I'm sure they'll help you find her."

"I know where she's gone, and so do you. And if I have to go to the police for help, I'll have to tell them about you, and Steeple Heyston."

"If that's a threat, Mr. Beaumont, it isn't much of one. I'll help look for her, but we need to call the police too."

"No," Gerald Beaumont said firmly. "We don't. She had . . . a problem a few years ago. She thought there was going to be an accident at the mine. She said she saw dead people who told her that one of the drifts was going to collapse. She was very badly affected by it, and she had to be put in a place where she could rest for a little while."

"Jesus."

"That's partly why we came here, to get away from all that. That's why I'm not going to the police, why I'll deal with it myself if I have to."

"And the mine . . . did it collapse?"

"As a matter of fact it did, but it was during the strike and no one was down there at the time. This new thing, it started after you went to Steeple Heyston, Mr. Tolley. If something . . . if Marjorie is hurt, do you think it will stop with her? I'm going over there now. I expect to see you."

A small hatchback car was parked in the space at the end of the track to Steeple Heyston, and the gate in the hedge stood open.

Tolley left the headlights of his Volkswagen on and climbed out and called to Gerald Beaumont. The darkness swallowed his voice. It was bitterly cold, dawn a curdled grey buried deep in the clouds beyond the railway embankment.

He stepped up to the gate, frosty grass crackling under his shoes, and scanned the hummocky meadow where the village had once stood, but there was no sign of anyone.

Tolley went back to the car and sounded the horn, went back to the gate and called Gerald Beaumont's name again. As he reluctantly started across rough ground towards the line of trees around the ruins of the manor house he saw something small run out of the darkness there, run straight towards him.

He froze, his blood knocking heavily in his chest: but it was only the Beaumonts' collie. It stopped halfway and started to bark, and Tolley went towards it, saying, "Good boy, good boy. Where's your owner? Where is that son of a bitch?"

The dog whined, turned back towards the trees. When it saw that Tolley wasn't following, it started to bark again.

Tolley called Gerald Beaumont's name again, and heard, faint and far off, a harsh squealing, metal on metal. Every hair on the back of his neck rose as a kind of tide of coldness swept up his body. A black figure stood on top of the embankment, small but distinct against the advancing light of dawn. It was still for a moment, then seemed to swoop down the steep slope, moving as swiftly as a gliding bird across the meadow towards the gate, cutting off Tolley's line of retreat.

He turned and ran towards the trees, the dog following at his heels for a few moments, then breaking away. Tolley ran on, breathing hard and hardly daring to look back, nothing in his head but the thudding of his pulse and the blind imperative to flee, flee before the thing was upon him.

He ran straight through the clump of trees, blundered through the church gate. Gravel scattered under his flying feet; he slammed against the heavy wooden door, wrenched at the handle.

It gave. Tolley stumbled through the door and slammed it shut, found the iron bolt and pushed it home just as something crashed into the door on the other side.

A great wind got up around the church. Something fell with a clatter, and a thick stench of burning began to fill the black air. Tolley found the book of matches he'd taken from the hotel bar, lit one and held it up, saw that the little square of hardboard that had patched the broken window had fallen in, and then a gust of foul air whirled around him and blew out the match. He lit another at once, cupping it in his hand. To be alone in the dark was intolerable.

Whatever was on the other side of the door began to turn the handle back and forth. Tolley retreated, and something struck the back of his knees before toppling to the stone flags. The match stung his fingers and he dropped it and lit another. He'd knocked over a bench. A pile of books that had been stacked on one end lay at his feet. Prayer books. He picked one up; its limp cover fanned like the wings of a dead bird. He knew then what he had to do.

First, he had to have light.

He took one of the thick candles from the altar and used several matches to get it alight. All the while, the wind howled and keened, and the hammering at the door never let up. Tolley scrabbled through the thin pages of the prayer book until he came to the Service for the Burial of the Dead, and began.

The wind did not die as he read the first psalm, but the banging of the door became staccato and uncertain, and ceased entirely when he reached the middle of the lesson.

As he read on, the howl of the wind dropped away to a mumbling moan that seemed at times to break into words. *Danger, danger.* And as he read, it seemed that he was no longer alone in the church, that a dark shadow occupied the middle of the front pew. He didn't dare to lift his eyes from the page as he read, but the shadow tugged at the corner of his vision, undefined, insubstantial, but definitely there.

And then, his throat dry, Tolley came to the end of the lesson, and realized that he would have to read the last part at the grave. When he hesitated, the wind rose again and the candle flame guttered flat and almost went out. There was nothing for it: the forms had to be gone through.

The shadow melted from the pew as, holding the candle before him, Tolley walked down the aisle and fumbled with the heavy bolt that fastened the door. It slid back. He turned the handle, jerked the door open.

Wind blew in his face, blew the candle flame sideways.

As he walked through the overgrown graveyard to the isolated pair of gravestones beneath the yew, Tolley felt a kind of pressure at his back, but steeled himself not to look around. He faced the two graves and by the light of the candle began to read the final part of the service.

"Forasmuch as it hath pleased Almighty God of His great mercy to take unto Himself the soul of Orlando Richards, here departed, we therefore commit his body to the ground . . . "

As he read, the words became more than words: every one a weight that had to be lifted and laid, each a single stone in the solemn edifice he was constructing. He came to the final prayer and, despite his aching throat, read it loudly, triumphantly. After the final *amen*, he heard, far off in the winter dawn—for it was dawn now, although still so dark that he could distinguish no colors—a cock crowing, the traditional end to a night of magic.

Tolley blew out the candle and, with the blunt edge of his car key, inscribed the name of Orlando Richards on the headstone.

It's over, he thought, as he walked away from the church. I've done my duty, atoned for what my great-grandfather did.

As he went through the narrow belt of trees, skirting past the ruined chimney of the manor house, the collie came bounding towards him, barking frantically, dancing around Tolley and running back towards the ruins, turning and barking. Tolley followed it.

"What is it, boy? Quiet now. Where's your master?"

And then he saw Gerald Beaumont.

The man's body was slumped in a tangle of rose-briars at the base of the tall chimney stack. His face was a mess of blood and bone, but Tolley recognized the Norfolk jacket, and the flat cap that lay in stiff weeds beside him.

Tolley turned aside and threw up. As he straightened, wind blew around him out of nowhere, rattling the bare branches of the surrounding trees. Tolley pulled off his signet ring and flung it away and screamed, "Leave me alone!" but the wind gathered itself into a scream and whirled a toppling tower of dead leaves around him.

He started to run, the collie chasing at his heels. Wind winnowed frosty tufts of grass, whirled leaves into the shape of a human figure before collapsing and blowing on, always in front of Tolley, who remembered now what Marjorie Beaumont had said about the ghosts of women, that they were stronger than those of men.

And their hate was stronger, too, strong enough to last a century even after the object of her hate had fled its first malignant flowering, strong enough to destroy Beaumont, poor bastard, who had only been at the edge of things.

The ghost of Orlando Richards had not been the danger after all. He had died in the burning train wreck, and nothing Tolley's great-grandfather had or hadn't done would have saved him.

Perhaps he had been trying to warn Tolley and the Beaumonts; perhaps he had somehow restrained the ghost of the woman who had died in the same accident. And now Tolley had laid him to rest.

Panting, Tolley pushed through the gate, saw with dull shock the figure waiting beside his car. For a moment he thought that his heart would stop; then the dog bounded ahead, and he realized that it was Marjorie Beaumont, and he wondered how he could tell her about her husband.

But then she spoke, her voice halting and heavy. It was her voice, but Tolley knew at once that she was not using it.

"Here's your inheritance."

The bloody head of the walking stick caught the first light of the sun when she swung it at him.

Grandmother's Slippers

SARAH PINBOROUGH

SARAH PINBOROUGH is a horror, thriller, and young-adult fiction author who has published ten novels. Her latest releases are *The Shadow of the Soul*, the second of the Dog-Faced Gods trilogy, and *The Traitor's Gate* (under the pen name Sarah Silverwood), which is the second installment in the Nowhere Chronicles. Her short stories have appeared in several anthologies, and she has a horror screenplay currently in development.

Pinborough was the 2009 winner of the British Fantasy Award for Best Short Story, and has three times been short-listed for Best Novel. She has also been short-listed for a World Fantasy Award. Her novella *The Language of Dying* (from PS Publishing) was short-listed for the Shirley Jackson Award and won the 2010 British Fantasy Award for Best Novella.

"I was recently house-sitting for a friend who was spending her time going to and fro from Scotland during her mother's final weeks," reveals the author. "When her mum passed on, my friend was stuck at the airport waiting for a flight to be there in time to say good-bye.

"Her flight was delayed (the man next to her in the checking-in queue declared that he was going to blow himself up, and the whole terminal was evacuated), and she missed that last good-bye.

"Obviously, she was very upset by that, but it got me thinking about all the things that are wrapped up in those last words and how important it is that we get the chance to say them."

IT WAS A WEEK AFTER THE FUNERAL that Jason first saw the slippers. It hadn't been a good week, truth be told. Once his mother had got back from Scotland he'd hoped that some semblance of normality would be restored. Gran had, after all, been dying for a very long time, but while the rest of the funeral guests had muttered somewhere beneath the brims of their black hats that it was probably a relief for her to just let go, his mother had greeted every such suggestion with a stony glare. As it was, when she'd finally flown home two days later, she'd poured a large glass of wine, lit a cigarette, and declared that it was "All just too bloody final" before disappearing into the garden to smoke in peace.

Jason hadn't been entirely sure how to deal with that. Nor the snippy comments she made that implied somehow that he wasn't grieving *enough*. If he was honest, he wasn't grieving *at all*. He had loved his grandmother in that abstract way generations divided by too many years and too many miles did, but he was thirty-seven and going through a marriage breakup, and when Great-Aunt Edna had called the previous year with the cancer diagnosis, he'd done a mental *that's that, then*, and put Gran out of his head and got back to arguing with Emily.

He'd half-expected his mother to be secretly relieved that it was all over—Gran had been eighty-nine years old, and as her body had failed her marbles had quickly followed—but it would appear that his mother wasn't quite as pragmatic about these things as he was. The morbid atmosphere that had hung over their house like the proverbial pall during Gran's last months refused to be dispelled now that the body had been laid to rest and the world could move on. His mother just wouldn't allow it.

She was out walking the dog when he first saw the slippers. It was Saturday morning and he was looking for tools to put up a couple of extra shelves. He'd tried the shed, beneath the sink, and the garage, before remembering the cupboard under the stairs. The junk cupboard. It had been dad's stash, before he'd moved out. Where he dumped all those things that he felt were vitally necessary to buy but which then lay untouched for years, gathering cobwebs. When he'd left, Mum had made him take all the drills and planers and saws with him. The new wife could find somewhere for them. Old habits died hard, though, and Jason was sure that if his mother had since bought herself some DIY tools, the cupboard under the stairs would be the place she put them.

Instead of a toolbox, however, he saw the slippers. They sat neatly side-by-side and facing outwards.

What took you so long?

There was mud on the edges of their worn blue padding. He stared for almost two full minutes before fully accepting that they were there. He knew they were Gran's slippers, even before he picked them up and nervously took a sniff of the man-made fibers. No one wore slippers like that any more—thick sole, highly flammable nylon or polyester, somewhat quilted. The material had small pale blue flowers against the darker blue. He wondered where she'd got them. The Co-op probably. Back in the days when they sold buttons and zips and cheap school shirts rather than food. These slippers came from a time of Co-op stamps and savings, rather than credit card debts and pound stores.

Alone in the hallway, he sniffed in their scent. Beyond the fibers was something else . . . the smell of her house. He was surprised at the flood of memories that came with it. A coolness where the heating was never on quite long enough. The softness of the sheepskin rug beside the spare bed. Edinburgh morning rolls. Robinson's marmalade. The click of the gas fire. The smack of her lips when she sipped her tea. Her reading glasses. The set of her curls, done once a week by Jeannie down the road.

He looked down at the slippers again. Therein lay the problem. These were not his Gran's most recent slippers. These were slippers from thirty years ago at least. Probably forty. His Gran had never been the sort to throw things away, and these slippers had been made to last.

These were the slippers he remembered her wearing when she still had her council flat in Leith when he was a small boy. When she'd always given him ten pence for sweets from the shop, and she and Mum had laughed over coffees in the British Home Stores café on Princes Street. What the hell were they doing here, in the cupboard under the stairs?

Waiting.

The answer came in an instant and he shivered slightly. That was ridiculous. Maybe his mother had brought them back with her. She said that they'd given all Gran's clothes to charity shops (No local ones. The last thing Aunt Edna, no spring chicken herself, would need was seeing a stranger walking down the road in her sister's Sunday coat. That might bring on a second funeral rather too quickly for anyone's liking), but perhaps she'd kept these as some kind of memento.

And put them under the stairs? In a forgotten place? The voice sneered.

He ignored it. He placed the slippers very carefully back in the cupboard—facing into the stairs this time—and closed the door. After a moment, he flicked the small bolt across.

After all the to-ing and fro-ing and weeks here and there, his mother hadn't been at the home when his Gran had decided it was time to die. She'd been on her way, but not actually there. His pre-grief-stricken mother would have probably commented that "That was bloody typical" of his grandmother. "Another way to make me feel guilty for something." Instead, his mother had simply cried at Luton Airport until her flight was called and then delayed and then called again.

By the time she reached the hospital, Gran's skin had slackened and she was cold to the touch. He imagined that what lay in the bed by the time his mother got there wasn't very much like Gran at all. When he'd arrived in Scotland a few days later for the funeral, he hadn't gone to the mortuary. He was sure he saw a tinge of envy on his mother's face from behind her cigarette smoke that he'd avoided that sight. But then it was very hard to tell exactly what she was thinking or feeling. "I should have been here," was all she would say. "I should have said good-bye, you know, while she was breathing. She might have heard me." Then she would cry some more and Great-Aunt Edna and the ladies from the church and the bowling club would comfort her.

When his mother got back from her walk, and the dog was drying in the conservatory, Jason made them both a cup of tea and idly chatted about this and that before bringing up the slippers. He didn't mention them in an outright way, but instead alluded to reminiscing about his Gran and the slippers had fixed in his head. His mother frowned. "What the hell are you on about?" she said, sipping her tea while eyeing the wine on the rack even though it was barely lunchtime. "Gran's slippers," he muttered lamely. "Her old blue ones. Just wondered if she'd still had them."

His mother looked at him as if he was mad, which perhaps he was. His face flushed, and then hers clouded over slightly with memory. "God, I'd forgotten all about those." Irritation crept in at the corners of her mouth and she frowned. "Why would she have kept those? Who keeps old slippers?"

Jason just shrugged lamely and felt about fifteen-years old. He didn't mention the slippers again. He was learning that irritation and grief seemed to go hand-in hand.

He went back to the cupboard the next time his mother was out. His mouth dried when he saw the slippers. Side by side and facing outwards. Somehow they'd turned around.

Not a nice trick to play, that one.

He grabbed the pair, holding them at arm's length as if they might infect him with something, and then shoved them in a carrier bag, before walking swiftly to the end of the road and dumping them in the bin. He smiled when he saw the council worker wheeling the dumpster barely a hundred yards away. Soon the slippers would be long gone. *That was that, then*, he thought, and headed back home.

But it wasn't. He woke up three nights later to a dull thumping sound coming from downstairs. Somewhere in the heart of the building. It was past 2:00 a.m. and the house was dark. *Thump. Thud. Thump.* A long pause. *Thump. Thud. Thump.* He tried to ignore it. (If it was a burglar, then they could just jolly well get on and burgle the house. He had no intention of tackling them—after all, that was what insurance was for, wasn't it?) But it refused to fade. A steady dull thud every few seconds. He pushed the duvet down from his face and listened. The noise was too even and regular for it to be an intruder. What was it? His curiosity getting the better of him now that the sense of imminent danger had passed, he climbed out of bed.

He crept down the stairs in his dressing gown and paused in the hallway. The thudding was coming from the cupboard under the stairs. He stared at it through the gloom. The wood actually shook slightly with each thump, as if whatever was on the other side was getting impatient and irritable. Could it be a cat? he thought. Or maybe a rat? Of course it could, he decided, even though he opened the door with trembling hands.

The toes of the slippers nudged out across the threshold of the darkness within.

About bloody time.

Jason's stomach turned to water, and he felt his guts tighten in a way that normally accompanied a bad and uncontrollable bout of something unpleasant. He couldn't wait until the morning to throw them away again. He ran out into the street in his dressing gown and dumped the slippers for a second time. Further away from the house this time, and each slipper in a different bin. He didn't care if anyone saw him. The good people of Turnham Green would be far too polite to ever mention it.

He checked the cupboard when he got back, and it was empty. After a moment he locked it anyway, before spending the rest of a restless night waiting to hear that steady thump return. It didn't, and throughout the next day at work he was exhausted. On the way home, he bought earplugs.

His mother's spirits did not improve as the days went past. Jason found this surprising, primarily because he couldn't remember a time when his mother had actually liked his Gran. She'd got irritable as she'd got older, and developed something of a martyr complex that used to drive his mother insane. Before she'd become too infirm, when he and Emily weren't even married yet, she'd come down on the train to visit. A tension would creep into the house along with her suitcase and bags of Murray mints, a tension that fixed itself between mother and daughter.

She never quite relaxed, his Gran, when she was old. It was always just the one glass of wine—couldn't possibly have any more—and "You know me, I don't like a fuss," before passive-aggressively demanding a fuss. Jason had found it almost entertaining, but her visits had driven his mother mad, and by the end of each one, the smiles through gritted teeth would have been abandoned and his mother would snap responses to his Gran as Jason and his dad stayed well out of the way.

His Gran's visits made his mother almost as mad as those times that his father had declared—especially in the worst years before he buggered off with the cliché secretary—that she was *turning into her bloody mother.*

Jason had tried that one on Emily once (even though he quite liked her mother), and the response had been astounding. And not in a good way. It would appear that the one person a woman dreaded growing up like was the one person that had looked after and loved her the most. What did they find to hate so much, he wondered?

He came home from a drink after work to find the cupboard open and the slippers at the bottom of the stairs. They weren't quite as clean as they had been, and on the right slipper, the one tilted upwards so that its toe was resting on the edge of the first stair, there was a small stain from something that might have been Coca-Cola mixed with cigarette ash. It was almost midnight, and all the lights in the house were out. The soft insides of the slippers were bright in the gloom.

His eyes moved up the stairs with dread. His mother. They were after his mother!

This time, he took them out into the garden and burned them.

For the next week, it became something of a battle. The slippers had *intent*. Always signaling their presence in the house by the under-stairs cupboard door being inexplicably open—the malevolent footwear was no longer easily confined. Once, Jason found them at the bathroom door while his mother was locked inside having a long soak. He was sure she was crying in there too, although she'd vehemently deny it if he asked. He'd heard it through the door as he'd wrestled the slippers from the carpet and destroyed them once again. They were getting heavier. More stubborn. But he wouldn't give up. What would happen if he did? Would they drown his crying mother in the bath?

His mother might have liked to keep her crying to herself, but she let her bitterness fly in barbed comments, mainly in his direction. He was there, after all. *Why didn't he stop worrying about her and get on with worrying about his own life?* was amongst her favorites. At those moments though, her eyes were red and puffy and he saw through the harshness of her comments. It was hard, this process of watching someone grieve. He hadn't expected there to be quite so much grief. She spent a lot of time out in the garden, a tight expression on her wan face, smoking furiously. He didn't know what to say to her. He didn't really try. Mostly, he was too concerned with the slippers.

Each time they came back they were a little dirtier, and the growing smell made it clear that this was grave dirt, not ordinary mud. Maybe one day the dirt would consume them and they wouldn't find their way back to the house. He hoped so. Because if not, he might die from exhaustion. The slippers seemed tired too. They grew weightier with each visit, and the material was starting to fray at the edges by the soles. He wondered who would give up first—him or the slippers? Thus far, it was a difficult one to call.

It was the times that he wasn't at home that worried him the most. The days had been slipper-free, but he couldn't stay in every night, and what would happen if they chose to come back when he was out? What if they reached his mother? He started avoiding using the main house phone, which sat in the hallway on a table a few feet away from the under-stair cupboard, and planned any evening drinks via text on his cell. The slippers probably couldn't hear—and technically weren't ever in the cupboard—but he wasn't taking any chances.

When Great-Aunt Edna rang to check in as she did every few days, Jason found that he no longer wanted to lie about the state of his mother. He didn't have the energy to. He wasn't ready to share his current situation with his grandmother's slippers, but if Great-Aunt Edna wasn't grown-up enough to offer some advice on how he could help his mother, then they were all in something of a pickle.

"I've tried talking to her," he said, "but she just snaps at me. She's snapping at me a lot. Not that I mind overly. I can cope with that. I've been married." He surprised himself with his use of the past tense. "But she cries at night. When she's asleep. That worries me." It was good to share. He couldn't go quite as far as to say, "What really worries me is what might happen if I don't get to the slippers in time," but it was good to pass on the burden of his mother's grief to someone else, if only for a minute or two.

Aunt Edna sighed. It was a wheezy cigarette rattle in his ear. "You just have to wait, Jason. She needs to make her peace."

"She keeps going on about not having said good-bye," Jason said. "Maybe I should take her back up to Scotland to the grave. She could say good-bye there." *And I could bury the bloody slippers once and for all.* It was strange how he had separated the slippers from his grandmother in his head. It was as if all the bitterness and impatience and resentment that had been in the old woman now filled them as her corpse rotted. He didn't have an issue with his grandmother, *per se.* But her slippers were a different matter.

"It's not good-bye that's bothering her, dear," Great-Aunt Edna said, as if he were a child again. "It's all the other things she never said. It's *those* she has to lay to rest, not your grandmother."

"What other things?" Jason asked.

"One day you'll understand," Great-Aunt Edna said, with the cryptic tone only ever used by the extremely old. He wondered if Edna would understand if he talked about the slippers. Probably not.

They hung up and he watched through the kitchen window as his mother sat on the garden bench and smoked some more. The past few months had aged her, and somewhere inside that made him feel sad. He wondered how to put it into words, but found that he couldn't; so he left it there, in a small space in his heart.

It was supposed to be a reconciliation dinner—that's what Emily had called it when she'd phoned him. She had sounded excited.

It turned out, despite her best efforts otherwise, to be a divorce dinner. Life could be ironic like that. It was she who had demanded that he leave, and now it was he that found he didn't really want to go back.

Emily had cried, and he'd been as pleasant about it as he could, but there was nothing really more to say. The marriage was over. Life was too short to fight the inevitable. The presence of death had been too strong in his world of late to imagine spending the rest of his life, however long or short that might be, with someone as uptight as Emily.

He didn't tell her that, of course. He told her that he would always love her (even though he wasn't, in fact, sure that he ever had), but that it was time for them both to move on.

He was surprised at how much better he felt by the time he got back to his mother's house, even though it was nearly midnight and he had been shattered before he'd even gone out.

The moment broke, however, as soon as he was home. The door clicked closed behind him and he was locked within a silent stillness. Three things hit him, almost immediately. The first was that, once again, the under-stairs cupboard door was open. Wide, this time. Determined. The second was the awful stench of rot that gushed out from that dark void, filling the entire downstairs. But the third was what disturbed him the most—the imprint of footsteps on the stairs. Dirty. Foul. Dragging.

He gripped the banister. His heart in his mouth, he started to climb, following the footprints all the way to the top. Ahead, his mother's bedroom door was open a crack. He crept towards it, his palms sweating. The house was silent. This close to her room, he should have been able to hear her soft, sobbing, half-words mumbled through jumbled grief-ridden dreams.

He looked down. The muddy footprints that crossed the doorway taunted him as, with his heart in his mouth, he pushed the door open wider.

He gasped silently, sucking air in rather than expelling, and then he held it. Tears sprung in the corner of his eyes, and for the first time since he'd opened the cupboard door, he understood.

He saw his grandmother for only the briefest moment. The blue slippers on her feet looked new and matched the dressing gown buttoned up to her neck. *How could he have forgotten that dressing gown?* Her hair was curled like it used to be when Jeannie did it, and although old, she was still healthily thick at the waist.

She was sitting on the edge of the bed, one hand stroking his mother's sleeping head. She looked up at him and smiled, and in that moment she was so real that he wondered if perhaps he'd got it all horribly wrong and that he was the ghost.

He backed away, pulling the door closed behind him, and headed to his room . . . leaving them to say the things they wished they had, and for the first time feeling a pang of grief for his Gran and the slippers she'd worn when he was only a boy.

The Mystery

PETER ATKINS

PETER ATKINS was born in Liverpool, England, and now lives in Los Angeles. He is the author of the novels *Morningstar*, *Big Thunder*, and *Moontown*, and the screenplays for *Hellbound: Hellraiser II*, *Hellraiser III: Hell on Earth*, *Hellraiser: Bloodline*, *Wishmaster*, and *Prisoners of the Sun*.

His short fiction has appeared in such best-selling anthologies as *The Mammoth Book of Best New Horror*, *The Museum of Horrors*, *Dark Delicacies II*, and *Hellbound Hearts*, while a new collection of his stories, *Rumours of the Marvellous*, was recently published by Alchemy Press/Airgedlámh Publications.

"'The Mystery' first appeared in *Spook City*," explains Atkins, "a three-author anthology also featuring fellow Liverpudlians Clive Barker and Ramsey Campbell and edited by another, Angus Mackenzie.

"I grew up about two hundred yards from The Mystery—a real park in South Liverpool—and this piece came about when my wife wondered how I could possibly have avoided using such an evocatively named place as the basis for a story.

"Which made me wonder, too . . ."

"For upwards of two hours, the sky was brilliant
with lights."
—*The Liverpool Daily Post, Sept. 8th, 1895*

THERE'S ACTUALLY no mystery at all.

Not if you went the Bluey, anyway.

It used to be the grounds of a house, a big one. No Speke Hall or anything, but still technically a Stately Home. It had been called The Grange and was pulled down in May of 1895.

Four months later, minus an ornamental lake which had been filled in, the grounds were opened as a park for the children of Liverpool by the city council. It was officially named Wavertree Playground but was almost immediately dubbed "The Mystery" by local people, because the person who bought the land and donated it to the city had asked for anonymity.

The Bluecoat School, a boys' grammar, backed onto The Mystery, and if you were a pupil there, even seventy-five years later, it was made pretty damn clear to you that it was one of our old Governors who'd forked up for the park. Philip Holt—one of our four schoolhouses was named for him—was a maritime magnate in the days of the great ships and the Cast Iron Shore. The money needed to clear the land and create the park was probably no more than loose change to the man whose Blue Funnel Line practically owned the tea trade between Britain and China.

So. No mystery there.

I'll tell you what *was* a mystery, though. The fucking state of the Gents' bogs.

The Liverpool of the mid-1960s was a city suffering a dizzying drop into recession. No more ships, no more industry, no more Beatles—*Tara, Mum. Off to London to shake the world. Don't wait up*—but even so, the public toilets at the northwest corner of the Mystery were astonishingly disgusting. "Derelict" didn't even come close.

They'd been neither bricked up nor pulled down. It was more like they'd been simply forgotten, as if a file had been lost somewhere in the town hall and nobody with any responsibility knew they even existed. Utterly unlooked after in a third-world sort of way and alarming to enter, let alone use. No roof, no cubicle doors, no paper, what was left of the plaster over the ancient red bricks completely covered with graffiti of an obsessive and sociopathic nature, and last mopped out sometime before Hitler trotted into Poland.

But, you know, if you had to go you had to go, and I'd had many a piss there back in the day. If you didn't actually touch anything, you had a fighting chance of walking out without having contracted a disease.

But to see that soiled shed-like structure still there on an autumn afternoon thirty years later was more than a little surprising.

I had some business to attend to and shouldn't really have allowed myself to be distracted, but I felt a need to check it out. The boys appeared just as I approached the stinking moss-scarred walkway entrance.

There were two of them, both about thirteen, though one at least a head taller than his friend. Although they weren't actually blocking the path—standing just off to the side, ankle-deep in the overgrown grass—they nevertheless gave the impression of being self-appointed sentries, as if they were there to perhaps collect a toll or something.

"Where are you going, then?" The first one said. His hair was russet and looked home-cut and his face was patchily rosy with the promise of acne.

"The bog," I said.

They looked at each other, and then back at me.

"*This* bog?" said the first.

"Fuckin' 'ell," said the second. He was the shorter one, black Irish pale, unibrowed and sullen.

"You don't wanna go in *there*," said the first.

"Why would you go in *there*?" said his mate.

I shrugged, but I wasn't sure they noticed. They were staring at me with the kind of incipient aggression you'd expect, but weren't actually meeting my eyes. Instead, they were both looking at me at about mid-chest height, as if looking at someone smaller and younger.

"Why wouldn't I?" I said.

"He might get ya," said the black-haired one.

"Who?"

"The feller," said the redhead.

"What feller?" I asked him.

He looked surprised. "Yerav'n 'eard of 'im?" he said.

"No."

"Fuckin' 'ell," said the shorter one.

"He's there all the time," his friend said. "Nights, mostly."

"Yeah," Blackie nodded in support. "Nights."

"Yeah?" I said to the taller one, the redhead, who seemed to be the boss. "What does he do?"

"Waits there for lads," he said.

"What for?"

"You know."

I didn't. He shook his head off my blank look, in pity for my ignorance. "He bums them," he said.

"Shags them up the bum," said his companion helpfully.

"Why?"

"Fuckin' 'ell," said the first one, and looked at his friend with a *we've got a right idiot here* expression. "Because he's an 'omo, that's why."

"A hom," said the second.

The first looked thoughtful. Came to a decision. "We better go in with ya," he said.

"For safety, like," said the second, with only a trace of his eagerness betraying itself. "He might be in there now."

"Oh, I think I'll be all right," I said. "If he's in there, I'll tell him I'm not in the mood."

My tone was confusing to them. It wasn't going the way it was meant to, the way it perhaps usually did.

"Yeah, burrit's worse than we said," the first one told me, as if worried some opportunity was slipping away. He looked to his friend. "Tell him about the, you know, the thing."

"Yeah, he's gorra nutcracker," Blackie said. "You know warramean?" He mimed a pliers-like action in order to help me visualize what he was talking about. "After he's bummed ya, he crushes yer bollocks."

I remembered that. It was a story I'd first heard when I was much younger than them. An urban legend, though the phrase hadn't been coined at the time, conjured into being in the summer of 1965 and believed by nearly every nine-year-old boy who heard it.

They were still looking at my chest, as if staring down a smaller contemporary.

"How old am I?" I asked them.

"You wha'?" the redhead said.

"How old do you think I am?"

They shared a look, and the taller one shrugged. "Dunno," he said. "About eight?"

"Might be ten," the other one said, not to me but to his friend, and the redhead shot him an angry look as if he didn't want to be bothered with details or sidetracked by debate.

I snapped my fingers loudly, close to my face, and drew their eyes upwards.

They looked confused. Their eyes weren't quite focusing on mine, and I still wasn't sure they could really see me. There was something else hovering behind their confusion; an anxiety, perhaps, as if they feared they might be in trouble, as if something would know they were being distracted from their duty and wouldn't be very pleased with them. As far as they were concerned, this was a day like every other and *needed* to be a day like every other, and any disruption in the pattern was alarming to them, in however imprecise a way.

I didn't doubt that this was how they'd spent a fair portion of their time, back when it was linear. Having a little chat and preparing some eight-year-old victim for a good battering. They'd probably done it before, and more than once. Done it regularly, perhaps, until their belief in the very predator they used as bait had become their undoing.

"Take a look at this," I said and took something out of my pocket to show them.

A few minutes later, back on the main footpath, I took a look back over my shoulder. It was very dark now and neither the toilets nor the boys were anywhere in sight. The moon had risen in the cloudless sky and I took a glance at my watch. It was an old-fashioned watch and its dial was un-illuminated, but I was fairly certain it said it was still four in the afternoon.

I'd kept up a brisk pace while checking the time and, when I looked up again, the house was directly ahead of me, though I hadn't noticed it earlier. Its size alone suggested it was probably magnificent in the daylight, but its lawns were unlit and its windows shuttered and it appeared simply as a great black shape, a mass of deeper darkness against the midnight blue of the sky.

Just outside its black iron gates, half-open as if in tentative invitation, a little girl was standing on the gravel of the driveway.

She was dressed in a simple knee-length smock dress and didn't look up at me as I walked towards her. She was concentrating on her game, her mouth opening and closing in recitation of something. It was a skipping song, as best I remembered it, but she was using it as accompaniment for the rapid bouncing of a small rubber ball between the gravel and her outstretched palm.

"Dip dip dip,
My blue ship.
Sailing on the water
Like a cup and saucer.
O, U, T spells—"

Oh, that's right. Not a skipping song at all. A rhyme of selection or exclusion, a variant of "eeny meeny miney mo." The little girl, long and ringleted hair pulled back from her forehead by a wide black ribbon, seemed to remember that at the same moment I did and, just as she mouthed the word *out*, her hand snapped shut around the ball, her eyes flicked up to meet mine, and she thrust her other hand out to point its index finger dramatically at me. Her eyes were jet black and her now-silent mouth was pulled in a tight unsmiling line.

"I'm out?" I asked her.

She didn't say anything, and nor did her fixed expression waver. I let the silence build for a few moments as we stared at each other, though I blinked deliberately several times to let her know that if it was a contest it was one she was welcome to win.

"Your concentration's slipping," I said eventually. "Where did the ball go?"

Her little brow furrowed briefly and she looked down at her empty hand. She pulled an annoyed face and then looked back at me.

"Are you going into the house?" she asked.

"In a manner of speaking," I said.

She gave a small tut of derision. "Is that supposed to be clever?" she said.

"No," I said. "Not really."

"Good," she said. "Because it's *not* clever. It's just stupid. Are you going into the house or not?"

"The house isn't really here," I told her.

"Then where are you standing?" she said. "And who are you talking to?"

Without waiting for an answer, and keeping her eyes fixed on mine, she began to lean her head sideways and down. Keeping her unblinking eyes fixed on mine, she continued the movement, slowly and steadily, with no apparent difficulty or discomfort, until her pale little cheek rested flat against her right shoulder and her head was at an impossible right angle to her neck. At the same time, in some strange counterpoint, her hair rose up into the air, stately and unhurried, until the ringlets were upright and taut, quivering against the darkness like mesmerized snakes dancing to an unheard piper.

I grinned at her. She was good at this.

We exchanged a few more words before I walked through the gates without her, following the wide and unbending path to the house itself. The imposingly large front door was as unlit as the rest of the exterior and was firmly closed. But I knew that others had come to this house before me, and that the door, despite its size and its weight and its numerous locks, had opened as easily for them as it would for me.

The rest of the vast reception room was pretty impressive, but the portrait over the fireplace was magnificent.

The picture itself was at least eight feet tall, allowing for some grass below and some sky above its life-size and black-suited central figure, who stared out into the room with the confident Victorian swagger of those born to wealth and empire. A foxhound cowered low at its master's feet and, in the far background, which appeared to be the grounds of the house, a group of disturbingly young children were playing Nymphs and Shepherds.

The room, like the long hall along which I'd walked to come to it, was illuminated by many candles, though I'd yet to see anyone who might have lit them. Through a half-open door at the far end of the room, though, I could see a shadow flicking back and forth, back and forth, as if somebody was about their business in a repeated pattern of movements.

As I came into the anteroom, the young woman who was pacing up and down looked up briefly from the clipboard she was holding. She appeared to be barely twenty, dressed in what I guessed to be the kind of nurse's uniform women might have worn when they were dressing wounds received in the Crimea, and the stern prettiness of her face and the darkness of her eyes said she could have been an older sister of the little girl I'd met outside the gates.

There was a single bed in the room and, though it was unoccupied, its sheets were rumpled, as if the woman's patient had just recently gone for a little walk. There were wires and cables and drip-feeds lying on the sheets, and the other ends of some of them were connected to a black-and-white television monitor that attempted to hide its anachronism by being cased within a brass and mahogany housing of a Victorian splendor and an H. G. Wells inventiveness.

The young woman, having registered my presence with neither surprise nor welcome, was back to her job of glancing at the monitor and then marking something on her clipboard.

The image on the monitor—grainy and distorted, washed-out like a barely surviving kinescope of some long-ago transmission—was a fixed-angle image of moonlight-bathed waves, deep-water waves, no shore in sight, as if a single camera were perched atop an impossible tower standing alone in some vast and distant ocean.

I looked at the image for a moment or two while she continued to pace and to make check marks on her clipboard.

"So what does that do?" I asked eventually, nodding at the monitor.

She stopped pacing and turned to look at me again. Her expression, while not unfriendly, was conflicted, as if she were both grateful for the break in routine and mildly unsettled by it.

"It used to show his dreams," she said, and turned her head briefly to look again at the endless and unbreaking waves. "But it's empty now."

She looked back at me and tilted her head a little, like she was deciding if I was safe enough to share a confidence with. "It's frightening, isn't it?" she said.

"Frightening?" I said. "I don't know. Perhaps it just means he's at peace."

"No, no," she said, her voice rising in a kind of nervous excitement. "You've misunderstood. That isn't what I meant." And then she caught herself and her voice went flat as if she feared lending emotion to what she said next. "I mean we might be having his dreams *for* him."

She looked at me half-expectantly, her eyes wide, like she was hoping I might tell her that she was wrong, but before I could answer a bell began to ring from a room somewhere deeper in the house.

"Teatime," she said. "You'd best hurry."

The children sat at trestle tables and ate without enthusiasm and there were far too many of them.

Their clothes were a snapshot history lesson: tracksuits and trainers, pullovers and short pants, britches and work-shirts, smocks and knickerbockers. The ones who'd been here longest were an unsettling monochrome against the colors of the more recent arrivals, and it wasn't only their outfits that were fading to grey.

Despite the dutiful shoveling of gruel into their mouths, I knew that they weren't hungry—there was only one inhabitant of this house who was hungry—and I wondered briefly why they even needed to pretend to eat, but figured that habit and routine were part of what helped him chain them here. Not a one of them spoke. Not a one of them smiled. I decided against joining them and headed back down the corridor to which the nurse had pointed me.

I saw something unspeakable in one of the rooms I passed and felt no need to look in any of the others.

The reception room was still empty when I got there. Patience is encouraged in these situations but, you know, fuck it. I decided to break something. There was an exquisite smoked glass figurine resting on top of the piano. I didn't even pick it up, just swept it away with the back of my hand and listened to it shatter against the parquet floor.

I hadn't intended to look, but a rapid skittering caught my eye and I bent down, barely in time to see a tiny something, wretched and limbless, slithering wetly beneath the sofa. I was still crouched down when there was a noise from somewhere behind me, unusually loud for what it most sounded like: the sticky gossamer ripping of a blunder through an unseen spider's web.

I stood up quickly, turning around to look. There was still nobody in the room but, though the large picture over the fireplace was intact and undamaged, its central figure was missing.

"You're a little older than my usual guests," the master of the house said from immediately behind me.

I span back around, very successfully startled. There was nothing overtly threatening about his posture, but he was standing uncomfortably close to me and I wasn't at all fond of his smile.

"A little older," he repeated. "But I'm sure we can find you a room."

"I won't be staying," I said. My voice was steady enough, but I was pissed off at how much he'd thrown me and pissed off more at how much he'd enjoyed it.

"You're very much mistaken," he said. "My house is easy to enter but not so easy to leave."

I understood his confidence. He had a hundred years of experience to justify his thinking that I was one of his usual guests. He could see me, so I had to be dead. Just as most ghosts are invisible to people, most people are invisible to ghosts. But, just as there are a few anomalous ghosts who *can* be seen by people, so are there a few anomalous people who can be seen by ghosts. And he'd just met one.

"Do you know what this is?" I said, and brought the tesseract out of my pocket. They've been standard issue at the department for the last couple of years. Fuck knows where they get them made, but I have a feeling it isn't Hong Kong.

I let it rest in my palm and he looked at it. He tried to keep his expression neutral but I could tell his curiosity was piqued. It always is.

"What does it do?" he said.

"Well, it doesn't really *do* anything," I said. "It just is."

"And what do you want me to do about it?"

"Nothing," I said. "Just look at it for a while."

I gave it a little tap and it slid impossibly through itself.

The room shivered in response, but I don't think he noticed. His eyes were fixed on the little cube and its effortless dance through dimensions.

"There's something wrong with it," he said, but the tone of his voice was fascinated rather than dismissive. "I can't see it properly."

"It's difficult," I agreed. "Because part of it shouldn't be here. Doesn't mean it's not real. Just means it doesn't belong in the space it's in."

The metaphor hit home, as it always did. I don't know why the tesseract works so well on them—I mean, it's utterly harmless, more wake-up call than weapon—but it's definitely made the job easier. He looked up at me. His face was already a little less defined than it had been, but I could still read the fear in it. He was smart, though. Went straight for the important questions and fuck the nuts and bolts.

"Will I be judged?" he said.

"Nobody's judged."

"Will I be hurt?"

"Nobody's hurt."

"Will I be—" He stopped himself then, as an unwilled understanding came to him, and he repeated what he'd just said. Same words. Different stress. "Will I *be?*"

I looked at him.

"Nobody'll be." I said.

It was too late for him to fight, but the animal rage for identity made him try, his imagined flesh struggling against its dissolution and his softening arms reaching out for me uselessly.

"You know who hangs around?" I said. "People with too little will of their own, and people with too much. Let it go. We're just lights in the sky, and their shadows."

"I'll miss it!" he shouted, his disappearing mouth twisting into a final snarl of appetite and terror.

"You won't miss a thing," I said, and watched him vanish.

I'd been in there longer than I thought and, as I walked back through the park towards the Hunter's Lane gate, true night was falling. But it was far from dark. There'd been so many souls in the house, young and old, predator and prey, that the cascade of their dissolution was spectacular and sustained.

For upwards of two hours, the sky was brilliant with lights.

Like an anniversary. Like a half-remembered dream. Like a mystery.

Poison Pen

CHRISTOPHER FOWLER

CHRISTOPHER FOWLER was born in Greenwich, London, and currently lives in the King's Cross area of that city. He is the award-winning author of thirty novels and ten short story collections, and creator of the Bryant & May mysteries.

His memoir, *Paperboy*, won the Green Carnation Award. He has written comedy and drama for the BBC and has a weekly column in the *Independent on Sunday*. Fowler is also the crime reviewer for the *Financial Times*, and has written for *The Times*, *Telegraph*, *Guardian*, *Daily Mail*, *Time Out*, *Black Static* and many other periodicals.

His latest books are an homage to Hammer horror called *Hell Train*, *The Memory of Blood*, and a two-volume collection of twenty-five new stories entitled *Red Gloves*. Forthcoming are two further novels, *Dream World* and *The Invisible Code*.

"This supernatural tale has its origins in a factual event," Fowler reveals. "A few years ago my best friend became sick. Knowing he was going to die, he had taken great pains to distribute his worldly goods fairly, but a number of unexpected events changed the rules as he lay dying.

"He passed away, and I was made the executor of his will. The complexities and ramifications of this task slowly spread to engulf two families, two homes in different countries, several cars, a boat, and five companies. Trying to remain objective and impartial was virtually impossible.

"It soon felt as if his memory was being sullied by the intrusion of so many accumulated objects—as if they were taking on a life of their own and turning those who were fighting to possess them into monsters. It was a grotesque and shattering experience, and has still not quite concluded.

"Perhaps I wrote the story to remove the bitter taste from my mouth. The moral, for me, was this: revere the person, not the belongings."

ANDREW BAYER

UNCLE ANDREW PLAYED the Stock Exchange and used his gains to fund his passions—but what were his passions? Nobody knew. He told his friends that he was a collector, but there were no collections at his Buckinghamshire mansion or his London flat.

Now he was in southern France, tearing along the Grande Corniche in his classic white 1968 Mercedes convertible, and the curving emerald hills had just parted to reveal the port of Monaco below. The autumn air was cool and smelled of pine and lavender. The morning sky was the same aching azure as the Mediterranean, and a few thin, grey clouds still hung like spiderwebs in the trees below the road.

Andrew pushed his speed to fifty, the most he could risk on a road with a forty-meter drop on one side and no crash barriers. He was late for lunch with Lycus Gerolstein, his lawyer, who would be waiting for him at the Salon Des Etoiles, ready to celebrate their latest purchase with a glass of fine champagne.

Coming from the opposite direction, a Niçoise estate agent was lighting her cigarette with one hand and arguing on her cell phone with the other, which didn't leave her any way of controlling the wheel of her Porsche Boxster. She was trying to arrange for some Russians to view a *pieds dans l'eau* property in Fontvieille, but they were being very difficult about the appointment times. She argued, threatened, and cajoled but they wouldn't come earlier, and she sensed she was losing the sale.

What she should have been doing was watching the central divider as she rounded the bend, because moments later she blithely crossed it, forcing the car coming from the opposite direction—a classic white convertible Mercedes—off the tarmac and out into the clouds.

The great vehicle sailed as gracefully as a galleon for a few seconds, then seemed to realize that it weighed over a ton, and dropped into the valley below. Andrew might have been able to get out, except that his hand-stitched 1968 seat belt had not been manufactured for speedy removal. He was still trying to unbuckle it when he hit the cliff face and bounced all the way down to the roof of the rococo Banque de Grimaldi building on the Avenue des Citronniers in Monte Carlo. The noise was so loud that it made diners briefly stir themselves from their lobster salads.

Andrew Bayer's classic car was stuck out of the bank's roof with its rear wheels still spinning. Inside the grand financial institution, his corpse, tethered by the effective seat belt, dripped blood over piles of bank notes. The accident made the front page of *Nice Matin* next day, right next to a car insurance advert. The irony did not go unnoticed.

In England, twenty-three-year-old Mark Bayer heard about the death of his favorite uncle, happy-go-lucky Andrew, and was heartbroken. He had been closer to Andrew than he was to his own father, who had worked in loss adjustment all his life and treated Mark as if he was a failure, just because he had chosen to become a graphic designer and get some pleasure from his career.

Mark had inherited Uncle Andrew's easygoing attitude. Recently he had spent more time than usual with the old man in London, for his uncle had been undergoing sporadic treatment for lung cancer at the Harley Street Clinic. Uncle Andrew was wealthy and knew how to enjoy himself, which made the rest of his serious-minded family regard him as a wastrel. Two years earlier he had retired to his grand country manse with his second much younger wife, a woman who had appeared on his arm after a trip to Boston, where he had been attending some kind of collectors' convention.

But what had he been doing in the South of France when he died? Nobody seemed to know, not even his wife.

Mark and his family attended the cremation service, which was held in Monte Carlo. Uncle Andrew had a brother and a sister of similar ages, a daughter from his first wife, and the aforementioned much younger second wife. The family was therefore split into three separate interested parties, and at any time at least one of these was arguing with the other two. Their loyalties shifted and switched like warring states in an Eastern European nation.

All in all, it was not the best recipe for a happy send-off.

The much younger second wife turned up in a tight-fitting Dior trouser suit and a white hat better suited to Ladies Day at Ascot. She outraged Mark's family, who were looking for any excuse to take umbrage.

During the service, a vicious argument escalated between Andrew's first and second wives, during which the first wife, whose name was Cheryl, questioned the second wife, whose name was Catherine, about her motives for marrying a wealthy man who was almost twice her age. Catherine replied that she had fallen in love with men like Andrew before. "Tell me," spat Cheryl, "at precisely what moment do you usually fall in love with your elderly millionaires?"

The family members quickly became embroiled and lined up on either side, carping across the divide. At a drinks party afterwards there was another fight when Mark's father, who was paying for the wake, had his credit cards humiliatingly rejected by the venue's management. Money and inheritance were openly discussed—subjects Mark's mother regarded as vulgar in the extreme. The English, she remarked pointedly, did not expose their financial affairs in public. This last remark was clearly aimed at Uncle Andrew's second wife, who was American and regarded the entire Bayer family as a bunch of bitter limey snobs with very little, as far as she could see, to be snobbish about. The wake ended on a very sour note indeed.

A few days later in London, the entire family attended the reading of Andrew's will at Lycus Gerolstein's office. Here, seated around the lawyer's boardroom table, they heard that Uncle Andrew's possessions, including another classic car, a boat, a country house, jewelry, a London apartment and bequests of cash, were to be divided up between various family members. It seemed that everyone's wishes had been catered for. Only one of the children had been deliberately and notably excluded from the will—Mark.

The young designer was surprised by the fact that he had been left nothing, as it contradicted what Uncle Andrew told him when they'd last met. In fact, Andrew had gone out of his way to promise that he was leaving something very special to his favorite nephew. "You were always the one I liked the best," Andrew had confided. "I know you'll make something of yourself. I want to ensure that you'll be truly happy in your life, so I'm leaving you the greatest of the gifts in my possession."

But he had left nothing. There was not even a mention of the boy in the will.

Mark was upset at first. He thought the old man had loved, trusted, and confided in him. Perhaps he had caused some offence over their final lunch and hurt his uncle's feelings? Even Mark's younger brother Ben had been bequeathed some money. Mark thought back over their last meeting, breaking it down into moments, but could think of nothing he had done to upset Uncle Andrew.

The family was very sorry to lose their patriarch. The amiably disreputable old fellow had been a touchstone for them, someone they could go to for advice and help, always kindly, always fair, a calm center to the frequently bitter whirlwind of Bayer family spats, recriminations and alliances. Now that he had suddenly been taken from them, they felt as if they had been cast adrift. There was no one to whom they could turn. Gabriel, Andrew's younger brother, was flaky and neurotic. Joan, his sister, was a melancholia-prone hysteric. Life without their mentor would be very different indeed.

At first the Bayers sought to pursue proceedings against the estate agent driving the other car, but she was in a Nice hospital with a broken neck, and Lycus, the family lawyer, advised them not to start an action against her in a French court of law. The process, he warned, would be protracted and constricted by red tape, and would probably last, Jarndyce-style, until there was no money left, but that was the French for you.

With conflicting emotions, Mark listened to his family's growing grievances. The complaints were petty; why had Uncle Andrew left Mark's parents jewelry but little money? Why had he only bequeathed his brother a classic car? Nothing quite made sense. Soon, a poisonous pall began to creep over the formerly happy family, and the things Uncle Andrew had left behind began to be evaluated, coveted and compared.

Mark looked on in discomfort as his parents pored over their copy of Uncle Andrew's will, endlessly reinterpreting every word. He had never thought of them as greedy people, but now it seemed they were becoming obsessed with the amounts they had been left. He had heard that this was the common result of losing a senior family member, but the process still disturbed him. Worse, it traduced his memory of the avuncular old man and made him think more harshly of the surviving Bayers. Assuming that these ill humors would be short-lived, he returned to work and family life, albeit diminished, continued as before.

GABRIEL BAYER

Exactly one month after his uncle had died, Mark received a phone-call just as he was starting to fall asleep at the keyboard of his computer. He had been putting in long hours, trying to drum up business for his ailing design practice.

"Mark, is that you?" asked a familiar voice.

"Uncle Gabriel?" Mark liked his other uncle, even though Gabriel struck him as emotionally unstable. Gabriel was forty-seven and twice divorced, and had a difficult relationship with his two unruly children, but his heart was in the right place.

"I'm sorry to call you at this time of night, Mark. I know you always keep late hours."

"Are you okay?" It was unusual for Gabriel to call.

"I don't know. I don't think so. Look, I know how close you were to my brother. You were always his favorite. I thought you might understand."

"Understand what?"

"I just saw Andrew."

"Yeah, I keep thinking I see him too."

"No, I mean I really saw him, alive."

"What are you talking about?"

"I know this is going to sound ridiculous, but I was driving back from the office this evening and passed him standing on the side of the road. He was waving at me."

"Uncle Gabriel, you know that's impossible."

"I know, but I swear to you it was definitely him. He was wearing the clothes he died in, that awful shiny blue suit he always wore in France and that awful straw hat—you know, the one the English always think they need to put on in the Riviera."

"Have you told anyone else about this?"

"God, no, of course not. They'd think—well, you know." Gabriel had suffered a nervous breakdown soon after his second divorce.

"I think maybe it's delayed shock," was all Mark could say. "I imagine it's a common phenomenon."

"I know. It just felt so weird, what with me driving his old car and everything. I looked in the rear-view mirror and there he was. I looked again a moment later, and he'd vanished." Gabriel had been left his brother's other car, another classic Mercedes, his favorite, a plum-colored 1970 saloon with white leather seats and whitewall tires. There were only fifteen of the left-hand-drive models remaining in the world.

"I don't suppose there's been any word on what he was doing in Monaco that day?"

"I've asked around. Nobody has a clue. He told Catherine he'd be away for a few days. She was used to him going on his collecting trips." As far as Mark could discern, Uncle Andrew visited private antique sales, but nobody knew if he ever bought anything. Apart from the few bits and pieces he'd left his family, he seemed to own no special collections. There was nothing but ordinary furniture in his country house.

They talked for a while, and Gabriel rang off, a little happier. But it wasn't the end of the matter.

The following morning, Gabriel Bayer said good-bye to his nineteen-year-old son, Jake, who still lived at home with him, and headed into work earlier than usual. The flat, straight roads that ran through the Norfolk Fens were obscured by patches of thick mist. Gabriel tuned to Radio 4 and listened to a heated discussion about the future of the Anglican church. He had just passed Melton Constable when the radio fazed and faded. On either side of him, misted patches of marsh water glowed softly in the early morning light. He fiddled with the radio's tuner, trying to relocate his program, when the dark man loomed at him.

The figure was standing stock-still in the center of the road. Its arms were raised in warning. Gabriel swung the wheel just enough to avoid hitting him, and glimpsed his brother Andrew's alarmed face peering out from under his white straw hat as he passed. The vehicle's wheels had lost their purchase on the mist-slick road, and no matter how hard Gabriel tried to correct the drift of the car it slid farther in the opposite direction.

A classic Mercedes has a solid tempered steel chassis. As the two front wheels spun free of the tarmac and slipped over the verge, they hung above the velvet green surface of the marsh for what felt like an age. Slowly, inexorably, the vehicle tilted and dropped into the dark, still water of the fen. Gabriel fought to unclasp his belt, but found himself in the same situation as his brother. The blinding weed-green liquid began pushing at the seals of the windows. It sprayed in through the radio, the steering column, the radiators. Gabriel was hysterical now, unable to do anything except twist about in panic. He could have escaped if he had only retained his presence of mind, for the fen was not deep. But the water was muddy and impenetrable, the embodiment of icy death. As the Mercedes settled, it rolled over and filled, and there was nothing Gabriel could do about it.

Nobody thought to check up on his whereabouts until darkness had already fallen. It took another day for the police to dredge the fen and locate his corpse in the weed-camouflaged car.

CHERYL BAYER

Mark was in his favorite Wardour Street café, an independent coffee shop with permanently steamed-up windows, when he bumped into Uncle Andrew's lawyer, Lycus Gerolstein. He had a pale oval face and thinning grey hair that added to his air of reticence. A stern but seemingly fair-minded man, he was greatly trusted by his loyal clients.

"May I?" he asked, joining Mark at his table. "I thought I might find you here. There was something I wanted to talk to you about. You know you were always your uncle's favorite."

"Yes," said Mark, "it's funny he decided not to show it. Not that I mind, I just don't understand what happened."

"Well, that's what I wanted to explain. Your uncle made some big changes to his will in a series of handwritten codicils before his death."

"What kind of changes?"

"Switching bequests from one side of the family to the other, that sort of thing. I tried to talk him out of them, because I felt the original will was fine as it stood. Hell, it had taken us many months to plan and refine it, to make sure that everyone in the family was treated with equanimity."

"You don't think he was coerced into making the alterations, do you?"

"I wasn't there when he made them, but I can tell you the signatures on the codicils are definitely Andrew's, although they're pretty shaky. Lately I've had my suspicions."

"When did he make these alterations?"

"Well, as you know, your uncle was in hospital quite a few times."

"He was having blackouts. At first he just told me it was high blood pressure. But I spoke to the doctor and discovered he was due to have chemotherapy for lung cancer. After a while, he admitted the truth and his treatments began."

"Obviously, I knew your uncle was unwell," said Lycus. "And when people become sick, families tend to gather in preparation for the worst. I checked with the hospital, and was told that several relatives visited him while he was there. I have a feeling the codicils appeared around then. As I say, I can't be sure until I've done some more checking. I just thought you should know."

Lycus rose to go, but placed a hand on Mark's shoulder. "At times like this, family members you know and love can behave strangely. This is just a friendly word of warning. I'd keep an eye on them if I were you."

As Mark headed back to the office he rented, a dank attic with an alarmingly sloped floor in one of the last unrestored properties in Soho, he mentally drew up a list of suspects. Who might have manipulated the old man for his money? The idea revolted him. He looked around the office, at his obsolete computer, and the walls that were wet from the leaking ceiling. He was painfully short of cash. Projects had been hard to come by lately, and although he felt a little envious of his brother and his cousins, he could not bring himself to ask them for a loan. It just didn't feel right. Surely his uncle would have left him money if he had wanted him to have it.

Pushing the thought to the back of his mind, he settled down to the morning's work.

Some time later on the other side of the city, Cheryl Bayer wrote out her name on a piece of paper and studied it with a critical eye. She had kept her former husband's name after the divorce but now, for the first time, the forty-six-year-old retail manager was thinking of ditching it. Andrew had left her his four-room flat in Stratton Street, Mayfair, choosing to bequeath his huge Buckinghamshire house to his younger second wife, Catherine. Why, she wondered, did the first wives always get the raw deals?

Okay, the flat was worth a small fortune, but it still didn't seem fair when you looked at what everyone else had got. Cheryl was trying to sell the place privately, and decided she would continue to live in it until she found a purchaser. The property had hardly been touched since the 1950s and probably needed rewiring, but she resented the idea of paying out hard-earned money to fix it before the sale.

She studied the signature once more. That was it then. She would change back to her given name and finally put her marriage to Andrew behind her. She balled up the paper and tossed it into the bin.

Finishing her second bottle of red wine—she would have to watch the drinking if she was going to find another husband—she went to bed, and lay listening to the taxis sloshing along the wet street outside. She thought about Andrew, trying to remember how he had looked in their happier times, but already those memories were growing dim. What were the chances of contesting his will—could she even do it now that it had been implemented? The whole thing was so unfair. Why should the second wife get so much?

It was no use. She couldn't sleep. Getting back out of bed she walked through the half-emptied flat without turning on the lights. As she approached the kitchen mirror, she looked at her reflection and instinctively knew that something was wrong. Her shaded figure shimmered and buzzed apart as if it was made of flies, and reshaped itself into Andrew. He was leaning against the kitchen wall behind her, with his hands raised in a friendly gesture. He was smiling at her benignly. With a gasp, she span around, but found nothing there. She hoped Andrew had not been able to read her unkind thoughts. When she looked back at the mirror he was gone, and she realized her sleep had overlapped into her drunken wakeful state, and he had never been there at all.

No more red wine. She decided to make some tea.

There was something wrong with the electric kettle. It was making a funny noise. Perhaps she had overfilled it. She honestly couldn't remember what she had done. She tentatively touched the side, but it didn't feel as if it was heating. She tapped the plug, tried the wall switch. The kitchen lights weren't working for some reason.

She wiggled the kettle plug more violently.

She saw the spark, and watched as it jumped with a sharp crack from the plug to the wall, vanishing under the wallpaper. It seemed to have actually gone behind the outlet. She could see it glowing red, burrowing through the paper. Suddenly it surfaced, burning upwards in a fierce crimson line. She knew she had drunk far too much, but she had never actually hallucinated before. She slapped her hands over the progressing spark, trying to stop it, but it continued to burn a path, searing and blistering the flesh of her palms. Now it was rising fast and branching into other patterns, burning channels across the kitchen wall, stopping once to flare and hiss, burning onwards again.

She stepped back and studied the wall, incredulous, trying to understand what was happening. Some kind of pattern was forming. It looked almost like handwriting. She wondered if she should try to call someone, or whether the fault would simply burn itself out. She knew she should have had the electrics checked.

The realization of what she was looking at hit her. The burning ziggurat appeared to be her ex-husband's signature. God knows she had seen it enough times when he had signed money over to her. The thought was so silly she started to giggle. At precisely this moment the lines all flared, and the entire kitchen wall burst into a singe fierce sheet of flame.

JAKE BAYER

It seemed as if the rain would never let up. Mark Bayer had attended few funerals in his life, but in one month his presence had been required at three. He watched the gathered family guiltily smoking under the eaves of the crematorium like schoolchildren, and almost felt sorry for them. During the service, everyone had talked about how much Cheryl had doted on her husband, but Mark was beginning to wonder. After the divorce she had become an angry drunk. Nobody mentioned that.

Two of the relatives closest to Andrew were dead. It was almost as if his uncle had planned their fates from beyond the grave. But Mark couldn't bring himself to suspect that such a kind, conciliatory old man would want to bring harm to his family.

Cheryl had been burned bald and blackened, which had presumably saved the crematorium some time. Her flat had been gutted and rendered into an empty shell that brought vulgarity to the precious Mayfair street. The coroner noted that the former Mrs. Bayer had been drinking heavily and would not have been able to exercise clear judgment, and although he was puzzled by the striped burns on her hands, a verdict of death by misadventure was passed.

With no assignments to work on, Mark took the next morning off to go and visit Joan and Warren, his parents. Over lunch in their favorite restaurant, a monstrously overdecorated *trattoria* in Highgate, North London, he attempted to confront them about the codicils to Uncle Andrew's will, but they neatly deflected his questions. If they knew the truth, it seemed they were not about to tell him.

He was starting to suspect everyone. Even those closest to him were now behaving differently in the aftermath of his uncle's death. As Mark questioned his parents, he started to see how aggrieved they became when discussing Andrew's wealth, and how disappointed they were with what they had been left.

Everyone except Mark had been left amounts of money, but his mother had also inherited a somewhat peculiar emerald necklace, and his father had been presented with an art deco diamond skull cuff link and tie pin set. However, it was obvious that his parents had been hoping for more; Andrew's spectacular Buckinghamshire house, perhaps. Surely they took precedence over his childlike second wife? Wasn't blood thicker than youthfulness?

Mark looked from Warren to Joan as they forked sweetbreads

and *osso bucco* into their mouths, and saw them in a different, less flattering light.

Uncle Gabriel had a nineteen-year-old son studying at Cambridge. Jake Bayer had been left a brand-new Kawasaki motorcycle by his uncle, to replace the one he had had stolen the previous year. Gabriel had never approved of his son's love of motorbikes. Now that Jake was fatherless, he found that he was allowed to ride the glistening machine.

On impulse, Jake set off to visit his girlfriend in Manchester, and powered up the M1 hoping to catch her before she went out for the night. He, too, had become infected by the thought that the other side of the family was profiting more heavily from his uncle's death. He had lost his father (not that they had ever been close) and had been given the admittedly beautiful Kawasaki Ninja Performance Edition machine, which his uncle had bought in readiness for his twenty-first birthday. But that was all he'd been bequeathed. His Aunt Joan and Uncle Warren had been left valuable jewels, and Andrew's second wife had inherited a huge mansion. It seemed unfair. Of course, his cousin Mark had been left nothing, but the guy was a loser, trying to build a tiny graphic design company in a recession, refusing help from anyone.

The lowering skies were brownish grey and the black road ahead was slick with rain, so he decelerated and concentrated on the traffic around him. With his father gone, Jake was the most senior male on his side of the family, and responsibility was expected of him.

A few hundred yards ahead, the articulated supermarket truck that had been pacing the Kawasaki for two junctions also decelerated sharply. According to the signs, one of the lanes was closed for the next mile. Most of the main truck haulage between London and Manchester was conducted on this route, and you had to remain watchful in wet weather.

Damn, the truck was coming close.

Jake loosened the throttle, watching the fast approach of the truck's back-plate, and knew he would have to slow down fast. It was okay, though, because there was nothing behind him. He checked the wing mirrors expecting to see a clear straight stretch of glistening blacktop. Instead, he saw his uncle's face. He was saying something, trying to warn him.

Shocked, Jake slammed on his brakes.

When he looked in the mirrors again, Uncle Andrew had been replaced by the steel grille of another truck, just feet from his rear fender and approaching at an insane speed.

The two great trucks slammed into each other, with Jake at their center. The motorcycle flipped onto its side and was crushed as flat as a milk bottle top.

It proved impossible to fully separate Jake Bayer from the Kawasaki. His head was found under the wheel arch of the second truck. His left foot turned up two days later on the slip road of a Little Chef restaurant.

JOAN BAYER

As soon as Mark heard of his cousin's death, he became convinced that this string of accidents was no longer coincidental. But the main question which haunted him was this; even if Uncle Andrew had somehow planned for his family to be hurt, why would he want to harm his young stepson? It seemed as if the items specified by the will were somehow cursed to inflict damage on their inheritors. But how could that be possible? Uncle Andrew had loved his family.

Mark tried to discuss the matter with his brother Ben, who clearly thought he was crazy. He knew there was no point in going to the police. He tried talking to his parents again, but the deflection he had encountered before now turned to outright hostility. Everyone was bitter and confused by this inexplicable and disastrous turn of events. Mark sat in his gloomy office and tried to figure out an answer. His brother had been left money. Surely, if there really was a curse he would be spared—after all, how could a gift as universal and as abstract as cash ever hurt him?

Over the next few weeks, the aftershocks of death continued to ripple through the Bayer family. Jake's girlfriend was devastated by her loss, and discreetly dropped out of school. Autumn crushed the life from London's trees and winter set in hard. It felt as if nothing could be healed.

Andrew's mother finally went to see the family lawyer about contesting the will. She felt that as Andrew's sister, she should have been left considerably more, so Lycus Gerolstein agreed to put her case to the rest of the family. However, they unanimously refused to grant her an extra tranche of cash from her brother's inheritance fund, and as a consequence, the divisions between them all grew deeper. Mark was at a loss to understand what was happening. He had always thought of his family as—well, typically English. They were scattered across countryside and city, eminently sensible, rather too respectable, slightly dull, slightly superior, but now they seemed vindictive, bitter, mean-spirited.

Mark's mother had changed more than anyone. Status and power had suddenly become ridiculously important to her. With his own salary running out and no new clients offering work, Mark had been forced to move back to his parents' house in Chiswick. That evening, he came home just as the first of the real winter storms was breaking, and found Joan preparing for her husband's annual office dinner. Shaking out his umbrella and leaving it against the banisters on the first floor hall, he knocked and entered his mother's dressing room.

He barely recognized Joan anymore. She had lost weight and Botoxed away her wrinkles. With her newly auburn hair swept up and the antique emerald necklace at her throat, she suddenly seemed like every other hungry social-climber who attended London's glitzy winter events. Now she spoke of little else than what had befallen the family, who had got what, and why they were not entitled to have it.

"Your uncle had always had his favorites," she told him, trying on new lipstick and popping her mouth at the mirror. "Catherine only married him for his money, everyone knows that. And she got exactly what she wanted. She's been left that house, which must be worth a couple of million. He even left her children the attached land, and they're not even his!"

Mark was miserable. He wanted his world to return to how it had been before the death of his uncle. He was sick of hearing about money. But their lives were broken and there was no going back.

"Well," said Joan with a final snap of her handbag, "I wouldn't be surprised if Andrew had kept a few other funds tucked away. He was always clever with his cash. Perhaps we should hire Lycus to look into the matter. He must know where everything is, he was as thick as thieves with your uncle." She turned to her son, as if suddenly becoming aware that he was in the room. "Are you sure you don't want to come with us tonight?"

"No, I'm trying to build a business plan," he told her.

"It's so unfair. You were supposed to be his favorite nephew. I think it's disgraceful, the way he's treated you."

"Where's Dad?"

"I'm meeting him there." She rose and looked about her. "Where did I put my jacket?"

"I think I saw it downstairs."

Joan kissed him and went out into the corridor. Mark put on his headphones and went to work on his laptop.

His mother stood in front of the hall mirror and tried to work out what was wrong with her reflection. It was the necklace; it refused to hang straight. The emerald pendant at its center was crooked, and the settings of the diamonds around it felt razor-sharp on her delicate skin. Annoyed, she unclipped the clasp at the back and attempted to realign the chain.

In the mirror, something was coagulating in the shadows behind her right shoulder, as if the very darkness was knitting itself into a shape. The penumbral figure was speaking to her. The flesh of Joan's neck prickled. She reached out a hand to the glass.

"Andrew?"

And then, just as quickly, it dissipated like smoke beneath her touch. Above her head an apocalyptic peal of thunder sounded, and the house trembled.

Mark's furled umbrella slipped from its position against the banisters and fell down into the hall. Its metal tip shot under the back of Joan's necklace, catching it, the handle yanking the chain down hard. Joan was wearing new high heels that slipped on the tiled floor and pulled her over. As she fell, the umbrella, now caught in the necklace, twisted as she landed on it, tightening the chain into a noose. The metal jewel settings sliced into her soft neck, neatly severing her carotid artery. She frantically tried to pull herself upright, but the umbrella twisted like a garrote and the jewels bit deeper. Her blood pooled in a scarlet mirror across the floor. For a brief moment she saw Andrew reflected, then she died.

OLIVIA BAYER

"Well, I continued working upstairs," Mark told the skeptical policeman who was covertly checking his pupils to see if he'd been taking drugs.

"You mean to tell me that your mother was struggling to catch her breath just one floor below and you didn't hear a thing?"

"No, I had my headphones on. I didn't know anything about it until I went downstairs to get a drink."

"And how much later was that?"

"I don't know, twenty minutes, half-an-hour."

"And you didn't even get up close to check on her?"

"Why would I? There was blood everywhere. I could clearly see she was dead." He knew that the image of his mother lying on the black and white tiles in a nimbus of her own blood would stay with him forever.

The officers who quizzed Mark after his mother's death were quick to rule him out of any involvement in what the forensics team termed a bizarre accident, because his computer log showed that he was at his terminal during the time of death, and it was clear that Joan Bayer had died alone. Mark's story perfectly matched the sequence of events, but the officers agreed that they had never heard of anyone dying in such a bizarre manner.

From this date on, Mark's father stopped speaking to his son. Mark moved out a few days after the funeral, and rented a tumbledown flat-share in Whitechapel. The strange story of the Bayer family deaths had been kept out of the press until now, but this latest addition to the roll call of the deceased received its first passing mention in the tabloids.

Mark had now begun to believe that some kind of embodiment of evil was hunting down his relatives, but although he tried to talk about it, none of the surviving family members were prepared to listen to him. Reading up about wills on the internet, he was shocked to discover how many inheritance settlements caused the breakdown of family relationships. Eventually he was forced to reach the only logical conclusion—that this terrible chain of events was simply the kind of bad luck that followed the sudden loss of a family patriarch.

Mark was now seriously broke, and because he had lately been preoccupied, he lost the support of his only freelance client. He was on the verge of asking his brother Ben for a loan from the money he had been left, but at the last minute decided not to request any assistance. He could not explain why he decided on this. He simply couldn't help feeling that everything Andrew left to his family had been irrevocably tainted.

Olivia, Uncle Andrew's twenty-one-year-old daughter from his first marriage, was a loner. She rarely spoke to any other members of the family. She loved the sea and lived in Brixham, Devon. As a consequence, her uncle had left her his twenty-two-foot Fletcher speedboat. She took it out even on the coldest days, roaring along the blue coastline for an hour at first light if the tides were favorable.

One morning, Olivia inexplicably failed to pump the petrol fumes from the tanks and nearly turned the boat into a fireball that would have killed her instantly. She was been an experienced mariner. It seemed so unlike her to make such a mistake.

Shaken by her own neglectfulness, she pumped out the tank and set off at speed, forgetting to untie the aft rope from its mooring capstan. Twenty yards out, the Fletcher slammed to a jarring halt, catapulting her backwards into the freezing water, and the racing propeller blade bounced down, ploughing into her screaming face, mincing it into fish-chum. By the time the harbor rescue team pulled her out, there was nothing left above the ragged stump of her neck.

Olivia Bayer's father had also left her money, and this was now inherited by Catherine, Uncle Andrew's second wife. There were just four direct descendants of the Bayer family left alive: Mark and his brother Ben; their father, Warren; and Catherine.

WARREN BAYER

Mark had taken to meeting up regularly with Lycus Gerolstein, his uncle's lawyer, because they shared a morbid curiosity about the family's ill-fortune. As winter dragged on, they sat together in the little coffee shop on Wardour Street, trying to come to terms with each new twist of fate.

"I've done some more digging," said Lycus one morning, opening his briefcase and pulling out a sheaf of papers. "As you know, your uncle was admitted to the Harley Street Clinic on three separate occasions. Each time, he had been suffering from blackouts and memory loss. During the recovery periods he temporarily lost the power of speech. The dates on each of the codicils match these periods. It's my belief that your uncle was in no fit state to sign anything. He wouldn't have known what he was doing."

"Then why were the revisions accepted?"

"We had no choice. His signature was on each of them, which made them legally binding documents. You understand, of course, that I am required to remain in a neutral position throughout this process."

"Do you know who else was present when the codicils were signed?"

"His second wife Catherine was there on the first occasion. Gabriel, his brother, was certainly present two months later, when your uncle was admitted once more." Lycus hesitated.

"And the third?" prompted Mark.

"Your father," said Lycus with an air of apology. "Warren went to the hospital with Andrew and stayed there overnight with him."

Warren Bayer was late for the meeting at his head office in Clerkenwell. The tube platform at Angel was uncomfortably crowded, but he had not been able to find a taxi in the rain. As he watched the red dot-matrix board revise the train arrival times, he touched the diamond skull-head cuff links Andrew had left him. Lately he had been burying himself in his work, trying to forget the tragedy that surrounded him. It was easier to place his grief at the death of his wife to one side than it was not to hate his own son for being in the house and doing nothing as she lay dying.

Just a few short months ago they had all lived in a state of distant equilibrium, but now the ruptures were tearing them all apart. Every action was subject to examination, every phone call a reason for suspicion. He hated the way he found himself behaving. It was just so damnably un-English.

Warren checked his watch. He was going to be late. The atmosphere on the platform seemed dense and stifling. A buffet of warm air announced the arrival of the train.

He studied the travel poster opposite, a fierce sienna photograph of a Middle Eastern desert. He looked hard at the center of the poster. A blackish-green spot was appearing, as if mold was starting to come through from the wall behind. The black pattern grew, forming itself into the vague shape of a man. He looked around to see if anyone else was noticing the phenomenon forming on the poster, but the other passengers were going about their business as usual.

Fascinated, Warren failed to hear the announcement that the next train would not stop. He looked back at the expanding shape, and it seemed for a moment that Andrew was there, calling to him, trying to tell him something, if he could only get a little nearer . . .

The sound of the arriving train rose in his ears, and there was Andrew in his shiny midnight-blue suit and white straw hat, stepping from the poster, desperately trying to communicate. In shock, Warren raised out his hands and stretched forward just as the hurtling underground train hit him, shattering both his wrists, splintering bone, tearing sinew and muscle.

He was spun around and cartwheeled in between the platform and the train, his severed hands with their cuffs and cufflinks still intact, sparkling in the shadows beneath the platform like forbidden treasures.

CATHERINE BAYER

Mark was seized by panic. Only three descendents were left alive. He tried to follow the chain of events that took place after the discovery of his uncle's illness, convinced that something had happened to ignite this contagion of damnation, but found nothing. At his father's service, he talked to his brother.

"Ben, you must promise me something," he said as they left the crematorium, a pleasant London park filled with clipped English trees and a great many bare rose beds neatly arranged like ledgers. "You mustn't spend any of the money Uncle Andrew left you."

"Don't start getting weird on me," said Ben impatiently. "It's not cursed, okay? Our parents died because they were messed up and distracted. I'm sure if either of them had been thinking clearly, they'd have survived. Shit like this happens to families all the time."

"Yeah, right. Our mother was killed by her necklace. Dad's hands were severed. Christ, even you should be able to see that these weren't accidents!"

"I agree, it's kind of creepy, but any explanation you try to come up with would have to be a whole lot creepier."

"How do you explain what happened to the rest of the family? You think they were all distracted? What if there really was an explanation for everything that has happened?"

"Like what? The old man secretly hated them all and cursed his belongings? If you believe that, you're as nuts as the rest of them." Ben tried to pull away but Mark held him back.

"Think what you like. I'm just asking you not to spend the money for now. Not until I've figured this out."

Mark walked away from his brother. He had always been close with Ben, but even they were being forced apart.

Catherine, Uncle Andrew's second wife, had chosen to stay away from this latest funeral. She was having problems of her own; she was becoming increasingly angry with her Russian builders. They worked hard, but they had a habit of leaving every door and window open. She had hired them to renovate the great neo-Georgian Buckinghamshire house Andrew had left her, and spent her days trying to keep out the wind and rain as the workmen walked mud through the hall. Now she could hear something slamming around upstairs, and knew they had left one of the windows wide again.

There was an icy draft coming from the main bedroom. She threw back the door and saw the problem; they had exited onto the scaffolding and left the place open to the elements. She went to the window and looked out, trying to see if she could see them. It was almost dark, and the scaffolds stretched off into tarpaulin-draped shadows.

The wind had risen. The tarpaulins banged and rattled like the billowing sails of a ship. The weather forecast had warned of gales. Her workmen had clearly finished for the night. How could they be so thoughtless? She reached up to close the window and saw the figure standing outside on the planked terrace, peering in at her. Its fierce eyes glowed in the dark. He was shouting something, but the noise of the wind was snatching his words away.

Catherine was too startled to move.

She was still staring at the shadow-form of her dead husband when the gale lifted the tarps and rolled the scaffolding pole from where it had been carelessly left on the walkway. The steel tube swung down, flipped over and shot through the window, punching a hole through Catherine's chest, hurling her to the far side of the room in a spray of glass, wood and blood. She remained there, skewered through the heart, as the figure broke up and dissipated into the turbulent night air.

LYCUS GEROLSTEIN

"Something has been bothering me for days," said Mark as they sat at their usual places in the little coffee shop. "You were supposed to have lunch with my uncle on the day he died. What were you meeting about?"

"I told you," said Lycus patiently, "Andrew wasn't happy with his current investment portfolio and was thinking of changing his accountant. He wanted my advice."

"You could have done that in London. Bit of an odd coincidence, wasn't it, you both being in Monaco?"

"Not really. I have a number of clients based there, and your uncle enjoyed driving along the Savaric cliffs. It crossed my mind that he might be keeping a mistress there."

Mark thought for a minute. Something was scratching away at the back of his brain. "Could I see the original will?" he asked.

"I don't see why not," said Lycus. "It's at my house. I thought I should keep it there, away from the rest of your family."

"There's only two of us left alive now," Mark reminded him. His heart was beating hard in his chest. He did not want the lawyer to see how anxious he was.

"Tell you what, why don't you come down tomorrow evening?" Lycus suggested. "I can show it to you then."

The following afternoon, Mark made his way to London Bridge and caught a train to Sevenoaks. He found Lycus Gerolstein's house set back on a densely wooded hill near the station. The lawyer had never married and lived alone.

"Come in, it's a frightful night," said Lycus, holding the door wide. "It feels like these storms will never end. I thought you might cancel. Actually I'm very glad you could make it, because there's something I've been meaning to discuss with you."

Mark settled himself in a deep sofa in the firelit lounge while Lycus poured some wine. "You know, you're going to be a very rich young man soon," said the lawyer.

"How would that be possible?" Mark suspected that his parents had left him money, but since his uncle's death the subject of inheritance had become objectionable to him.

"Catherine Bayer died intestate. Without a will, the house she had inherited from your uncle passes to you."

"Surely it would go to the children from her previous marriage?"

"No. Andrew specified that in the event of his wife's death you should inherit their house."

"I don't understand. Why would he do that? He deliberately kept me out of his original will."

"Perhaps he had a change of heart."

Mark sensed that the lawyer was lying. He felt sure that Lycus would have discussed the possibility with him earlier. "Why are you only telling me this now?"

"I already explained that I'm not allowed to take sides. I'm afraid that meant restricting information to interested parties. Don't you see, if your family had known exactly what was in the codicils, they might have acted against each other?"

"You're talking about premeditated murder, Lycus. No, I can't allow myself to believe that. I want to see the original will."

Lycus sighed and rose to his feet. "Very well. Follow me." He led the way upstairs, into a narrow extension that seemed older than the rest of the house. "This is all that's left of an earlier building—1720. Mind your head on the beams."

Lycus led the way to a large room with a vaulted wooden ceiling. At one end a wood fire crackled in a large stone grate. "This single room constitutes the whole of the original house," he explained. "This is where your uncle and I kept our collection. I've never shown this to anyone else."

The lawyer's study was lined with beech wood museum cases. Mark approached one and peered inside. African, English, and Spanish masks stared sightlessly back at him.

"They belonged to devil-worshippers," Lycus explained. "No

matter what each race believes in, one thing is constant to every creed. There's always a devil."

"I suppose that's because we're all afraid of dying," said Mark. "We need to believe in someone who will allow us to strike a bargain."

Lycus looked pleased. "You're exactly right," he said. "It's human nature to seek an escape clause. The structure of every religion requires a mirror image. Every deity needs its opposite."

Mark studied the carved fetish idols, their screaming faces and twisted wooden limbs. "Quite a hobby."

"Your uncle and I shared the same interests. We wondered if it was possible that the objects men made—the items they worshipped with, the things they owned—could become imbued with their spirits. Ever since priests first sold nails from Christ's cross, such items have had totemic value. They've always been in demand. Here we are."

Lycus opened a glass-topped case and withdrew an envelope. "Your uncle's will, and its codicils."

He slid out the vellum within and spread the pages across the glass. Mark stared at his uncle's signature, as delicate as a spiderweb. Beneath it was a line that read: *Signature of Beneficiary*.

Above the signature of Andrew Bayer it said: *Signature of Notary Official*. In the space beside it, Lycus Gerolstein had written his name.

He checked all the documents, the first will and the three codicils. In each case, Lycus Gerolstein had signed his name.

"You were there," said Mark, looking up. "You were the officiating witness for all of these."

"Well, I had to be, otherwise the document would not have held any legal power."

"So you always knew who had tried to coerce my uncle into changing his will."

"I told you before, Mark, it is a requirement of my profession to remain nonpartisan. I knew that almost every member of your family had tried to persuade Andrew to change his mind. Each of them had patiently waited for him to become enfeebled before persuading him to sign. When your uncle recovered, he remembered little of what he had done. I had to tell him. By the time he was healing from his third attack, the bequests were in a hopeless mess once more. I wanted to spare you that knowledge."

Lycus moved to a cabinet and withdrew a shallow walnut box, carrying it as if he was transporting an item of immense worth and fragility. Lifting the lid, he took out an ornately carved fountain pen and handed it to Mark. It was surprisingly heavy.

"What is this made of?" Mark asked, studying the chased silver overlaid on the cream casing. "Is it ivory?"

"Something far more precious. "

"What did you do once you realized the original will had been messed up with codicils?"

"I drew up one final version that would sort everything out. It was this version Andrew signed in Monaco the day before he died. In order to receive your rightful inheritance, you need to countersign it. Just a formality."

Lycus slipped out a thick grey sheet filled with tiny print and laid it down on his desk with great care. This page looked completely different to the others. He indicated the space at the bottom. "Just on the line, if you will." He casually waved a hand over the page.

Mark hesitated, looking at the pen again. "First tell me," he persisted, "what is this?"

"It's a writing implement that was long thought lost. Your uncle used it for all his important documents. A superstition of his."

Mark weighed the fountain pen in his hand once more. "It's made of bone. I went to art college, Lycus, I studied anatomy. It looks like it's carved from one of the metacarpals. The bones in the wrist that connect to the fingers."

Lycus stepped closer. "You're quite right, a rare antique, designed for necromantic purposes. Just a folk superstition," he said impatiently. "Sign."

Mark laid the fountain pen down. "No, I can't."

"What are you talking about?"

"The bequests brought death to my family. If I inherit, the same thing will happen to me." He recapped the pen and toyed with it, balancing it between his fingers.

"You have to sign, Mark," Lycus warned, "or you won't get a thing."

"I don't want anything."

"Don't be ridiculous. This will change your life. It will give you everything you ever wanted. You haven't got a penny to your name. You'll never have to worry about money again."

"I don't want to receive an unearned gift. I'd rather give it away."

"But that's absurd."

"Is it? You remember when we met after my uncle died? I kept thinking—why would a lawyer seek me out in a coffee shop, just to tell me that he thought the will had been compromised? Men like you don't do such things without a reason, Lycus. You wanted me to become suspicious. Dissatisfied. You know what I think?"

A faint smile traced itself on Lycus's face. "No, what?"

"I think everything you told me in those meetings was designed to get me here tonight."

"And why would I want to do that?"

"You need me to accept my inheritance."

Lycus shook his head in pity. "How would that benefit me?"

Mark snatched up the pen. "What's the secret?" he asked. "Who did this belong to?"

"Give me that." Lycus made a lunge for it, but Mark stepped back beyond his reach.

"It's not about who it belonged to, is it? It's who it was made from." Mark turned the pen's barrel to the light and noted the inscription carved into the polished bone. *Gemacht von der hand unseres herrlichen Leiters.*

"I think I finally understand the nature of my uncle's will. I was his favorite nephew. He told me he was going to leave me the most precious gift of all. And he has."

"What do you mean?" Lycus moved closer, playing for time.

"He gave me independence. By making sure that I was the only one who was excluded from the bequests, he protected me."

"Interesting," said Lycus carefully. "I think perhaps it's time you knew the truth about your uncle Andrew. His cancer treatments were becoming progressively less successful. Each stay in hospital weakened him, although he hid it well. He didn't want to cause you any pain. When he discovered he was dying, Andrew feared that in his frail state the family would try to coerce him over the will—which of course they did—so he met with me and asked me if there was a way that I could help him."

"And you had the answer. You were both collectors."

"Andrew had long ago realized what his family was really like. He wanted to see them revealed in their true colors, but he didn't have long to live. I told him that by signing his will in the manner I proscribed, with the instrument we could purchase, his spirit could remain on earth long enough to confirm his suspicions. He would be able to see that justice was done. I told him that each family member who acted uncharitably would be destroyed by the item they were bequeathed."

"Why would he have believed you?"

"I told you, he was a collector of the arcane. A will is the one document everyone needs to sign. What happens if such a document could truly decide your afterlife? Wouldn't you want to know? Especially if you had no other choice? Andrew believed me because it was I who found the pen."

"That was why he went to France. The two of you bought it in Monte Carlo. The one thing I know about Monaco is that it's a tax haven, a place where private items are secretly traded."

"Your uncle and I purchased the pen, and he used it to sign a final version of the will—a version only he and I ever witnessed. This one." He tapped the grey page on the desk. "Feel it. It's extraordinarily delicate to the touch. We rewrote the will on the flayed skin of a concentration camp victim, and signed it with the führer's own hand—or at least, a part of it. Imagine the power we created! The very next day your uncle died, and became a creature of the shadow-world."

"My uncle wasn't a vindictive man. He would never have wanted his entire family to suffer."

"Perhaps not, but he was embittered by the thought of his impending death. He could watch what happened after, but couldn't intervene."

Mark thought for a moment. "My uncle Gabriel phoned to tell me he'd seen Andrew, and then he died. What if Andrew was trying to warn him?"

"Perhaps you're right. Perhaps the real tragedy of Andrew's deal was that his bitterness left him as he expired, and he no longer wanted revenge. Instead he was forced to watch, powerless to intervene, while his relatives gave in to their base instincts, cruelly dying one after the other. He saw how all men can be brought down to animal behavior."

"It's you, isn't it? You want what everyone who collects this kind of stuff wants. Proof of the soul."

"I merely carried out your uncle's wishes. Of course, I wanted proof of the soul's immortality. The führer was an occultist, but that isn't what gives the pen its power. It holds his life essence. Just as all of the other items hold the souls of their owners."

"You mean the jewelry."

"I mean everything!" Lycus shouted. "Everything your uncle left behind came from our collection. The steering wheel of Gabriel's car once belonged to Joseph Goebbels. Cheryl Bayer's flat had been the home of Alistair Crowley. The emerald necklace was made for Ilse Koch, the so-called Butcher of Buchenwald. The cuff links had belonged to the serial killer Peter Kurten. The money, too, laundered from generations of Nazi looters through Swiss banks. Everything I persuaded your uncle to leave in his will had been purchased from collectors, often at a terrible cost. Even the rope on Olivia Bayer's boat had once been part of a hangman's noose."

"What about Catherine Bayer's house?"

"That hadn't belonged to anyone notorious. But she had. Before she met your uncle, she had been the mistress of a notorious Washington warmonger. Your family was right about her. She had an evil heart. I introduced them." He sounded rather proud of the fact. "You see, getting the pen and the parchment wasn't enough. The inheritances had to be filled with the same kind of dark energy. It was a brave experiment, to be sure, but one that paid off. A curious mind is a wonderful thing, Mark. Your uncle shared my fascination with the idea."

Mark pretended to continue studying the will. His hands were trembling. "Tell me something, Lycus. Did my uncle know he was going to die that morning on the cliffs?"

"Oh, he knew the cancer would catch up with him soon enough. But you know as well as I do, every gain must be met with a certain amount of sacrifice. Using the pen shaved a few weeks off his life, that's all. I think I really underestimated its power. It wasn't the only relic removed from the führer's bunker, but it's the only one that was used in necromantic ceremonies after the war. Now, I think it's time for you to countersign the will, if you would."

Mark made a show of bending over the parchment. Lycus leaned closer, his lips slightly parted in anticipation. Mark prepared to place the nib against the sheet of flesh.

And, with the flick of his wrist, he sent the bone-pen curving behind him, towards the heat of the fireplace.

"No!" Lycus dived for it but Mark met him, punching him hard in the stomach. As they fought, the pen fell into the hottest part of the charcoal and began to burn. "Get it out!" Lycus screamed, "you don't understand!" But Mark slammed the lawyer onto his back and held his boot on Lycus's throat.

"If the will's agenda is not completely fulfilled, my soul will have to be surrendered in Andrew's place!"

"You shouldn't have let your passions get in the way of a deal." Mark kept the terrified lawyer pinned down as the pen spat and cracked in the fire, which now glowed crimson. Lycus bucked sharply and threw him aside, diving into the fireplace, yelling as the flames attacked his hands. But no matter how hard he tried to grip the pen it kept slipping from his grasp, luring him deeper into the fire.

Wedged in the roaring fireplace, he turned back to Mark, the crimson inferno roiling over his arms, engulfing his head, tearing at his face, causing his eyes to burst apart. The flames swirled around him in a fiery tornado, sucking the flesh from his charring bones. There was an immense explosion of blood-red flame and his body was lost inside the pulsing orange logs of the fire.

Mark threw the will in after Lycus, watching as the flesh smoked and burned with a strange green flame.

Then he put on his jacket and left the house.

The rain was easing up. He had almost reached the station at the bottom of the hill when his cell phone started to vibrate in his pocket. He checked the caller ID: *Ben Bayer.*

"I'm really sorry, Mark," his brother began. "I was broke. I just spent a tiny amount of the money."

"How much?" Mark demanded to know.

"Just a hundred pounds. I was going to be thrown out of the flat if I didn't pay the rent."

"Lock the doors, Ben. Don't move a muscle until I get there." He closed the phone and set off with a renewed sense of purpose. The will had been destroyed. He prayed that he had acted in time.

Glancing up at the leaden storm clouds, Mark thought he saw his uncle's face, smiling down benignly.

Return Journey

RAMSEY CAMPBELL

RAMSEY CAMPBELL was born in Liverpool, England, where he still lives
with his wife, Jenny. His first book, a collection of stories entitled *The
Inhabitant of the Lake and Less Welcome Tenants*, was published by August
Derleth's legendary Arkham House imprint in 1964. Since then, his novels
have included *The Doll Who Ate His Mother*, *The Face That Must Die*, *The
Nameless*, *Incarnate*, *The Hungry Moon*, *Ancient Images*, *The Count of Eleven*,
The Long Lost, *Pact of the Fathers*, *The Darkest Part of the Woods*, *The Grin of the
Dark*, *Thieving Fear*, *Creatures of the Pool*, and *The Seven Days of Cain*, as well
as the movie tie-in *Solomon Kane*.

His short fiction has been collected in such volumes as *Demons by
Daylight*, *The Height of the Scream*, *Dark Companions*, *Scared Stiff*, *Waking
Nightmares*, *Cold Print*, *Alone with the Horrors*, *Ghosts and Grisly Things*, *Told by
the Dead*, and *Just Behind You*. He has also edited a number of anthologies,
including *New Terrors*, *New Tales of the Cthulhu Mythos*, *Fine Frights: Stories That
Scared Me*, *Uncanny Banquet*, *Meddling with Ghosts*, and *Gathering the Bones:
Original Stories from the World's Masters of Horror* (with Dennis Etchison and
Jack Dann).

PS Publishing recently issued the novel *Ghosts Know*, and the definitive
edition of *Inhabitant of the Lake*, which included all the first drafts of the
stories. Forthcoming is another novel, *The Black Pilgrimage*.

Campbell has won multiple World Fantasy Awards, British Fantasy
Awards and Bram Stoker Awards, and he is a recipient of the World
Horror Convention Grand Master Award, the Horror Writers Association
Lifetime Achievement Award, the Howie Award of the H. P. Lovecraft Film
Festival for Lifetime Achievement, and the International Horror Guild's
Living Legend Award. He is president of both the British Fantasy Society
and the Society of Fantastic Films, and for many years he reviewed films
for BBC Radio Merseyside.

"'Return Journey' was suggested by a trip to Llangollen, North Wales,"
explains the author, "where the vintage railway had been dressed up to
recall World War II, sandbags and all.

"My imagination didn't need much prompting after that, especially once the train went slowly into a tunnel . . ."

AS THE OLD TRAIN PUFFED out of the station, past the sandbags on the platform and the men dressed up as soldiers and a wartime poster with its finger to its lips, the three children who were managing to occupy the whole compartment apart from Hilda's seat began to demonstrate their knowledge of history. "I'm Hitteler," announced the girl with orange turf for hair, and shot up an arm.

"I'm Gobble," said the girl whose bright pink lipstick didn't quite fit her mouth.

Hilda didn't know if she was meant to be offended. When Hitler and Goebbels were alive they'd been just a couple of the many things her parents never discussed in front of her. It was left to the third girl to react, clicking all her ringed fingers at her friends and declaring "You'd get shot for that if we was in the war."

"We're not."

"They don't have wars any more."

"You'd get shot or you'd get hung," the ringed girl insisted. "Hung by your neck till you was dead."

They must have learned some history to use phrases such as that. Perhaps they remembered only the unpleasant parts, the opposite of Hilda. She was turning to the window in search of nostalgia when the ringed girl appealed to her. "They would, wouldn't they?"

"Did you know anyone that was?"

"Did you ever see any spies being hung?"

"I don't look that old, do I? I wasn't in the war, just in the wars."

They regarded her as though she'd started speaking in a dead language, and then they crowned themselves with headphones and switched on the black boxes attached to them. If they intended to shut up so much of their awareness, Hilda wondered why they were on the train at all—but she wasn't far from wondering that about herself.

She'd seen the poster on the outside wall of the car park of the telephone exchange where she worked. Since none of her colleagues had seen it, she'd felt it was aimed just at her. OLD TIME LINE, it had said, with a train timetable and the name of a town pretty well as distant as her hot and bothered Mini could reach for one of her Sunday jaunts. If she hadn't been aware of having settled into never driving anywhere that wasn't already part of her past, she mightn't have taken the chance.

The town had proved to be even more Lancashire than hers: steep hills climbed by red concertina terraces, factories flourishing pennants of grey smoke, streets so narrow and entangled they might have been designed to exclude any relative of the shopping mall that had taken over the view from her floor of the small house she shared with two pensioners whose rooms always smelled of strong tea. She would have liked to explore, but by the time she'd found a car park where the Mini could recover from its labours she'd thought it best to head for the next train. When she'd stumbled panting into the two-platformed station she'd had to sprint for the train the moment she'd bought her ticket, scarcely noticing until she'd boarded that the railway preservation company had gone wartime for the weekend, and at a loss to understand why that should make her wish she'd been less eager to catch the train.

She rather hoped she wouldn't need to understand while she was on it. The station and whatever it contained that she hadn't quite liked were gone now, and trees were accompanying the train, first strolling backwards and then trotting as a preamble to breaking into a run as the last houses stayed in town. The land sank beside the track, and a river streamed beneath to the horizon, where a glittering curve of water hooked the sun from behind frowning clouds to rediscover the colours of the grassy slopes. This was more like the journey she'd wanted: it even smelled of the past—sunlight on old upholstery, wafts of smoke that reminded her of her very first sight of a train, bursting out like a travelling bonfire from under a bridge. The tinny rhythmic whispers of the headphones were subsumed into the busy clicking of the wheels, and she was close to losing herself in reminiscences as large and gentle as the landscape when a guard in a peaked cap slid open the door to the corridor. "All tickets, please."

He frowned the children's feet off the seats and scrutinised their tickets thoroughly before warning "Just behave yourselves in the tunnel."

That took Hilda off guard, as did her unexpectedly high voice. "When is there a tunnel?"

"There has been ever since the line was built, madam."

"No, I mean when do we come to it? How long is it?"

"Just under a mile, madam. We'll be through it in less than a minute, and not much more than that when we come back uphill. We'll be there in a few puffs."

As he withdrew along the corridor the girls dropped their headphones round their necks so as to murmur together, and Hilda urged herself not to be nervous. She'd never been frightened of tunnels, and if the children misbehaved, she could deal with them. She heard the guard slide back a door at the far end of the carriage, and then darkness closed around the windows with a roar.

Not only the noise made her flinch. The girls had jumped up as though the darkness had released them. She was about to remonstrate with them when they dodged into the next compartment, presumably in order to get up to mischief unobserved. Excerpts of their voices strayed from their window into hers, making her feel more alone than she found she wanted to be. The tunnel itself wasn't the problem: the glow that spread itself dimmer than candlelight was, and the sense of going downwards into a place that threatened to grow darker, and something else—something possibly related to the shadow that loomed in the corridor as the girls fell abruptly silent. When the guard followed his shadow to Hilda's door she gasped, mostly for breath. "Nearly out," he said.

As he spoke they were. Black clouds had sagged over the sun, and the hills were steeped in gloom. In the fields cows had sunk beneath its weight, and sheep that should be white were lumps of dust. It wouldn't be night for hours yet; nobody was going to be able to stage a blackout, and so she was able to wonder if that was the root of her fear. "Thank you," she called, but the guard had gone.

She remembered little of the blackout. The war had been over before she started school. The few memories she could recall just now seemed close to flickering out—her parents leading her past the extinguished houses and deadened lamps of streets that had no longer been at all familiar, the bones of her father's fingers silhouetted by the flashlight he was muffling, the insect humming of a distant swarm of bombers, the steps leading down to the bomb shelter, to the neighbours' voices as muted as their lights. She'd been safe there—she had always been safe with her parents—so why did the idea of seeking refuge make her yearn to be in the open? It was no excuse for her to pull the communication cord, and so she did her best to sit still for ten minutes, only to be brought back to the war.

The temporarily nameless station was even smaller than the one she'd started from. The closer of the pair of platforms was crowded with people in army uniform smoking cigarettes as though to celebrate an era when nobody had minded. The three girls were beating the few other passengers to a refreshment room that had labelled itself a NAAFI for the weekend, and Hilda might have considered staying on the train if the guard hadn't reappeared, shouting "End of the line. All change for nowhere. Next train back in half an hour."

The carriage shook as the engine was uncoupled, and Hilda grabbed the doorway as she stepped down onto the platform, which displayed all it had to offer at a glance. Most of the female passengers were queuing for the grey stone hut behind the ticket office. The waiting room smelled of cigarette smoke harsh enough for Woodbines.

The refreshment room had to be preferable, and she was bearing for it when a pig's face turned to watch her through the window. For as long as it took her to confront it she had the grotesque notion that the building had become not a NAAFI but a pigsty, and then she saw the snout was on a human head.

Of course it was a gas mask, modelled by one of the girls from the train. Three empty masks were rooting at the inside of the window. By the time Hilda grasped all this she was fleeing up the steps onto the bridge over the tracks, and the realisation by no means slowed her down. She walked very fast until she was out of sight of anything reminiscent of the war—out of sight of the station. She saw the smoke of the engine duck under the bridge and rear up on the other side, where the rails used to lead to the next county—presumably the engine would turn so as to manoeuvre to the far end of the train—and then she was around a bend of the narrow road bordered by sprawling grass, and the flank of the hill intervened between her and the railway. She didn't stop until she came to a hollow in the side of the hill, where she not so much sat as huddled while she tried to breathe calmly enough to believe she might grow calm.

Breezes and sunlight through a succession of shutters of cloud took turns to caress her face. The grass on the hills that crouched to the horizon hiding the town where she'd joined the train blazed green and dulled, shivered and subsided. She didn't know whether she closed her eyes to shut out the spectacle of the agitated landscape or in an attempt to share the stillness it briefly achieved. While she gave herself up to the sensations on her face she was able not to think—was aware only of them, and then not of them either.

She wouldn't have expected to be capable of sleeping, but some kind of exhaustion had left her capable of nothing else. She didn't dream, and she was grateful for it. Instead, as her mind began to struggle out of a black swamp of unconsciousness, she found herself remembering. Perhaps her stupor was helping her to do so, or perhaps, she thought as she strove to waken, it was leaving her unable not to remember.

Her parents had kept her safe from everything about the war, but there had been just one occasion when she'd had to shelter without them. She'd spent a Saturday at her aunt's and uncle's across town, which meant her teenage cousin Ellen had been required to play with her. Long before it was time for Ellen to see her home the older girl had tired of her. Perhaps she'd intended to be more quickly rid of her, or perhaps she'd planned to scare Hilda as a sly revenge for all the trouble she'd been, by using the short cut through a graveyard.

They hadn't progressed halfway across it when it had begun to seem to Hilda as vast as the world. Crosses had tottered towards her, handless arms as white as maggots had reached for her, trees like tall thin cowled heads without faces had whispered about her as she'd scampered after Ellen into the massing darkness, and she'd been unable to see the end of any path. Ellen had to look after her, she'd reassured herself; Ellen was too old to be frightened—except that as the sirens had started to howl, a sound so all-encompassing Hilda had imagined a chorus of ghosts surrounding the graveyard, it had become apparent that Ellen was terrified. She'd run so fast she'd almost lost Hilda at the crossing of two paths dark as trenches, and when she'd halted, her voice had betrayed she'd done so largely out of panic. "Down here," she'd cried. "Quick, and don't fall."

At first Hilda hadn't understood that the refuge itself was one source of her cousin's distress. She'd thought it was a shelter for whoever worked in the graveyard, and she'd groped her way down the steps after her into the stone room. Then Ellen had unwrapped her flashlight, and as its muffled glow brightened with each layer of the scarf she removed from it, her breaths had begun to sound more like whimpers. The walls had been full of boxes collapsing out of their long holes and losing their hold on any of their lids that hadn't caved in. For a moment Hilda had thought someone was looking at her out of the box with the loosest lid, and then she'd seen it was a gas mask resting on the gap between box and lid. Gas masks were supposed to protect you, and so she'd run to pick it up in the hope that would make her braver. "Don't touch it," Ellen had not much less than screamed, but Hilda had pulled the mask off—

She didn't know if she had screamed then; certainly she did now. The cry rose to the surface of her sleep and carried her with it, and her eyes jerked open. The view that met them could have been more reassuring. The sun was considerably lower than last time she'd looked, and its rays streamed up like searchlights from behind black clouds above the town past the horizon. One beam spotlighted a solitary oval cloud, so regular she had to convince herself it wasn't a barrage balloon. She hadn't quite succeeded when she became aware not just of the lateness but of the silence. Had the last train departed? Long before she could walk back to town it would be dark, if she managed to find the right road.

As she shoved herself to her feet her fingers dug into the soil, and she remembered thinking in the graveyard vault that when you went down so far you were beneath the earth. She did her best to gnaw her nails clean as she dashed to the bridge.

The platforms were deserted. The ticket office and all the doors were shut. A train stood alongside the platform, the engine pointing towards the distant town. The train looked abandoned for the night, and she was about to despair when the stack gave vent to a smoky gasp. "Wait," she cried, and clattered down the steps. She hadn't reached the platform when the train moved off.

"Please wait," she tried to call at the top of her voice. Her dash had left her scarcely enough breath for one word. Nevertheless the rearmost door of the last of the three carriages swung ajar. She flung herself after it, overtook it, seized the inner handle and with a final effort launched herself into the corridor. Three gas masks pressed their snouts against the window of the refreshment room, their blank eyepieces watching her as though the darkness was. She shut them out with a violent slam and retreated into the nearest compartment, sliding the door closed with both hands and falling across a seat to fetch up by the window.

The station sailed backwards, and the humped countryside set about following. She was glad the masks were gone, but she wished the view would demonstrate the past had gone too. There wasn't a vehicle to be seen, and the animals strewn about the darkened fields were so still they might have been stuffed. She was trying to content herself with the rewinding of the panorama when she remembered that it would return her to the tunnel.

She didn't want to enter it by herself, especially since the lights of the carriage appeared to be dimmer than ever. She would put up with children so long as they didn't try to make anything of the dark. If there were any in her carriage she would have heard them by now, but perhaps there were quieter passengers. She stood up, though the movement of the train was against it, and hauled herself around the door into the corridor.

She was alone in the carriage. The empty compartments looked even less inviting than hers: the long narrow outlines of the seats reminded her too much of objects she was anxious to forget, the choked brown light seemed determined to resemble the wary glow of her memories. Surely there must be a guard on the train. She hurried to the end of the corridor and peered across the gap into the next one, down which she heard a door slide open. "Hello?" she called. "Who's here besides me?"

The carriage tossed, sending her off balance. She floundered towards the gap above the speeding tracks, and had to step across it into the middle carriage. It was swaying so vigorously that the lamps looked close to being shaken out, and she had to reassure herself that the sound like a nail scraping glass was the repeated impact of a blind against the window of the first compartment. If someone had drawn the blinds down for privacy, Hilda was loath to disturb them. Instead she ventured past in search of the door she'd heard opening.

Was the carriage out of service? The insides of the window of the next compartment were so grimy they might have been coated with soil. Through a patch that a hand must have cleared she saw movement—a stump jerking up and down—the movable arm of a seat, keeping time with the rhythm of the wheels. It must be a shadow, not a large black insect, that kept creeping out from beneath the arm and recoiling, though there were certainly insects in the adjacent compartment: fat blue flies, altogether too many of them crawling over those few sections of the windows that weren't opaque, more of them blundering against the rest of the glass, thumping it like soft limp fingers. She was trying to nerve herself to dodge past all that, because next to it was the door she'd heard, when she saw what was wedging the door open. She wanted to believe it had slid open with the lurching of the carriage, which had also thrown an item of lost property off one of the seats to be trapped by the bottom corner of the door—a glove with its fingers twisted into claws and as brown as shrivelled skin. Even if it was only a glove, it didn't look quite empty enough.

Perhaps she didn't see it stir, or perhaps the careening of the train made the fingers twitch. She only knew she was backing down the corridor, leaning against the outer wall for fear of being hurled against or into a compartment, her hands sliding almost as fast over the grimy windows as the twilit hills and fields were regressing outside them. She had to force herself to look behind her rather than retreat blindly over the gap. As she executed a faltering stride into the rear carriage, her lips formed words before she knew where she remembered them from, and then while she attempted not to remember. "It wasn't me," she mouthed as she fled along the carriage, and as she slid the door shut on the corridor that had turned too dim for her to see the end of it and clung to the handle "I didn't do anything."

She hadn't broken into the vault or vandalised the contents, true enough. Days later she'd overheard her father telling her mother that some children had, and she'd realised they must have left the gas mask. "Pity they weren't old enough to be called up," her father had said for her mother to agree with, "and learn a bit of respect," and Hilda had felt his comments could have been aimed at her, particularly since Ellen had persuaded her never to mention they'd been in the graveyard. After that, every time she'd had to go to the shelter with her parents—down into the earth and the dimness full of shapes her vision took far too long to distinguish—she'd repeated her denial under her breath like a prayer.

"I didn't do anything"—but she had. She'd lifted the mask from the open end of the box—from the head poking through the gap. Whoever had pulled out the box must have used the mask to cover up the head. It seemed to Hilda that some of the face might have come away with the mask, because the vacant eyes had been so large and deep that shadows had crawled in them, and the clenched grin had exposed too much besides teeth. Then the light had fled with Ellen up the steps, and as Hilda scrambled after her, shying away the mask and its contents, a steady siren had sounded the All Clear like a cruel joke. As though summoned by the memory of her having had the light snatched away, darkness erased the countryside outside the train with a stony shout of triumph.

She doubled her grip on the handle until the hot thick stale exhalations of the engine began to invade the compartment through the open window. Now that the journey was uphill the smoke was being channelled backwards, and she felt in danger of suffocating. She lunged across the seat to grab the handles of the transom and slide the halves together. They stuck in the grooves while her hands grew as hot and grubby as the smoke, then the halves stuttered together and met with a clunk. She fell on the seat and masked her face with her cupped hands, but when she saw her blurred reflection against the rushing darkness on both sides of her she uncovered her face. At least she'd shut out much of the uproar as well as the smoke, and the relative silence allowed her to hear something approaching down the tunnel.

No, not the tunnel: the corridor. She heard an object being dragged, followed by a silence, then a closer version of the sound. She was well-nigh deaf from straining her ears when another repetition of the noise let her grasp what it was. Somebody was sliding open the compartment doors.

It could be the guard—perhaps he was responding to her call from before they had entered the tunnel—except that the staggery advance sounded rather as though somebody was hauling himself from door to door. She strove to focus her awareness on the knowledge that the train wasn't supposed to stay in the tunnel much more than a minute. Not much more, her mind was pleading, not much more—and then she heard the door of the neighbouring compartment falter open. Her gaze flew to the communication cord above the entrance to her compartment just as two bunches of fingers that seemed able only to be claws hooked the edge of the window onto the corridor. The carriage jerked, and a figure pranced puppet-like to her door.

It might have been wearing a camouflage outfit, unless the dark irregularities on the greenish suit were stains. It was too gaunt for its clothes or for the little of its discoloured skin she could see. Above the knobbed brownish stick of a neck its face was hidden by a gas mask that had fallen askew. With each sway of the carriage the mask looked in danger of slipping off.

For the duration of a breath she was incapable of taking, Hilda couldn't move. She had to squeeze her eyes shut in order to dive across the compartment and throw all her weight against the handle of the door while she jammed her heels under the seat opposite her. As long as the door and the glass were between her and the presence in the corridor it surely couldn't harm her. But her sense of its nearness forced her eyes open, and the figure that was dancing on the spot in time with the clacking of the wheels must have been waiting for her to watch, because it lifted both distorted hands to fumble with the mask.

Hilda heaved herself up to seize the communication cord, and only just refrained from pulling it. If she used it too soon, the train would halt in the tunnel. Her mouth was yearning to cry out, but to whom? Her parents couldn't keep her safe now; they had never appeared when she'd called out to them in the night to prove they were still somewhere. Her fist shook on the rusty chain above the door and almost yanked it down as the fingers stiff as twigs dislodged the mask.

Whatever face she'd been terrified to see wasn't there. Lolling on the scrawny neck around which the mask had fallen was nothing but a lumpy blackened sack not unlike a depleted sandbag from which, far too irregularly, stuffing sprouted, or hair. All the same, the lumps began to shift as if the contents of the sack were eager to be recognised. Then light flared through the carriage, and Hilda tugged the cord with all her strength.

The brakes screeched, but the train had yet to halt when the lights, having flared, died. The train shuddered to a stop, leaving her carriage deep in the tunnel. She had to hold the door shut until help arrived, she told herself, whatever she heard beyond it, whatever she imagined her fellow traveller might be growing to resemble. But when the handle commenced jerking, feebly and then less so, she rushed across the invisible compartment and wrenched the halves of the transom apart and started to scream into the darkness thick as earth.

Grandfather's Teeth

LISA TUTTLE

LISA TUTTLE made her first professional sale forty years ago with the short story "Stranger in the House"—now the opening entry in her book *Stranger in the House: The Collected Short Supernatural Fiction, Volume One*, published by Ash-Tree Press.

Perhaps best known for her short fiction, which includes the International Horror Guild Award–winning "Closet Dreams," Tuttle is also the author of several novels, including *The Pillow Friend, The Mysteries*, and *The Silver Bough*, as well as books for children and nonfiction works.

Although born and raised in America, she has lived in Britain for the past three decades, and currently resides with her family in Scotland.

"That I began to write 'Grandfather's Teeth' on a day when I had a dental appointment is not insignificant," Tuttle admits. "The last period in my life when my teeth caused me so much pain, I could look forward to the glorious day when my braces would come off.

"Alas, there's no such happy outcome to the dental woes of the elderly person I have somehow, mysteriously, become.

"I can't claim that writing this horror story reduced my fear of either dentures or dementia, but I enjoyed the opportunity to share."

GRANDFATHER'S TEETH were not the worst thing about him, but they were pretty horrible.

Shelley squealed in disgust whenever she caught sight of the set of ivory-colored teeth arrayed in the pink plastic gums, whether carefully placed in a glass of water, or abandoned, high and dry on top of the television set, on a plate in the refrigerator, or halfway up the stairs; but for Dougie the teeth had a peculiar fascination, like a lot of horrible things, although the reason why was impossible to explain, especially to a girl. But it was that fascination which made him rush over and pick the things up whenever he spotted them somewhere out of place, and even clean them and restore them to the blue plastic box in the bathroom, although he accepted thanks from his mother and his aunts just as if he'd done it to save them the trouble.

It only happened a few times, because Grandfather didn't start dropping his teeth that much until he had seriously lost it, and by then his obscenity-laden rants had started alienating the neighbors, who fortunately remained neighborly enough to rescue him after he set his house on fire, and after that he was moved into a nursing home that specialized in elders with dementia.

Dougie and his sister were taken to visit Grandfather in the home, which was much worse than going to his house had been, because they weren't allowed to wander off, and there was nowhere to go and nothing to do but sit in the overheated television lounge, and pretend to be interested in the wildlife documentaries or cooking programs that the residents were all ignoring in favor of watching you, or sit in Grandfather's room and pretend to be having a conversation while staying out of grabbing reach. Having him pinch your cheek or give you a slobbery kiss wasn't very nice, but it wasn't as bad as whatever he did to Shelley at the end of their third visit. That had made her scream and then cry—she must have cried for a whole hour—and afterwards, although Dougie still had to go for a weekly visit, she was allowed to stay home.

Dougie could remember when his grandfather had been a kind, gentle man who seemed to know everything there was to know about birds and animals, and who had taught him how to make a kite, but that soft-spoken, intelligent man had gone, replaced by a big, bad-tempered baby who wouldn't even put his teeth in at mealtimes, so he could only eat mush.

Although he no longer used them, Grandfather's teeth were still kept in a box on the bedside table, within easy reach, in case he changed his mind. The sight of the cloudy blue plastic container sitting between the old radio and a box of tissues gave Dougie a funny squiggly feeling in his tummy, and he imagined reaching out his hand and picking it up, then squeezing the sides so the smoothly rounded top would pop open to reveal the set of false teeth snug within. Then he would take them out.

At the thought of feeling the fat, pink plastic gums and the cold hard incisors embedded there, his stomach hollowed and dropped like he was on a roller-coaster, and all of a sudden he had a stiffy. He couldn't believe it; how stupid was that; not even a fit nurse in sight. He was hunched over a little, trying to hide it, trying desperately to think of something even more disgusting and less horn-inducing than an old man's false teeth, when, with her usual brilliant timing, Mum asked if he was all right and did he need the toilet?

When Grandfather died no one was very sorry, because, really, the man they had known and loved was already dead; it had just taken his body awhile to catch up. Most of his possessions had been disposed of already: the furniture and books divided among his daughters, smaller memorabilia distributed to his grandchildren and other relatives. The apprehension his daughters had felt about letting him take anything valuable into the home had been justified; no one could say what had happened to his good watch or the radio, and even things with no worth beyond the sentimental were missing. The box returned by the nursing home was stuffed with pajamas and socks and handkerchiefs, and contained a few items that must have been stolen from other patients to make up the weight: some paperback novels, a pair of praying hands carved in dark wood, an ashtray.

Apart from the photo album and a small collection of framed photographs, Mum put everything else back into the box.

"What are you going to do with that?" asked Dougie, who had been hanging back, watching, as his mother took inventory of Grandfather's remains.

"Take it to the dump. They might have saved me the trouble and done it themselves. Did they really think anyone would want a dead man's dressing gown, or his ancient underwear? If *they* didn't want it . . ." Sighing, she rose, wiped her hands on her trousers, and left the room.

Alone, Dougie stood and stared at the box. He told himself it didn't matter if they were in there or not. No one could conceivably want a dead man's false teeth. But he couldn't help being curious. His mother had not included them among her monotone listing of contents, nor had he once glimpsed the occulted gleam of cloudy blue plastic as she'd pulled things out and pushed them back.

Hardly aware of having crossed the room, he found himself kneeling. She could come back at any minute, and how would he explain? The flaps pulled back, his hands plunged down; he was elbows-deep in fabric, holding his breath against the stench of stale linen, of old man, as he groped along the cardboard bottom. He felt the wooden hands, the cover of a book, then palmed something smoothly rounded, soft plastic yielding as his hand closed on it.

He'd just pulled it free when he heard her footsteps in the hall. Quickly, he stood up and stepped away from the box, shoving the small container deep into one of his pockets. The box was open now, but being caught trying to shut it would look more suspicious than just leaving it.

She came in holding the car keys. "Want to come?"

"Where?"

"I told you: the recycling center." She nodded at the box.

"Now? A special trip, like, just for that?"

She bent down to tuck in the flaps. "I was needing to go to Waitrose, anyway. And if there was anywhere you wanted to go . . .?"

Straightening up, she looked for his reply.

His hand went into his pocket to curl around the plastic shell as he shook his head. "No thanks. I'm good."

She left the room to go make the same offer to his sister, and, unobserved, he could have returned the teeth to the box, sent them on their way to oblivion with no one the wiser, but he did not.

When his mother and sister had left, he went into his room and closed the door. He relaxed, secure in the knowledge that he was alone, and would be undisturbed for at least an hour, even though he had nothing in mind that required such a high level of security.

He took out the small container, put it on his bedside table, and popped it open. Looking at the faceless grin inside recalled something heard on a wildlife program, probably one of those unintentionally absorbed in the lounge at the care-home, about the meaning of the smile in apes. When a chimpanzee grinned at you he wasn't amused; no, it was his way of showing subservience or fear: please don't hurt me, I'm harmless.

"Scared of me, huh?" said Dougie conversationally as he picked up the teeth.

They didn't feel quite the way he remembered them feeling, back when his grandfather was alive. Of course, then, when for reasons obscure probably even to himself, Grandfather would remove his teeth and put them on top of the television or inside the refrigerator, they were coated in dried saliva if not actually sticky. Now, they were clean and dry, but, strangely, not cold. They even felt warm, and somehow had a feeling of life about them. It was almost as if they were *vibrating*.

He was still trying to make sense of it when Grandfather's teeth flipped over in his hand and chomped down on the spot known to palm-readers as the mound of Venus.

It hurt like hell, and Dougie screamed and shook his hand in a useless attempt to get it off. It was only when he grabbed hold of the teeth with his other hand, attacking them from behind, that he was successful, and that was only because, when the teeth slackened their grip for a moment in preparation for a second, harder, bite, he felt that slackening, and was able to use it to his advantage and pull the teeth off.

He looked in horror from the teeth marks in his left hand to the set of teeth in his right. How? Why? Once again, his attempt to understand made him slow to react. Whether they moved on their own or somehow used the energy in the hand that held them might be impossible to judge, but the end result was the same. They moved and caught the end of his left forefinger, this time biting down hard enough to take it off. Of course, as soon as they had bitten through, the set of teeth fell away with the fingertip.

Dougie stared at his throbbing, bleeding hand, in pain but too shocked to scream. He began to whimper, and called out for his mother's help.

Then he remembered he was on his own.

He ran to the bathroom and snatched up a facecloth, which he wrapped around his mutilated finger, as much to hide it as in an attempt to stop the bleeding, and then he clamped his hand in the opposite arm-pit as he awkwardly used the phone to call emergency services. In the first gush of terror he said he'd been bitten, that the end of his finger had been bitten off. When asked for more details, he had the presence of mind to blame an imaginary dog, which he said had run off.

The calm-voiced operator took his details, told him what to do, said an ambulance and paramedic would be with him hopefully in a very few minutes, and then asked if he still had the fingertip. If he could find it on the ground, he should keep it on ice, and bring it with him, because the surgeon might be able to stitch it back.

He went back into his bedroom to search, waves of sickness running through him in hot and cold surges, flinching at every shadow, terrified that the teeth would leap out at him and bite off more fingers, or maybe this time go straight for his throat. But nothing happened;

nothing moved in the room except himself, and the only evidence that the teeth had ever existed was the blue plastic clamshell case lying open and abandoned on the table.

It was just as he was about to give up—he could hear the welcome sound of an ambulance siren coming closer—that he noticed a small, dark pool of blood on the carpet. Going near to it, bending down, he saw a gobbet of flesh in the middle of it, and the muted gleam of his own fingernail.

His finger would be slightly lop-sided in future, and the nail would probably fall out before (probably) growing back, but the repair of Dougie's finger was judged a success. He didn't get away with his story about the dog, even though it made it into the local paper: the doctors and nurses recognized the tell-tale signs of a human bite—confirmed by the imprints of a set of teeth around the base of his thumb.

Who bit you, Dougie? We know someone bit you, and it was a person, not an animal. What happened? Who are you trying to protect? You must tell us the truth."

The truth, of course, only made things worse. They didn't believe him. His insistence on blaming a set of false teeth (which he couldn't even produce; how should *he* know where they'd gone?) only shifted the suspicions of the grown-ups away from some imaginary, violent friend—(Mother: "He doesn't have any friends. At least, no one he brings home.")—squarely back to him. If there was no other person involved in the incident, adult or child, then Dougie must have used his late grandfather's false teeth to inflict the damage on himself. Why did he want to hurt himself? What did he think he was doing? Why had he stolen the teeth?

"It wasn't stealing," he said quickly, defensively. "Mum was only going to throw them away. Anyway, she already said we could have anything we wanted out of Grandfather's things."

And why had he wanted the false teeth?

But he didn't. He never wanted them. He hated the horrible, smelly things! He didn't know why he'd taken them. He didn't mean to do it; it was just, suddenly, they were in his hands. And biting.

He was made to stay in hospital for a few days while social services investigated his home situation. He thought that meant they would be searching for the teeth, but when his parents came to take him home, and he asked if they'd found the teeth and what they'd done with them, he knew by the look that went between his father and the social worker that not only had they not found them, they probably hadn't even been looking for them, because they actually thought he was crazy, and had only imagined, if not invented, the whole sick story.

He didn't care if he had to talk to a psychiatrist twice a week, to express his feelings and play word games; he didn't mind taking pills and being put on a special, healthy diet; even the prospect of being sent to a "special" school did not bother him nearly as much as returning to the house where grandfather's teeth were waiting for him.

Where were they? Would he be safer shut inside his own room, or was that the most dangerous place in the house? He decided, against his usual habits, to leave the door to his room open—noticing, as he went in, that his old door handle had been replaced by one without a lock. His bandaged finger started to throb, painfully, and he stood in the middle of the floor, his elbows tucked in against his sides, hands at chest-level in the T. Rex position, and held his breath, listening for any small sound—squeak or clack or shuffle—but there was nothing. Nothing happened, and he had to breathe. He had to move. He couldn't spend his whole life—not even the entire day—waiting to be attacked. He'd just have to be careful.

Before going to bed that night, Dougie looked everywhere he could think of in his room, using a flashlight to search out dark corners under his bed, but he did not find the teeth. He'd always been good at Easter egg hunts, so he was able to satisfy himself that, wherever they had gone, they were no longer in his room. He'd noticed the blue plastic case was missing, and assumed that, like the bleached-out patch on the carpet where his blood had dripped, was his mother's doing. Maybe she'd also found the teeth and destroyed them and just wasn't saying anything on the doctor's advice. He decided that unless his parents raised the subject he wouldn't say anything more about Grandfather's teeth. If they were outside the house, they were no longer his problem. If they were still lurking somewhere inside the house—well, he'd worry about that in the morning. He shut his bedroom door and went to bed.

When he woke it was not morning—it was nowhere near morning, since his room was even darker than when he'd gone to bed—and he knew the teeth were nearby. He didn't know how he knew, and he stayed absolutely still, hoping not to reveal his awareness, and tried to recapture whatever it was that had awakened him: was it the click of teeth meeting floor in a bizarre scuttle, or the soft thump of something falling onto his bed?

His arms were tucked in close to his sides beneath the covers, and he hated to even think of putting one out, reaching over to the bedside table where not only the lamp but those teeth might be waiting to bite another finger off, but there was no safety in lying in the dark, where the next he knew of the teeth might be as they met through the cartilage of his nose or ear.

As swiftly as he could, praying his thrust was accurate, Dougie sent out one arm towards the lamp. His fingers closed on the switch, and at once the room was flooded with warm yellow light. He breathed out in relief at the sight of the empty tabletop, and beyond that, apart from his shoes, socks, and jeans, the floor empty all the way to the door. He turned his head, and saw them, hardly an inch away, on his pillow.

They were so close, he could smell them, the sharp chemical tang of plastic overlaid with something more personal, biological—a trace of ancient saliva mingled with his own blood.

He opened his mouth to scream, and they flew inside. His scream was choked off before it could emerge, and he thrashed in agony. They were in his *throat*, they would *kill* him—he had a vision of the teeth eating their way out of his stomach, and of his own lingering, agonized death—but the gag reflex saved him. The teeth were too big to swallow, and his throat pushed them back.

Yet he could not spit them out. They would not be ejected. They were *doing* something, as fiercely active as a small animal nesting in his mouth. When he tried to pull them out, they snapped at his fingers, a painful nip that drew blood. He had to withdraw his hand; he didn't dare try again although what they were doing was so painful it made him cry.

They were breaking his teeth, forcing them out, pushing them down into the gums, making way for themselves, and they were brutally efficient. Scarcely more than a minute after they'd entered his mouth, the teeth were as firmly lodged as if they'd grown there.

Still too frightened to put his hands too near his mouth, Dougie ran to the bathroom, switched on the light, and looked in the mirror.

His face was sweaty and greenish with fear, his lips were puffy, and there was blood running in streams from his mouth, down his chin, like he was some deranged vampire-zombie cross. He grimaced at the mirror, peeling his lips back in the ape's fear-smile to reveal the set of perfectly even, gleaming white teeth, monstrous in his mouth.

The moan that came out of his mouth had nothing in common with that hideous grin. Gaining in volume, it finally cracked through the spell of sleep wrapped round the house.

Shelley was first to emerge, coming out of her room rubbing her eyes, sleepily asking what was the matter.

Dougie turned towards his sister. She looked like some kind of cute little cartoon bug, the way her skinny white arms and legs stuck out of her black sleep-shirt. He loved her, even if he would never say it. He didn't want to make her scream and cry, but Grandfather's teeth did.

Ill Met by Daylight

BASIL COPPER

BASIL COPPER was born in 1924 in London, and for thirty years he worked as a journalist and editor of a local newspaper before becoming a full-time writer in 1970.

Copper's first story in the horror field, "The Spider," was published in 1964 in *The Fifth Pan Book of Horror Stories*. Since then, his short fiction has appeared in numerous anthologies and has been extensively adapted for radio. Collections of his work include *Not After Nightfall, Here Be Daemons, From Evil's Pillow, And Afterward the Dark, Voices of Doom, When Footsteps Echo, Whispers in the Night, Cold Hand on My Shoulder*, and *Knife in the Back*.

One of the author's most reprinted stories, "Camera Obscura," was adapted for a 1971 episode of the television series *Rod Serling's Night Gallery*.

Besides publishing two nonfiction studies of the vampire and werewolf legends, Copper's other books include the novels *The Great White Space, The Curse of the Fleers, Necropolis, House of the Wolf*, and *The Black Death*. He has also written more than fifty hard-boiled thrillers about Los Angeles private detective Mike Faraday, and has continued the adventures of August Derleth's Holmes-like consulting detective in several volumes, including the collections *The Exploits of Solar Pons, The Recollections of Solar Pons*, and *Solar Pons: The Final Cases*, along with the novel *Solar Pons Versus the Devil's Claw*.

More recently, PS Publishing has produced the nonfiction study *Basil Copper: A Life in Books,* compiled and edited by Stephen Jones, and a massive two-volume set entitled *Darkness, Mist & Shadow: The Collected Macabre Tales of Basil Copper*. Forthcoming from the same imprint is a restored version of Copper's 1976 novel *The Curse of the Fleers* and a collection of all the author's Solar Pons stories.

"I must admit that my work in certain genres has been greatly influenced by the wonderful tales of M. R. James," explains Copper. "His own subtle and oblique way of constructing narrative has been my dictum: less is more. I also admire the work of the distinguished film director Lawrence Gordon Clark, who has translated some of James's finest stories to the television screen in a restrained and wonderfully evocative fashion. Clark has been trying to get my film treatment of James's 'Count Magnus' made for TV, for which I shall always be grateful.

"I hope that those who come to this tale for the first time will find some measure of enjoyment and, dare one say it, a *frisson* of the terror that takes hold of the protagonist. For, as Edward van Sloan so memorably observed in an epilogue to one of the classic Universal horror films, 'There *are* such things!'"

IT WAS LATE MORNING when Grant left St. Ulric's Church. He had come down there on an architectural project two months earlier, and now, on this bright spring day, he had dropped into a bar almost opposite for a pre-lunch drink. As he sipped his goblet of chilled house white he had a clear view through one of the front windows across the road and to the church beyond. That was when he first saw the old man. He wore dark clothes, and the architect thought for a moment that it was the sexton, a somewhat lugubrious character he had spoken to earlier in the morning, but then he realized he was mistaken.

The man's dark clothes had nothing about them appertaining to the church. In fact, now that Grant saw him more clearly, he looked like a tramp, for the watcher could have sworn the old man's overcoat was tied together with string. He was acting in a most peculiar manner, which had first attracted Grant's attention.

He swayed slightly, as if drunk, and though Grant, oblivious of the animated chatter of the occupants of the bar, shifted slightly to catch a glimpse of the man's face, he kept it averted. Then he suddenly darted into the church entrance, so perhaps he was connected with St. Ulric's after all, Grant thought.

"Something else, sir?"

The white-coated barman was at his elbow.

"Yes, same again, please. By the way, do you know that old chap hovering about opposite?"

The barman looked puzzled.

"I don't see anyone, sir."

Grant turned his attention back to the church entrance but the man had gone, no doubt 'round the main body of the building. There was a public footpath there.

He gave a short laugh.

"It's nothing important. An old chap was there just now."

The barman nodded, glancing at the former's leather case, which he had propped against the table leg.

"Ah, you'll be Mr. Grant, sir. Doing the survey of the church for Mr. Brough. Staying at The Bull, I believe."

Grant nodded. Brough was the rector.

"You seem to know a lot about me."

The barman smiled.

"It's a small place. And Mr. Brough enjoys a drink here from time to time. He spoke about you when you first came."

After Grant had returned to The Bull, where he had taken a room for the duration of his work on the church—it would be a long commission, for the building was in a very poor state, particularly so far as the foundations went—he had lunch and then found a corner of the coffee lounge and checked his latest notes and drawings. This occupied him for over an hour and afterward he decided to take a walk 'round the village in order to stretch his legs. He passed the old timbered post office on his way 'round and on impulse, seeing a phone booth outside, went in and dialed his fiancée, Sally, in London, to let her know how things were going. Then he returned to The Bull and continued working on his notes in the now deserted lounge.

Presently there was a pleasant interruption to his labors when a shadow fell across his drawings and the bulky form of the rector, the Reverend Charles Brough, materialized. A good-looking man in his early fifties, his black hair flecked with grey, he had established a good rapport with Grant and the latter had enjoyed the hospitality of Brough and his much younger wife at the rectory, a mellow 18th-century building the other side of the churchyard.

Grant, using his privilege as a guest at the hotel, quickly ordered the visitor a glass of sherry and the two men were soon engrossed in facts and figures regarding the renovation work on the church.

"Of course, you do realize it will be a very expensive job," the architect pointed out. "A good deal of under-pinning of the buttresses on the north side of the building, where water has been penetrating for years and some of the paneling and other interior fitments are showing signs of dry rot, to say nothing of woodworm."

The rector smiled briefly, raising his glass in salute.

"I don't think that will be too big a problem, Mr. Grant. The Diocese has promised us half a million pounds and we have a large-scale restoration fund underway."

Grant nodded.

"Oh, but you haven't taken my fees into account."

The rector gave a dry chuckle before continuing.

"Now that you have been on the spot and gone into all the details how long do you think the work will take? We have an excellent firm of church restorers, and though they have only undertaken what you might call running repairs in the past, they will be glad of this major commission in these difficult times."

Grant pursed his lips, putting down his sherry glass and tidying up his papers.

"According to the requirements you've laid down and the preliminary figures I've arrived at, around two years for the complete restoration. Perhaps a little longer. My associates will, of course, check the work thoroughly as it proceeds. And naturally I shall still have overall control."

Brough gave him an approving glance.

"That's about what the church council thought. I'll let them know your provisional findings at the council meeting next Monday evening. You'll be present, of course, and perhaps you'd like to have dinner at the rectory afterwards."

Grant thanked Brough for his invitation and the two men rose.

"I must get back to the church," the rector said.

"I'll come with you," Grant replied. "I have to take some more measurements and make further inspection before writing my notes this evening."

The two men fell into step as they crossed the road towards St. Ulric's, engaging in small talk, when Grant caught sight out of the corner of his eye a black-clad figure walking among the gravestones in the churchyard. He was too late to see clearly, and the man—for he was certain of the gender—had disappeared along the footpath by the time they reached the worn lych-gate.

"Did you see who that was?" Grant asked.

The rector glanced around.

"I didn't notice anybody. This is a public footpath, as you know. Something to do with the Lord of the Manor in medieval times, who gave the land for the building of the church, while retaining a public right of way. A great eccentric, according to old records."

"That reminds me," Grant continued. "I saw an old chap in shabby black clothes acting rather queerly near the church this morning. I wondered if you knew anything about him."

The rector shook his head.

"Doesn't ring a bell."

He gave a short laugh.

"We have all sorts of funny people around here. Eccentrics, harmless village idiot types. There are gypsies in the woods too, though they have no right to be there. Many of them use the footpath that runs down to a sort of small suburb to the north of the church. Several streets bisected by a stream. Most picturesque. You ought to take a look some time."

"I will," Grant promised him.

The two men were at the church porch now and Brough extended his hand.

"You're going into the church and I'm going to do some work in my study at the rectory. Shall I see you over the weekend?"

Grant gave the other an expression of mock regret.

"I'm going up to London to see my fiancée in the morning and shan't be back until Sunday evening."

The rector broke into a smile, revealing strong, square teeth.

"Ah, journeys end in lovers' meetings," he said jocularly.

Grant smiled too.

"Something like that."

He watched the powerful figure striding away down the brick path, but as he turned to go into the church something arrested his attention. Instead, he went across the sloping turf between the gravestones to where he had previously seen the dark form. He walked aimlessly, desultorily reading the worn inscriptions. They were mostly old tombstones here, with an occasional vault for some more prestigious local, he supposed. One in particular caught his eye. Principally because there was a fresh posy of spring flowers tied with string, lying on the damp grass. He glanced from it to the black letter inscription on the worn stone, half obscured by the inroads of ivy.

He read: JEDEDIAH BRIGGS. CALLED TO GLORY APRIL 30TH, 1770. Underneath was a rather puzzling inscription in much smaller letters: GREAT THOUGH IT IS TO LIE IN DARKNESS, EVEN MORE GLORIOUS IS IT TO WALK ABROAD AT THE NOONTIDE HOUR.

A curious sentiment, the architect thought, and during various church commissions carried out in his career, Grant had never seen a stranger. Even more bizarre, to his mind, was that the inscription carried no date of birth. He would ask the rector about it when they met on Monday. He supposed now that the figure he had seen might have left the rustic bouquet at the graveside; possibly some descendent of the deceased person, though over two hundred years was a long time to continue leaving such tokens. However, as he turned back to the church and his immediate concerns, the matter was swiftly erased from his mind.

Grant took an early train to London the next morning and passed a pleasant weekend with his fiancée. But there was some indefinable cloud that was hovering at the edge of his consciousness that he could not wholly shake off all the time that he was away from the village and his commission at St. Ulric's. Even Sally had noticed it and though she was too tactful to question him directly, he passed it off by speaking of the problems with the church foundations, which were causing some difficulties. It was nothing the rector had said nor had it to do directly with the church, but the somewhat moving image of the simple bunch of wild flowers lying on the grave, that recurred from time to time.

But when he caught the 9:30 train at Charing Cross on Sunday night all these relatively trivial matters were forgotten, and he and Sally parted amid laughter and suppressed tears on the girl's part. Meanwhile, he had promised to have her down to stay at The Bull soon, and it was with a lighter heart that he sat down in a corner of the crowded carriage to read one of the quality Sunday papers, which passed the first stage of the journey agreeably. Unfortunately he had to change trains once and the second stopped at every station so that when he finally arrived at his destination it had turned eleven o'clock.

It was a somewhat misty evening with the smell of damp earth and the faint fret of the distant stream in his ears as he hurried to the telephone booth to ring Sally to let her know of his safe arrival. There were few street lamps, and dark patches of shadow obscured the road at intervals while a watery moon gave little light, but Grant could have sworn that someone was keeping pace with him at the other side of the road. No one else had got out at the station and he had passed no one on his way down the street, though it was possible that some railway employee had just finished his duties and was making his own way home.

There was a gritting sound in the roadside gravel that fretted at his nerves and he stopped twice to see if the unknown pedestrian would reveal himself, but each time all was still apart from the faint rustle of the wind in the roadside trees and the far off murmur of the stream, now partly blotted out by the encroaching houses. The cheerful lights of The Bull were now showing ahead and once he had made his call and Sally's reassuring voice was in his ears, things fell into perspective so that when the dark form of a villager passed by the phone booth a minute or two later, the explanation was simple. Darkness, wind, and imagination had combined to present a very different picture. He rang off with a light heart and entered the welcoming vestibule of the hotel with a clear mind for the tasks of the following morning.

Grant slept well and after an excellent breakfast in the crowded dining room, he collected his equipment and then set out for the church. The day was overcast and dark clouds were rolling in from the west, but fortunately it was dry, as he intended to make further examinations of the exterior buttresses which had caused him some previous concern. The soil was sandy there and might create some problems with the underpinning. Grant was a very meticulous man, noted for the high quality of his work, and he did not want the builders to run into unexpected difficulties when they were on site.

But first, out of idle curiosity, he turned aside and retraced his steps of Friday through the older part of the graveyard to where the tomb of Jedediah Briggs stood. The first thing he noticed was that the bunch of flowers had gone. It was no great matter really; presumably some passer-by had made off with them. The second thing, however, was rather more puzzling for Grant now saw that what he had originally taken for a gravestone, appeared to be a sort of portico. A shallow flight of steps descended, presumably to a vault beneath, but they were now completely obscured by a tangle of weeds and ivy, with only the worn top tread showing.

Then he saw the friendly figure of the rector advancing towards him along the path.

"Had a good weekend?"

Grant nodded.

"Great."

Brough looked at him shrewdly.

"Worried about something? Nothing to do with your fiancée, I hope?"

Grant laughed.

"Nothing like that, thank goodness. I was thinking how curious this tomb was."

The rector bent towards the inscription on the worn stone.

"Old Jedediah Briggs? He was something of a local legend. A sort of 18th-century tearaway."

He chuckled.

"Only without the motorcycle, of course. But apparently he was quite well off at one time, and during those years he used to gallop about the parish in a phaeton lashing out with his whip at anyone who crossed his path."

"Nice fellow," Grant said.

"You may well say so. Then he fell on hard times and became bitter and even more vindictive. He hanged himself from a branch of one of the churchyard trees in the end."

"That's strange," Grant observed.

"Why so?"

"I thought suicides weren't allowed to be buried in consecrated ground in the old days. Yet here we have this elaborate tomb."

The rector shrugged.

"I believe this thing was put up in the late 19th century at the request of his descendants, who had him re-interred. Yes, you're right, it's a strange story. We have something about it in the old church records if you'd care to follow it up."

"Perhaps," Grant said. "But I wonder why it's become so overgrown when the rest of the churchyard is so immaculately kept."

The rector gave the other a strange smile.

"You'd better ask the sexton about that. Old Martin's a bit superstitious and says there's something odd about it. He's a silly old fool in some ways but a good church servant, so I don't press the point. Once or twice a year our team of local volunteers clear the graveyard."

The two men had turned away towards the church entrance by this time.

"Anyway, somebody must think well of him because someone left a posy of wild flowers there on Friday," Grant said.

The rector had his face averted and said nothing so Grant did not pursue the matter.

When Grant ascended to the little muniments room above the church porch, where St. Ulric's records were kept, the sun was low in the sky, throwing long shadows across the well kept turf surrounding the church, and the graveyard beyond. Through the tiny lancet windows the dark silhouettes of birds were flying back to the woods beyond, presumably to seek their nests, he thought as he turned away. The records were kept in a large oak aumbry secured to the stone wall with massive bolts, and Grant opened the door with a keen sense of anticipation, though he could not have said why.

He went through the shelves with quickening interest and took several of the huge volumes down. But to his disappointment the records for the latter part of the 18th century seemed to be missing, though the church history and its relevant documentation was extraordinarily complete otherwise. Just then he was somewhat startled by an odd creaking noise, and the door to the little chamber opened rather furtively, Grant thought; if a door could be furtive, he felt, with an inward smile as the white hair of old Martin, the sexton, was thrust into the gap.

"Ah, there you are, Mr. Grant, sir. Was there anything further you'll be wanting as I'll be away home in a few minutes. The rector said I should keep myself available in case you require my help."

Grant was smiling now, half due to the old man's grave and formal way of speaking, though nothing of this showed on his face.

"I don't think so, thank you. Oh, just a moment, though. There is something. Could you let me know what happened to the church records for the last half of the 18th century? Or were they perhaps destroyed in a fire or lost?"

A darkness seemed to descend on Martin's features, though his face, illuminated by the rays of the dying sun, was clearly delineated against the blackness of the passage behind him. He bit his lip before replying.

"As far as I recollect, Mr. Grant, they were taken to the County Record Office some years ago."

Grant wrinkled his brow.

"Why so? That seems rather odd, doesn't it, as it leaves a gap in these valuable records here."

The sexton looked discomfited.

"I don't rightly know, sir. I believe it had something to do with certain valuable information contained there. Mr. Brough would be able to help you."

For some reason Grant felt he had to persist in the questioning, despite the sexton's somewhat evasive manner.

"Forgive me for asking, but are you sure you don't know the reason this material was removed? As I have said it leaves a gap in the archives. And the County Records Office is a long way off."

Martin shook his head. There was a stubborn set to his features now.

"I know nothing, sir. But I'm sure Mr. Brough would be able to explain. And you can, of course, consult the records yourself. The offices are only an hour's drive away."

Grant nodded.

"Well, thank you, anyway. And don't let me detain you further."

With obvious relief Martin backed out the door with a mumbled good night, and a few moments later the architect heard his heavy boots clattering down the wooden stairs. On a sudden impulse Grant crossed to the narrow windows set in the opposite wall, fully expecting to see the sexton hurrying down the path. But there was no sign of him. What he saw instead was a thin figure dressed in shabby black clothes tied with cord, who seemed to glide between the gravestones.

As Grant stood transfixed at the casement, the man turned his face towards the lancet windows, as though he knew there was a watcher there. Grant was left with the impression of red-rimmed eyes that were shrouded in cavernous sockets surmounted by eyebrows that looked like whitened seaweed. The man gave him a twisted smile as though in recognition. Before he had passed the end of the building out of Grant's sight, the latter took the stairs two at a time to gain the church porch. But quick as he was, there was no one to be seen in all the long expanse of paving that stretched to the lych-gate. He gave up his researches for that day, and after tidying the muniments room and locking both it and the main church door, he made his way thoughtfully back to The Bull to prepare his notes for the parish council meeting.

It was a long evening and discussion, as always at parish level, went on interminably. Strictly speaking the church renovation was a Diocesan matter and had nothing to do with the parish council's jurisdiction, but there was an added complication because the rector and the church council wished to install toilets and other modern facilities within the church proper.

This would entail extensive drainage works involving the closure of the public right of way through the churchyard, inconveniencing people who lived in the small suburb beyond, and would mean them having to walk more than a mile 'round in order to reach their homes. However, Grant had come up with a plan to erect a raised plank walkway across the graveyard while the drainage work was in progress, which met with the meeting's approval.

It was half past ten before the gathering closed and finally Grant and Brough walked across to the rectory where the former had been invited to a late supper. He spent a pleasant time with the rector and his wife, and it was past midnight when Grant got back to the inn. He slept badly and had a frightful dream, no doubt arising from the previous night's debate, when some members of the parish council had raised objections to the drainage work, which would involve, as they put it, desecrating the graves of the dead, in particular the vault in which the remains of Jedediah Briggs were interred. They did not say that in as many words, but their remarks had obviously implanted a seed in the architect's mind.

The dream began, as so many do, in a very inconsequential way, with Grant saying goodbye to his fiancée at Charing Cross Station. Then, as always, he was immediately transposed to the village and the graveyard in particular. But instead of it being night, as one might have supposed, it was broad daylight, though the village was silent and deserted; absolutely devoid of human beings. Then there appeared a dark figure, gliding effortlessly between the gravestones. Grant turned to run but was able to make only a few steps, as though in slow motion, like some macabre sequence in a film. But a hand was on his shoulder and the owner of the tattered black overcoat, whom he had previously seen in reality, gave him a crooked smile and beckoned him to follow.

The pair went down dank steps towards the Briggs vault and there was a charnel stench in the dreamer's nostrils. He tried to run but fell headlong towards the vault door, which gave with a crash. He woke drenched with perspiration, thankful to see early daylight leeching through the curtains of his room. He remembered the words of one parish council member, in reference to the digging up of the graveyard: "If it goes ahead, I warn this meeting, no good can come of it." He eventually fell into a refreshing sleep.

For the next few days Grant was involved in a heavy workload, finishing his drawings and specifications. Nightly he was posting his rough drawings and specifications to his London office, where his staff of draughtsmen would prepare the final plans. During his tours of the church building and its surroundings, Grant was surprised to find that the area round the vault of Jedediah Briggs had been cleared of ivy and foliage, just as it had been in his vivid dream. But the explanation was simple: the rector remarked that the church working party had been along on their half-yearly task of clearing up the churchyard.

Brough was abruptly called back to the rectory, following a message relayed by his wife, to the effect that the bishop had rung regarding the work on the church and would be ringing back in half an hour. Left to himself, Grant circled the massive vault building, which was in remarkably good condition, considering its age. It was a bright, cloudless day, with the pleasant aroma carried from a distant bonfire and the sound of passing cars was more often than not drowned by the reassuring chorus of birdsong.

The time passed very quickly and Grant was kneeling on the grass making notations in the jotting pad he always carried, when he became aware that a deep silence had fallen and even traffic noises had faded. At almost the same moment a dark shadow fell across the nearest tombstone. Grant looked up with a welcoming smile, thinking that the rector had returned, but it was not Brough. A black-coated figure, that was becoming all too familiar, passed swiftly by with averted face towards the mausoleum. As Grant got to his feet, energy flooding back into his frame, he started forward with a hoarse cry. He ran quickly across the turf but when he arrived at the back of the tomb there was no one to be seen. Nothing in the wide expanse of the churchyard either.

He leaned against the lichen-encrusted wall, perspiration pouring down into his eyes. Considerably shaken, it was some time before he again became aware of familiar sounds; passing cars, no longer muted; the cries of birds; and the distant shouts of children from a nearby school. His nerves at last calmed, he made a careful examination of the exterior of the tomb. Was he suffering from hallucinations? he wondered. It was true he had been working extremely hard and Sally had often urged him to ease up. But it was nothing like that. The person he had seen was tangible enough, though it was true that no one else had apparently seen him.

Nothing unusual about that either, because Grant had been alone, as he was on this occasion. He went down the ancient stone steps with beating heart and tried the great oak door, which had weathered extremely well considering it had been *in situ* for over 220 years. There was something carved into the woodwork, which time and weather had blurred, so that he could not make it out. It was probably in Latin anyway, and his memory in that department was rather rusty. There was an enormous circular iron handle. He tried it gingerly but to his relief it was securely locked. His relief was mingled with embarrassment because he was not normally of a superstitious or nervous nature. He wiped his face with his handkerchief, put the notebook in his pocket, and went back up towards the churchyard entrance. It was time for lunch and the reality of everyday things.

Grant had much to do in the next few days, and as time passed the events of recent weeks began to seem fanciful. But one night there was a sudden and quite unexpected thunderstorm of enormous power and ferocity, with torrential rain which continued all night. The storm had eased by early morning, and when Grant left his breakfast table at The Bull the rain had ceased and a cheerful sun was drying off the earth, though there were visible traces of the night's havoc with torn branches strewn across the roads and a few ancient trees down in the countryside beyond.

When he hurried downstairs with his briefcase and equipment he was met by the hotel manager who said there was an urgent telephone call for him. He was worried that it might be bad news about Sally as he crossed to the reception desk, but it was Brough, who informed him that the churchyard had sustained considerable storm damage. A few minutes later he was able to see for himself. Two oaks had been uprooted, smashing some of the tombs and standing monuments, while lightning had apparently struck the Briggs mausoleum. The top of the heavy stonework had been cracked and there was a gaping hole in the sidewall near the bottom of the steps.

Brough had a worried face.

"The workmen are due to start on some of the church underpinning in a week or two. Do you think this will make any difference?"

Grant shook his head.

"Not unless there is similar damage to the church foundations. But I'll make a thorough inspection and let you have a verbal report before lunch."

Brough had relief on his face.

"That's good."

As Grant went back up the path to the church porch the small knot of curious spectators, which included the sexton and one of the churchwardens, was slowly dispersing. In the afternoon Grant spent more than two hours in the little muniments room, working on his notes and rough sketches. He felt there might be some difficulty in moving a number of the monuments in the south aisle of St. Ulric's, and he was concerned in case their considerable weight might cause a collapse when the builders started excavating the church foundations on that side in order to commence the underpinning.

He wrestled with ideas for more than another hour, but eventually felt there was nothing for it but to program the removal of the massive tombs before work on the underpinning began. Things would not be entirely satisfactory; they never were in his experience of church renovation, but the itinerary he had planned was the best he could think of for the moment. When he finally left the church, the afternoon was waning and an early dusk was setting in, due to the low cloud mass which hovered over the village. There was no one about in the churchyard or in the street beyond, and the sexton, Martin, had left an hour before. As he neared the section where the tomb of Jedediah Briggs lay, some impulse again made him turn aside to survey the damage the storm had caused.

As he came closer, he could now see that the great oak door, which had seemed so secure, now hung awry on its hinges, no doubt due to the damage to the gaping hole in the wall beyond. There were dark shadows on the stone treads and he was horrified to see that the jostling shapes were composed of dozens of rats, which were emerging from the broken doorway. Grant shrank back, but the seething mass darted aside and at the same moment someone came up behind him. Grant turned, expecting to see the rector but it was the black-clad figure of the old man he had several times glimpsed hovering about the churchyard.

The architect was nauseated by the malodorous charnel stench that emanated from the creature's clothing. He thrust a withered face into Grant's own, and at the same time a claw-like hand seized his arm in a crushing grip, incredible in one so old. He had a welcoming smile on his face as he said in a high, sweet voice, "Come with me, my son. Welcome to Paradise!"

As though in a dream, Grant was led inexorably towards the steps leading to the shattered doorway of the tomb. They were halfway down and Grant could not shake off the paralysis which had overcome him, when a huge brass altar cross was suddenly thrust into the old man's face. He gave a hideous cry of fear and fell downward through the door, which Grant had remembered as being solid, but nevertheless disintegrated in a cloud of dust, as the architect fell fainting into the rector's arms.

Brandy was being forced down Grant's throat. He coughed and the swimming vision finally settled into the reassuring faces of Brough and one of his churchwardens. The architect was back in the church, lying on one of the pew benches with a cushion beneath his head.

"What was it?" he gasped, when the fit of shuddering had passed. "What was it?"

The rector shook his head.

"We will leave that for the moment," he said gently. "You have been unconscious for nearly an hour but the police doctor told us there was nothing to worry about. All is being taken care of."

Grant struggled up.

"I owe you so much, rector."

The other gave him a wry smile.

"Let us say we were fortunate. I had occasion to come back to the church to collect some notes for a lecture. I saw you being dragged across the churchyard by a strange old man in black clothes and I assumed it was the person of whom you had previously spoken. Then I also noticed that you were walking like a drunken man with a desperate expression on your face. There was something so sinister in the sight that I was momentarily paralyzed and you were almost at the vault steps before I recovered myself."

Grant took another sip of the brandy, feeling strength returning.

"That thing . . ."

The rector bit his lip.

"There was something inexpressibly unholy in that horrifying tableau. So I rushed into the church and seized the altar crucifix and struck it blindly into the creature's face. I say 'creature' advisedly because there was something loathsome and evil about it. The thing let go your arm and fell downward into the vault."

"I cannot thank you enough, sir."

Brough inclined his head. He was about to speak when they were interrupted by the wailing of police sirens outside. Grant started to his feet, but the rector laid a hand on his arm.

"I should not go out if I were you. The police, the press, doctors, and the ambulance men are there."

There was a tremor in his voice now.

"They have discovered terrible things in that vault. Opened coffins. Many bodies, some of them in advanced stages of putrefaction. Police computer systems have already identified a number as being those of persons missing in the county over the past few years."

He shuddered.

"Utterly evil. Unspeakable things."

"And the old man?" Grant said in a trembling voice.

The rector turned away.

"Nothing but bones and dust. It is beyond belief."

Grant left the village a week afterward, his work completed. In the interim the vault contents had been removed, the tomb dismantled, and the area turfed over, and the bishop then re-consecrated it as sacred ground. The architect took a month's convalescence and he and Sally were married in the late summer. Understandably he was reluctant to undertake church restoration work after his experiences and now sends one of his junior colleagues instead. A strange aftermath of the affair at St. Ulric's is the appearance of a small streak of white in his otherwise black hair. His wife has often asked him to snip it off but he prefers it to remain as a salutary warning and reminder of the evils that walk abroad at noonday. The quotation was garbled, owing to his faint recollection of the piece, but his wife got the message.

The Place

JOHN GORDON

JOHN GORDON was born in Jarrow-on-Tyne, England, and now lives in Norwich with his wife, Sylvia. As a child he moved with his family to Wisbech in the Fens of Cambridgeshire, where he went to school. After serving in the Royal Navy on minesweepers and destroyers during World War II, he became a journalist for various local newspapers.

His first book for young adults, *The Giant Under the Snow*, was published by Hutchinson in 1968 and gained praise from Alan Garner, among others. It was reissued in 2006 by Orion, along with editions in Italy and Lithuania, and as an audio book.

Since then, Gordon has published a number of fantasy and horror novels, including *The House on the Brink*, *The Ghost on the Hill*, *The Quelling Eye*, *The Grasshopper*, *Ride the Wind*, *Blood Brothers*, *Gilray's Ghost*, *The Flesh Eater*, *The Midwinter Watch*, *Skinners*, *The Ghosts of Blacklode*, and *Fen Runners*.

The author's short stories are collected in *The Spitfire Grave and Other Stories*, *Catch Your Death and Other Stories*, *The Burning Baby and Other Stories*, and *Left in the Dark: The Supernatural Tales of John Gordon*. He was one of five writers who contributed to the Oxrun Station "mosaic novel" *Horror at Halloween*, edited by Jo Fletcher. His autobiography, *Ordinary Seaman*, was published by Walker Books in 1992.

"There was a derelict house in the fen countryside near where I lived when I was a boy," reveals Gordon. "It stood well back from the road, and there was a long driveway from it leading to a ruined gateway flanked by stone eagles that were reputed to fly down to drink in the river nearby, and the house itself was haunted.

"I ventured in my mind beyond that gateway to find this story . . ."

"YOU MUST HAVE BEEN very afraid," she said.

"Well, I didn't like it much."

"I should have died."

"Yes." He fell silent, and when he resumed he spoke slowly. "I was too afraid to open the curtains. At least while the light was on in the room. Whatever it was out there could have looked in and seen me and I couldn't have seen it, whatever it was."

"You could have put the light out."

"Then I would have had to cross the room in the dark, go right up to the curtains, and . . ."

"Stop. You make me shiver." She paused. "Why didn't you go to the phone?"

In spite of the darkness, she could see his smile.

"Don't tell me you had forgotten the phone," she said.

"No, I hadn't forgotten."

"You are going to tell me the lines had been cut."

"No, the phone was working."

"Thank goodness."

"I heard it ring."

"Well then." She let out her breath, relieved.

"The phone is in the hall," he said.

"Oh, I see. In the dark."

"No. I told you I'd put on every light in the house. The hall was very bright." He thought for a moment. "It must have been bright."

"Must have been?" she asked. "Didn't you go out there?"

He spoke as though he had not heard her. "I'm sure it was bright, because the lights in the room hadn't failed. They didn't ever flicker." He lifted his head and spoke to her again. "You know what it's like on a windless night in summer with the lights burning. It was all quite calm."

"Except you."

"Except me."

"Who was ringing?" she said.

"I don't know. I didn't leave the room. Somebody else answered the phone."

"What a relief!" She was laughing. "So there was somebody else in the house, after all."

He remained silent and her laughter died.

"There was somebody else in the house, wasn't there?" she insisted.

"I don't know why I'm telling you this," he said. "Not now, just before we are married."

"Maybe it's a test." She came closer. "To see if I love you in spite of all."

"Even if my house is Bluebeard's castle, and all my previous wives are lying there murdered?"

"Our castle. I fell in love with it before I even knew you."

He glanced away down the avenue of trees. "Yes," he said, "this place does have that effect. On most people. I was the same. That's why I have to tell you everything about it." He drew in his breath and let it out like a sigh. "Everything that I told you earlier is true. The house was empty except for me."

"But somebody answered the phone."

"There was a sound like footsteps. Then the phone stopped ringing."

"Don't go on," she said. "Not while we're out here in the dark."

"All right."

"All right? You mean you're not going to tell me what happened next?"

"Well you said . . ."

"You've got to!"

He allowed himself to smile again. "There's not much more to tell. I sat there. There were no more phone calls, no more footsteps. And towards dawn the scratching and tapping at the window stopped altogether. Then I went to bed."

"To bed?"

He nodded.

"I don't know how you could. I should have fainted. They would have found me white-haired in the morning. Dead or gibbering or something."

"It's my own place," he said. "One learns not to be too afraid."

"And nothing since?"

"Nothing."

She fell silent, and after a while he said, "I don't care what happened. It's a beautiful house. I can't wait to live in it . . . with you."

They were at the end of a long avenue of trees. He put his arm around her waist, and they looked back towards the house.

"Its windows are so small from here," she said. "It looks tiny, yet it's a big house. A very big house. And the grounds are huge."

"I sometimes don't know myself where they end and then I find myself on other people's property. I rather like that."

"You are odd," she said. "When I live here I won't ever want to go outside the boundary."

"I felt like that, and so did . . ." He broke off. "I'm sorry."

"There's no need to be sorry." She spoke gently. "I know it was her house. You've told me all that."

"I was like you," he said. "It was the place that attracted me. She may have been living here still if it wasn't for me."

"No." She shook her head. "It was she who ran away. She just left all this—and you. I know it wasn't your fault."

He said, "She changed so suddenly. Nothing had happened until that day, and then it was just the smallest of arguments. I can't even remember what it was about. I've tried. I've tried many times to bring it back but it eludes me."

"I know." She had heard him speak of it before, but made no effort to stop him. The more he spoke of it the quicker the memory would be, if not obliterated, at least softened.

"She let me go into the house first. She held back because she was angry. And the door closed behind me. I remember how I felt as it shut—it slammed. I hadn't touched it, but it slammed—and I remember suddenly feeling delighted, wanting her to feel that I had slammed it. But more than that. I suddenly felt in possession of the house—her house. But now she was outside, on the other side of the shut door, and the house was mine. It was as though the house wanted me and not her."

They walked on a few paces nearer the house before he resumed.

"I was, I suppose, slow in opening the door. Just too slow. Just a fragment of a second too slow. And when I did so she had turned and was running away along the avenue."

"This avenue?"

"I don't know. It may have been."

"And you never saw her again?"

"No. I waited. Then one day they wrote and told me she had died. They wrote. They did not give me time to reach her. They had had the funeral before I could get there. They had not wanted me. I don't know what she had told them."

They walked on in silence.

"So you came back here," she said.

"I had to. I love the place."

"I can't blame you," she said. "I would feel the same"

He stopped and turned towards her. "So we have no secrets. I have told you everything."

"I know," she said.

"And you?" he asked. "You have no secrets?"

She shook her head. "And it was afterwards you thought the house was haunted?"

"Just that one night."

"You were under a great strain."

"It was after it happened that the place began to feel emptier and emptier. And then you came along."

"It was the house." She teased him. "The house came first." She looked away. "These avenues," she said, "they all lead straight to the house. How many are there?"

"I've never counted them. And you are mistaken. They are not all straight. Sometimes you lose sight of the house altogether."

"But not tonight. And the moon is directly over it, so we couldn't lose it even if we tried. It really is lovely."

"But haunted."

"That was your last secret. But now you've told me, so it doesn't matter any more. It's all gone; vanished." She kissed him. "Let's get back to the others. We're so far away you can't even hear them."

"Perhaps everybody's gone. It's late."

"All the better. I'd like to have it all to myself, and I hate a party that goes on too long."

"But they're my friends," he said.

"There's always another day."

"I want to see them."

"You don't think they've been frightened away, do you?"

"What makes you say that?"

"Ghosts," she said.

He shook his head.

"I'm sorry. I shouldn't have made a joke of it. It must have been very frightening."

He made no response, and she said, "You must not blame yourself for being afraid. It was bad enough having a ghost outside the house, but to have one inside as well . . ."

"There was only one. The footsteps inside were the only sounds an old house can make. And telephones eventually have to stop ringing. They can't go on forever. The only ghost was the one outside, trying to get in."

"But it didn't. And it went away and never came back."

He seemed not to have heard. "I should at least have opened the curtains."

"Why do you blame yourself?"

"I could have learned something. All I had to do was open the curtains. But I was too afraid."

"You missed nothing, my darling. It was only a tree tapping at the window."

"There are no trees that close," he said.

"A creeper?"

He shook his head.

"It was a moth, or something, attracted by the light."

But he was striding on now, and she had to run a pace or two to catch up. He was gazing ahead.

"They've gone," he said. "They've all gone!"

Lights burned in every window, laying patches of brightness on the paving of the terrace. There was no car. Not even the sound of a motor in the distance. At the heart of the avenues the house spread its own radiance like a silent star.

"I'm glad," she said. "We don't need anybody."

"They've deserted us."

"I don't care. We've got it all to ourselves." She walked across the gravel to where the light from the open door folded itself down the steps and reached out like a carpet to greet her. The hall was beautiful, full of dazzling light. Within it there were many doors leading to the intricacies of the house itself. The staircase curved away to the momentary darkness of the landing. There was so much to explore, and now she could do so because it was all hers. She paused on the steps. "Let's go in together," she said.

But he had crossed the gravel to gaze into the tunnel of trees into which the cars must have disappeared. He did not answer. A tiny spasm of annoyance at his neglect crossed her mind, and she stepped into the hall alone.

It was then that she saw that history was repeating itself—the quarrel, the drawing apart which put one inside the house and the other outside—and she acted to prevent it.

She held the door to stop it swinging to if a gust of wind should funnel through the house, and she turned to beg him to come with her. But already he was entering the blackness of the avenue. No matter. She was in control. She could decide what happened next. She opened her mouth to call out and bring him back.

At that instant, as though to obliterate any sound she could make, the telephone on the little table behind her began to ring. She started and swung round. The door, reacting to her sudden movement, slid away from her and slammed shut. She reached for the lock, but it was stiff and complicated and as she fumbled at it the phone dinned at her from its perch—like a black goblin, scolding and shrieking.

She left the door and went towards it to silence it. As she moved, a little more of the landing came into view. Matching her, pace for pace, there seemed to be a figure moving towards the head of the stairs. Yet all the guests had gone.

She spun and ran into the nearest room. The second door slammed behind her and she was alone. She remained where she was, her back against the door. Thank God for all the light. She sat down. He was only just outside. He would soon be back. She heard, through the ringing of the phone, his steps in the hall. Then, mercifully, the phone fell silent.

She breathed deeply, twice, and let her head fall forward. In a moment, when her heart steadied, she would get up and go to him.

The hall was quiet now. It must have been the light shining up through the railings of the landing that had persuaded her there was a figure there. She smiled and let her mind explore the hall, and beyond it to the other rooms. They were all bright, empty, and calm. She breathed easier and raised her head. It was time to go to meet him.

She was still sitting when, beyond the closed curtains, something tapped on the glass.

The Bridegroom

R. B. RUSSELL

R. B. RUSSELL runs the award-winning Tartarus Press with his partner, Rosalie Parker, in the Yorkshire Dales in the North of England.

He has had two collections of short stories published, *Putting the Pieces in Place* and *Literary Remains*. A story from the first collection, "In Hiding," was short-listed for a World Fantasy Award. A further collection, *Leave Your Sleep*, is forthcoming from PS Publishing.

"'The Bridegroom' is a story that unfolded as I put down the words, without any planning," explains Russell. "What the result reveals about my unconscious mind will be left to others to explain."

JULIET HYLAND WAS thoroughly bored with the company of Harriet Dot, but too polite to simply get up and walk away from the older woman. Well over a generation separated them and they had little in common. Juliet recognized the only thing that had brought them together was their singleness, perhaps even their loneliness . . .

. . . And Juliet resented this, just as she resented all of the many readjustments she had been forced to make since Nicholas had died. She had deliberately chosen the secluded seat in the gardens of the hotel so as to be on her own. She had been trying to work out why she had made her annual visit to Easthaven, and all that she could think of was that it was a defiance. Why should she not stay at the hotel, just because her husband was no longer able to accompany her?

Harriet Dot had not stopped talking, and Juliet decided to listen to her, if only to drag her thoughts away from widowhood.

"Easthaven was a very popular resort in Victorian times," the old woman explained. "And back then the Albert Hotel provided accommodation for only the wealthiest visitors. The private pleasure gardens were the envy of the other hotels, you know. The small ravine running down to the beach is natural. It's the result of centuries of erosion by a stream through the local sandstone. Well, something like that might've been a problem, but not to the Victorians. The hotel planted it with rhododendron and azalea bushes. There's a whole series of pathways and steps that go down to the beach.

"And I do believe," Harriet added, with an authority that was confident that it could not be gainsaid, "that the design of the ravine gardens was the work of Capability Brown."

The absurdity of the comment rang loud and discordant. Juliet asked, without thinking: "Are you really sure about that?"

It was a mistake to question Harriet's authority on such an unimportant matter. The regular rhythms of her monologue had been soothing because they hadn't required any engagement. Now, however, Juliet found that she had to talk with the woman.

"I'm sure I read it in a leaflet produced by the tourist board," Harriet replied.

"I'm sorry; perhaps you're right. It's just that I've always associated Capability Brown with the century before."

"Oh?"

"Yes, and with rolling landscapes created for country houses."

"Have you ever walked down through the ravine gardens?" Harriet asked, as though direct experience would be proof enough.

"Yes," came the unwilling reply. "Quite often." Juliet hoped that the woman would simply resume her inane chatter.

"Really? On this stay? Or have you been to the Albert Hotel before?"

"I've been before."

"Oh, you should have said! You shouldn't have let me talk on so! Then you probably know all about it, and how there used to be a narrow cast-iron bridge across the ravine, and an open funicular railway down into it? And there were little kiosks apparently."

"Most of those would predate my first visit," Juliet smiled weakly. "Though, I'm sure the bridge was still in place when I came the first time. It was nearly twenty years ago."

"Really?" Harriet laughed nervously. "Well, they were all Victorian fancies, you know. I expect you've seen the photos in the hotel bar. The funicular probably wouldn't be allowed today, not with all the 'health and safety' we have to put up with. The European Union's probably why they finally took down the bridge."

Juliet had been on the point of offering further information about her very first visit. However, Harriet was already talking about another local hotel, and then changes she had observed in the seaside town, all of them for the worse, so far as she was concerned. Juliet looked down at her hands and at her wedding ring. Before she had stopped listening to Harriet Dot, she had heard just how and why the woman had never been married. Juliet thought it odd that Harriet, who had offered so much information about herself, had never once asked about Juliet's husband. Not that she really wanted to speak about him to somebody so unsympathetic.

As Harriet started to talk about her sister, Juliet's boredom grew once again. After another diplomatic ten minutes of appearing to listen, she announced: "I think I shall go back to my room. I want to have a bath and a change of clothes before dinner."

"Perhaps we could dine together?" suggested Harriet. "As we both seem to be staying here on our own."

"Perhaps."

"Shall we say seven?"

Harriet Dot had taken the equivocal reply as positive. "It's a little early for some people, I know, but I can't eat too late. It's my indigestion; I'll never get to sleep before eleven unless I eat early."

Juliet promised to book a table for two, but as she walked back across the lawn she seriously considered checking out. There were so many better reasons for leaving early than simply escaping from the tiresome Harriet Dot, but she did not know when the trains would leave for London, and finding her way across the capital on a Friday night and getting a connection back home would be exhausting. It would make more sense to depart the following morning so that she could have the whole day ahead of her.

In the reception it seemed unaccountably busy and she had to wait to book the table for dinner. Then she went up to her room with a heavy heart. She remembered how over-awed she had been by her first visit to the hotel with Nicholas. She had been going to explain to Harriet Dot that the place had seemed so sophisticated that she had told her new husband that perhaps they should leave because they were not "good enough."

Juliet considered her own discomfort quite amusing, but she actually smiled as she remembered how Nicholas had risen to the challenge. He had previously sought the advice of his father and believed that he then knew how to act in a smart hotel. Juliet remembered how he had asked the waiters for recommendations as to what to eat and drink so casually that he had almost hidden his own ignorance. He had even tipped the staff as though it was second nature to him!

Juliet took far longer bathing, selecting and putting on her clothes, and applying her makeup than she would normally have done. She rarely wore jewelry, but that night she put on a silver necklace and earrings that had been a recent impulse purchase. When she was ready to go down to dinner she looked in the full-length mirror on the back of the door and saw herself all dressed up in the setting of the small, single room. Her entire appearance seemed wrong. The necklace and earrings were too showy and she removed them. She carried them back to the dressing table, and then carefully took off all of the recently applied makeup. She had used a little moisturizer and now removed her wedding ring so as to rub the remains of it into her hands. When she picked the ring up, that too felt inappropriate. She put it with the rest of the jewelry, and then left the room before she could think about what she had done.

There were a number of guests arguing with the maître d' about their reservation when Juliet arrived at the dining room. It was busier than she had ever remembered it, but she could see Harriet Dot sitting alone at a table on the far side of the room. As Juliet was wondering how to negotiate her way past the group in front of her, she had a premonition of the dull meal she was about to endure. Without any further thought she decided to walk out through the reception.

She had no idea of where she was going. Her shoes with a small heel were unstable on the gravel, so she walked over to the grass and removed them, deciding to carry them. The grass was cold on her feet, but soft, and she continued on over the lawn, her eyes slowly adapting to the lack of light. The cloudy sky above was oddly silver, almost phosphorescent, and everything against it was black. She was tired, but glad to be walking and not sitting, listening to and resenting an old woman who was simply like her—lonely. Juliet considered that she didn't actually dislike the woman. If anything, she was afraid of her; she was afraid that she was destined to become a Harriet Dot herself.

She continued on with these depressing thoughts until she reached the ravine. She wondered whether Nicholas felt as lonely as she did, wherever he was now. She felt for the comfort of her ring and remembered why it was not there. She would put it back on, she resolved, as soon as she returned to her room.

By that time she could see quite clearly, aided by the curious light in the sky. Through the black trees and bushes she glimpsed the sea and that, too, was quite bright. She wondered if it reflected the light in the sky, or whether it was the sky that reflected the light of the sea? It was an odd effect, although Easthaven, whose streetlights could not be seen from that part of the gardens, probably contributed. She looked back and immediately the lights of the hotel itself spoiled her newly acquired night vision.

Juliet looked away. She leaned against the low fence and stared down into the impenetrably dark ravine. She wished that she might have seen the gardens as they had been in their heyday, when the paths had been lit by small gas lamps and there had been brightly lit kiosks selling sweets and hot chestnuts. Like Harriet Dot, Juliet had once read in a leaflet all about the hotel in Victorian times.

As time passed her eyes were adapting once more to the lack of light. She could make out the individual petals on the late-blossoming flowers around her, although the leaves of the rhododendrons were still black.

It was then that Juliet noticed, to her left, the footbridge over the ravine. Her first reaction was to laugh. How could she have not realized that it had been so recently replaced or restored? Had she not told Harriet Dot that it wasn't there anymore? Why hadn't the woman contradicted her? Juliet was concerned that she had probably ended their conversation too abruptly and had been rude to the old woman. She glanced back at the hotel where poor Harriet would still be waiting at the table, perhaps telling the annoyed waiter that her companion really would be joining her very soon. By being late for dinner Juliet was compounding her rudeness.

She resolved to return to the hotel and apologize. She took one look back at where she had seen the bridge and suddenly it was no longer there. She closed her eyes tight for several seconds, and then looked again. Her vision was still not as good as it had been previously, but it was better. No, there was no footbridge over the ravine.

Juliet walked back to the hotel wondering just what had caused the illusion. Tiredness, no doubt, and the uncertain light; she was suddenly overcome with fatigue, and would have gone straight back to her room if it was not for her obligation to Harriet. She put her shoes back on when she reached the hotel entrance, and was pleased to see that it was much less busy.

In fact, the hotel was almost empty. In the dining room one solitary couple was finishing their dessert and Harriet Dot was nowhere to be seen. Juliet reasoned that she had been outside for longer than she had realized, but had so much time really passed? It was busier in the bar and she looked in there, hopefully, for Harriet. It was then that she noticed the long-case clock was showing that it was a half past eleven.

Juliet was willing to believe that a half an hour had passed since she had left the building, perhaps even a whole hour, but over four? She asked a man beside her what the time was and he pointed at the clock. He was amused by her insistence that he check his own watch, which he did, and he confirmed the late hour. Thoroughly confused and disoriented, Juliet turned to leave the bar and then saw the photograph of the cast-iron bridge over the ravine.

The image was in sepia tones and included ladies and gentlemen in Victorian clothes, but it was still the footbridge she remembered, and believed that she had so recently seen. This odd illusion didn't bother her so much as what had happened to four hours of her evening. And of even more concern was what Harriet Dot would be thinking of her.

The next morning Juliet awoke ravenous and remembered that she had not had dinner the night before. She tried not to think about the evening, but dressed hurriedly and went down to the busy dining room. By an unfortunate coincidence Harriet Dot arrived for breakfast just as she did.

"I am so sorry about last night," Juliet apologized.

"Were you unwell? You left the garden in a hurry and I was worried about you."

"I was, rather," she lied. She was about to say that she had stayed in her room but there was a danger of being found out. "I made myself come down for dinner," she explained, believing it was the kindest thing to do. "But it was so full in here that I had to go out for air. I started walking, and then couldn't face seeing anyone."

"I did wonder," Harriet nodded. "There's a wedding party here, you know. And, unfortunately, they'll be back for the reception later this afternoon. No doubt it'll go on into the evening, which is unfortunate."

They were shown to a table together and Juliet said that she found it hard to be annoyed by wedding parties, no matter how boisterous: "The first time I came here was for my honeymoon," she was finally able to tell the woman. "And every year after that we celebrated our anniversary here; familiarity has never quite removed the sparkle for me."

"And your husband is now . . .?" Harriet was obliged to ask.

"He died nine months ago. It was a heart attack."

Harriet reached over and put her hand on Juliet's.

Juliet Hyland set out along the coast path immediately after breakfast and arrived in West Cove at twelve. It had been a strenuous walk and she devoured the pub lunch and drank two large glasses of wine without noticing any effect. She had put the miles between herself and Harriet Dot with some enthusiasm, but the return to Easthaven was inevitable and could only be put off for so long. As she set back out she felt heaviness in her legs for the first time that day.

The path she had walked with such ease that morning now seemed rough and uneven. The distance stretched out before her and it was further than she remembered between recognizable landmarks. Juliet felt the muscles in her calves start to tighten, and her pace slowed. A light rain began to fall but she continued, doggedly, to walk onwards.

She was back at the edge of Easthaven when she noticed that the light was failing, and she congratulated herself on having returned while she could still see where she was going. At so many points she had considered stopping, if only for a few moments, but she knew that, if she had done so, it would have been twice as hard to resume her walk. Tired, but pleased with herself, she walked up the drive to the hotel and could tell that the wedding party had returned and that the reception was underway. There were cars parked all along the driveway and there was music thudding from the ballroom at the back. Many more lights were blazing than usual, and outside the main entrance was an assorted throng of merry smokers.

It wasn't until Juliet was walking through reception that she realized what a fright she must look—red in the face and bedraggled. She didn't care; none of the people knew her, and many were already drunk. As ill luck would have it, though, Harriet Dot appeared between her and the stairs. She was with a group of women of similar age, and all were drinking tumblers of some bright red liquid. Juliet was pleased; the old woman had decided to join the wedding party rather than complain about it.

"What have you done to yourself?" the woman asked as she noticed Juliet.

"I've walked to West Cove and back," she replied proudly. "And now I will go up to my room, send for some food, and have a long, hot bath."

"All the way to West Cove!" exclaimed the assorted women, who were impressed.

"Did you have lunch at the Queen's Head?" asked one of them. Juliet said that she had, and was pressed for details of exactly what she had ordered. She told them and agreed that it had been excellently cooked and good value. They said that she had done the right thing in ordering the second glass of wine, and thought that she had been very brave to walk back rather than simply phone for a taxi.

Juliet was about to say good-bye to them and put her foot on the first stair when an overwhelming fatigue took hold of her. Pausing to talk to Harriet Dot and her new friends and had been a mistake; she had lost her forward momentum and was now unable to continue. As she was considering going around to the lift, another woman offered Juliet a glass of the red liquid they were all drinking.

"Have some punch," she suggested. "It will do you good."

Juliet decided that she might be right and took the warm glass gratefully.

"I'm going to have to go upstairs, though, and do something about my wet clothes and hair," she said to Harriet. She took a mouthful of the drink and felt an immediate warming effect.

"Let *us* look after you," said another woman, who linked her arm through Juliet's, and soon the whole group were leading her to a room off the reception area.

"This is where the bride prepares," said a woman who introduced herself as Helen. Another, by the name of Margaret, was delighted to discover an almost full bottle of champagne and topped up her glass of punch with it.

Juliet was relieved of her wet coat and sat down in a chair facing a mirror. She was horrified to see what she looked like, especially alongside all the carefully made-up women. She was too tired to get up though, and suddenly one woman was drying her hair for her with a towel and another had removed Juliet's shoes and was giving her a foot massage. She laughed at the silliness of it and drank back her punch. When her glass was topped-up with champagne she decided that the mixture was surprisingly palatable.

There were delighted squeals from two of the party who had discovered a box containing a lovely white, embroidered blouse. Juliet could see that all of the women were rather drunk and she enjoyed watching them, thinking that they were still just like young girls really.

"This would suit you," Harriet said, holding out the blouse to Juliet.

"It's very nice," she admitted.

"Try it on," suggested another woman.

"No, it belongs to somebody else. The bride?" asked Juliet.

"Oh, go on. Where's the harm," said another.

Juliet continued to protest, but then let them unbutton and remove her damp shirt. When they had put the blouse on her she admitted that it did feel and look lovely.

Juliet couldn't remember the name of the woman who was now using a dryer on her hair; it was Anne or Carol, possibly. Piling the hair up on top of her head, the woman found a large Spanish comb and fixed it all very professionally. It wasn't something Juliet had ever thought of doing before; it felt a little odd, but looked rather good. She then closed her eyes and listened to the laughing, good-natured talk, and found that she had relaxed. The punch and champagne were soothing her aching legs, and, well, she reminded herself that she was on holiday.

Juliet opened her eyes as a slightly intimidating woman came forward and began to apply makeup. It felt uncomfortable because she wasn't accustomed to somebody else putting it on for her, but she wasn't in the mood to argue. She succumbed to the foundation, powder, blusher, lipstick, eye shadow and eyeliner. It was a waste of time, she told them, as she would soon be removing it all and going to bed, but it seemed to give them pleasure.

When the woman had finished she backed away, and Juliet saw herself in the mirror for the first time since she had appeared in it as a bedraggled mess.

She looked lovely. She had problems fighting back the tears; it had been ten, perhaps fifteen years since her reflection had appeared so young. She tried to thank the laughing women around her, but was unable to hold back the emotion.

They were very good to Juliet. A large brandy was brought, tissues for her nose, and the woman who had previously appeared so intimidating was sweetness itself as she repaired the damage to the makeup. When Juliet again looked at her reflection she was able to find pleasure in her appearance, even pride.

She was handed a long, flowing white skirt; it was just one of many items that the women had found in the boxes and had been passing between each other. She removed her own, still damp, skirt and put on the replacement. She admired herself in the mirror while the women praised her and she enjoyed their admiration. The alcohol made her feel happy and confident, and now she felt that her energy had returned. In the midst of the women she was escorted into the ballroom where they all made a grand entrance.

As if on cue some rock and roll song was struck up by the band and the women started to dance, unselfconsciously and with some abandon. It was years since Juliet had danced. The floor had previously been empty, but members of the wedding party stood up and joined them. She danced with an elderly man who introduced himself as Margaret's husband. Then she danced with a young fellow who said that he was the Best Man. The next man to dance with her did not say who he was, but she instinctively knew that she was dancing with the groom. The dance floor was crowded, the music was louder than before, and there was a great deal of laughter. She looked at the groom, with whom she was now dancing very close, and decided that he was good-looking. They made a fine pair, she told herself, and for a moment she continued the enjoyment that came from being the center of attention. She remembered how she and Nicholas had looked at their own wedding reception, and wondered how she would have felt if some impostor had gate-crashed her party.

Juliet decided to leave. They were at the edge of the dance floor and Juliet felt herself being whirled around, allowing herself to spin towards a door that had been left slightly open to admit cooler air. Suddenly she was out of the door and into the night, running across the dark hotel garden. The music seemed to follow her, as did the laughter. As she ran, the laughter, if anything, was louder, and she was frightened by its pursuit.

And then she ran into something and nearly fell forwards over it. For a few seconds she felt herself suspended in air, but then was back on her feet. She had run into the fence around the ravine garden, and had nearly fallen into it.

She immediately thought of Harriet Dot's complaints about "health and safety" and laughed with relief. She was about to look around at the hotel behind her when she saw the bridge over the ravine.

It was unmistakably the Victorian cast-iron footbridge. She closed her eyes tight and when she opened them it was still there—a certain, physical presence. Juliet was confused; the previous evening she had experienced an illusion, but she couldn't remember whether it had really been there or not. She walked over to where it set out across the ravine, and suddenly a hand was in hers.

"Come with me," said the voice, and she looked up to see the bridegroom.

Juliet resisted, and he let go of her hand and walked forward.

"It's fine," he said, in the softest of voices, and turned, walking backwards away from her, smiling.

His features were indistinct, but she knew that it was the man she had danced with and she felt a longing for him. But she could not walk forward.

Juliet took a deep breath. The figure had stopped in the middle of the bridge and was holding out his hand to her. Although she could not be sure why he wanted her to follow, she knew that she wanted to be with him. She wanted him to hold her in his arms and support her and reassure her that everything would be all right.

"Go to him," said a voice with authority from behind. Juliet turned and recognized Harriet Dot. "He's your husband."

"No, he's not. He's the bridegroom."

"If you won't recognize him as your husband, then I will."

Juliet watched as Harriet Dot slowly and purposefully walked out across the bridge.

"But who is he?" Juliet asked helplessly, realizing that she had missed out on some magnificent opportunity. She would have rushed forward and pushed Harriet out of the way, but tiredness swept over her. She felt so weak, and it was as much as she could do to remain standing.

Juliet closed her eyes for a moment, and when she opened them again everything before her had vanished.

Juliet awoke the next morning in the hotel bed with every part of her body aching. It was not just her legs—every muscle felt tired and refused to cooperate. It was as much as she could do to dress and go downstairs. She was not hungry, and did not go through to breakfast. She did not even look into the dining room to see who was in there.

She was surprised not to have a hangover. Her eyes were tired but her head felt reasonably clear. Her thoughts were unimpaired, but she did not want to think why she had to go down into the ravine gardens.

It took some time to find where Harriet Dot was laying, as though sleeping, just off the pathway, among the azaleas. She looked quite content. At least a decade had slipped away from her face. Juliet kneeled down and stroked her cheek. She thanked the woman, before standing again, very stiffly, and going back to the hotel. When she reported Harriet's death to the receptionist it started a process of formalities that were surprisingly quiet and dignified.

It was a policewoman who came up to Juliet's room to ask her a few questions later that morning. She sympathized that Juliet had lost a friend, and Juliet didn't admit that she had known Harriet Dot only slightly.

"We need to know about next of kin," the policewoman said. "Is there a husband?"

"Yes," said Juliet automatically.

But when she thought about it later, she realized that she didn't know.

Is There
Anybody There?

KIM NEWMAN

KIM NEWMAN is a novelist, critic, and broadcaster. His fiction includes *The Night Mayor, Bad Dreams, Jago*, the Anno Dracula novels and stories, *The Quorum, The Original Dr. Shade and Other Stories, Life's Lottery, Back in the USSA* (with Eugene Byrne), and *The Man from the Diogenes Club*, all written under his own name, and *The Vampire Genevieve* and *Orgy of the Blood Parasites*, which were published under the pen name Jack Yeovil.

His nonfiction books include *Ghastly Beyond Belief* (with Neil Gaiman), *Horror: 100 Best Books* and *Horror: Another 100 Best Books* (both with Stephen Jones), *Wild West Movies, The BFI Companion to Horror, Millennium Movies,* and BFI Classics studies of *Cat People* and *Doctor Who*.

He is a contributing editor to *Sight & Sound* and *Empire* magazines, writing the latter's popular "Video Dungeon" column. He has also written and broadcast widely on a range of topics, and scripted radio and television documentaries.

His stories "Week Woman" and "Ubermensch" have been adapted into episodes of the TV series *The Hunger*, and the latter tale was also turned into an Australian short film in 2009. Following his BBC Radio 4 play *Cry Babies*, he wrote an episode ("Phish Phood") for BBC Radio 7's series *The Man in Black*. He has also directed and written a very short film, *Missing Girl*.

Newman's most recent books include expanded reissues of the Anno Dracula series and *The Hound of the d'Urbervilles* (from Titan Books), and a much-enlarged edition of *Nightmare Movies* (from Bloomsbury).

As the author explains: "All I remember about writing this story is that when Maxim Jakubowski asked for a contribution to a collection of Internet-themed fiction, it struck me that there was an equivalence between the spiritualist table-rapping craze of the early twentieth century and Googling as an attempt to wrest answers to any question out of the void.

"Fraudulent medium Irene Dobson/Madame Irena is a mildly recurrent character in my work—she first appeared in my play, *My One Little Murder Can't Do Any Harm*, and pops up briefly in my novel *Jago*."

"IS THERE A PRESENCE?" asked Irene.

The parlor was darker and chillier than it had been moments ago. At the bottoms of the heavy curtains, tassels stirred like the fronds of a deep-sea plant. Irene Dobson—Madame Irena, to her sitters—was alert to tiny changes in a room that might preface the arrival of a visitor from beyond the veil. The fizzing and dimming of still-untrusted electric lamps, so much less impressive than the shrinking and bluing of gaslight flames she remembered from her earliest seances. A clamminess in the draught, as fog-like cold rose from the carpeted floor. The minute crackle of static electricity, making hair lift and pores prickle. The tart taste of pennies in her mouth.

"Is there a traveler from afar?" she asked, opening her inner eye.

The planchette twitched. Miss Walter-David's fingers withdrew in a flinch; she had felt the definite movement. Irene glanced at the no-longer-young woman in the chair beside hers, shrinking away for the moment. The fear-light in the sitter's eyes was the beginning of true belief. To Irene, it was like a tug on a fishing line, the satisfying twinge of the hook going in. This was a familiar stage on the typical sitter's journey from skepticism to fanaticism. This woman was wealthy; soon, Irene would taste not copper but silver, eventually gold.

Wordlessly, she encouraged Miss Walter-David to place her fingertips on the planchette again, to restore balance. Open on the round table before them was a thin sheet of wood, hinged like an oversized chessboard. Upon the board's smoothly papered and polished surface was a circle, the letters of the alphabet picked out in curlicue.

Corners were marked for YES—*oui, ja*—and NO. The planchette, a pointer on marble castors, was a triangular arrowhead-shape. Irene and Miss Walter-David lightly touched fingers to the lower points of the planchette, and the tip quivered.

"Is there anybody there?" Miss Walter-David asked.

This sitter was bereft of a fiancé, an officer who had come through the trenches but succumbed to influenza upon return to civilian life. Miss Walter-David was searching for balm to soothe her sense of hideous unfairness, and had come at last to Madame Irena's parlor.

"Is there—"

The planchette moved, sharply. Miss Walter-David hissed in surprise. Irene felt the presence, stronger than usual, and knew it could be tamed. She was no fraud, relying on conjuring tricks, but her understanding of the world beyond the veil was very different from that which she wished her sitters to have. All spirits could be made to do what she wished them to do. If they thought themselves grown beyond hurt, they were sorely in error. The planchette, genuinely independent of the light touches of medium and sitter, stabbed towards a corner of the board, but stopped surprisingly short.

Y

Not YES, but the Y of the circular alphabet. The spirits often used initials to express themselves, but Madame had never encountered one who neglected the convenience of the YES and NO corners. She did not let Miss Walter-David see her surprise.

"Have you a name?"

Y again. Not YES. Was Y the beginning of a name: Youngman, Yoko-Hama, Ysrael?

"What is it?" she was almost impatient.

The planchette began a circular movement, darting at letters, using the lower tips of the planchette as well as the pointer. That also was unusual, and took an instant or two to digest.

M S T R M N D

"Msstrrmnnd," said Miss Walter-David.

Irene understood. "Have you a message for anyone here, Master Mind?"

Y

"For whom?"

U

"For Ursula?" Miss Walter-David's Christian name was Ursula.

N U

"U?"

"You," said Miss Walter-David. "You."

This was not a development Irene liked a bit.

There were two prospects in his chat room. Women, or at least they said they were. Boyd didn't necessarily believe them. Some users thought they were clever.

Boyd was primarily *MSTRMND*, but had other log-in names, some male, some female, some neutral. For each ISDN line, he had a different code name and e-address, none traceable to his physical address. He lived online, really; this flat in Highgate was just a place to store the meat. There was nothing he couldn't get by playing the web, which responded to his touch like a harpsichord to a master's fingers. There were always backdoors.

His major female ident was *CARESS*, aggressively sexual; he imagined her as a porn site Cleopatra Jones, a black model with dom tendencies. He kept a more puritanical, shockable ident—*SCHLGRL*—as backup, to cut in when *CARESS* became too outrageous.

These two users weren't tricky, though. They were clear. Virgins, just the way he liked them. He guessed they were showing themselves nakedly to the room, with no deception.

IRENE D

URSULA W-D

Their messages typed out laboriously, appearing on his master monitor a word at a time. He initiated searches, to cough up more on their handles. His system was smart enough to come up with a birth-name, a physical address, financial details and, more often than not, a .jpg image from even the most casually assumed one-use log-on name. Virgins never realized that their presences always left ripples. Boyd knew how to piggyback any one of a dozen official and unofficial trackers, and routinely pulled up information on anyone with whom he had even the most casual, wary dealings.

IRENE D: Have you a message for anyone here, Master Mind?

Boyd stabbed a key.

Y

IRENE D: For whom?

U

IRENE D: For Ursula?

N U

IRENE D: U?

URSULA W-D: You.

At least one of them got it. IRENE D—why didn't she tag herself ID or I-D?—was just slow. That didn't matter. She was the one Boyd had spotted as a natural. Something about her blank words gave her away. She had confidence and ignorance, while her friend—they were in contact, maybe even in the same physical room—at least understood she knew nothing, that she had stepped into deep space and all the rules were changed. IRENE D—her log-on was probably a variant on the poor girl's real name—thought she was in control. She would unravel very easily, almost no challenge at all.

A MESSAGE FOR U I-D, he typed.

He sat on a reinforced swivel chair with optimum back support and buttock-spread, surveying a semicircle of keyboards and monitors all hooked up to separate lines and accounts, all feeding into the master monitor. When using two or more idents, he could swivel or roll from board to board, taking seconds to chameleon-shift. He could be five or six people in any given minute, dazzle a solo into thinking she—and it almost always was a she—was in a buzzing chat room with a lively crowd when she was actually alone with him, growing more vulnerable with each stroke and line, more open to his hooks and grapples, her backdoors flapping in the wind.

I KNOW WHO U ARE

Always a classic. Always went to the heart.

He glanced at the leftmost screen. Still searching. No details yet. His system was usually much faster than this. Nothing on either of them, on IRENE or URSULA. They couldn't be smart enough to cover their traces in the web, not if they were really as newbie as they seemed. Even a net-shark ace would have been caught by now. And these girls were fighting nowhere near his weight. Must be a glitch. It didn't matter.

I KNOW WHAT U DO

Not *DID*, but *DO*. *DID* is good for specifics, but *DO* suggests something ongoing, some hidden current in an ordinary life, perhaps unknown even to the user.

U R NOT WHAT U CLAIM 2 B

That was for sure.

U R NOT WHAT U CLAIM 2 B

"You are not what you claim to be?" interpreted Miss Walter-David. She had become quickly skilled at picking out the spirit's peculiar, abbreviated language. It was rather irritating, thought Irene. She was in danger of losing this sitter, of becoming the one in need of guidance.

There was something odd about Master Mind. He—it was surely a he—was unlike other spirits, who were mostly vague children. Everything they spelled out was simplistic, yet ambiguous. She had to help them along, to tease out from the morass of whatever it was they wanted to communicate with those left behind, or more often to intuit what it was her sitters wanted or needed most to hear and to shape her reading of the messages to fit. Her fortune was built not on reaching the other world, but in manipulating it so that the right communications came across. No sitter really wanted to hear a loved one had died a meaningless death and drifted in limbo, gradually losing personality like a cloud breaking up. Though, occasionally, she had sitters who wanted to know that those they had hated in life were suffering properly in the beyond and that their miserable postmortem apologies were not accepted. Such transactions disturbed even her, though they often proved among the most rewarding financially.

Now, Irene sensed a concrete personality. Even through almost coded, curt phrases, Master Mind was a someone, not a something. For the first time, she was close to being afraid of what she had touched.

Master Mind was ambiguous, but through intent rather than fumble-thinking. She had a powerful impression of him, from his self-chosen title: a man on a throne, head swollen and limbs atrophied, belly bloated like a balloon, framing vast schemes, manipulating lesser beings like chess pieces. She was warier of him than even of the rare angry spirit she had called into her circle. There were defenses against him, though. She had been careful to make sure of that.

"Ugly Hell gapes," she remembered from *Doctor Faustus*. Well, not for her.

She thought Master Mind was not a spirit at all.

U R ALLONE

"You are all one," interpreted Miss Walter-David. "Whatever can that mean?"

U R ALONE

That was not a cryptic statement from the beyond. Before discovering her "gift," Irene Dobson had toiled in an insurance office. She knew a typewriting mistake when she saw one.

U R AFRAID

"You are af—"

"Yes, Miss Walter-David, I understand."

"And are you?"

"Not anymore. Master Mind, you are a most interesting fellow, yet I cannot but feel you conceal more than you reveal. We are all, at our worst, alone and afraid. That is scarcely a great insight."

It was the secret of her profession, after all.

"Are you not also alone and afraid?"

Nothing.

"Let me put it another way."

She pressed down on the planchette, and manipulated it, spelling out in his own language.

R U NOT ALSO ALONE AND AFRAID

She would have added a question mark, but the Ouija board had none. Spirits never asked questions, just supplied answers.

IRENE D was sharper than he had first guessed. And he still knew no more about her. No matter.

Boyd rolled over to the next keyboard.

U TELL HIM GRRL BCK OFF CREEP

IRENE D: Another presence? How refreshing. And you might be?

CARESS SISTA

IRENE D: Another spirit?

Presence? Spirit? Was she taking the piss?

UH HUH SPIRT THAT'S THE STUFF SHOW THAT PIG U CAN STAND UP 4 YRSELF

IRENE D: Another presence, but the same mode of address. I think your name might be Legion.

Boyd knew of another net shark who used Legion as a log-on. IRENE D must have come across him too. Not the virgin she seemed, then. Damn.

His search still couldn't penetrate further than her simple log-on. By now, he should have her mother's maiden name, her menstrual calendar, the full name of the first boy she snogged at school, and a list of all the porn sites she had accessed in the last week.

He should close down the room, seal it up forever and scuttle away. But he was being challenged, which didn't happen often. Usually, he was content to play awhile with those he snared, scrambling their heads with what he had found out about them as his net-noose drew tauter around them. Part of the game was to siphon a little from their bank accounts: someone had to pay his phone and access bills, and he was damned if he should cough up by direct debit like some silly little newbie. But mostly it was for the sport.

In the early days, he had been fond of co-opting idents and flooding his playmates' systems with extreme porn or placing orders in their names for expensive but embarrassing goods and services. That now seemed crude. His current craze was doctoring and posting images. If IRENE D was married, it would be interesting to direct her husband to, say, a goat sex site where her face was convincingly overlaid upon an enthusiastic animal-lover's body. And it was so easy to mock up mug shots, complete with guilty looks and serial numbers, to reveal an ineptly suppressed criminal past (complete with court records and other supporting documentation) that would make an employer think twice about keeping someone on the books. No one ever bothered to double-check by going back to the paper archives before they downsized a job.

Always, he would leave memories to cherish; months later, he would check up on his net-pals—his score so far was five institutionalizations and two suicides—just to see that the experience was still vivid. He was determined to crawl into IRENE D's skull and stay there, replicating like a virus, wiping her hard drive.

URSULA W-D: Do you know Frank? Frank Conynghame-Mars.

Where did that come from? Still, there couldn't be many people floating around with a name like that. Boyd shut off the fruitless backdoor search, and copied the double-barrel into an engine. It came up instantly with a handful of matches. The first was an obituary from 1919, scanned into a newspaper database. A foolish virgin had purchased unlimited access to a great many similar archives, which was now open to Boyd. A local newspaper, the *Ham&High*. He was surprised. It was the World Wide Web after all. This hit was close to home—maybe only streets away—if eighty years back. He looked over the obit, and took a flyer.

DEAD OF FLU

URSULA W-D: Yes. She knows Frank, Madame Irena. A miracle. Have you a message from Frank? For Ursula?

Boyd speed-read the obit. Frank Conynghame-Mars, "decorated in the late conflict," etc. etc. Dead at thirty-eight. Engaged to a Miss Ursula Walter-David, of this parish. Could the woman be still alive? She would have to be well over a hundred.

He launched another search. Ursula Walter-David

Three matches. One the Conynghame-Mars obit he already had up. Second, an article from something called *The Temple*, from 1924—a publication of the Spiritualist Church. Third, also from the *Ham&High* archive, her own obit, from 1952.

Zoinks, Scooby—a ghost!

This was an elaborate sting. Had to be.

He would string it along, to give him time to think.

U WIL BE 2GETHER AGAIN 1952

The article from *The Temple* was too long and close-printed to read in full while his formidable attention was divided into three or four windows. It had been scanned in badly, and not all of it was legible. The gist was a testimonial for a spiritualist medium called Madame Irena (no last name given). Among her "sitters," satisfied customers evidently, was Ursula Walter-David.

Weird. Boyd suspected he was being set up. He didn't trust the matches. They must be plants. Though he couldn't see the joins, he knew that with enough work he could run something like this—had indeed done so, feeding prospects their own mocked-up obits with full gruesome details—to get to someone. Was this a vengeance crusade? If so, he couldn't see where it was going.

He tried a search on MADAME IRENA and came up with hundreds of matches, mostly French and porn sites. A BD/SM video titled *The Lash of Madame Irena* accounted for most of the matches. He tried pairing MADAME IRENA with +SPIRITUALIST and had a more manageable fifteen matches, including several more articles from *The Temple*.

URSULA W-D: Is Frank at peace?

He had to subdivide his concentration, again. He wasn't quite ambidextrous, but could pump a keyboard with either hand, working shift keys with his thumbs, and split his mind into segments, eyes rolling independently like a lizard's, to follow several lines.

FRANK IS OVER HIS SNIFFLES

Among the MADAME IRENA/MEDIUM matches was a *Journal of the Society of Psychical Research* piece from 1926, shout-lined FRAUDULENCE ALLEGED. He opened it up, and found from a news-in-brief snippet that a court case was being prepared against one Irene Dobson, known professionally as Madame Irena, for various malpractices in connection with her work as a spirit medium. One Catriona Kaye, a "serious researcher" was quoted as being "in no doubt of the woman's genuine psychical abilities but also sure she had employed them in an unethical, indeed dangerous, manner."

Another match was a court record. He opened it: a declaration of the suit against Irene Dobson. Scrolling down, he found it frustratingly incomplete. The document set out what was being tried, but didn't say how the case came out. A lot of old records were like that, incompletely scanned. Usually, he only had current files to open and process. He looked again at the legal rigmarole, and his eye was caught by Irene Dobson's address.

The Laburnums, Feldspar Road, Highgate.

This was 26, Feldspar Road. There were big bushes outside. If he ran a search for laburnum.jpg, he was sure he'd get a visual match.

Irene Dobson lived in this house.

No, she had lived in this house. In the 1920s, before it was converted into flats. When it had a name, not a number.

Now she was dead.

Whoever was running this on Boyd knew where he lived. He was not going to take that.

"This new presence," said Miss Walter-David. "It's quite remarkable."

There was no new presence, no Caress. Irene would have felt a change, and hadn't. This was one presence with several voices. She had heard of such. Invariably malign. She should call an end to the seance, plead fatigue. But Ursula Walter-David would never come back, and the husbandless woman had a private income and nothing to spend it on but the beyond. At the moment, she was satisfied enough to pay heavily for Irene's service. She decided to stay with it, despite the dangers. Rewards were within reach. She was determined, however, to treat this cunning spirit with extreme caution. He was a tiger, posing as a pussycat. She focused on the center of the board, and was careful with the planchette, never letting its points stray beyond the ring of letters.

"Caress," said Miss Walter-David, a-tremble, "may I speak with Frank?"

Caress was supposed to be a woman, but Irene thought the first voice—Master Mind—closer to the true personality.

IN 52

"Why 1952? It seems a terribly long way off."

WHEN U DIE

That did it. Miss Walter-David pulled away as if bitten. Irene considered: it seemed only too likely that the sitter had been given the real year of her death. That was a cruel stroke, typical of the malign spirit.

The presence was a prophet. Irene had heard of a few such spirits—one of the historical reasons for consulting mediums was to discern the future—but never come across one. Could it be that the spirits had true foreknowledge of what was to come? Or did they inhabit a realm outside time and could look in at any point in human history, future as well as past, and pass on what they saw?

Miss Walter-David was still impressed. But less pleased.

The planchette circled, almost entirely of its own accord. Irene could have withdrawn her fingers, but the spirit was probably strong enough to move the pointer without her. It certainly raced ahead of her push. She had to keep the planchette in the circle.

IRENE

Not Irena.

DOBSON

Now she was frightened, but also annoyed. A private part of her person had been exposed. This was an insult and an attack.

"Who's Dobson?" asked Miss Walter-David.

SHE IS

"It is my name," Irene admitted. "That's no secret."

ISNT IT

"Where are you?" she asked.

HERE THERE EVERYWHERE

"No, here and there perhaps. But not everywhere."

This was a strange spirit. He had aspirations to omnipotence, but something about him was over-reaching. He called himself "Master Mind," which suggested a streak of self-deluding vanity. Knowledge wasn't wisdom. She had a notion that if she asked him to name this year's Derby winner, he would be able to furnish the correct answer (an idea with possibilities) but that he could reveal precious little of what came after death. An insight struck her: this was not a departed spirit, this was a living man.

Living. But where?

No.

When?

"What date is it?" she asked.

GOOD QUESTION

Since this must be a sting, there was no harm in the truth.

JAN 20 01

IRENE D: 1901?

N 2001

URSULA W-D: I thought time had no meaning in the world beyond.

IRENE D: That depends which world beyond our guest might

inhabit.

Boyd had run searches on "Irene Dobson" and his own address, independent and cross-matching. Too many matches were coming up. He wished more people had names like "Frank Conynghame-Mars" and fewer like "Irene Dobson." "Boyd Waylo," his birth-name, was a deep secret; his accounts were all in names like "John Barrett" and "Andrew Lee."

Beyond the ring of monitors, his den was dark. This was the largest room in what had once been a Victorian town house, and was now divided into three flats. Was this where "Madame Irena" had held her seances? His raised ground-floor flat might encompass the old parlor.

He was supposed to believe he was in touch with the past.

One of the Irene Dobson matches was a .jpg. He opened the picture file, and looked into a small, determined face. Not his type, but surprising and striking. Her hair was covered by a turban and she wore a Chinese-style jacket, buttoned up to the throat. She looked rather prosperous, and was smoking a black cigarette in a long white holder. The image was from 1927. Was that when she was supposed to be talking to him from?

WHAT DATE 4 U

IRENE D: January 13, 1923. Of course.

Maybe he was supposed to bombard her with questions about the period, to try and catch her out in an anachronism. But he had only general knowledge: Prohibition in America, a General Strike in Britain, talking pictures in 1927, the Lindbergh flight somewhere earlier, the stock market crash a year or two later, *Thoroughly Modern Millie* and P.G. Wodehouse. Not a lot of use. He couldn't even remember who was prime minister in January 1923. He could get answers from the net in moments, though; knowing things was pointless compared with knowing how to find things out. At the moment, that didn't help him.

Whoever these women were—or rather, whoever this IRENE D was, for URSULA W-D plainly didn't count—he was sure that they'd have the answers for any questions he came up with.

What was the point of this?

He could get to IRENE D. Despite everything, he had her. She was in his room; she was his prey and meat, and he would not let her challenge him.

I C U

I C U

I see you.

Irene thought that was a lie, but Master Mind could almost certainly hear her. Though, as with real spirits, she wondered if the words came to him as human sounds or in some other manner.

The parlor was almost completely dark, save for a cone of light about the table.

Miss Walter-David was terrified, on the point of fleeing. That was for the best, but there was a service Irene needed of her.

She did not say it out loud, for Master Mind would hear.

He said he could see, but she thought she could conceal her hand from him.

It was an awkward move. She put the fingers of her left hand on the shivering planchette, which was racing inside the circle, darting at the letters, trying to break free.

I C U ID

I C U R FRIT

She slipped a pocketbook out of her cardigan, opened it one-handed and pressed it to her thigh with the heel of her hand while extracting the pencil from the spine with her fingernails. It was not an easy thing to manage.

U R FRIT AND FRAUD

This was just raving. She wrote a note, blind. She was trusting Miss Walter-David to read her scrawl. It was strange what mattered.

"This is no longer Caress," she said, trying to keep her voice steady. "Have we another visitor?"

2TRU IM SNAKE

"Im? Ah-ha, 'I'm' Snake? Yet another speaker of this peculiar dialect, with unconventional ideas about spelling."

Miss Walter-David was backing away. She was out of her seat, retreating into darkness. Irene offered her the pocketbook, opened to the message. The sitter didn't want to take it. She opened her mouth. Irene shook her head, shushing her. Miss Walter-David took the book, and peered in the dark. Irene was afraid the silly goose would read out loud, but she at least half-understood.

On a dresser nearby was a tea tray, with four glasses of distilled water and four curls of chain. Bicycle chain, as it happened. Irene had asked Miss Walter-David to bring the tray to the Ouija table.

"Snake, do you know things? Things yet to happen?"

2TRU

"A useful accomplishment."

NDD

"Indeed?"

2RIT

There was a clatter. Miss Walter-David had withdrawn. Irene wondered if she would pay for the seance. She might. After all, there had been results. She had learned something, though nothing to make her happy.

"Miss Walter-David will die in 1952?"

Y

Back to Y. She preferred that to *2TRU* and *2RIT*.

"Of what?"

A pause.

PNEU

"Pneumonia, thank you."

Her arm was getting worn out, dragged around the circle. Her shoulder ached. Doing this one-handed was not easy. She had already set out the glasses at the four points of the compass, and was working on the chains. It was important that the ends be dipped in the glasses to make the connections, but that the two ends in each glass not touch.

This was more like physics than spiritualism, but she understood it made sense.

"What else do you know?"

U R FRAUD

"I don't think so. Tell me about the future. Not 2001. The useful future, within the next five or ten years."

STOK MRKT CRSH 29

"That's worth knowing. You can tell me about stocks and shares?"

Y

It was a subject of which she knew nothing, but she could learn. She had an idea that there were easier and less obtrusive fortunes to be made there than in Derby winners. But she would get the names out of him, too.

"Horse races?"

A hesitation.

Y

The presence was less frisky, sliding easily about the circle, not trying to break free.

"This year's Derby?"

A simple search (*Epsom +Derby +winner +1923 -Kentucky*) had no matches; he took out *Kentucky*, and had a few hits, and an explanation. Papyrus, the 1923 winner, was the first horse to run in both the Epsom and Kentucky Derby races, though the nag lost in the States, scuppering a possible chance for a nice long-shot accumulator bet if he really was giving a woman from the past a hot tip on the future. Boyd fed that all to IRENE D, still playing along, still not seeing the point. She received slowly, as if her system were taking one letter at a time.

Click. It wasn't a monitor. It was an Ouija board.

That was what he was supposed to think.

IRENE D: I'm going to give you another name. I should like you to tell me what you know of this man.

OK

IRENE D: Anthony Tallgarth. Also, Basil and Florence Tallgarth.

He ran multiple searches and got a cluster of matches, mostly from the '20s—though there were birth and death announcements from the 1860s through to 1968—and, again, mostly from the *Ham&High*. He picked one dated February 2, 1923, and opened the article.

TYCOON FINDS LOST SON

IRENE D: Where is Anthony? Now.

According to the article, Anthony was enlisted in the Royal Navy as an Able Seaman, under the name of T.A. Meredith, stationed at Portsmouth and due to ship out aboard the H.M.S. *Duckett*. He had parted from his wealthy parents after a scandal and a quarrel—since the brat had gone into the Navy, Boyd bet he was gay—but been discovered through the efforts of a "noted local spiritualist and seeress." A reconciliation was effected.

He'd had enough of this game. He wasn't going to play anymore.

He rolled back in his chair, and hit an invisible wall.

IRENE D: I should tell you, Master Mind, that you are bound. With iron and holy water. I shall extend your circle, if you cooperate.

He tried reaching out, through the wall, and his hand was bathed with pain.

IRENE D: I do not know how you feel, if you can feel, but I will wager that you do not care for that.

It was as if she was watching him. Him!

IRENE D: Now, be a good little ghosty and tell me what I wish to know.

With his right hand lodged in his left armpit as the pain went away, he made keystrokes with his left hand, transferring the information she needed. It took a long time, a letter at a time.

IRENE D: There must be a way of replacing this board with a typewriter. That would be more comfortable for you, would it not?

FO, he typed.

A lash at his back, as the wall constricted. She had understood that. Was that a very 1923 womanly quality?

IRENE D: Manners, manners. If you are good to me, I shall let you have the freedom of this room, maybe this floor. I can procure longer chains.

He was a shark in a play pool, furious and humiliated and in pain. And he knew it would last.

Mr. and Mrs. Tallgarth had been most generous. She could afford to give Master Mind the run of the parlor, and took care to refresh his water-bindings each day. This was not a task she would ever entrust to the new maid. The key to the parlor was about Irene's person at all times.

People would pay to be in contact with the dead, but they would pay more for other services, information of more use in the here and now. And she had a good line on all manner of things. She had been testing Master Mind, and found him a useful source about a wide variety of subjects, from the minutiae of any common person's life to the great matters which were to come in the rest of the century.

Actually, knowing which horse would win any year's Derby was a comparatively minor advantage. Papyrus was bound to be the favorite, and the race too famous for any fortune to be made. She had her genie working on long-shot winners of lesser races, and was sparing in her use of the trick. Bookmakers were the sort of sharp people she understood only too well, and would soon tumble to any streak of unnatural luck. From now on, for a great many reasons, she intended to be as unobtrusive as possible.

This morning, she had been making a will. She had no interest in the disposal of her assets after death, when she herself ventured beyond the veil, for she intended to make the most of them while alive. The entirety of her estate was left to her firm of solicitors on the unusual condition that, when she passed, no record or announcement of her death be made, even on her gravestone. It was not beyond possibility that she mightn't make it to 2001, though she knew she would be gone from this house by then. From now on, she would be careful about official mentions of her name; to be nameless, she understood, was to be invisible to Master Mind, and she needed her life to be shielded from him as his was from hers.

The man had intended her harm, but he was her genie now, in her bottle.

She sat at the table, and put her hands on the planchette, feeling the familiar press of resistance against her.

"Is there anybody there?"

YYYYYYYYYYYYYYYYYYYYYYY

"Temper temper, Master Mind. Today, I should like to know more about stocks and shares . . . "

Food was brought to him from the online grocery, handed over at the front door. He was a shut-in forever now. He couldn't remember the last time he had stepped outside his flat; it had been days before IRENE D, maybe weeks. It wasn't like he had ever needed to post a letter or go to a bank.

Boyd had found the chains. They were still here, fixed into the skirting boards, running under the doorway, rusted at the ends, where the water traps had been. It didn't matter that the water had run out years ago. He was still bound.

Searches told him little more of Irene Dobson. At least he knew someone would have her in court in four years time—a surprise he would let her have—but he had no hopes that she would be impeded. He had found traces of her well into the 1960s, lastly a piece from 1968 that didn't use her name but did mention her guiding spirit, Master Mind, to whom she owed so much over the course of her long and successful career as a medium, seer, and psychic sleuth.

From 1923 to 1968. Forty-five years. Real time. Their link was constant, and he moved forward as she did, a day for a day.

Irene Dobson's spirit guide had stayed with her at least that long.

Not forever. Forty-five years.

He had tried false information, hoping to ruin her—if she was cast out of her house (though she was still in it in 1927, he remembered), he would be free—but she always saw through it and could punish him.

He had tried going silent, shutting everything down. But he always had to boot up again, to be online. It was more than a compulsion. It was a need. In theory, he could stop paying electricity and phone bills— rather, stop other people paying his—and be cut off eventually, but in theory he could stop himself breathing and suffocate. It just wasn't in him. His meat had rarely left the house anyway, and as a reward for telling her about the extra-marital private habits of a husband whose avaricious wife was one of her sitters, she had extended his bindings to the hallway and—thank heavens—the toilet.

She had his full attention.

IRENE D: Is there anybody there?

Y DAMNIT Y

Wait

CONRAD WILLIAMS

CONRAD WILLIAMS is the author of the novels *Head Injuries, London Revenant, The Unblemished, One, Decay Inevitable, Blonde on a Stick,* and *Loss of Separation.*

He has written more than 100 short stories, some of which are collected in *Use Once Then Destroy* and the forthcoming *Open Heart Surgery.*

Williams has won the Littlewood Arc prize and the International Horror Guild Award, and is a three-time recipient of the British Fantasy Award. His first edited anthology, *Gutshot: Weird West Tales,* recently appeared from PS Publishing.

"'Wait' came about directly after a visit to Poole's Cavern in Buxton, Derbyshire," the author explains. "At the end of the system is a boulder choke. A radar scan in 1999 established that a greater network of chambers lies beyond it.

"It was quite awe-inspiring to think that we were feet away from a place that has not been seen by human eyes since the glaciers carved it out two million years ago.

"And then I began to think about means of access and how every entrance can also be an exit . . ."

THE SNOW HAD NEVER really gone away. It swirled in his head, in memories of Julie's cheap little ornament. And here was the same whitened motorway turnoff. Here the same crystallized countryside swelling against the verge. He had to stop the car at the accident site, although he had persuaded himself over the three-hour duration of his drive up here that he would not.

He parked in a lay-by and walked back. The telegraph post was no longer there. The car had almost torn it out of the ground, and might have done so had it not destroyed the passenger side of the car first.

Julie had not stood a chance.

The doctors he spoke to reassured him that she was unlikely to have felt anything, the impact was so swift, so massive. There was nothing to suggest an accident had taken place here.

Don had received a face full of broken glass, but he was otherwise unmarked. He could walk. He could get in and out of bed. He could turn his head. Everything that Julie could not. Even the cuts on his face had healed without leaving obvious scars. The scar he needed to heal was inside him. That was partly the reason for this trip. To confront the moment of his wife's death, and to carry on to the place they had meant to be journeying. To find a way forward.

They had been a scant ten minutes away from Sheckford, that awful day. Now Don went back to the car and switched on the engine. He pulled out into the road. A blade of sunshine sliced through clouds and turned the snow golden. Apart from the streak of red far off in the distance, on one of the hills surrounding the town.

A lorry thundered by him, dragging up a great fan of slush that covered his windscreen, blinding him for a moment. His heart racing, he cleared the filth from the glass, his head full of collisions and the feel of all those icy pebbles of windscreen assaulting his face. The shock of cold air as his car was bisected. No scream. No sounds at all.

Now the red was gone from the hill. Or maybe it was a different hill, a different angle, an illusion formed by the sun and the strange refracted light coming off the crystals of snow and ice.

Maybe it was in his own eyes.

The doctor had explained to him that all that exploded glass had to go somewhere. There would have been some splinters he wouldn't even feel. The force of the impact would have sent them into his flesh so fast, so smoothly, that there would have been no blood. There was the likelihood that he would carry minute slivers of glass around in his flesh for the rest of his life. Some survivors of bomb blasts, he was told, had suffered hundreds of tiny splinters of glass passing right through their bodies.

He was a year further away from her. He was a year closer to her.

Don would not let himself get distracted again. He completed his journey concentrating fully on his driving, checking his speed, his rear-view mirrors and keeping his hands at ten-to-two on the steering wheel. He let out a long, low sigh when he arrived at the hotel car park and turned the engine off. He listened to it ticking like some horrible countdown. Keep busy. Keep moving.

He got out of the car and strode past a woman holding a leash, calling into a clump of bushes for a dog that would not come. From the sounds of her, she'd been calling for some time. A red glove came up and rubbed at her face, perhaps in an attempt to coax the worry from it.

He checked into the hotel and tossed his suitcase onto the bed. The exact room they would have taken a year previously.

Why are you doing this to yourself?

He turned but of course there was nobody else in the room. He stared at the reflection of himself in the full-length mirror fitted into the panels of the wardrobe doors. The mirror was not the best quality. Red paint edged it, indicating that at some previous time it had been part of some other furniture. The silver backing was scarred and there was foxing in the corners. A look of shabby chic, he supposed the hotel was going for, but it appeared out of place when compared to the rest of the room, which was formal, Edwardian, verging on the cold.

"God, you'd have hated this, Ju," he whispered.

He sat on the edge of the bed and stared at his fingers. Julie liked his fingers. She had described them as surgeon's fingers, as early as their first date. He could do nothing for her, though, with these delicate fingers. He could not stave off death. He couldn't find the life in her and coax it back, make it bloom, make it overpower the hurt that took her away. He felt bad that he had escaped with little more than bruises and shock (poor thing) while she had the life slammed from her in less than a millisecond. He wished she were merely lost, like that dog in the bushes.

He unpacked, desultory, quietly panicked by his decision to come here. He didn't know what to do. He had been filled with plans when he took that journey up with his wife. They were celebrating their third anniversary. Glass, ha ha. But also he'd meant this trip to be a way for them both to shed the tension that had been building up in London. Julie's homeopathic shop in Camden had been hit hard by the recession. She relied on the Christmas shopping period to tide her over the following half-year, but trade had been anything but brisk. She had had to let one of her assistants go and, although she enjoyed a steady supply of small orders via the website, and as a practicing herbalist was able to lean on the money she made from her patients, it was not enough to help them scramble out of the red. Another twelve months like this would have buried the business. Instead, they buried Julie, and all the worry over the business meant less than nothing. It was sold. It was over.

As for Don, he was teaching guitar to a class of young boys and girls at the local primary school. They had more often than not been bought the instrument for Christmas, or their birthdays, but little thought had gone into it. The parents tended to buy expensive items, without pause to consider if the guitar would be too big or small, the neck too wide for the child to be able to shape a decent barre chord. In the main his pupils had no natural aptitude. No promise. One boy had picked up the guitar like a double bass. Another held the guitar in the correct manner but, astonishingly, had used his strumming hand to fret chords and vice versa. It was enough to make him want to restring his Gibson via their scrawny little throats.

It had been such a long time since he had relaxed, or even tried to. He stared out of the window at the square and the people milling around it. The opera house and the park were possible places to visit, but he didn't feel like being among other people. He shaved because it ate up some time. As he did so, he thought about guitars and people. He wanted to write a song about Julie, but he didn't know how to begin. All the great songs written by guitarists for important people in their lives. John for Julia; Eric for Conor; Joni for Kelly; George for Patti. Mothers and fathers, sons and daughters. Lovers. There ought to be something in him for Julie, but every time he thought of music, he felt guilty. How could he even begin to consider the positioning of notes on the stave when she would never again be able to do the things she loved?

He felt a twinge in his cheek and ran his finger over the skin there. He hadn't nicked himself shaving but there was a lump in his cheek. *Great*, he thought, *I survive a major road traffic accident only to fall foul of cancer*. He checked in the mirror. Maybe the blade had taken the top off a pimple he hadn't noticed. The edges of the lump were raised. It felt tender. He tried squeezing it, convinced now that it was filled with pus and he would have to clean it or run the risk of it becoming a boil, or worse. He stopped immediately. The slightest pressure told him that there was something solid beneath the skin.

He called down to reception and asked for ointment, plasters, and painkillers. He poured vodka from the miniature in his minibar and drank it in one swallow. When the packets and pills came, brought by a young man whose expression clearly spoke of his disdain for anybody who asks for such things from room service, Don tenderly applied to his cheek some of the ointment—which contained a substance he recognized from Julie's work in homeopathy, something that was good at drawing out foreign bodies—and placed one of the plasters over it. He stomached the pills with more vodka. He changed into a shirt and trousers, went down to the bar and had a cocktail, read the newspaper and, when the bar started to become busy, retired to his room, more than a little drunk, where he slept fitfully.

At one point during the night, he was sucked deep enough into sleep to suffer a nightmare. He dreamed he was hiding from something that was trying to sniff him out. Something that had poor eyesight, but keen olfactory organs. Something that was intensely hungry for Don.

He had hidden in a city filled with black glass. But its surfaces made poor reflections, clinging jealously to their color as if they would reveal terrible pictures if they were allowed to clear. There was no light anywhere. Whenever Don thought he had discovered somewhere safe, cracks would appear in the glass and he would see his pursuer's thin, long fingers, scabbed and pitted, picking through the fractures in a bid to get nearer to him, near enough to be able to swipe at Don's clothes. This happened, finally, and he felt the fingers like needles piercing the skin of his thigh. He was swept towards the crack in the glass and unceremoniously dragged through it. He was choking on splinters. And if he looked through the thin aperture, an aperture whose edges he was unraveling messily upon, he could see the shadow of its face and the writhing puncture at its center ringed with shattered white teeth, surely too thin and weak to be able to do all *this*.

"Name's Kerner. Grant Kerner. How's your breakfast?"

Now that Kerner had drawn attention to it, Don realized he no longer wanted his food. It was swimming in grease. The bacon was undercooked, the tomato blistered black on the outside, solid and cold in the center. And he was still mindful of the unhealthy, yawning mouth he had witnessed in his dreams. He couldn't remember the last time he had been hungry, or enjoyed a meal. He pushed the plate away and drew his coffee nearer. Caffeine and alcohol seemed to form the limit of his appetites these days.

Kerner was eating muesli loaded with extra whole hazelnuts and dried apricots. Don's jaws ached just watching him.

Kerner was obviously one of those people who liked to winkle information out of people and he perhaps saw Don as something of a challenge. He kept on at him throughout Don's second cup of coffee and while he wrapped miniature pots of jam in a serviette and stashed them in his coat pocket.

"I'm a photographer," Kerner said, although Don had not asked him his occupation. "I take pictures of crippled things. Cars, buildings. Broken architecture. People, if I can get away with it. Things that don't work the way they ought to. What do you do?"

Don thought of his job. For so long he had been going through the motions, it was as if he was working from a script every day. In a way he was, following the slavish schedules set down by a government eager to have its target figures bolstered by achievable test results.

He showed the children how to play basic chords, the first few essentials: A, D, and E, corrected them when they went wrong—which was often—and put on excruciating "musical" events for their parents to attend. Interaction was at a minimum. He thought the children could see right through him, though they were all under ten years of age. He wondered if he resented them, since Julie's death. He wondered if maybe he was taking out the fact that he was fatherless, and had never intended to be—certainly not at this age—on them.

"I'm unemployed," Don said. He tried to think of a job so far removed from who Kerner seemed to be that he wouldn't ask him any follow-up questions about it. "I used to work in Human Resources."

That worked. Kerner's smile froze a little; he nodded, gazed outside. "That your car?" he asked brightly, apparently happy to find another conversational topic.

"The Focus? Yeah." Don closed his mouth. We used to have a Volvo. You know, safest car in the world. *Until I totaled it. And my wife.*

"I drive a Lexus."

"Nice."

"Yeah," Kerner said. "I like to drive gone midnight. Empty roads. Good up here. Some good roads. Hairpin bends and suchlike."

"It's just a metal box to get me from one place to another." Don had bought a second-hand car a week after the accident. He forced himself into the driver's seat. He would not allow it to lock him down. *Metal boxes. Wooden boxes. Snow globes.*

"Well, I must go," Kerner said, and drained his cup. "Some good light here in the mornings. Click-click and all that. Peace out, rainbow trout."

Don watched Kerner move through the dining room to the door. The other man was of a similar age to Don, he reckoned, but there was a world of difference in their physiques. Kerner's limbs were slender, he was lithe and stealthy. He panthered across the room. Don hated his own rounded posture. He was all clump and jostle. Too many hours hunched over his guitar. He resolved to do something about it—cut back on the alcohol, eradicate the fast food from his diet, try to exercise more—but even as he left the hotel lobby and walked across the square to his car, he knew this would never be the case. Some people were born to the shape they would occupy all their lives.

I'm going to take you to the school I attended. I was a model pupil. Don't laugh. I was a senior prefect. I never had a day's absence. I took eight O levels and scored As for all of them.

Don sat in his car wondering how he had arrived here; the journey was a blur. It angered him that he should still be able to switch off whenever he drove, considering what had happened. He got out, stalked away from his little metal box, his mobile coffin, and loitered by the school gates. So this was his old seat of learning, Sheckford Junior. So what? It might have meant something had she been with him.

There's the veranda where I used to sit with Belinda Smart, under our coats, feeding each other toffees. There's the playground where Johnny Dobson fought back against Mr. Addison. There's the school field where I got ambushed on my birthday and I was egged to within an inch of my life. Now it was all just memories. Then and now. No context. His life was a flatline without detail. Bedtime stories, and not very good ones at that.

He walked along the edge of the school grounds until he reached the gym. Everything the same. Everything changed. His youth was so close sometimes, he felt he could feel it beneath his fingers. He saw himself every day in any number of mirrors, and it was Don, it was him. But a photograph from even as recent as five years ago displayed to him a massive change in how he looked. His skin greyer now, his eyebrows lighter, his eyes more sunken. But he had not seen it happen. He had been tricked.

He was a prisoner to the calendar, he realized. He thought in little boxes that were to be ticked off and filled with things to do. Almost every day he thought back to what he had been doing ten years ago, twenty years ago, further. He lived in the past, by his diary. He was a history man, his head full of dead leaves. It was a form of reassurance, he knew. There were too many roads into the future and he didn't like not having a map for it.

Movement. He turned and gazed out over the school fields (*pelting Debbie Epstein with snow, winning the high jump and just missing out on the 800 meters title, kissing Penny Greig for the first time near the pavilion*) and saw a couple gesticulating wildly at each other as they raced across the grass towards the main road. She was having to run to keep up with him, her red scarf flapping at her throat like a terrible wound. She spotted Don and pointed at him. The man's head snapped up. Little hair. It was like a pink oval, a beige egg sitting on an elaborate eggcup. They arrowed towards him. The man was rolling his sleeves back as if setting himself for a scrap.

"Martin," she was calling. Don shook his head, but then realized she wasn't attempting to address him.

"Have you seen Martin?" Her voice was brittle. She was at the edge of tears.

"My boy," the man explained, and he was full of accusation. "Our boy. He was playing in our garden on Kent Lane, just down there at the foot of the fields. Keepy-uppy. In our garden."

"I was washing dishes," said the woman. "I could see him. And then

I went to empty the washing machine and when I came back he was gone and the back gate was swinging open."

"Maybe he kicked his ball over the wall," Don said.

"Martin is six," the man said, as if that was explanation enough.

"He can't reach the latch," the woman said.

"I haven't seen anyone," Don said. "I just got here."

The man looked him over as if Don might somehow be concealing Martin on his person. "The police," he said at last. "We have to bring the police into this."

"Oh, God," the woman said. And then she screamed Martin's name.

Don drove back to the hotel and forced himself to face up to what was going on. His coming here was nothing to do with a pilgrimage. It wasn't a personal tribute. It was running away. All of those responsibilities back home; they'd still be there when he returned. Debts and deadlines and demands. Julie was the soft barrier that prevented him injuring himself against all that bureaucracy. She organized, she delegated, she controlled. It might have lapped around their ankles occasionally, but the water never rose around their throats, as it seemed to be doing these days.

Now Julie was gone, every day was like crashing his car. There were impacts everywhere. He missed her so desperately it was as if he could still feel the mass of her in his hands. Her smell was in every room she'd inhabited. There were shadows and shades of her in everything he owned. When the sun shone she was splintered within it; when it rained, each drop carried a fragment of her reflection.

He had tried to find that snow globe of hers, after the crash. She took it everywhere with her. It had been a gift from her childhood. A lucky token. He had wandered around in the ruins for an age until the ambulances arrived, his face dripping into the snow around the wreckage, poking with his toe amidst the mangled aluminum, the torn fabric seat covers, the shreds of her. It was gone.

This is madness, he thought now, but there was no way he could stop being dragged under. To tackle that might mean he had to force her out of his life altogether and he was not ready for it.

The stress of the afternoon was in him like hot pins. The way that poor woman had screamed for her son. It was animalistic. He could understand her need. He had wanted to howl like that, for Julie. It built up inside you. You forgot who you were.

He tried to make the room comfortable enough so that Julie might come to him in some way. He needed to be warm and clean and relaxed. He bathed and drank a glass of whisky. He put her favorite music station on the radio. He sat by the window and closed his eyes. He determined what each sound was and relegated it to the back of his mind. There was space here for her.

He felt himself slide towards sleep. But she was not there to greet him. She had not been a part of this intimate darkness since before her death. It was as if, in dying, she had ceased to exist for him during the moments when he ought to be most receptive to her. Gazing at photographs of her was like assessing a stranger. She mugged for the camera. She was never her natural self. He felt panic at the thought that, day by day, this memory of the truth was gradually leaving him. It scared him more than the nightmares that were so ready to enter that vacuum he'd created just for her.

That evening, after another challenging meal in the hotel restaurant, Don sat in the bar nursing a glass of Scotch. He'd decided on an early night and a quick escape back to London in the morning. He'd look into therapy. He'd consider a holiday away from the UK. He needed to map out his career. Find a new hobby, some new friends. Do the unthinkable. Find someone else. *Why not just dig her up and spit into what's left of her face?*

"Hello again!"

"You bastard."

"Excuse me?"

"Sorry . . . Grant, isn't it? I'm very sorry. I was talking to myself. I was thinking about someone."

Kerner was observing him with a mixture of skepticism and distaste. "Really," Don pressed. "I'm sorry. That was aimed at me, actually."

The doubt in Kerner dissolved. Maybe he could see something in Don's own features, his posture. Defeat, quite possibly.

"Then I apologize for interrupting you."

"I'm glad you did. There's only so much abuse I can put up with."

Kerner laughed; the tension lessened. He assessed Don as if for the first time. There was a sense of him weighing up what to do next. Don could feel an invitation growing within; he was all too ready to refuse it. But he surprised himself by accepting, when Kerner asked if he would like to accompany him on a visit to Kayte's Cavern.

They walked. It was not far. There was a place to buy tickets and cheap souvenirs. A café. All of it closed now. A little display, showing the history of the cave and what had been found there. Roman coins and bones and bronze brooches. Over time, it had been a burial ground, a shelter, and the hideaway for a robber, the eponymous Nathaniel Kayte, who used the darkness and the depth and the churning noise of the water sluicing through it to his advantage when hiding from his pursuers.

Later it was a tourist trap. People traveled great distances to see the flowstone curtains, the stalactites and stalagmites, the great chambers of pale crystal, glowing in the dark as if lit from within. After that it became a big draw for the Victorians, who were led by candlelight deep into the cavern and then, the flames blown out by their canny guides, asked for more money if they wished to be taken back to safety.

"Isn't it a bit late for this?" Don asked again. "I thought you meant we'd go in the morning."

"Caves are dark whether the sun's shining or the moon's up, no?" Kerner said. "My mate's on duty tonight. We can get in without paying. And anyway, the cavern's closed while they do some exploratory digging. I think they're going to go deep. Open up some new chamber that has never before been seen by human eyes." Kerner deepened his voice at this last sentence, turning to Don and peering at him with theatrical menace.

"What's your interest in this place?" Don asked Kerner as a black-clad figure in a peaked cap swung open the gates and directed them to the cavern's mouth. "I thought you photographed broken things."

"Not exclusively. Anyway, I'm not working. I might not even switch my camera on."

There were signs saying NO ENTRY and DANGER. Another which read: CLOSED TO THE PUBLIC UNTIL JANUARY. Don felt a pang of claustrophobia when he saw the size of the entrance. He would have to bend over slightly, and then the gap narrowed and the ceiling came down farther and it was as if he were being swallowed by some gigantic, scabrous throat.

When the cave was first discovered, back in the 1500s (Kerner explained), long before explosives were used to blast a more comfortable passage, you had to crawl through on your belly.

Don felt water drip on to his neck. He could feel the damp in the air. There were footlights guiding you into the cavern along a concretized strip, but then the cave floor took over and it was uneven, treacherous. There was a giddy moment when he wasn't sure if he was even the right way up.

We become so used to flatness, to stability, he almost said to Kerner. The horizon and the vertical. Take the straight lines away and we lose direction.

Kerner seemed to have no such problem. The bigger man bustled through the gap as if he were pushing himself to the front of the queue on sale day.

"Shouldn't we have a guide?" Don asked.

"No guides for us," Kerner said. "I know this place like the back of my gland. I slipped Mac back there a tenner. He's happy to warm his hands on another cup of tea. We're doing his patrol for him. We're doing a public duty."

Don didn't like that. He had never strayed too far away from the rules. Even when teaching, he stuck to the tried and tested. A gradual accumulation of knowledge. A natural progression. Chords. Barre chords. Finger-picking. Scales. Power chords and riffs were not on his syllabus. It was lazy. It was a fast track to sloppy playing. You had to have the foundation. Deep roots. Core. He was an oak, Don decided now, enjoying the analogy. It was distracting him from the pressing in of the cave walls. He was an oak to Kerner's weak bough, flapping in the wind.

"You've been in here before then?" Don asked, to stop himself from laughing.

"Many times. I could serve as a guide myself, I reckon."

"Do you have a torch?" The entrance lights only illuminated so far. Up ahead, the blackness was deeper than anything Don had ever known. He had never thought of the dark possessing a physicality, but that's what it seemed like. There was substance in it. You'd be forgiven for thinking you had to pierce some part of it in order to get through at all.

"We don't need a torch," Kerner said.

"What are you, part owl?"

Kerner chuckled. And then light exploded around them. Don felt suddenly foolish. The space within the cavern was voluminous. The ceiling of it was sixty, seventy feet from where they were standing. Its geology seemed a living thing. It was sinuous in some places, jagged in others. He sensed Kerner watching him, his finger on a light switch hidden behind a curtain of rock.

"Timer switch," Kerner said. "Switches off automatically, after a while. This place closed down in the 1950s. Lack of interest. Nobody to fund it. It was taken over in the 1970s. Given a real spring clean. They put in the electricity then. No more of those dodgy gas lamps the Victorians used."

"The rock," Don said. He wasn't sure what he meant to follow that with. It seemed anything he might say would not do justice to his surroundings.

"Amazing, isn't it?"

"That it is."

"Limestone, in the main," Kerner said, clearly relishing his role. "You're looking at rock that was formed around three hundred and fifty million years ago, when modest little Derbyshire was part of a continental landmass close to the equator. Volcanic activity pushed the limestone up and into the fractures that were created, hot minerals poured. So you've got your galena, your fluorspar, your barites, your calcite. Veins and seams. Ore. This glittering wonderland. This cave was formed by water. Rain becomes acidic when it passes through organic matter, like soil, as I'm sure you know. It dissolved the limestone. Streams eroded it further. You can hear the water crashing through. We'll see it up ahead. All this water coming through here, it's been going on for two million years."

My God, thought Don. He thought of Julie. She would have loved this. She had been dead for one year. The water coming through here, it was difficult to imagine it would ever stop. It would still be sluicing through two million years hence. The cave wider, deeper, but essentially the same. People coming and going so quickly, like glyphs on the pages of a flicker book.

The colors were amazing. Blues and greys and greens. Orange heating up to red. Stalagmites reached up to stalactites, fangs in a closing jaw.

"How big is the cave?"

"Who knows," Kerner said. "It extends farther than anybody thought. Come on, I'll show you."

They advanced through the cave, and it expanded around them. Handrails and steps had been put in. The electric lights, subtly positioned, showed off the ripples and thrusts of rock while ensuring there was no chance of becoming lost. Behind them, the lights shut off, like portions of a stage during a play. It was all very dramatic.

Don gradually relaxed. Kerner was a knowledgeable and amiable guide and Don grew to become grateful for his company. They walked through various sections, separated by natural kinks in the path they were following; all were given grandiose names: Hall of the Kings, The Chamber of Hanging Knives, Grey Lion's Lair. The names were attributed to the shapes in the rock. Some looked like crowns, or daggers, or a flowing mane. It was like hunting for faces in the fire, or the clouds.

The path ran out at a boulder choke surrounded with safety rails and more threatening red signs. Don had been so engaged by the alien surroundings, the assault of the cold and the clean, mineral flavor in his nostrils and throat, that he'd completely forgotten about the lump on his cheek. But now, as its pain re-announced itself to him, he stopped and pressed his hand to his skin.

"Okay?" Kerner asked.

"Yeah, just . . . I don't know. Spot or something."

"Oh, I noticed that too, but I didn't say anything."

Don tried to laugh it off but the sound came out all wrong. Beautiful place, unkind acoustics. "I'm turning into a teenager again," he said.

"You should maybe see a doctor. It might be an infection. You don't want it to become an abscess or anything like that. They'll have to cut a big chunk out of you. Bad scars. I have photographs of people, post-op. People who had tumors. One guy who was bitten by a flea or a tic or something. Half his face turned rotten, virtually slid off him. Imagine that."

Don tried to ignore him. He removed the sticking plaster from his skin and pushed ahead, leaving Kerner to his study of a small, visible stretch of churning water. His fingers fretted at the sore. The surrounding skin was puffed up and tender. There was a hard core beneath. It wobbled under the dome of taut skin, making him queasy. Maybe it was the air pressure that was nagging at it. Or the cold. Something was being drawn out. Maybe it was just time. The body healed itself of most things, given enough time.

"Look, see," Kerner said. He was pointing at a small hole in a cluster of rocks at the foot of the choke. "They dropped cameras through that last year and found a huge . . . I don't know how you'd describe it . . . amphitheater of white rock. They dubbed it 'the blizzard bowl.' Crystal city. Like landing in one of those daft ornaments, you know. What are they called?"

"Snow globes," Don whispered.

"Snow globes, yeah. That's the chappy. Anyway, the idea is they're going to send a man down there. Apparently there's a guy known as Rat lives in the village. Spelunker *extraordinaire*. He can squirm his way into holes like that. No fear in him. He's going to see what's what and then they're going to open the whole thing up. I mean, it's anyone's guess. How far can you go? There might be worlds upon worlds beyond that blizzard bowl. Who knows what we might find? There are new species being discovered every day in the rainforests."

There was a moment, just as the lights were turned off, and they began the walk back to the cavern entrance, when Don thought he heard the scrabble of movement, but he chose not to mention it, because he didn't want to appear nervous or stupid to Kerner. The slide of insecure pebbles. A rat, or a bat. It was nothing.

"Let's have a pic," Kerner said, when they were outside. He got Mac to take a photograph of them, standing in front of the cavern entrance, and then they were ushered out of the grounds and it was much colder out here and the stars were studs of glass scattered across an oily hard shoulder.

"Nightcap?" Kerner asked.

Don shook his head. "I'm wiped," he said. "Thanks for an interesting evening."

"Sad to leave ya, Eurasian beaver."

"Good night."

Again. Did it become a ritual if it happened more than once?

A hot bath. The Scotch. The music she loved. *Oh, I could drink a case of you.* He mustered the memory of the smells that made her who she was. Tea tree oil. Fennel. He thought back to the last time they had made love. The flush of red on her chest. The eyes closing. The quickening of her breath. *Don, Don.*

Sleep was over him and around him, closing, like a thin blanket, but it was not yet in him. His breath deepened. His eyes rolled back. He submitted himself. Sleep sank into him like something taking a bite. And just at the moment he felt himself go under, he was aware, in the dark, of a shape at the foot of his bed. It was heart-shaped, a muted grey, and it took awhile to understand that it was the shape of someone's back: the arms and head lost to shadow. Slowly, it shifted. He heard the shiver of nylon moving against itself. He saw the nubs of vertebrae in a spine curve subtly against the fabric of a cardigan. And it was *her* cardigan. His heart leaped. Until:

Why are you doing this?

He flinched. Her voice was too close, as if she were whispering in his ear. And there was something wrong with it. She sounded as though she was thirsty. The voice, full of holes.

I love you but you have to let me go don't blame yourself

"Julie? Julie, what can I do? Where are you?" He stared at the figure at the end of the bed as it stretched and writhed. "Don't leave me. It was so sudden."

I have to go I want to go to the white I want to run through the snow you can set me free

The shush of her nylons . . . but she never wore tights.

"Julie?" He jerked upright in bed, blinking himself awake. The shape toppled forward, turning. Her hair fell across her face so he could see only a sliver of gleaming eye through the mouse-blonde bands of it. She raised her thin limbs and showed him where she'd cut through the veins of her arms with the shattered remnants of her snow globe.

The blood hissing like water from punctured hoses, eternal.

I'd have killed myself anyway, eventually . . . don't blame yourself

In the second it took him to wrench himself free of the bedclothes, winter sunshine was streaming through the window and his alarm clock was droning and she was gone. He turned back to see his pillow, streaked with red. A pebble of glass sitting there like something the tooth fairy had forgotten to collect.

"Whoa, pal. Easy. What bit you this morning?"

Don had dropped his glass of cranberry juice. He watched the spreading red stain around his breakfast plates and tried to stop his hands from shaking. Surely everyone could see that. They'd think he'd been drinking at daybreak. Or that he had something terrible to hide. Kerner watched him while he chewed his interminable muesli. His question hung in the air. Don ignored it.

He poured coffee and tried to hide in its steam. The plaster on his face felt tight and itchy, but he wasn't going to sit there with a wet hole flapping in front of all these people while they tucked into their grilled tomatoes.

After his shower that morning he'd noticed there were other points on his face beginning to flare up. Most worryingly, there was an ache building behind his left eye. Another in his chest. The windscreen had shattered into a million pieces. How many of them had disappeared inside him? How many were now worming their way out, rejected by his flesh after the slow journey of a year? In the horror of it, came the thrill. The glass might have connected him to his wife. What if, as he had read once, it was possible for slivers of glass to pass through your body? Perhaps some of them had become embedded in her. He was in her, then, after a fashion. And now that he was here, in Sheckford, some numinous frequency, made in blood, had been opened between them. It was the kind of thing she believed in. The end was never the end. We were all passengers in transit.

"There's something wrong with my camera," Kerner said. "Just found out this morning."

"I think there's a camera shop in the village. Maybe they'd have a look at it for you." Don hated the sound of his own voice. It was weak, pathetic, more so since his eventful night.

"Not this. Specialist job, I reckon. Fault somewhere. And not with my picture-taking abilities, for once. It's as if I'd forgotten to take the film out and rewound it and taken more exposures over the top."

"Have you checked that?"

Kerner gave him a look. He checked his watch. "Hmm," he said. "Says here that it's still the twenty-first century. That must mean I've got a digital camera."

The sudden, spearing conclusion that he didn't like Kerner. Don was glad his camera was knackered. He hoped it would cost him a fortune to repair it.

"Look, see," Kerner said, pushing his bowl to one side and setting the expensive camera on the table. He pressed a few buttons and the screen on the rear flashed up a picture: the one Mac had taken the previous evening.

Don came around the table and squinted at the glass oblong. "Christ," he said.

The two of them, standing in front of the cavern entrance, the blue guide lights set into the floor illuminating them from below, giving them an unhealthy, cyanotic glow. Shadows falling on the uneven rock behind them: Kerner's, Don's, and someone else's.

"See that?"

"Yeah. It can't be Mac's shadow, can it?"

"Hey?" Kerner leaned in closer. "I hadn't actually noticed that. I was talking about that . . . glow, in your chest."

Now Don saw it. In roughly the position where his heart might be, a fist-sized lump of grainy light, like the diffuse aura cast by a sodium street lamp. He pressed his fingers to his breastbone.

"What could it be?" he asked. His voice sounded perilously close to choking. Tears ganged up. But Kerner seemed not to notice.

"Could just be some hot pixels on the sensor, maybe. Maybe a lens problem. But I have some pictures I took before and after, and they seem clean. That shadow you point out though . . . it's obvious something's not right. Bollocks. It's quality glass that. Spent a fortune on it . . ."

"I have to go," Don said.

Kerner nodded, smiled. His fingers fidgeted with the buttons on the camera body. "*Adieu,* caribou."

Go home. Leave this place. Let it sink into time, let it become a fossil in your memory.

But how could it? This was as much Julie's place as his now. They were inextricably linked by Sheckford, the things that happened to them here.

He was back in his room, standing in front of the mirror, his shirt off, staring at his chest, willing the glow to reappear. *It's you, isn't it? Julie?*

He switched on the light and his breath caught. Two shadows. But one was merely a copy of the other, bounced back by the silvered glass. He pressed his fingers against his skin and felt something hard. It was like a swelling. All of the other hot spots of pain in his skin sang out. He buttoned his shirt and returned to the bedroom. There was a sense of someone having just departed. The mattress seemed to be rising slightly, where it might have cushioned a body moments before. There was a slight shift in the temperature of the room. A microscopic change in its pressures.

I want to go to the white I want to run through the snow

The crystal snow globe had been so important to her. It had been with her for much of her life, and it had helped to end it too. She had often told him how lovely it would be to live in a snow globe, to be protected from all the evils in the outside world by that perfect glass. The silence, the beauty.

He was out of the hotel and walking hard along the street before he had any concrete notion of where he was heading.

His mind was filled with white.

Mac let him through the gate but was unsympathetic when Don told him he might have lost his car keys in the cavern. "It's not really my job to go hunting for lost property. I'm a security guard."

"I'll go," Don said.

"I don't think so. This isn't a drive-through restaurant. You don't just pop back whenever you feel like it."

A twenty-pound note changed his mind.

Don steeled himself at the entrance, but only because the pain in his chest ramped up a notch. It was like heartburn, only a hundred times worse. He thought he might retch, but nothing would come when he leaned over. Something felt sharp just beneath the skin. Something was coming.

He could hear the water plowing over and under and through the rock as it had done for so many millions of years. It had churned through this cavern at the moment of his birth and at the moment of Julie's death. He staggered along the pathway, grateful for its enormous sound; it meant he did not have to listen to his own skin tearing open.

He reached the boulder choke and stared at the foot of it, where the tiny opening was like a pupil in a dead eye. He imagined great acres of untouched white crystal beyond it, like a field of virgin snow before the children have wakened, like Heaven.

"Julie?" he called out, but his voice was unable to best the roar. It hurt too much to try again. He felt his chest fail, and lifted his hands as if he might prevent himself from tipping out on the cold, wet path. What was there in his chest cut his hand. Blood sped from him, slicking his fingers. It was difficult now, to find purchase on the slippery curve of the glass in him.

He saw movement at the lip of the aperture. Julie? But of course it wasn't. What could he have hoped from this? Julie was cold and dead as the piece of glass within him.

Long, white nails attached to long white fingers. The skin of something eternally damp, of something that had never known sunlight. It skittered out, all elbows and fish-thin ribs pulsing beneath translucency. A sore-looking jaw, red-rimmed, loaded with icy needles that glittered like hoarfrost, shreds of the missing packed between them. It made a sound that was almost beyond a frequency audible to him. It sounded like metal scraped across glass. It turned an eye to him that was as pale as moonstones.

Don turned to run, but his foot slid in his own filth. The chunk in his chest shifted. As he gripped it and pulled, closing his eyes to the terrible suck as the glass came free, the lights went out and the thing fell on him, all too keen to lend its assistance.

City of Dreams

RICHARD CHRISTIAN MATHESON

RICHARD CHRISTIAN MATHESON is a novelist, short story writer, and screenwriter/producer. He is also the president of Matheson Entertainment—a production company he formed with his father, Richard Matheson—which is currently involved with multiple film and television projects.

His credits include *Sole Survivor*, a four-hour Fox television miniseries based on Dean Koontz's best-selling novel; *Delusion*, an original horror suspense film for VH1; *Demons*, an original dark suspense film for Showtime, and the adaptation of Roger Zelazny's *The Chronicles of Amber* as a four-hour miniseries for the Syfy Channel.

Matheson also created and wrote *Majestic*, a one-hour paranormal series for TNT based on the work of Whitley Strieber, and he is currently in development with director Bryan Singer on the six-hour miniseries *Dragons*. The author also recently created *Splatter*, a web-based horror project with Roger Corman, directed by Joe Dante.

Some of Matheson's seventy-five short stories are collected in *Scars and Other Distinguishing Marks*, with an Introduction by Stephen King, and *Dystopia*. His debut novel, *Created By*, was a Bram Stoker Award nominee, and his new, dark novella about Hollywood, *The Ritual of Illusion*, is available from PS Publishing.

Matheson has described the inspiration behind "City of Dreams": "On my parents' backyard deck, it's possible to hear snippets of conversation, like bits of an escaped séance, from the nearest neighbor's home.

"The spectral effect of these half-murmurs and incomplete stirrings, as if a Rorschach for the ear, tends to invite interpretation and, though high pines and moody breezes divide the acre-plus properties and mask detail, theories arise, as mimosas are sipped, as to what the hell is going on over there.

"Several years ago, the house next door sold rather suddenly and a new owner moved in: identity unknown. Moving men filled the empty house with unmarked boxes, and security cameras were installed at key perimeter zones. It seemed something big and embroiled was up over there. On the deck, speculations brimmed.

"Was it Nixon, in shattered exile? Dylan? Johnny Carson, drained by decades of feigned interest? Joe Namath, tending to his aching dimples? Garbo? Brian Wilson, hanging-ten off his melting psyche? John Gotti gone to the mattresses? Gore Vidal grinning carnivorously, dodging burdens of ennui?

"We entertained all icons, fallen or exalted, from every venue of fame, and had a full story to go with why they'd ended up next door. Whether by tragedy, glory, intended crime, sick passion, or alibi, as in all persuasive narrative, twisted motive was central to our theories of their residence. We never got to the bottom of any of them, but an addictive pastime was born.

"Years later, I wrote a story that considered the fixations of a screenwriter who overhears a secretive, unseen neighbor, of imagined prestige, who has just moved in next door. I bruised its comic tones with some heartache and added an overly sensitive parrot. It's one of my favorite pieces.

"As it turned out, a celebrity did move in beside my parents, all those years ago. They have never yet been seen on the property. Mimosas continue to pour."

IT WAS JUNE WHEN the Royal moved in.

I knew because high, metal fences started going up, perimeter shrubbery doubled, and two sullen Dobermans began patrolling. Then, overnight, an intercom, numerical keypad, and security camera were mysteriously installed at the bottom of the Royal's driveway, which ran alongside mine. Whenever I drove by, the lens would zoom to inspect me, staring with curt inquisition.

The Royal was obviously concerned who visited.

Had the Royal been hurt? Was future hurt likely? Were death threats being phoned in hourly? It seemed anything, however dire, was possible. I was already feeling bad for the Royal.

I didn't know if the Royal was a him or her. Rock diva? Zillionaire cyber tot? Mob boss? Pro-leaguer? My mind wandered in lush possibility.

But all I ever saw was a moody limo that purred through the gate and crunched up the long driveway. By the time it got to the big house, the forest landscaping hid it—a leafy moat. I found it all rather troubling. In my experience, concealment is meaningful; trees can be trimmed, the fears which lurk behind them are a different story. Ultimately, one cannot hide, only camouflage. Orson Welles certainly understood this; in *Citizen Kane*, tragic privilege never seemed so rapturous, nor incarcerated.

As days passed, I tried not to listen to what went on next door. I'd play jazz CDs, sip morning espresso, scan the entertainment section for reviews to distract my attentions. But my community is exclusive and quiet, and birds' wings, as they groom, are noticeable. It made it hard to miss the Royal's limo as it sighed up the driveway, obscured by the half million dollars of premeditated forest. Once parked, doors would open and close, and I'd hear footsteps, sometimes cheerless murmurs; the limo driver speaking to the Royal, I assumed. Russian? Indo-Chinese? Impossible to tell. Then, the front door to the house would slam with imperial finality.

It went on like that for two weeks.

I began to think, perhaps, I should be a better neighbor, make the Royal feel more welcome; a part of the local family. Which is somewhat misleading considering the neighborhood is an aloof haven and I barely know anyone. I'm like that; keep to myself, make friends slowly. I'm what they call an observer. Some dive, I float with mask and snorkel. But the instinct seemed warm, welcoming.

I was also getting very curious.

I was up late writing one night, and decided to mix up a batch of chocolate chip cookies. My new screenplay was coming along well, if slowly, and I thought about love scenes and action scenes as I peered into the oven, watching the huge cookies rise like primitive islands forming. They were plump, engorged with cubes of chocolate the size of small dice; worthy of a Royal, I decided.

I let them cool, ate three, wrapped the remaining dozen in tinfoil. Crumpled the foil to make it resemble something snappy and Audubon, the way they make crinkly swans in nice places to shroud leftovers. I wrapped a bow around the neck, placed the tinfoil bird into a pretty box I'd saved from Christmas, ribboned it, found a greeting card with no message. The photo on the front was a natural cloud formation that looked a bit like George Lucas.

I used my silver-ink pen that flows upside down, like something a doomed astronaut might use to write a final entry, and wrote: *Some supplies to keep you happy and safe. Researchers say chocolate brings on the exact sensation of love; an effect of phenylethylamine. (Just showing off.) Welcome to this part of the world.*

My P.S. was a phone number, at the house, in case the Royal ever needed anything. I also included a VHS of François Truffaut's *Day for Night*, a film I especially love for its tipsy discernment.

I debated whether to include any exclamation marks, thought it excess, opted for periods. Clean, emotionally stable. Friendly but not cloying. Being in the film business, I knew first impressions counted.

It's one reason I'm sought after to do scripts, albeit for lesser films with sinking talents. But I'm well paid and it allows me to live in this secured community near L.A., complete with gate guard, acre parcels, and compulsory privacy. I'm an anonymous somebody; primarily rumor. I wish I could've been Faulkner, but there you are. I'm a faceless credit on a screen; my scant reply to a world's indifference.

I left the cookies and card in the Royal's mailbox, at the bottom of the driveway, and spoke tense baby talk to the Dobermans as I made the deposit, like one of those pocked thugs in *The French Connection*. The package fit nicely, looked cheerful in there. Too much so? I considered it. Every detail determines outcome; it's the essence of subtext, as Frank Capra once observed. And certainly, if the Royal were truly an international sort, I wanted there to be room for some kind of friendship. I could learn things. Get gossip that mattered; the chic lowdown.

I waited two days. A week.

Nothing.

I'd sit by my pool every morning, read the paper, scan box-office numbers, sip espresso. But I wasn't paying full attention. I was watching my Submariner tick.

At 10:30 sharp, the heavy tires would crunch up the driveway and the door ritual would begin. I couldn't make out a word and tried to remember if I'd left my phone number in the P.S. Even if not, there was always my mailbox. Concern was devouring me by ounces and I disliked seeing it happen.

In self-protection, I began to lose interest in the Royal; the inky sleigh, the seeming apathy, the whole damn thing.

At least that's what I tried to tell myself.

Sergio Leone says the important thing about filmmaking is to make a world that is "not now." A *real* world, a *genuine* world, but one that allows myth its vital seepage. Sergio contends that myth is everything. I suppose one could take that too far.

Two weeks passed quickly and I'd heard nothing. I felt deflated, yet oddly exhilarated to be snubbed by someone so important; it bordered on eerie intoxicant, even hinted at voodoo. Despite efforts otherwise, the truth was I continued to wonder what the Royal thought about me, though it hardly constituted preoccupation.

I'm a bit sensitive on the topic because my ex-wife often said I paid unnatural attention to those I considered remarkable, though I found nothing strange in such focus. The way I see it, we all need heroes: dreams of something better, perhaps even transcendent. A key piece of miscellany: she ran off with a famous hockey player from Ketchikan, Alaska, a slab of idiocy named Stu. *Time* and *Newsweek* covered their nuptials. Color photos, confetti, the whole bit. A featured quote from her gushed: "I've never been happier!"

Real pain. Like I'd been shot.

I feel it places things, as regards my outlook, in perspective. She certainly never could. Strangely enough, I've been thinking about her lately; how she drove me into psychotherapy after she left and took our African Grey, Norman, with her and never contacted me again, saying I'd made them both miserable. Over time, I heard from mutual friends that she was claiming, among other toxic side effects of our marriage, that I'd caused Norman to stop talking, and that once they'd set up house elsewhere, he became a chatterbox. I took it personally; couldn't sleep for weeks.

More haunting facts of my teetering world.

The fate of the cookies preyed on my mind for days, affecting work and sleep, a predicament rife with what my ex-shrink, Larry, used to term "emotional viscosity," a condition I suspect he made up, hoping it would catch on and bring him, and his unnerving beard, acclaim. Still, I wrote halfheartedly and my stomach churned the kind of butter that really clogs you up.

Another few days went by and I made no move. Any choice seemed wrong; quietude the only wisdom. I was feeling foolish; mocked. My heartfelt efforts had been more irrelevant than I'd feared. I continued to work on my screenplay, and joked emptily with my agent, who seemed an especially drab series of noises compared to the person I knew the Royal must be.

It's true, I had no real evidence. The Royal might be an overwhelming bore. Some rich cadaver in an iron lung, staring bitterly into a tiny mirror.

But I didn't think so.

In fact, I was beginning to think anyone who went to such trouble to avoid a friendly overture had something precious to protect. On a purely personal level, if cookies, a card, and a badly executed foil swan could scare a person, their levels of sensitivity had to be finely calibrated. Perhaps the Royal had been wounded; given up on humanity. I've been there. I wish somebody like me tried to crack the safe; get me the hell out.

But when's the last time life had a heart? Let's face it, unsoothed by human kindness, souls recede. It's in all the great movies: pain, sacrifice, hopes in dissolution.

It's how people like me and the Royal got the way we are. We flee emotionally, too riddled by personal travail to venture human connection. Sort of like Norman. We're just recovering believers, choking on the soot of an angry world.

I understood the Royal. Yet I had to move on; get over it.

But it was hard. Maybe I was simply in some futile trance, succumbed to loneliness and curiosity. I admit I'm easily infected by my enthusiasms. You read about people like me; the ones who do something crazy in the name of human decency only to find themselves stuffed, hung on a wall; poached by life.

So, despite rejection, I found myself listening each morning, over breakfast, to the Royal's property, gripped by speculation. Awaiting the door ritual, sensing the Royal over there, alone, needing a friend. It was sad and nearly called out for a melancholic soundtrack; something with strings; that haunted Bernard Herrmann ambivalence.

It made me recall a line I once heard in a bleak Fassbinder movie; this Munich prostitute whispered to her lover that a person's fate "always escorts the bitter truth." She blew Gitane smoke, pouting with succulent blankness and, to my embarrassment, it just spoke to me. I don't know why. It got me thinking, I suppose, the ways movies can; even the sorry, transparent ones.

It was the first time I began to consciously wish I could do a second draft of me, start things over; find my life a more worthy plot, tweak the main character. Maybe even find a theme. A man without one has nowhere to hide.

Ingmar Bergman based a career on it.

Two days later, the note came.

In my mailbox, dozing in an expensive, rag-cloth envelope. It was hand-written, the letters a sensual perfection.

We must meet. How about
drinks tonight over here.
Around sunset?

I must have read it a hundred times, weighing each word, the phrasing and inclusion of the word "must." It seemed not without meaning.

I debated outfits. Formal? Casual? I was able to make a case for either; chose slacks, a sweater. I looked nice; thought it important. Before heading over, I considered a gift. Cheese? An unopened compact disc? Mahler? Coltrane? But it strained of effort and I wanted to seem offhand, worth knowing. The way Jimmy Stewart always was: presuming nothing, evincing worlds.

I used the forgotten path between the two driveways, dodging the Dobermans, who seemed to expect me, tilting heads with professional interest, beady eyes ashimmer.

I walked to the front door. Knocked. Waited two minutes, listened for footsteps, and was about to knock again, when the door opened.

She was *exquisite.*

Maybe twenty. Eyes and dress mystic blue, dark hair, medium length. Skin, countess-pale. She wore a platinum locket, and gauged me for a moment.

"Hello," she said, in the best voice I've ever heard, up till then, or since.

We spent an hour talking about everything, though I learned little about her. At some point, she said her name was Aubrey and I'm sure I responded, though I was lost in her smile, her attentions colorizing my world.

It seemed she told me less about herself with each passing minute, which I liked; she was obviously the real thing. Genuine modesty looks best on the genuinely important.

She asked me about my work and carefully listened as I spoke about why I loved the music of words and the fantasy of movies; of creating perfect impossibilities. Her rare features silhouetted on mimosa sunset, and she said she'd always loved films, especially romantic ones, and when her smile took my heart at gunpoint, I felt swept into a costly special effect, a trick of film and moment, as if part of a movie in which I'd been terribly miscast; my presence too common to properly elevate the material.

She took my hand, and when we walked outside and watched stars daisy the big pool, I thought I must be falling in love. I still think I was, despite everything soon to befall me.

After a slow walk around her fountained garden, she said she was tired and needed her rest, that she'd come a very long way. I wish I'd thought to ask for details of that journey; an oversight which torments me to this second.

Aubrey slowly slipped her delicate hands around my waist and it almost seemed like loss had found us; a moment nearly cinematic in composition.

She said she had a gift for me, and led me to a wrapped package that rested on a chaise, near the pool.

"I made it," she said.

"A painting?" I guessed, reaching to open it, until she gently stopped me.

"Tomorrow," she suggested. "When you're alone."

It seemed she was being dramatic. I wish it had been anywhere near that simple.

"Good night." Her full lips uncaged the word, as she looked up into my eyes, vulnerably.

I protested, wanting to know more about her, but she placed her mouth to my ear.

"I've always looked for you out there," she said softly, voice a despairing melody. "In the dark. I've wondered what you were like."

"What do you mean?" I finally replied, lost.

She never answered and I watched her disappear into the mansion, with a final wave, and what I would describe in a script, if I had to tell the actress what to convey, as veiled desperation.

The next morning, I slept so deeply I didn't even hear the car that sped up my driveway. It wasn't until the knocking that I finally awakened.

When the detective spoke, I felt the earth die.

"A break-in?" I repeated in a voice that had to sound in need of medical attention.

He explained the missing piece was valuable, purchased in London, at auction. The chauffeur had told the police the owner of the house was a collector, but gave no further details.

"It was a gift. She gave it to me." I explained.

"She?"

"Aubrey." I could still see her plaintive eyes, desperate for connection. "The woman who lives there."

He said nothing.

Asked if he could see it.

I nodded and took him to my living room, where it leaned against the big sofa. He slowly, silently, unwrapped it and my world began to vanish.

The poster was full-color, gold-framed.

It was from the 1930s, and the star was a stunning brute named Dan Drake; unshaven and clefted. His beautiful co-star was Isabella Ryan, and she was held in his embrace as the two stood atop Mulholland Drive, windblown; somehow doomed. Behind them, a stoic L.A. glittered, morose precincts starved of meaning. Though striking, no splendor could be found in its image, merely loss. The movie was titled *City of Dreams*, but I'd never heard of it.

Isabella's eyes and dress were mystic blue; her flowing dark hair and pale skin more regal than the platinum locket adorning her slender neck.

From any angle, no matter how inaccurately observed, she not only resembled Aubrey, she was her.

It was shocking to me in a way I'd never experienced, and I nearly felt some cruel director zooming onto my numbed expression for the telling close-up.

Both stars had signed at the bottom.

To everyone who ever loved. Yours, Dan Drake.

Beside his, in delicate script was:

I've always seen you out there. You're in my dreams. Love, Isabella Ryan.

She seemed to be looking right at me, disguising a profound fear.

Charges were never brought against me, and the sunken-faced detective said I'd gotten off easy, that my neighbor, still unnamed, didn't want trouble and was giving me a second chance. The Royal only wanted the poster back, nothing more. For me, this generosity stirred further mystique, intolerable distress.

It's futile to determine who I'd actually spent the evening with; I don't believe in ghosts unless they are of the emotional variety; aroused by seances of personal misfortune, you might say.

But this thought brings no peace, no clarity.

I looked up *City of Dreams* in one of my movie books and found it: *1942, MGM. Black and white. Suspense. 123 minutes.* There was a related article about Isabella, an airbrushed studio photo beside her husband, the obscure composer Malcolm Zinner. Zinner was bespectacled, intense. It appeared their marriage had been loveless.

The book said she'd had a nervous breakdown, but then don't they all? She'd never done another movie after *City of Dreams*, despite promising reviews, and died in a plane crash, in 1953. The book said her real name was Aubrey Baker.

Truffaut said that film is truth, twenty-four frames per second. Mine seems to be moving rather slower these days, my heart circling itself. I feel drenched by confusion; a lost narrative. I am drawn to unhealthy theory and wonder if perhaps I am dying.

Maybe I've just seen too many movies.

My ex-wife used to say the thing about irony is you never see it coming; that's how you know it's there. Also, the bigger it is, the more its invisibility and caprice. She used to talk like that, in puzzles. I'm not sure what she was getting at, but there you are.

All I know is a movie poster with a long-dead beauty had been the most genuine thing I could remember in a lifetime of misappropriated and badly written fictions; it seemed a bad trend. Not even a particularly worthwhile plot, but I was never much good at that part.

Meanwhile, the Royal, it appears, is out there somewhere, hidden by lawyers; filtered and untouched. Bereft, bled by abuse and event; disfigurations of neglect.

It's been two months now, since that evening by the pool, and still no sign of the Royal, who remains at large in elite silence. I suppose I've given up thinking we'll ever actually meet, barring the extreme twist.

Sometimes, I find myself staring at the hand-written invitation, which I saved, though I have no idea who really wrote it. I stare until the words lift from the paper and fly away, scattering grammar into sky; an image Vittorio De Sica might have sparked to.

After considerable search, I finally found a copy of *City of Dreams* at a specialty video store, which had to track it down for me. When I watch Aubrey, despite her astonishing beauty, I keep thinking she looks trapped; not by bad dialogue or plot, but an apprehension of her life to be. Its imminent ruin.

Today, I tried to tell my agent why the dumb script I've been working on is late, and when he heard all of what had happened, he sighed and said writers were always getting themselves in crazy messes. He said he thought I'd probably seen Isabella's movie when I was a kid and forgotten about it.

He nearly accused me of drinking, again, and wondered if maybe I'd had too much one night, wandered around the Royal's house and seen the poster; decided I had to have it, succumbing to stupid nostalgia. To bring back my only good childhood memory; going to the movies.

The rest had been loveless, terrifying; an ordeal that lasted for endless seasons of pain.

I'm sure he's right. I do drink when I get lonely. I could take many evenings out of your life failing to convey the dread and hurt I often feel. I've had nights where I stared pointlessly, out at the world, and thought that no one could ever love me, just as, it seems, Isabella watches it from her lurid, heartbreaking poster, searching for the one face out there, in a heartless city, who will truly care.

Buñuel said every life is a film. Some good, some bad. We are, each of us, paradoxes in an unstated script; pawns who wish to know kings, souls divided, hearts in exile. We're all tragic characters, one way or the other; the vivid Technicolor glories, the *noir* hurts, the dissolve to final credits.

Fellini believed movies were magic, itself, awakened by light. That theaters were churches, dim and velvet; filled with incantation. All I know is that when you feel lost and wounded, movies always welcome you, like a friend, inviting you to forget the painful truth; embracing your most lightless fragilities, the sadnesses which bind you.

To dream of better things.

Life pales.

A House on Fire

TANITH LEE

TANITH LEE was born in North London. She did not learn to read—she is dyslexic—until almost age eight, and then only because her father taught her. This opened the world of books to her, and by the following year she was writing stories.

She worked in various jobs, including shop assistant, waitress, librarian, and clerk, before Donald A. Wollheim's DAW Books issued her novel *The Birthgrave* in 1975. The imprint went on to publish twenty-six more of her novels and collections.

Since then Lee has written around ninety books and nearly 300 short stories. Four of her radio plays have been broadcast by the BBC, and she also scripted two episodes of the cult TV series *Blakes 7*.

Her recent books include *Greyglass* and *To Indigo* from Immanion Press, and ongoing reissues of *The Birthgrave* and *StormLord* trilogies from Norilana Books, along with a short story collection, *Sounds and Furies*. Another recent collection, *Disturbed by Her Song* from Lethe Press, was short-listed for the LAMBDA Award for gay, lesbian, and transgender fiction.

In 1992 she married the writer/artist/photographer John Kaiine, her companion since 1987. They live on the Sussex Weald, near the sea, in a house full of books and plants, with two black-and-white overlords called cats.

"I think the idea for this story was with me for about eighteen months before I took the opportunity to write it," recalls Lee. "The idea's basis came from John—a suggestion of juggling the traditional concept of ghost-haunts-house. I then figured out the method of death(s), and the only possible title instantly arrived."

Edwin Marsh Onslowe strangled his mistress, Mrs. Violet North, in the early February of 1885. In order to conceal the crime, he then set a fire in her otherwise unoccupied and remotely situated house, which accordingly burned to the ground during the night. As their elicit affair had been scrupulously hidden by both parties, Onslowe was not even suspected of having anything to do either with the fire itself, or with the demise of Mrs. North. The latter was in fact judged carelessly and accidentally to have burned to death. Some time later, however, Edwin Onslowe presented himself at a police station and freely confessed to arson and murder. He was subsequently found guilty and hanged.

The reason he gave for his confession has, ever since, remained the subject for perplexed debate.

—*Derwent's Legal Mysteries*

THE HEAT OF THE FIRE on his face—

It was burning. *Burning* . . .

Traveling up on the train through a fading afternoon into the first encroachment of dusk, he was a little excited. More at the element of adventure, of course, than at seeing Violet again. She was hardly any longer a novelty.

In fact they had met five years before, and from the very start had carried on their rather intermittent affair in just this way, which was that of *subterfuge*. It had been for her sake. A married woman with a great amount to lose, she had had to be persuaded, or to persuade herself. Besides, their earliest meetings took place in spying, gossipy London, in a succession of small hotels somewhere between the Strand and the Hibernian Road.

To each of these they went separately, meeting near the agreed venue, pretending thereafter to be a married couple bound for Charing Cross Station and the boat train, and having to break an arduous journey in order to rest for three or four hours. Edwin, this scenario in mind, would always arrive with a pair of spurious bags—the other luggage having "already gone on ahead." No doubt that would have been quite enough to sustain their ploy. They were never challenged, treated with unsuspicious courtesy, and served tea at the end of their sessions. However, Edwin had instantly enhanced the little play.

Both he and she were to dress in modest clothes rather unlike their generally more elegant garments (for Violet, through her legal husband was rich, and Edwin, if hardly wealthy, still quite well off). Edwin, too, might employ a wig, even a false moustache. These he would apply, and later slough, in some convenient if chancy doorway or alley found en route. They would, each of them, talk in less polished accents and more hackneyed terms, as befitted apparel and hotel.

They would keep this up from the moment of publicly meeting until the bedroom door closed fast on their supposed siesta. Which was, evidently, the exact opposite of restful. Emerging after, they would continue their roles, mildly genteel little nobodies, until they parted, then without any visible sign of affection or even of ever having known each other, somewhere in the warren of streets.

Violet herself seemed to enjoy their game. Sometimes she would, once inside the hotel bedroom, dissolve in laughter, muffled initially by his hand, and then his eager mouth.

Certainly to begin with, Edwin was ardent, enticed by Violet's body—she was then just twenty-one years of age. But over the succeeding half-decade he must admit their liaison sank, for him at least, to a habit—one he might not much miss if given up. Nevertheless, the "game" *always* amused him.

He was playing it, naturally, when he journeyed out of London on the train. He sat in a second-class carriage, not overly full at that time of day or year, and watched the thick smoke and steam of passage drift by, and the wildlands of the more southerly northwest come and go between, in gathering afternoon, sunset and dusk. He was attired as a poorish office clerk, who liked to go walking in the country should he get a vacation. The inn he meant to stay at, too, just outside Pressingbury, was precisely the sort such a person would choose. Edwin had gone to some pains, as ever in his Violet episodes. But this, admittedly, had been a more complex project, made necessary by her having taken possession of some big old country house.

Violet had sent him a short letter, addressing him by the invented name of *Mr. Harbold.* She was newly in the house, and would he not come up in February. Then they could discuss the "important business" at hand.

Edwin, accepting the invitation with slight, if not completely tepid interest, had no notion what the "business" was, if indeed it were anything more than another code in their game. The faint irksomeness of the trip was offset for him by playing once more in disguise. He would stay tonight at the inn, then go off on his "little walking tour." The second day and night he would spend with Violet, returning from her new house directly to the town, and thence to London.

Violet's husband, Henry Augustus North, was at this time in India. More than fifteen years her senior, he had been there now almost a quarter of a century, in a mercantile rather than a military capacity. Now and then, of course, he was in England, as he had been when first they met. But now, as then, he never stayed long. The climate of England did not agree with North. Just as, Violet had convinced him, that of India, even untried, would never agree with *her.*

Edwin left the train at Pressingbury Halt. By then he was tired and hungry, buoyed up only by his disguise (he now was Mr. Harbold) and the play he would carry on at the inn to safeguard Violet's reputation. He walked the two miles to his lodging as twilight closed on the landscape. Edwin paid no attention to the beauty of the scenery, the steep boulderings of hills changing to the black furred backs of giant beasts, the eerie sparkle of a white waterfall, the glittering litter of the cool late-winter stars. It would be a longer walk tomorrow to the isolated property. And Violet would be demanding. (Rather like her husband, Edwin had not seen her for several months.) As he reached the inn and traipsed inside, Edwin did wonder, briefly, if tomorrow's might be, after all, the last time he spent with her.

As it happened, he had met a young woman only the week before, at the races. Iris Smithys was less high up the social ladder than Violet North, but only nineteen, with perfect figure, unmarked skin, and dancing eyes full of a sudden heat when they had met his own. Yes, truly, this might well be the last occasion he and Violet played any of their little games. They must, both, then, make the most of it.

"Edwin—my very dear—! How wonderful that you've arrived!"

She had grown old. In less than seven months her summer had been shed from her. Her flesh seemed dry, to see, to touch . . . No, this was absurd. She was not yet twenty-seven . . . Unless, as sometimes the female sex did, she had *lied*.

"Violet. More lovely than ever," he murmured, holding her close in the clandestine hallway.

"Alas no, my dearest. I'm not at my best, I know. It's been a troubling while. I wanted not to bother you with any of it until I had some knowledge of where I stood."

Alarm took a grip on Edwin, replacing the annoyed repulsion he had felt on viewing her drabness.

In spite of all Edwin's care—had old North discovered the adultery? Was he perhaps even now storming towards England across the ocean, polishing a pistol as he prowled the decks?

Her reply rushed the blood from Edwin's cheeks.

"We are to be divorced," said Violet, and burst into such a torrent of tears, it was as if a fountain had been turned on inside her eyes.

Edwin clamped himself in iron control.

"Are you in any danger, Violet?" He meant, naturally: Am *I* in any danger?

To his bemused relief she shook her head. "No, no—my very dear . . . Oh Edwin, it's been such a dreadful strain—yet now, perhaps, at last, something wonderful may come from it!"

Edwin was in several minds on this, but he followed Violet meekly into a large morning room that led off the hallway. He had seen no servants either within or without the house, and when presently Violet informed him she had dismissed them all for three days of holiday, he was unsurprised if perturbed. Obviously, to keep even the most trusted and loyal retainer on the premises during Edwin's sojourn would be unwise. But how, servantless, they were to manage he partly dreaded. He thought she would have no culinary skills beyond the making of a pot of tea, or the peeling of an apple.

But Violet was all enthusiasm. She ushered him to a chair and brought him, on a tiny tray, a glass of sherry and a plate of biscuits, with the oddly jaunty air of a silly child acting. Even so, her gloom seemed abruptly to have left her. She looked in the firelight (had *she* lit the fire?), softer and less unappealing as her face relaxed. "You see," she said, sitting on a stool at his feet, "this may come to be the best thing in the world, my love."

Gravely Edwin waited. "Yes?"

It was then, for the very first, the house made its presence known to him.

Edwin, as noted, was—despite his earnest game-playing—not especially observant, and particularly not of anything that was not *animate*. That is, a human being might attract his attention, either for some extreme of conduct, fair or foul, or likewise physical appearance. Even a dog or horse, or large bird, might also gain his regard, if sufficiently aggravating, smelly or threatening. The earth, however, unless in quake or eruption, could never do so. Not even the sea itself, unless he had been on it in the midst of a storm, something that so far he had sedulously avoided. The world was only shapes, lights and shadows, weather, and potential stupid accidents and assaults such as pitfalls or rabid sheep. Meanwhile all static objects, which must necessarily include the architecture of any building, whether a temple of the ancient Greeks, a pyramid of the uncanny Egyptians, or a slum behind a stable (rather resembling the place he had grown up in before a legacy came his way) had less impact on him than music on a stone.

He had had today a *very* long walk to reach his destination, aided only by Violet's badly drawn map. Therefore, this big and rangy house perched on the top of a hill, surrounded by rough if private woodland, and with a strange tall rectangular façade, had left him, until that moment in the morning room, entirely untouched.

The more curious then, maybe, the reaction that swept stilly yet intensely into and through him.

So powerful was the impression, although utterly unnameable and nearly untranslatable, that for a second or so he failed to hear his mistress's twitterings.

If he had *had* to name it, *identify* it, as, rather later indeed he would struggle to do, he would say, *did* say, that he felt the house did not *like* him. Ridiculous though this was, it was the furthest he could get towards the root of the feeling. It did not *like*, nor did it *trust* him. And far, far worse than any prying servant, it seemed—through its hundreds of corners, its thousands of boards and cornices and angles, its countless ranks of windows—to be *watching* him with a terrible and immutable *attention*.

"Forgive me, Violet. This is a fine sherry—my thought was distracted for an instant. What did you say?"

"Oh, my dearest Edwin, I know it must all be such a startlement! Perhaps I should wait awhile. We can discuss everything after luncheon. I am so glad—so very glad you're here at last!"

Needless to relate, rather than discuss anything at all, they took the habitual "siesta" after lunch.

Edwin, who had not looked forward to this, now learned that some of the very good, if cold, food left by the vacant cook had cheered him, as had the wine. And in the dim curtained bedchamber on an upper floor, he found that, instead of comparing Violet with Iris Smithys, he was enabled to *conjure* Iris into and over Violet's willing, yearning flesh. He did not, then, fail to enjoy the afternoon. As for Violet, she was almost religious in her worship. Good God. She loved him. He had never fully accepted such a foible in her before. At the hour it added gloss. Then quite quickly it began to make him uneasy. And this was when, taking post-carnal tea as they had been used to do in the hotels, he felt again the "eyes" of the house upon him. Its ears were *listening.* The house was "weighing him in the balance," he was afterwards to declare. And the *house* had fathomed him as the idiotic Violet never had, or surely could. As even *he*, probably, had not.

Finally, when evening drew on, they sat in a big dark parlor inadequately lit by oil lamps (no gas, let alone electricity, had been brought to the house). And here Violet explained all that had recently occurred between her and Henry Augustus North, its impending events and ultimately seemingly unavoidable outcome.

North himself, the old duffer, had fallen in love not only with the Indian climate, but with some native woman, some alleged princess or *Rani*—or some such peculiar title. For her he had given up the Christian faith, and was now proposing to marry her. To this end he would allow Violet to divorce him, so no scandal should attach to her. The Rani was also, it transpired, well-to-do. North accordingly gave over a great many funds, shares, estates, and general interests to his soon-to-be-former wife. These things included the old house in the hills.

Violet said she had been calamitously upset by all of this; it seemed she must have reckoned him mostly faithful, even if *she* were not. She had felt, she announced, shamed, abandoned, scorned, and ruined. Yet, on coming to the house, she had fallen in love (oh, love again) with it immediately. It was a domicile, she told Edwin, said to have inherent healing qualities. For example, some male ancestor of the present Mr. North, during the previous century, had been miraculously cured here of a loathsome disease, while any woman brought to bed with child on the premises delivered a hale and fortunate baby, and herself suffered no harm.

Such stories normally contemptuously tickled Edwin. Now he frowned. But Violet went on, expatiating at enormous length, with the exuberance if not the flare of a professional storyteller, on the house's mystical pre-history. How the ground, the hill and its woods, were formerly some blessed site in "times of yore," how all the bricks and stones, beams, even cements and joists that glued and stitched the place together, had been taken from marvelous and legendary areas, not merely in England, but over all Europe—a type of wood from some sacred antique forest, a rare marble said to have been created from ice and the blood of a saint. More than this, during the erection of the house, which, the tale had it, went on about the middle of the 1600s, not only planners and architects but every mason, carpenter and artisan of any sort was tested, and proved to be pure in heart and intellect before he took a part in the building.

Perhaps, at another season, Edwin, here, might politely have stifled a yawn. Now he was deluged by a unique and almost horrified irritation. Like the yawn, he held it in. And eventually Violet reached her conclusion. This involved her statement that, in the end, she had come to understand her husband's latent and luminous kindness to her in his giving of the house. She had, since being here, also recovered much of her general vitality, and hoped for a complete renewal. For these reasons she had finally sent for Edwin.

"You bloom, dear Violet," he drawled, and sipped the glass of champagne, whose bottle he had had to open.

"Yes, Edwin, I'm better, and will be better still—" (For her sake he hoped so.) "But, in addition, do you see what a chance we have now—that is, once the divorce is settled?"

Distracted by the scrutiny of shadows and silences, drained by false lovemaking, rather, he must admit, *on edge*, Edwin stared at her. He had no idea what Violet meant. He should not have been so slow. But never mind it, next moment, with a glowing smile, she was to enlighten him.

"Edwin, you and I—we can at last be absolved of any guilt, and rescued from our lonely longing. We can marry, Edwin. I can be your wife! No stigma can connect to me. And I shall be wealthy now in my own right. We shall be rich, Edwin! And—my own beloved—we shall be *one*, as surely God has always meant us to be."

Dinner was cold as well. He found now it did not cheer him so much, not even with the excellent Burgundy, and purplish port, not even the imported and splendid cigars she had contrived to get him.

He saw, too, her eyes beginning to gleam once more with the renewal of lust. He had managed that earlier, but again? Edwin thought not.

He began to make his excuses. They were sufficiently feeble. He seemed, he said, to have caught a chill during his walk to the house; he was not well. And it had been something of a shock, her news, he must admit. He had been so concerned for her . . .

Oh, women. Such fools, but so sharp always when their primal needs went unmet, so *clever*, with the base intelligence of some lower animal—Violet had sussed him out instantly. Her eyes burst forth their tears once more. Did he not want her? But they could be married—all her considerable money should be his. Did he not *love* her? She had always thought he did. Why else—*how* else—had he persuaded her to dishonor, dragged her into wicked adultery. She loved *him*. He was her world.

"Violet, you misread me now," he blurted, frightened of her feral urgency. The most civilized of females, he had long known, could turn in a second from Belle to Beast. "I'm not myself this evening. I must go to bed, forgive me. We can talk again tomorrow." And he rose, male authority pulled about him like a steely mantle. Violet responded with inertia. As sometimes even the most hysterical of women did. They had been so dominated, commanded, almost from the cradle. It was God's law. Man was king. "Tomorrow," he frigidly promised, slinking out of the door. "We will discuss all this then." He did not risk a perhaps consoling paternal kiss on her forehead. Through her flood of tears, he saw the flames of crucifying truth burning her up, like a narrow pale house on fire within, the casements splintering at the heat, and the scarlet and gold of arson blazing from its riven skull.

Out in the passage, where the candlelight was thin and isolated, Edwin Marsh Onslowe felt the weirdest throb, a sort of non-physical lurch, crunch through the building. It was, it went without saying, only the differentiation of the cold night beyond the walls and the internal warmth of lamps and fires, metal and wood expanding, contracting. Such things were not supernormal.

With luck, she would weep herself to sleep, and at first light he could, in the nondescript disguise of clerkly Mr. Harbold, quit the unsettling house, and the awful company of Violet North, forever.

It was not to be. Certain matters, it seemed, were already, as the Eastern poets said, written in some momentous book.

Notwithstanding the prologue, he was tired, and sleep came swiftly. He had no dreams he recalled. Yet his slumber was fretted by a kind of half-conscious anxiety—the premonition of Violet's revenge—traducing him, filthying his name, of hiring men to murder him even, or, oddly worse, somehow forcing him, despite everything, to marry her, and so decay beside her for fifty years of dreary hell.

In actuality, Violet stole, about three in the morning, into the separate bedroom prepared for him, a room (clearly) she had not expected him to select.

Asleep, he woke in panic as she flung herself upon him, her flailing weight, her burning hot skin, and tear-melted eyes, screaming and sobbing out all those emotions she had, until that minute, so stringently clamped for twenty-seven years in the prison of her heart.

The fear he felt was colossal. Probably it made his excuse.

As before, when she had sometimes giggled so loudly and insanely in those hotel bedrooms, or indeed in other stages of their passion when she grew too noisy, he clapped his right hand over her mouth. In the past, he would have kissed her next. Not now. Exerting another strength he had, which perhaps he could never have foreseen he might possess, left-handed he seized her throat. At which his right hand let go of her face and flew to join its partner. Grasping her neck in both hands (that seemed to him in those moments incredibly large, too large to belong to him) he did not merely choke the life from her, but snapped the bones of her upper spine free of her skull, as if they had only been the slender stems of glass goblets.

When Edwin had finished killing Violet, he did another—to himself, later—astonishing thing. He rolled her body straight off the bed onto the floor. There it lay then, in its coil of nightgown and robe, for the rest of the hours of darkness, while he slept in a deep and dreamless stupor on his back, at the center of the mattress.

The commencement of dawn light on the ceiling woke him. It was rosy, one of those icing-sugar winter dawns often shown on picture cards of happy skaters, or small animals frolicking in wintry woods. Edwin lay, slightly confused, staring up at it, thinking it first the reflection of his fire, but the fire in the grate was out, naturally. He could not, for a little while, recollect where he was. Then he remembered he was in Violet's country house. And then he remembered all of it.

He sat up very slowly, and in a shrinking terror looked down over the side of the bed to the bundle of washing and loose hair on the carpet. Then he buried his head in his hands and wept in despair. Rather as Violet had done, but Edwin did not really think of that.

In the greater part of humankind there resides an instinct for survival. It is this which can clutch at straws and effect a rescue from them. It is this which can, now and then, outwit fate.

After some time Edwin, as he believed, pulled himself together and got up. Having dressed, he went down through the house to the kitchens, where he soon located some cold beef, a loaf, and butter. Since tea and coffee had not been made, of course, he did not bother with them but charged himself with a brandy and soda in the drawing room.

In the new day—a bluish but very cold one, with frost visible on the windows, and on the edges of boughs and walls—the house, with its unlit hearths, looked quite deadly to him. Although, as has been said, Edwin lacked imaginative perception, he felt the hollowness of the place, as if it, too, were frozen both out and in. But this fancy was one he did not dwell on. He had by now mastered himself. He had done something shocking and harsh, even if driven to it by extreme provocation. He doubted any man alive, unless an uplifted priest or a fool, could have done otherwise. It seemed almost as if she—Violet—had given herself to him as a sacrifice. But again, such a notion was not to be considered now. For Edwin must make a plan.

The excellent and rejuvenating fact was that, as he had come here in his disguise of the humble, irrelevant Harbold, *Edwin* had had no role in any subsequent event. Nor could he be suspected of having one. Nobody at all had ever known of Edwin's connection with Violet North. While, and in this he did trust her fully, Violet would never have betrayed her relationship with him. She had always been far too afraid of losing her husband, or more properly, the financial parasol North had maintained over her head. As for the invented Harbold himself, even he had evidenced no link with Violet. He had gone off on his doltish country walk, vanishing from the inn, a dull little nobody soon forgotten.

It only remained, therefore, for Edwin to go home—if perhaps now in a slightly altered disguise. This posed no difficulty. He had always taken a few spare articles of dress with him, even a secondary wig, on his jaunts with Violet; it was, for him, part of the fun. And in this manner, *Harbold* need not be seen again *anywhere*. While Edwin must have been in London all the time, at his quiet lodging, immersed in his own harmless projects.

Edwin went to change his clothes and don the other wig, which was a rather nicer one than he had given poor Harbold. That done, Edwin went very carefully over the house, and through each room he had, however briefly, occupied. In the process of doing this, inevitably, he came upon Violet's body again, still laid out like rolled-up washing beside the bed. Edwin was by then completely in control of himself. So much so in fact that he thought her very unseemly. Caught by a curious whim, he had half an urge to move the corpse, to stuff it possibly into its own bed, but he sternly resisted such childishness. Instead he returned alone to the master bedroom, where Violet and he had spent the previous afternoon. Here he paused, brooding.

Of course, it could not be denied, there was *every* evidence *here* that the woman had been with a lover. Scowling, Edwin took in various signs he was too fastidious to name to himself—they had been careless here, as not in the cheap hotels. And she had troubled to tidy nothing. It was a pity, he thought then, with admirable practicality, he had not killed her before any of *that* took place. Could there be clues here after all that might, despite all odds, reveal his actions?

Just then the house gave off a massive cracking creak. It must remind any who had ever heard such a noise of the snapping of bones.

Edwin's nerve, for a fragment of a second, also snapped. He shouted at the house. "It's the damned cold! Just the cold makes such a sound in you! You need a bloody fire to warm you up."

Epiphanies are often bizarre, and come in many forms.

That which came to Edwin caused him physically to stagger. But then he stood in utter silence, staring about him, his hands already flexing, his mind already racing. And the house, too, the house was entirely silent. Silent as the grave.

Setting the fire was very easy. Her unmodern residence was full of candles, tapers, matches, lamps, and oil. Edwin went about his task quite methodically, but also with a certain exhilaration. He could not hide from himself that he nearly relished this ultimate act of cleansing, after all the foolish mess Violet had made for him. He understood he did her also a great service. No opprobrium now could ever attach itself to her character.

So thorough Edwin was (and so sensible, pausing even to partake of a quick luncheon in order to keep up concentration and stamina), that the sun was low when, his own luggage safely out on the lawn, Edwin struck and scattered the first of his incendiaries.

He presently beat a hasty retreat, for the fire obligingly took hold everywhere, and with a slightly surprising efficiency. But then, he had been immaculate. He had made a proper job of it. What bewilderment the returning servants would receive, he vaguely thought, when he had got himself off along the drive and down onto the wooded slopes of the hill. By then he could smell the tang of smoke out in the fresh cold of a darkling dusk. Turning at length, he looked back, and saw to his immense relief and satisfaction an unearthly glow and flicker—rather like, conceivably, that of the northern lights—going on in the upper air above the trees. Then, even as he gazed transfixed, there came a huge, wide *bang*, like thunder, and through the twilight overhead darted an explosion of spangling elements, as if insects burst from some shell.

A cinder dashed on Edwin's cheek, a miniscule scorch sharp as a tiny sting. At this, it occurred to him that, with luck, even the old trees on the hillside might very well also go up in smoke. Wisely then he ran, his bag clutched tight, and the downhill path quite helpful now he was past the larger tree roots, and soon well lighted by the burning house behind.

Not until he had reached flatter ground, due to make southwards now along deserted country tracks, did Edwin permit himself one further viewing of his masterpiece.

By that time all he could make out was a vast black cloud rising hundreds of feet into the sky, that let out of itself quite regular bright fountains, and through which occasionally some dull crimson shape evolved, more like a noise than a sight, a sort of *roar*, a soundless *bellowing*.

It was a wearisome plod on foot and without detour to the station. But from there a late train took him to the town of Pressingbury. He could, in his smarter character, stay tonight at the Pressingbury Arms. Tomorrow there remained only the uneventful journey to London, and a little well-deserved peace.

Some seven days later, rested and recovered, Edwin Onslowe invited Iris Smithys to accompany him to the seaside, since the weather in the south-east had become clement. She consented and they visited the pier at Hastings, resplendent with its Eastern Pavilion. Iris flirted deliciously with Edwin all morning, and ate a fish luncheon with him, but declined a mutual spell in one of the more attractive hotel bedrooms.

This angered Edwin. He felt, perhaps correctly, Iris had strung him along. They returned to London in sullen non-communication.

Truth to tell, once parted from the girl, he was rather reluctant to go back to his flat on Tenmouth Street, behind the Temple. He passed a further hour or so at a public house, but found the pub fire far too hot. It had been a very mild day.

The heat of the fire on his face. It was burning, drying his skin so that his flesh seemed to stick to his bones. His hot eyes filled with water . . .

Rising cursing from this dream, the first dream he had fully recalled for months, Edwin opened the window of his bedroom and peered into the street below. Gas-lamps blurred and flickered. But even in the fresher air he could smell the poisons of the room's blocked chimney. He must speak to the bloody landlord again. God knew, he paid enough rent.

Quite often Edwin indulged in buying all the reputable newspapers, and reading them at home. He had accordingly done this for three consecutive days, and so found, on the evening of the third, several references to a dramatic rural house fire. In the item Violet was still, very properly, spoken of as Mrs. Henry North, and a brief comment made on the tragedy of her comparative youth and the likelihood that, the body's having been found in the bedroom, she had wakened too late to fly. Most likely also the blaze was caused, the more proselytizing journal added, by careless use of an unguarded flame. It added a paragraph on the very severe danger of leaving lit candles in passages, or banked fires burning overnight.

Though icy, the week had been very dry, and both the house and much of the surrounding and ancient woodland were consumed. Violet herself, as Edwin learned from a more scurrilous rag the next day, had been fairly consumed, her corpse only identifiable by a remnant of her wedding ring, which was composed of white silver rather than gold.

Edwin Onslowe found himself cool throughout his reading of these facts. He had kept his head, and would continue to do so. Sometimes, it was true, he did feel slightly sorry for her, if only for a moment. Then he recalled how upset she had been on learning he did not love or wish to marry her. Her life thereafter would only have been a misery to her. Really, she had made a lucky escape.

On the evening of the fifth day Edwin dined at his club in Bleecher Street. Coming back about eleven-thirty at night he found, on entering his flat, that a rank smell of smoke hung around it. He, despite the paper's warning, had as ever left a fire in the apartment, albeit safely caged behind the fireguard. Edwin concluded something had happened in the chimney, and promptly descended the house to wake his landlord. As a rule, landlord and tenants did not have direct dealings, and the nightshirted gentleman was not best pleased to meet with Edwin at a quarter to midnight. However, it was arranged that the chimney should be investigated on the morrow.

The next day then was occupied throughout by a visitation of sweeps and similar mechanicals. The chimney was swept and pronounced in order, and other appliances vindicated of blame.

Worn out by this tiresomeness, yet somewhat looking forward to the *following* day (on which he was to escort Miss Smithys to Hastings), Edwin had that night dropped into a heavy sleep.

After the Hastings trip, Iris' aggravating behavior, and the odd dreams of burning heat, Edwin woke rather later than usual, about nine, and getting up, could still smell, as in the night, horribly strong and fetid smoke in every room of the apartment. Once more the landlord was summoned, and the man having this time ungraciously climbed the four flights, declared there was no smell at all.

"Well, I've been forced to open all the windows. Fortunately the weather's mild, or I'd no doubt have caught a chill."

"'Tisn't that mild," rejoined the landlord, scanning the frosted avenue below. "Maybe it's your nasal corridors that are at fault, Mr. Onslowe. When the wife takes cold she can smell smoke in her nose from the catarrh. Common phenomenon," he added loftily.

"I am not your damn—I am not your wife."

"Well," said the landlord, "I'd recommend you visit your physician, Mr. O. I'm not about to call out the sweep again when the chimneys aren't at fault." So saying he left.

Edwin soon also vacated the premises, needing, he felt, clean air. He would have to move, he decided, as he strode through the grasslands of Hyde Park, staring in disapproval at the feeding sheep. Some smaller apartment in some nicer venue, why not?

After luncheon Edwin returned to his rooms, and did notice an elusively smoky odor out on the street. A fog perhaps was building itself up from the puffing chimneys of thousands of homes and places of commerce. After all, from these alone there was a constant basic underflavor of smoke that, like the horse dung, one seldom noticed. Probably he had *imagined* the excess inside his flat. (Edwin evidently did not realize he had little imagination.) Nevertheless, on undoing his door he was assailed at once by a choking miasma so awful he began to retch. Inclined to rush out again, he yet rushed forward, alarmed that something was indeed burning. Nothing was. The room lay warm yet grey, the hearths all dead.

Only then did it come to him what the real cause of this "phenomenon" might be. And at the idea, his heart leapt and clutched at his breast. The clothes he had worn on the night of his departure from Violet's house, the very wig, the shoes, the bag itself—they remained in his wardrobe, and must be imbued by smoke. He had not considered the need do anything to or with them, save store them as before. Certainly, he had detected no telltale smell of cinders or burned material on them previously, not even in the hotel at Pressingbury, let alone on the London-bound train. Yet surely here lay the cause of the rancid and bitter stink. Shut up in the dark (like his crime, had he considered it), no doubt the staleness had intensified, and his nose, more acute than those of others, grew quickly aware.

These remnants of the "game" must go. Out, out of the flat, out of his life. He would dispose of them as soon as evening fell.

He did not don another disguise. He had told himself, quite strictly, such immature pursuits should cease. Even so, he waited until full darkness sank on the city. It was a dark that not even the gas street lighting, not even the blaring windows of shops and taverns could properly disperse. There was also, indeed, he believed, a hint of mist. It swirled about the corners of things, and breathed out from the mouths of passersby.

He took the bag and all its contents, which comprised both "costumes" from his visit to Violet, and walked along with casual briskness. He had not conceived a plan. Yet somehow it had been borne in on him that to follow the river a way might well be the best course. Tonight the tide was high. What could be more apt than to pause awhile, then let his burden fall. If any stray found it after, pulled down or upstream by the sea-tending Thames, it could mean little.

He noted idly as he went along, something slightly peculiar about the gas lamps. Even, now he gave attention, the occasional brazier at a street corner. The fires in both seemed oddly extended, and in some cases to be actually *fizzing*. They gave off, he felt, unnecessary heat. Someone should look into it.

Edwin came out on the fine, elongated terrace of the Embankment. It was a calm night, and down on the black serpent of the water, a fire-funneled steamer and a couple of small tugs plied their passage. Edwin glanced at the Egyptian Obelisk, erected only a few years before, a silly folly he had always thought it. But now, something in the tall narrow *upwardness* of it momentarily unnerved him. From its topmost point a kind of glinting ray seemed intermittently to spark—some trick of the murky evening.

A few more persons passed him. Then came a stretch where no one was save he. All about, in the near distance, the busy metropolis galloped and hurried. But up against this artery of watery night he stood, for a space, alone. Edwin did as he had meant to. He leaned a little, the bag raised up by his chest. Below, straight down, beyond the stone steps, there expanded what looked like black liquid coal. A mile deep it seemed, but could not be. Deep enough.

Presently the bag dropped, noiseless, until it touched the surface with only the least audible of splashes. But then. Time felt as if it had stopped—or, not exactly stopped . . . time had *hesitated*. Edwin beheld the bag's conglomeration of falsehood and old smoke entering the river with the solid motion of a thing far heavier. And as the river took it, then closed again above it, out on the skin of the water a hundred brilliant golden eyes came crackling and buzzing. They were little fires, little dancing yellow flames, each with a coil of bluish smoke. In utter astonishment Edwin stared at them, as they budded and bubbled there, shining so bright. Until with a popping hiss, as one they all went out, leaving only a long, thick wreath of smolder that filed slowly away between the gaps of the night.

During the next weeks, a pair of journals carried a reference to Mrs. North's burial somewhere on the Isle of Wight. A number also bore news that her husband, a merchant-trader then resident in India, had been suspected of arranging his wife's death, since he wished to marry elsewhere. However, without a shred of evidence he was soon cleared of all blame. By then a damp and sluggish February had lapsed into a rampaging, iron-clad March. Edwin Onslowe, it must be said, had given slight heed to either papers or weather. He had other matters on his mind.

The night after casting his bag of disguises into the Thames, with such an odd result, he had dined in the West End. The meal was overcooked, and while coming back, a thickening of the fog gave him a cough.

Back in his rooms he found the air no better, and once again inwardly determined to move. He slept badly, constantly waking up thinking he had heard a loud cracking noise, as if a large bough had broken from a tree. But no trees stood near his lodging. Getting up at first light, he saw the street again sugared by frost, and on touching the windowsill pulled off his hand with a cry. It would seem the surface was so cold it had felt scaldingly hot—a curious sensory error he had heard described, yet never formerly experienced. His fingers remained sore for half an hour.

That day he called on Iris Smithys, who permitted him to take her to luncheon. She would allow nothing else, and on parting, informed Edwin she would probably be unable to continue their "friendship," as another gentleman in her life had taken offense at it.

As Edwin marched back through the city, he was conscious of sweating with rage. And near St. Martin's, another unpleasant event befell him. One of those braziers with which London appeared then to be overstocked, let off a huge gout of sparks and red cinders just as he went by. Edwin, as if attacked by bees, leapt about in panic, beating out the fiery debris which had landed on his coat and in his hair, his hat on the pavement and his hands and face smeared with black. Rather than show concern, a nearby group of traders came closer to laugh at him. And when in fury he bawled profanities, he was accosted by the burliest and least wholesome of them, who manhandled Edwin, remarking, "Must be a bleedin' lunatic, you. Clear off, or I'll call the coppers." Edwin prudently went on his way.

In his flat he found many minute scorches on his face, a singed eyebrow, and tiny holes burned in his greatcoat. The scorches, even the singe, faded during the evening. The punctures in the coat also seemed to heal—some visual trick, no doubt, of the unreliable gaslight in his rooms, which had started to flicker distractedly and give out a strange resinous smell. He turned off the lights and resorted to candles. But these smoked, and were too hot to put up with.

He passed a wretched night, coughing and sweating so he feared he had a fever. And again he was frequently woken, from any brief sleep he had, by some noise, the source of which he could never locate, but that would seem to indicate a large rat in the attic, stumbling about and knocking the brickwork loose.

The *heat* of the fire on his face—

It was burning. *Burning . . .*

Why in God's name was he standing here, so near to this dangerously incendiary sight, however compelling? The tall house was almost by now engulfed in the vast tidal waves of the fire, the flames seeming of extraordinary size, as if made in some other world of giants, where even the elements must exist on a bigger scale. Out from the chimneys they poured in scarlet plumes, while the roofs ran like molten gold.

And behind him, all down the hill, the dry old woods had already caught, their winter boughs breaking into hot foliage, rose-red or yellow as the eyes of tigers. The sky even was like a dense amber dome.

He coughed ceaselessly. His lungs were tangled by the thick brown smoke. His eyes no longer ran with water, they bulged, and the moisture in them seemed to be boiling—he must at least shut his eyes, but he could not. And he could not turn and run.

A massive explosion, like a cannon shot, resounded from the house's core. Up through the cooking orange jam of air, the entire architecture seemed to rise. It did so with a weird, slow powerfulness. While off from every angle of it, the stones and bricks, the wood and marble and glass, went flying. One more deadly swarm. High, high the amalgam of chaos soared, then shattered and came spinning back towards the earth.

Already slabs and shards fell all around him, each detonating as it struck the ground. Oh, he must run away—he *must . . .*

Pleading, Edwin Onslowe woke in his London bed. He fought with his sheets, the blank dark night, his boiled eyes starting from his flame-roasted face.

And then he flopped down again with a pitiful mewing.

How long he lay thereafter, still coughing a little, the tears now unbottled and laving his parched skin, he never knew. *It was done. It was over.* So he told himself. *You simpleton, a dream. What else?*

How dark it was now. Were the street lamps even alight? Puzzled, reaching for normalcy, he made to rise. But in that moment a soft amorphous glow began. Edwin lay back. He had only thought the light was gone. Look, there it was, shining through the curtains and upward along the edges of the ceiling, a pale rosy light, like that from a low-burning hearth.

Perhaps three seconds it cheered him. Then he saw that in color it was quite wrong, not to mention in strength. For see how it grew, and as it did the room filled with heat.

All his ceiling glowed now, a vivid restless red. And as through his curtain spiked an upsurge of light shafts like knives, he heard the loud blows and cracks above him of the blazing attics beginning to give way . . .

Edwin sprang from the bed, but did not reach even the window. A smothered dizziness, a stampede in his head—as unconsciousness axed him to the carpet, he knew he would lie there at the bedside, in his nightshirt resembling a roll of washing, until the flames had eaten all of him from the bone, and baked the bone to calcined and unidentifiable black.

The landlord demanded extra rent in lieu of proper notice. Edwin refused. "Count it," he coldly said, "your penalty for a rotten chimney and poorly maintained gas fitments."

Finding and securing another apartment had, of course, taken up a generous amount of March. Edwin had been meticulous, and wisely so. He did not mean to saddle himself with such a punishment twice.

No wonder he had had bad dreams in that vile place. No wonder his eyes sometimes flecked over with hosts of brilliant little sparkles (like sparks?), or darkened with cloudiness (rather like smoke, perhaps). This was all due to his upset nerves. The flat in Tenmouth Street was, he believed by then, a potential death trap. Not only the temperamental gas, and the reeking chimneys, but the water had started to run boiling hot from the vaunted "modern" faucets. Besides this, most of the surfaces in the rooms intermittently burned his hands. Once a *teacup* left hurtful, blood-red marks on palm and fingers for seventy minutes (he had timed the horror). Strangely, there were never blisters.

Inevitably, he continued to experience terrifying nightmares under such circumstances. He had convinced himself, however, as a rational man must, that no matter how real they seemed, they were only the result of so many petty, or alarming annoyances in the waking world. Even so, the nightmares affected his health. He felt always sweaty and feverish, and noted uneasily, with embarrassment, a faint rank charcoal odor lingering in his most newly laundered clothes, as if his own body by now emitted it. His hands, if not scorched by something, carried dirty smears that apparently spontaneously appeared on them—nonsense, naturally. Attending to his fingernails, black grit was often removed. When in other environs, aside from the fever, and the random visual disturbances, he seemed to think he was much better. Although it was a little odd, too, the number of small fires he noted everywhere— sometimes even reflections in puddles seeming startlingly to flame. Or sunset in some window, igniting, crackling, flashing . . . But there. He was under such strain.

The new apartment lay in rather a run-down street of Lambeth. There were fewer amenities, and the rooms were more cramped. But it boasted a fine view of a little public garden, and was, if anything, inclined to be draughty and cold, which he, always now so overheated, positively relished.

He was to move in on April 2. The night before, forced to sleep at Tenmouth Street, which sometimes lately he had avoided (putting up in a small hotel—he slept only in snatches but dreamed as a rule far less), Edwin dosed himself with a chemist's powder.

Whatever happened, tomorrow he would cross the river—cross running water—and be free of all this insanity.

Such a notion—the crossing of water—did not remind him that this exact gambit was used in popular fiction in order to elude a vengeful spirit.

Had he, recently, thought of Violet? Maybe he had, but if so only deep within his not yet fully recognized unconscious.

Steeped in the powder, he slept. But he thrashed and groaned, the drug altering his nightmares into a sort of burial by clinker and soot.

Morning arrived. Edwin drove himself to be sprightly. And the second day of April smiled upon him. Weak sun held off the rain. The removal van and reliable horse conducted those movables that were his away to Lambeth without a hitch. By the dinner hour, Edwin was installed, fussing with positions of chairs and tables as happily as some old lady with her ornaments. He did not care. Now all should be well.

He dreamed he was with Violet on the train to Hastings. He wished he were not, was bored and irritable. Until she suddenly vanished into thin air. Delighted, he took no issue with her disappearance. Next instant, others in the carriage were pointing out of the window at a burning edifice up on a tall hill.

All of them seemed frightened, and Edwin also grew afraid. Indeed, they were all well advised to be, for gradually, as the train ploughed on, the burning house came swelling down the hill after them, and, netted about with woods on fire and glass bursting like fireworks, ran on the track at their side.

All the other passengers then fled the carriage, but Edwin could not move, though the train windows grew ever hotter and melted like wax.

In the first of the most terrible earlier dreams Edwin had woken, or thought he had. That time, he thought he had tried to reach the window, but fainted. He certainly found himself next day lying by the bed.

Now, erupting from the dream of the train running neck and neck with the burning house, Edwin flung upright. Where was he? Tenmouth Street? No, no, he was shot of that place. Nevertheless, after all, even into Lambeth the nightmares had hunted him and pulled him down.

Edwin moaned. How impenetrably dark the room was. Of course, he had new curtains, very thick. No light could enter from the street.

He reached for matches, but had forgotten to put them by. He must get up and cross the room, turn on the gas above the mantelpiece . . . or draw the curtain back an inch, perhaps.

A single unwary notion came to him as he swung his feet towards the floor. Was it Violet? Was it actually possible that Violet . . . haunted him? *Don't be a fool.*

The floor, lino rather than carpet, was cool to his feet. Thank God. And the blackness was without any smell, neither any sound. Oh, he would light a lamp, have a brandy, play a game of Patience. All would be well; he could not expect to slough all his trouble in a single evening.

As his hand touched the curtain, like the trick of a cheap but cunning magician, a thousand little golden embers winked on all over it. They twinkled and fluttered, scrambling up the folds. His eyes, it was only that; it would pass in a moment . . . Ignoring the illusion, even though it burned his hand, he dragged the heavy material aside. And there, directly below, instead of a street and a small garden, Edwin beheld the side of a craggy wildwood hill, sloping downwards into sheer darkness, under a starless sky. But even so, the stars were waking up. They were in the trees. They were red and gold. They glittered and jostled, and long threads of purple vapor spiraled up from them. There came a sound like the hissing of snakes.

"No," Edwin said, with a nonsensical firmness, to the room, the night. But it was much too late for *No.*

The swarm of sparks came out from every direction, whirling at him, covering him, and by their solar flare, he saw his own hands beating at them, and in the round mirror opposite to him was the face of a madman shrieking . . .

Such a mirror had never been his. It was another mirror, that maybe he remembered. It had hung in that house.

By the naked flicker of sparks, of hurrying flames that skittered now everywhere, Edwin saw the cramped room had expanded to several times its size. Its ceiling had risen and was graced by cornices, and over there a solid beam—it was not the room in Lambeth, let alone in Tenmouth Street.

"A dream—!" shrilled Edwin.

The heat came in a torrent, a towering shout. For a scintillant second he could look straight through every wall. He saw the architecture of the huge old house, its narrow upright structure, the struts of stone or wood that pinned its brickwork, the tessellations of its roofs, the castle-shapes of chimneys, ziggurats of stairs, the weaving web of corridors and annexes, halls, and antechambers, the furniture that clad it, the drapes and papers and carpets that dressed it. He saw all this by the fiery torch of regnant flame, for the fire already gouged and conquered every avenue. The smell of smoke now was so acrid it had transmuted his lungs also to fire. He rushed from side to side, and slender vestiges of things floated or slammed towards him, gilded with their bright soprano pain.

Violet—he thought—*Violet*. But here, too, he was quite wrong. It was not Violet—poor, pathetic, tear-sodden ninny—not *she* he had brought inadvertently away with him from those two nights of homicide and arson. All about him now, crackling and cracking, timbers breaking, atoms raining down in lava showers, all about him screaming with its own speechless fury and despair, all about him was the vengeful ghost of what he, Edwin Marsh Onslowe, had also slain. Built on a site of blessing, constructed with care and talent from all that was benign, a healer, a protector. Replaying for him its endless dying agony. Of course, it was not any *human* psyche that had pursued him. It was the *ghost of the murdered house*.

The bedroom door, as Edwin wrenched it wide, burned the flesh from his hands. Howling, vomiting, he blundered through the ghastly radiance of passages, between the black bones of walls, and down its volcano-glass of blazing stairs. But there was no way out. Even had he found one, beyond the door, the gate, the land was burning too, its ancient trees, the very sky.

A hundred shattered mirrors showed him also how *he* had become. He was burned black, his facial bones a slate of scoria. He was so scalded that he shivered as if with icy cold. He, like the house, was quite dead, yet did not die. From his own mouth his unbreath issued out more flames. His boiled eyes bulged and glared. He did not know his name, he did not know himself.

Only what he had done. And that this, *this* would never end.

Edwin was discovered the next morning lying in an alleyway some five streets from his new apartment. He wore only his nightshirt, was both bruised and dirty, and some of his hair had been torn out.

The constable, who subsequently escorted him back to his lodging, confirmed that Edwin seemed to have received some dreadful shock, but he was by then subdued and decorous. He agreed to all the constable's requirements with a look of "almost relief." At the flat Edwin tidied himself and dressed. The two men then went by cab to the nearest police station.

> Regardless of the fact that Edwin Onslowe's reason for admitting to the murder of Violet North, perhaps understandably, was never credited, his concise outline of his acts and motives convinced the arbitrators of the law. Guilt, meanwhile, as is well known, may assume varied aspects. Onslowe himself is said to have stated that, since his arrest, the remorseless haunt, or as others took it to be, nightmare, had donned a less awful if still persistent form, which involved mostly his watching, from outside, the house burn down. To Mrs. North

herself, Onslowe never referred with any interest, let alone display of regret.

One further anecdote, conceivably, is worth noting.

Prior to his execution, Onslowe spoke with the priest, then customary. But Onslowe is reported to have told this gentleman immediately: "I neither hope for, nor fear, anything in any life after death. Following death there is nothing at all. For if there were another life, why do ghosts remain to trouble us in this one? My Hell I've suffered. Once dead, my dear sir, I expect—confound it—to get some peace."

—DERWENT'S LEGAL MYSTERIES

Party Talk

JOHN GASKIN

JOHN GASKIN was educated at the City of Oxford High School and Oxford University. In his early years, Gaskin worked on British Railways and as a banker before taking a lectureship at Trinity College, Dublin, where he became a Fellow and held a professional chair in philosophy.

Since 1997 he has mainly written fiction, including a volume of poems and two collections of short stories, *The Long Retreating Day: Tales of Twilight and Borderlands* and *The Dark Companion*. He is also the author of the nonfiction study *A Traveller's Guide to Classical Philosophy* and a full-length tale of murder and haunting, *A Doubt of Death*.

Gaskin lives in a remote part of Northumberland, UK, and doubts that he will ever be connected to the Internet.

"A year or two ago I was planting roses against the wall of a village church, and found strange things," he recalls. "A little later I was at a lunch in one of the larger houses overlooking a deserted railway, and a river . . ."

> The guests are met, the feast is set:
> May'st hear the merry din.
> —Coleridge

SHE HAD THE SWEET SMELL of faded roses that I associate with polite mortality in decay. I would have preferred talking to someone else at the Selwoods' lunch party—after all, buffets are designed to shuffle sheep and goats—but she held me with deep-set eyes that might almost have been blind, or perhaps they were focused upon something beyond me or the house. I could not politely escape.

"You write ghost stories," she stated in a gravelly whisper that seemed to require no movement in the mask-like tightness of her face.

"I have published a few—not real ghost stories, mere tales of the uncanny, the boundaries between chance and significance, agency and accident, eidetic imagery and actual perceptions."

"But you do not believe in ghosts, 'real' or otherwise."

"No. I have to confess I don't. At least not as the intention of dead persons bringing about new events in the world. But I believe in the power of the living brain to influence directly other physical things in the world with results it does not expect or always understand—like the poltergeist effect."

My analysis elicited no comment.

She was sitting at the high-backed end of an expensive Victorian chaise longue, somewhat over-clothed (as I thought) for a well-heated house, even if it was January in the Cheviots. I was aware of a large and vague wrap of material round her shoulders, a grey head scarf of dusty silk drawn tightly over her head, a garment that might have been a jacket or a coat, and a long dark skirt. I could not see her feet, but there were smears of mud on the carpet near her that appeared to have been carried in from the garden, not from the graveled forecourt of the house where I had entered. There were black gloves over her evidently thin fingers. She gestured towards the far end of the chaise longue.

"Sit down."

For a moment I had sight of her open mouth. "I have a tale you must hear," she said.

I mumbled something about not wishing to keep her from the rest of the company. But the rest of the company was receding from us, intent upon itself or upon food in the adjacent dining room, and there was no one at hand to offer rescue. I settled at the far end of our chair in a position that made it easy not to look at her too intently. I must have grimaced.

"Yes, you'll find it as hard as stone—horsehair and leather under silk tapestry. They always preferred show to comfort, even in Gosforth. It wouldn't have been tolerated in my day. Everything was for comfort then—except for the bedrooms and the plumbing. I remember the chill of the bedrooms. I was eighteen. I'm accustomed to it now."

She paused, as if looking back into a place to which I was not admitted. Then to my embarrassment I heard her say:

"You do not wish to hear me, Dr. Smyth. But you have no choice now your glass is all but empty. Be still and I shall take you deeper than its emptiness."

It was a ridiculous style of speaking, and I should have braced myself for a period of the sleepy half-attention in which one hopes to be able to say "yes," "no," "how nice," and "what a pity" in the right places—except that I was uncomfortable, it was cold near the window, and for some reason I was acutely wide awake. She was speaking again.

"I left school that spring and was supposed to be filling in time learning German before wintering at a finishing school in Switzerland where they only spoke French. I believe my father thought German might encourage me to listen to more Bach cantatas. German was not in fashion at the time and cantatas are some of the drearier manifest-ations of religion. I rebelled. The rebellion took the form of Thomas, the gardener's boy who, unlike German irregular verbs, was beautiful and tempting. It was beyond my mother's ability to come to terms with what she found us doing uncomfortably behind a hedge one afternoon.

"Tom was mercifully called up almost immediately afterwards. I was banished to the care of my mother's aunt, a robust-minded woman of considerable experience of the world who had never married and lived in a lonely house several hundred miles away. My love was warm and strong. Home, as I discovered too late, was comfortable and safe.

Todburn Hall, as it was called before they rediscovered the old religious connection, was large and untenanted by youth or laughter. It seemed to me that my great-aunt lived in a plush cocoon of velvet and chilly comfort. She tried to receive me well and be kind in the practical ways she understood, but I was vexed with life and gave her little help."

The voice ceased, and I glanced sideways against the pale light of the window. The sun had disappeared behind winter clouds and the ribbon of river lay grey and cold a field or two away below the house. I could see only her vague silhouette against the blank glass. The spreading web of her clothes filled the end of our chair like a shadow.

But the voice had resumed—a penetrating whisper that was both clear and quiet, like listening inside the private world of some exquisitely engineered earphones.

"I was lonely, but it was not loneliness for people or company in general. It was the raw, torn-off space beside me that had been the fresh animal smell of Tom, the soft bloom of his skin, his talk, his touch, his strength. I walked by the river. I painted pictures in dark and fervent colors. I cried out in my heart. I was morose and withdrawn when my aunt tried to draw me out of myself. She knew more of life than I could then recognize or would ever know, but there were no words she could find to bridge the gap between us. Every generation thinks its own pain is unique. That is the glory and the pity of life.

"Her solution was to divert my attention with hearty activity. Having already drawn the garden and made a catalog of its contents for her, checked the silver inventory, painted the view of the river in several unsuitable versions, and read to her a number of Oscar Wilde's stories—the longest was missing from her collection. She later told me it was lost when she was in charge of the British Expeditionary Force's hospital in Alexandria.

"As I was saying, having completed all these tasks, I found myself one afternoon—about a month after my banishment—tidying a strip of garden against the south wall of the village church.

"A number of disused gravestones had been set close against the wall of the transept. They were old stones, much defaced, but they were close and I felt watched as I worked on my knees below them. A foolish fancy! It is the keeper of the gate that watches, not the gate.

"I was to prepare the ground and plant a dozen roses donated by my aunt—Rosa Mundi they were called. Yes, Rose of the Earth. Beauty from the dust. None survive now. Some did not survive my planting, particularly at the eastern end of the wall where the soil was mostly sand and fragments, like the ground at Xanthos. You do not know it . . ." Her voice faded away as if in exhaustion, and for a moment I hoped to see her fall asleep, but she resumed more strongly.

"Roses have deep roots, and I did not at first recognize what I was finding. The earth was dry, and in one area seamed with brown fibrous material like peat. It was in this that I dug up part of a bone. I was at the corner of the transept, where the wall turned back to join the chancel a few yards away. At the corner and just past it, one of the old headstones had been positioned leaving a few inches of dark space between its back and the church wall.

"I threw the thing down there out of sight—and other bits that left no doubt at all concerning my finds. It was as I was disposing—with some distaste—of part of a broken bone with discolored teeth still in place that a shadow moved on the wall in front of me. My back was to the path through the graveyard, and I turned sharply. I had heard no one approaching, and was feeling uneasy about concealing my finds behind someone else's memorial.

"It was only a young clergyman who was watching me—probably the curate I thought. Those were the days when country livings were properly staffed.

"'What are you doing with those?' he asked.

"'Planting them. My aunt, Miss Addison, is a member of the Select Vestry, and she has given them to the church. I'm doing it for her.'

"'No, I mean with the bones.'

"'I . . . well they're only bits and pieces. I suppose they have been brought to the surface as other graves have been dug. I presumed that behind a gravestone would be a suitable place.'

"'Yes indeed," he said, before bending down to look, closer to me than appeared to be necessary. 'You've finished planting?'

"'Yes. I'm tidying up.'

"'And this . . . brown stuff—it's not like the rest of the earth.'

"'No. It's a layer, about eighteen inches down. I hope the roots will reach it and gain some nourishment. Do you think I've gone too deep?'

"'I don't know. Earth like that should not be near the surface. But your roses will certainly draw life from it.'

"He stood up and looked at the gravestone where I had concealed the bones. I had not been able to see the name earlier. The lettering was much eroded and it was the angle of the sun, now flush with the face of the stone, that showed up the antique lettering as shadows. The name was Elenor Ward. There was no mention of family or husband, merely the year of her birth and that she had died at the age of sixteen. She was commended to the mercy of God. I sensed before I was told the mercy she might have needed from men, and almost certainly did not get.

"'An old parishioner learnt her story when she was a child, and told me about her one day when I was standing here,' he said. 'She was . . .' he hesitated, 'to have a child by one of the village laborers, an unrepentant sinner. She wasn't the first he'd got into trouble, but she was the last—at least in this place. He went away before the child was born. That's her grave, not just a moved stone like the rest. She's under there. But I'm sorry. This is morbid talk and I haven't even introduced myself. My name is Thornton, Peter Thornton. I'm assisting here for the summer.'

"I told him my name and that I was staying at Todburn Hall.

"'Good gracious!' he exclaimed with what seemed to me contrived and certainly unnecessary concern. 'That's almost three miles away. Have you transport?'

"I explained that I had not. I preferred walking along the south side of the river and crossing at Pauperhaugh.

"'May I have the pleasure of walking with you a part of the way?' he inquired. I could find no reason to refuse his company, and we strolled along pleasantly enough in the August sunshine. He showed me a short cut over the railway. It was probably forbidden, but trains were few and could be heard long before they came round the bend and could see anyone on the rails. As we walked, some dark worm of curiosity made me return to the story of Elenor Ward.

"'Did her child survive?' I asked, as if it were the most natural question in the world.

"'I was told not. None of the creature's offspring survived him. There was something wrong about him. They were stillborn. I suppose there are tales like that in most old parishes if one listens, tales embellished by time and the desire for justice in this world.'

"'And the father—what happened to him?'

"'As I said, time does not relate. My informed source was not that well informed.'

"Then we spoke of other things. He was interested in hearing about Todburn Hall, having visited my aunt there on parochial business.

"'It's a lovely reuse of Hanoverian ideas,' he said. 'Perhaps a little heavy in details, but so much better than that damp museum of a place the original family had down by the river. But it's a pity, if I may say so without offense, that the main front faces north, and is so near to the road. It can gain very little light and only a lot of dust on that side.'

"'Yes,' I agreed, 'but upstairs, like the ground floor, it's almost entirely corridors and landings on the north—apart from maids' bedrooms. I have a delightful room at the head of the stairs looking south. I can get the sun there all day if I want, and see it setting up the river every evening, and the morning train puffs away quite prettily in the distance round Pike Hill. It tells me the time if I'm not already up.'

"'Are you staying long?' he asked as we reached the bridge.

"I said I did not know.

"'I hope I'll see you again—at church on Sunday I mean.' But that was not what he meant.

"The remainder of my walk along the gritty road to the house was not agreeable. For one thing I was tired and feeling the lack of Tom.

Mr. Thornton had reminded me of the need, not supplanted it. For another, there was something small down the side of my boot that irritated without being uncomfortable enough to justify undoing all the lacing.

"At the side door of the house I found what it was—a thin tooth, brown and stained. It was careless of me to have let it lodge there, and I should have thrown it away into the garden without a thought. But I didn't. To do so felt somehow sacrilegious, at least a disrespect to the dead whom I had disturbed—as if they could care!

"Rather than leaving it on the windowsill of the porch where my aunt or a maid could see it and would ask questions, I took it to my bedroom and placed it on the chimneypiece, intending to drop it in the churchyard again on Sunday.

"That evening after supper I was sitting pretending to read. We were still enjoying the long sunsets of the north, and I did not think it cold, but Aunt May suddenly got up and closed the French windows.

"'There's a chill in the place,' she announced. 'It's the river air. I hope you didn't catch cold walking home? The Rector much approves of the roses. Thank you for planting them. I phoned him about the Sunday school outing and he mentioned that his curate had met you. Such a nice young man. Pity about his father. I hope you didn't find the planting too hard?'

"'Not at all. It was most interesting digging up all the bits of bone. If I'd gone on I could almost have made a man of him again.' I don't know if my levity was inadvertently or intentionally sarcastic, but my aunt bridled.

"'Oh dear! I'm so sorry. They will have been fragments from old graves that have been re-used. You left them alone? One isn't supposed to touch things like that, although I don't know why. We smashed up living men easily enough in the last war.'

"'I put them behind Elenor Ward's headstone, and Mr. Thornton said that would not be wrong.'

"'Elenor . . .?'

"'Round the corner at the end of the rose bed. Mr. Thornton said—'

"'Oh yes, of course. That unfortunate girl! They say she killed her lover you know.'

"'Mr. Thornton didn't tell me that.'

"'He wouldn't. It was never proved and he's too charitable to repeat old gossip. I should be, but I'm not. It's more interesting than modern parish chitchat. She and the others—there were others—had reason enough. He took his pleasure where he could get it without asking—a brutal, ugly creature by all accounts, more like a Cairo street dog than a man. He disappeared, God knows how or where, but she was blamed.

"'Will you take a cup of cocoa with me before we go to bed? I'm still cold, and cocoa always reminds me of nights in the desert with the wounded. I never saw a man die that really wanted to live you know, but I remember one that really wanted to die, and did, merely because his school friend had been killed beside him in the trenches near Gaza. Silly boy! Life is more than love.'

"I said I would take cocoa, partly to humor her, partly because I was becoming concerned about myself for a reason I need not mention, and I knew she normally put some mild sleeping draught in the cocoa for herself and, since it was the same making, I would gain the same benefit.

"My great-aunt was right about the chill. My bedroom had not retained the heat of the afternoon sun, and I didn't know whether to open the window to let the summer air in, or keep it closed against the dampness of the river.

"I slipped out of my clothes and into a nightdress as quickly as possible. The tester bed was large and needed to be warmed by the heat of one's own body. I lay on my back, looking up at the ceiling through the space where the canopy ought to have been. The four posts were there, and the top rails joining them, but there was nothing more than a box-pleated frill of tapestry round the outside to look at, and a spider out of reach in the middle of the ceiling, motionless and waiting for a victim. I hoped it would not drop onto the bed.

"The room *was* cold, and I ought to have opened the window to freshen it, but I couldn't summon up the will to get out of bed again. I thought about Tom. I worried about the future. I tossed about. I told myself I was tired. I insisted that I should sleep. But sleep would not come. Perhaps my aunt had been too sparing with whatever she used.

"The air felt oppressive, and there was no clarity in breathing: a cold stuffiness permeated everything. Eventually I sank into a state of semi-inertia, motionless in body and lethargic in mind. The last gleam of summer light faded away into the north, leaving the walls dark and my uncurtained windows visible only as pale oblongs hanging in space. There was no wind, and the sound of the river where it hurried over shallows was not strong enough to penetrate the room. I might have heard the harsh screech of an owl, or a curlew trilling down on the water meadows below the house, or far away on the moor, but there was nothing, and I lay in isolation from the world.

"I was not aware of falling asleep, but I must have done so, for I experienced again the walk from the churchyard with Mr. Thornton. He was by my side talking foolishly. I walked with the helpless acceptance of a sleeper, except that I knew that if I could turn there would be something at my side I would not wish to see. But it was a dream. At the bridge, Mr. Thornton turned away, but the other remained with me like a footstep scarcely heard in an empty street at night. The road wavered, bent upwards, and divided itself again into the windows of my room.

"I hear nothing now, but then I could sense even the smallest of creatures walking or scratching on wood or among leaves. Perhaps the spider wrought his business. But he had moved to a new place. Something was feeling along the woodwork beyond the foot of the bed— little pushings and scrapings which were not the living silence of one's inner ear that never departs except with death.

"I was now thoroughly awake, but subject to the strangest delusion. Normally one moves without thought. I found myself thinking very intently about moving, but unable to put the matter to the test for fear of finding that I could not. The scraping had stopped, but I could detect behind the swishing of the blood in my ears some other disturbance. The blankets were becoming heavier. I do not understand how I failed to notice the beginning of that dreadful experience, but something was covering the bed. My feet were held down by a weight that was moving up my legs like a carpet of lead being slowly unrolled. I was on my back. The weight was on my belly, trapping my arms, creeping over my breasts, suffocating and sick. I wanted to shrink into the bed, to be lifted away, to die—anything to escape the horror of what was being done to me. But two things held me in being for later. One was an agonizing thrust of pain as if something had broken within me under the pressure. The other was a protracted flickering of lightening somewhere to the south, beyond the river, that lit up the whole room and let me see everything in it with the clarity and certainty of full light.

"My aunt could not have been asleep, for within seconds, even before the long undulations of thunder had caught up with its lightening, she was knocking urgently at the door. She came in before I could speak. I had fallen out of bed and knocked over a chair and small table in my struggles, but my first reaction was to look down to see if I was bleeding. Of course I was not, but embarrassment in my generation was almost as strong a motive as fear.

"She was a wise and practical woman behind the formal exterior, and must at once have seen that something far beyond thunder and bad dreams had moved me, and brought her to my room. She put her arm round me, and sat with me on the side of the bed. I was shivering uncontrollably and couldn't tell her. To her everlasting credit she did not ask.

"'You'd better come back to my room for the night,' she said after a few moments. 'It's got the biggest bed between Weldon and Windyhaugh, so you'll be perfectly comfortable and safe. I'll make tea, and you'll take sugar in it whether you like it or not.'

"I went with her thankfully. She had an electric kettle and tea things in the room, and a little nursery light that burned in a corner. I lay close to her but did not sleep.

"With the return of light she took me back to the room to collect my clothes. It was cold, and she flung open the windows. The rain-washed freshness of grass and the honeyed smell of the earliest heather wafted in with all the sweetness of the world. Then she examined the room. It was as I had left it—bedclothes flung about and the table on its side.

"'What's that disgusting object?'

"She was pointing at the chimneypiece. A funnel of dirty grey, like rotting lace, was woven into the angle between shelf and wall. Shrunk into it, but still moving, was the tip of an obscene pink worm. I thought I was about to faint; instead I was violently and horribly sick.

"'What's the matter child? You must tell me. Something happened here.'

"I told her what I could, what I had felt. But I could never bring myself to tell any other living person what I had seen. I do not know how much she believed to be real, but it was enough. Some things cannot be spoken. She found the tooth beside the pillow. I explained how I had brought it into the room, and where I had left it.

"'I'll take it away,' she said. 'It will go back where it belongs.'

"On the Sunday she pushed it into the ground where, as she said, Elenor or another, must have hidden the body. 'Quite clever,' she observed judiciously, 'like hiding a book on a bookshelf.'

"Before Daniel, my aunt's gardener, could be summoned to remove the web, its tenant had disappeared. The maids took my things to a small room next to Aunt May's where later my worst fears became manifest. She was very matter-of-fact and invented an acceptable story. My father was already away in France and died in an accident without ever being told. My mother did not wish to know. I never went to Switzerland. I heard Tom was one of the few killed in the big German push across the Ardennes. His baby was stillborn a month later—or so they insisted. I did not see him. The pain was like being torn by stones. I never wanted to recover. I took my departure by the railway as soon as I was well enough to move. It was easy enough in the end. The darkness was deep and cold. Sometimes I see the man who must hear my story. When his time is near he has no choice."

"My dear Harry, what *are* you doing? You look quite stunned! They've all been at the food, and you haven't had anything yet."

Vivienne Selwood almost rushed at me, and I stood up in some confusion with my back to the window.

"I'm sorry. I haven't been attending. I've been listening to . . . to . . ." I made a helpless gesture, and turned to indicate my companion in the hope of a belated introduction, but she had slipped away. "To the old lady who was sitting here. I didn't get her name."

"Old lady? What old lady? Really you men do exaggerate! What was she like?"

"Well . . . very old. A dry, grey face, shrunken mouth and deep-set eyes, dark clothes and black gloves. She seemed to have no—"

I broke off, aware that what I was saying might give offense if I was describing a relative or old friend of the Selwoods'.

Vivienne laughed. She was very beautiful, and when she laughed her fair Nordic features had a power that negated argument. "I don't think any of my guests would like to hear themselves described like that!"

She paused.

"But there may be someone living up near the old railway who fits your description. Dad told me he'd spoken to someone like that. It was last year; but he died in November, so we can't really ask him now can we?" She laughed again. "Tony and I don't know all the locals yet, but if she came here she was certainly an uninvited guest. You didn't get her name?"

"No. She mentioned a clergyman—Thornton—and I think she said her aunt or grandaunt's name was Addison."

"There are dozens of *Harrisons* in this area. I believe one lived here before the Malings and there was some sort of tragedy. But do come and have some food before the farming contingent demolishes everything. Tony has some rare whisky he wants you to try, and the other Scots are *dying* to sound you about the Bank's share price."

Before following her I looked across the valley at the still perceptible line of the abandoned railway. It curved into an oblivion of hills to the south. There was no one to be seen, and the mud on the carpet had already turned to dust.

The Hurting Words

SIMON KURT UNSWORTH

SIMON KURT UNSWORTH was born in 1972 in Manchester, England, and despite extensive research he still has not found evidence of any mysterious signs or portents being seen on the day of his birth.

His stories have appeared in the Ash-Tree Press anthologies *At Ease with the Dead*, *Exotic Gothic 3* and *Shades of Darkness*, as well as in *Lovecraft Unbound*, *Gaslight Grotesque*, *Creature Feature*, *The Black Book of Horror 6*, *Never Again*, *The Mammoth Book of Best New Horror #21* and *#22*, and *Black Static* magazine.

His story "The Church on the Island" was nominated for a World Fantasy Award and was reprinted in *The Mammoth Book of Best New Horror #19* and *The Very Best of Best New Horror*. The author's first collection, *Lost Places*, was published by Ash-Tree in 2010, and forthcoming are two more collections, *Quiet Houses* and *Strange Gateways*, from Dark Continents and PS Publishing, respectively.

"'The Hurting Words' is a story about six years in the gestation," explains Unsworth. "It was conceived because of, and evolving from, a genuine incident in a creative writing class I attended, where I received back too many copies of a piece of writing I'd done and couldn't work out who the extra one was from.

"For the longest time (well, about five years), it was stuck at a point near the middle, with the tale refusing to move. But thanks to the gentle midwifery of (among others) the Monkeyrack Writing Mob, Barbara Roden, Gary McMahon, and Stephen Jones, it finally emerged complete, healthy and squalling.

"I stole my friend Sarah's surname for a main character and haven't given it her back yet, and I feel quite sorry for my villain."

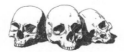

THERE WERE five of them.

Trevelyan counted the bundles of paper again, separating each from the others, and there were still five when there should only have been four. Sighing, he thrust them back into his bag; he did not have time to check them all now and would have to look at them later.

It was a simple idea; Trevelyan and four other staff members who had started at the same time as he acted as proofreaders and critics for the various reports, grant submissions, and research articles that the others wrote. It did not matter if they were from different disciplines, were in different departments, they simply made what comments they felt they could and the authors did with them what they wanted. The previous Monday, Trevelyan had placed copies of his draft article *Frankenstein's Monster: An Impression of Schizophrenia?* into four pigeonholes, and on this Friday afternoon, he should have had four replies. There were five.

It wasn't until that evening that Trevelyan looked at the papers. His original idea, that he had picked up a rogue paper or had photocopied one too many of his own article, he quickly dismissed. Each of the returned drafts before him was different. Jenni Grey had made a series of comments that were useful and his fellow English Literature lecturer McTeague's return was, unusually, almost unmarked. Breen had, as befitted an orderly physicist, filled the margin with his notes written in lurid purple ink and Darber had simply listed all the typos and grammatical errors at the end of the article. And then there was the extra one.

Whoever had written these notes had spent time doing it; every page was covered in a neat black script that filled the space around his text. Here and there, words or phrases had been scored out and new ones written across them so that the paper had become a palimpsest. The new comments were dry, academic, written in short sentences that speared their meaning quickly. On the final page of the article, the unknown author had written a longer piece

Dear Boy, this is almost passable work, containing some ideas with facets that are not without interest but that need further work. I would caution you, however, against committing the great heresy of literary criticism: do not look back and impose your own culturally relative views on what you read. Frankenstein's Monster may well, to your mind, be a good metaphor for the creeping terror of schizophrenia, yet Shelley would have had no concept of schizophrenia. Madness, yes. Bodily disintegration and the plight of the poor and ill, yes. The workings of places like Bedlam and its unfortunate residents, also yes. But schizophrenia? No. Ask yourself: had "schizophrenia" as a concept even been "invented" back when Shelley wrote her novel? Perhaps it might be better to say that Frankenstein's Monster is a good metaphor for illness generally, for decay and loss of control, rather than to tie it to such a specifically 20th-century concept as "schizophrenia"?

DRR

"What?" asked Trevelyan, aloud. The earlier comments had been useful, but this last one missed the point entirely. His paper was *about* the way in which readers imported their own interpretations onto things, especially when the original writing was as powerful as Shelley's was. It was what made classics classics: their ability to be constantly reinterpreted and reinvented. Dracula, for instance, might be about the creeping influx of foreign cultures or the unstoppable march of science and technology, or it might be about the spread of AIDS, and in twenty years time it might be about something else entirely. This was one of the themes that Trevelyan's article had sought to illustrate using *Frankenstein*, and it was this that his unknown critic had apparently missed.

It must be a joke, he decided, albeit a complicated one. The depth of knowledge displayed indicated someone with a good grip of literature and theory, which pointed to McTeague, but he was humorless and it did not seem to be his style, not really. Perhaps it was a way for McTeague to say all the things to him that he felt he couldn't in person? Unlikely; he was well known for arguing with his colleagues over the slightest thing, and did not shy away from outspokenness. It was more likely one of Darber's odd creations, thought Trevelyan. The psychology lecturer had the time and the sort of mind needed to find this sort of thing funny. He resolved to keep an eye on him.

The Five met every few weeks, and by coincidence their next meeting was that night. Jenni Grey and Breen, newly engaged, arrived at the bar at the same time as he did, and Darber came in shortly after, and they spent a few minutes catching up and exchanging news. When McTeague came in, he came straight up to Trevelyan and stood over him, saying "Stay away from me." He spat as he spoke, and his fists clenched. Trevelyan saw the fists and tried to move back, saying "Alex, what?"

"I know what you're doing," said McTeague. "It won't work."

"Alex, what's wrong?" asked Jenni, standing.

"He knows," said McTeague, nodding at a bemused and concerned Trevelyan, who was still watching the older man's clenching and unclenching fists. His hands were large, the knuckles prominent, the veins snaking around them like rope.

"Alex, sit down and have a drink," said Darber.

"I won't sit with him, nor drink with him" said McTeague, one finger jabbing towards Trevelyan. "Ask him why." And with that, he turned and ran from the bar.

"Alex?" asked Jenni softly to his retreating back. Once he had gone, she turned to the others, her face a question in skin.

"Strange," said Darber. "And what did you do to irritate him, Raymond?"

"I've no idea," said Trevelyan.

"He's—" said Jenni, but trailed off. "He's not himself. He made some comments on a paper of mine," she said finally, quietly. "They were . . . odd."

"Be honest, they were rude" said Breen, and Trevelyan finally relaxed a little. Maybe it was McTeague who'd written his mysterious criticism after all. If he was about to burn out, it might explain it. *McTeague*, he thought. *Poor, humorless McTeague, with his staid readings and articles on the classics and his dry lectures, has finally begun to lose his mind.* It was a simple case of one of academia's smaller fish beginning to founder and Trevelyan, who had never really been that friendly with the older man, dismissed him from his thoughts.

That night, McTeague killed himself.

The funeral took place on a bright day, the mourners' shadows melting like tar across the grass and headstones. Trevelyan, sweating in his only dark suit, stood by Grey and Breen for the graveside service. Grey was weeping openly while even Breen looked sad, and Trevelyan was uncomfortably aware of how dismissive his last thoughts about McTeague had been; guilt lay in his stomach like undigested dough. Perhaps if he had gone to McTeague, spoken to him, he might not have climbed out of his fourth-floor office window and thrown himself to the ground below, leaving his last mark on the earth in blood and flesh on the concrete apron in front of the English Department offices.

Perhaps he would still be alive.

Trevelyan went to the memorial after the service, although it made him uncomfortable. He felt as though he bore a mark that let people see how he had treated McTeague, told what he had thought about him. Attending the gathering was a punishment for his inactivity, self-imposed, to make him feel better and he wondered if other members of the Five felt the same; they were all there. Jenni certainly did and cried almost continually, sometimes quietly and sometimes more noisily, cursing herself for not being a better friend to the dead man.

"I don't think you could have helped him," said Darber, wandering across from one of the loose groups of people by the buffet. "I saw him last week, before the incident in the bar, and he was very odd then. Distracted. He told me that he was tired of being 'got at,' but he wouldn't tell me who was getting at him."

"Did you try and help him?" asked Jenni angrily.

"No," said Darber, either not noticing or ignoring Jenni's anger. "There was no point. He and I didn't really get on and anyway and I only saw him for a moment. I called into his office to give him back the draft of his paper; I'd forgotten to put it in his pigeonhole and I'd made some comments I thought he'd find valuable. He wouldn't take the paper from me. I thought it was odd, certainly, but not odd enough to make me worry. I tried to talk to him, but he seemed disinclined to speak."

Disinclined? thought Trevelyan as Jenni fell softly into more tears and Darber walked away. *Poor McTeague, if that was his last human contact!*

During the next weeks, and as the bolus of his guilt receded, Trevelyan thought of McTeague less and less. The coroner's verdict came and went, confirming what everyone already knew: McTeague had killed himself as a result of unknown stress or stresses in his life. His lectures were parceled out between his colleagues and his photograph taken down from the Current Staff board. Trevelyan continued amending his article, correcting and reworking it according to the feedback he had received and thought useful. The Monday after it was finished, he took copies of it to put in the Five's pigeonholes, realizing with a sad little jolt that they were the Four now, and that McTeague's pigeonhole had already been re-allocated; the strip of tape across its bottom edge now held a new name. He wondered if all the traces of McTeague's existence at the university were being erased as quickly and easily; certainly, no one seemed to want to talk about the man now he was dead. Even Jenni had not mentioned him the last time Trevelyan and she had met. Indeed, Trevelyan had the distinct impression that she deliberately avoided the subject. Perhaps her guilt, like her friendship with the dead man, was greater than Trevelyan's. He did not know.

That night, Jenni rang. She was crying, her conversation broken by sniffs and little animal hitching sounds, and it took Trevelyan a while to calm her enough to explain why she had called him.

"You want me to what?" he asked after she had finished.

"Come with me to poor Alexander's office," she replied. "Now that the coroner's verdict is in, the police have released his things. The university want the room cleared, and they asked me to do it because they know I was his friend. You work in the same department, so you can help. Please? I need company, I'm not sure I can go there alone. I asked Davey, but he can't do it."

Davey? thought Trevelyan, before realizing that Jenni meant Breen. Even Breen never used his first name, simply signing himself B or *Breen.* It didn't seem to fit, somehow.

The foyer to the English and Philosophy Building was quiet, the air relaxing into the building's emptiness. Jenni was waiting for him, huddled into her coat, slumped back on one of the chairs that lined the walls. Her face showed the reddened signs of recent tears, although her eyes were dry. She smiled weakly, standing and saying, "Thanks for this. For coming with me, I mean. I couldn't have done this alone, not go through his things. It'd be like grave robbing. I mean, I know I'm not keeping any of it, but I'd feel really uncomfortable, you know?"

Trevelyan nodded, knowing exactly what she meant; the thought of searching through McTeague's possessions, of boxing them up and passing them on or back, felt insulting, as though they were sullying his memory. It was as if, by packing away his things, they would be packing away McTeague himself, constraining him and storing him like so much useless detritus.

At the office, Trevelyan let Jenni enter first, thinking she might need a moment alone. In the quiet, Trevelyan heard Jenni sob once, and then a yellow lozenge of light fell through the open doorway, seeping across the carpet like old honey. Briefly, Jenni's silhouette was caught in it like a fly in amber, and then it was gone and Trevelyan followed her into the room.

It was a mess. The police search had left things in scattered, untidy piles and this, coupled with McTeague's own hoarding nature, had left an office claustrophobic with contents. The surface of the desk was lost under papers and books, ragged strips of torn paper sticking out from their closed pages as makeshift markers. Shelves lined the walls, the books they contained piled against each other like broken teeth; more books sat atop the cases, excess from the shelves that had no proper home. Magazines, also with torn paper markers jutting out from their closed pages, were stacked in uneven towers next to the bookcases. Two battered grey filing cabinets stood either side of the window, their drawers labeled with handwritten and peeling stickers. Next to the door, Trevelyan saw, the porters had left a stack of empty boxes.

"You look at the books," said Jenni quietly. "I'll start sorting through his desk."

The books were easy; almost all belonged to the department, so he placed them in boxes, sealing them when they were full, labeling them and pulling them into the corridor. The magazines he boxed separately; they would go to McTeague's mother. The filing cabinets were, oddly, almost empty. Once they were done, he was almost finished; only one more thing to sort.

"What's this?" Trevelyan asked, pointing to a clear bag by the waste bin. Jenni, just finishing sorting through the desk drawers, looked around briefly and then said, "The paper from the bin. The police took it to see if there was anything in there that might give them some idea of why he did it, but there was nothing. I think they hoped they'd find a draft suicide note, but there's just lots of academic notes, they said." Trevelyan noticed that, as she spoke, Jenni had looked at the window fearfully and then looked away. He had felt it himself, as he sorted and packed. It drew at him, made him want to open it and look down, to experience a little of what McTeague experienced, to see a little of what he saw. It had been raining that night, he remembered; McTeague's last view of the world had been dark and wet.

The carpet below the window was stained, and in amongst the remnants of the police fingerprint powder on the window ledge were tiny rings where the raindrops had dried and left behind their ghosts. As Trevelyan knelt to pick up the bag of old papers, something brought him up short. At first, he wasn't sure what it was except a sense that he had seen something out of place, something jarring, and then he realized.

Writing.

Inside the clear plastic bag, most of the sheets had been folded roughly, crumpled in the past and then smoothed again, and the wrinkles across their surfaces looked old and tired. Black type crawled across them, and webbed around the type were handwritten notes, and Trevelyan recognized the handwriting.

Using the point of a key, Trevelyan tore open the heavy bag. Taking out sheet after sheet of the paper, each different from the last but also terribly, awfully similar, he placed it on the floor. Finally, with perhaps thirty pieces spread out in front of him, Trevelyan leaned back on his haunches and let out a long, uncomfortable breath.

"What is it?" asked Jenni, looking over at him and the paper.

"I'm not sure," replied Trevelyan. "I think it's what Alexander was working on when he died, but look," he said, gesturing at the paper about him. Each piece was covered in comment, written in the same brittle handwriting Trevelyan recognized from the additional copy of his own draft research paper. Sometimes, the comments appeared helpful and considered. Trevelyan read one that said *This sentence seems overly long: perhaps you could split it into three sentences?* Others were shorter, more terse: *Lazy writing! Be concise, man!* Trevelyan saw one sheet where an entire paragraph had been scored out with a heavy black line and the word *NO!* written in the margin next to it.

"I got one of these," said Trevelyan. "I think Alexander wrote it, as well as his own normal feedback. It was strange."

"It's not his writing," said Jenni. "Besides, why would he write those things to himself? Some of them are downright nasty." She was holding a sheet upon which a series of sentences had been crossed out and the phrase *Have you learned nothing from earlier comments? Idiot.* was written.

"If he was stressed and suffering," said Trevelyan, "he might have done it to try to make himself feel better."

"How could this make anyone feel better?" asked Jenni, dropping the paper back onto the floor. "It's horrible stuff. Have you finished? Can we go?"

Trevelyan took the papers home with him in the end. Sitting in his study, he read them again and finally thought he could discern their order. If he was right, they showed an increasing aggression to the handwritten comments and a concurrent deterioration of the quality of McTeague's typed text. The handwritten comments became bullying, hectoring and finally downright unpleasant, and it made him sad to know that McTeague—*Alexander*—had essentially bullied himself to suicide. The sheets were a mute testimony to it, a good-bye note written in oblique parts, desolate and angry and bitter. He sealed them in an envelope and placed them in his drawer; he would pass them to Jenni and let her decide what to do with them.

He spent the rest of the night making his final changes to his *Frankenstein* paper and printing it. *No more feedback*, he decided; *now this stands or falls on its own merits.* Leaving it in the center of his desk, he went to bed. It had been a long day and sleep felt like a reward for labors completed.

When he picked up the envelope from his pigeonhole, Trevelyan didn't have time to read what it contained, instead putting it in his bag with his other paperwork. The envelope was large, had neither sender's address nor stamp on it and only his name on the front in block capitals: R.E. TREVELYAN. He didn't remember it until the following night, carrying it into his lounge and opening it whilst lying on his sofa, tearing away the flap of the envelope and upending the contents onto his chest. Trevelyan caught a whiff of something dry, as though the envelope held long-untouched air full of dust and powder, and then a sheaf of white paper tumbled out.

At first, he couldn't work out what he was seeing. It was his work, his paper on *Frankenstein*, but covered in markings. Was it a rejection? No, there was no enclosure from the journal, not even a standard

"Thank you but no thank you" slip. Besides, the journal's editor and he had discussed his paper before he submitted it, and whilst it wasn't quite a commission, it wasn't a blind submission either. Had the editor sent it back with his thoughts written on? No, surely any comments or revisions would have been written up properly, or he would have rung Trevelyan to talk them through? He looked again at the comments, and as realization dawned he sat up and the papers fell to the floor in an untidy pile.

He recognized the handwriting.

It was McTeague's, or at least it was the writing he had assumed was McTeague's, and it should have died with him, buried in a near-anonymous graveyard that Trevelyan was sure the man had never visited in life. And yet, here it was scrawled over the paper, *his* paper, in cramped, obsessive lines. It was almost too dense to read at points, the letters tangling together and overlapping so that the words themselves were squeezed, as though whoever was writing was desperate to fit as much on the page as possible. The underscores and crossings out were so thick that the ink had bled sideways, feathering into the surrounding words like gathering storm clouds.

Trevelyan's first thought was that he had put the wrong paper into the envelope, had accidentally sent an earlier one to the journal, but he dismissed that idea straight away. He knew his own work, and what he could see of the typed text under the handwritten commentary was the final version of the article, and he had only printed one copy. So how had it got here? And how had someone managed to scrawl over it?

The comments themselves were as vitriolic as before, he saw. One sentence, *Lazy material, man!*, leaped out at him immediately, and he found many others like it. There was a barely restrained fury to the comments, to the parade of words (*no! weak! idiot!*), that made them difficult to read. On the last page, Trevelyan found another addition, written in a space of its own and larger, as though to ensure it was read.

You have listened to nothing, learned nothing from my earlier comments and suggestions. As a result, this paper is flawed and lazy, and I cannot allow it to go to publication. When you have the good grace to make the amendments that I have suggested, perhaps then I may be more amenable to allowing it to face public scrutiny. Until then, however, I insist that it stays unread by all except you and me.

DRR

After he had finished reading, Trevelyan very carefully put the papers back into the envelope, stood, and went to his study. He placed it in his bag and went to leave the room, but stopped. In the half-dark, he thought about the paper, about the comments, about McTeague and Jenni and himself, and then in a low voice, he said, "No. It's my paper. It goes in the form I want." And then, trying not to think at all, trying to pretend that things were normal, he went to bed.

He didn't sleep. In a darkness that felt brittle and full of edges, Trevelyan lay in his bed and helplessly teased at the situation like he would a holed tooth with his tongue. If not McTeague, then who? And it wasn't McTeague, it couldn't be—messages from dead men were the stuff of stories, the things he read and wrote about and taught, not things that happened in the warmth of a campus summer. So, another member of the Five (*Four*, he thought sharply, the *Four*)? But if so, why? What was the point? It didn't make any sense; at least with McTeague, there had been a kind of obscene, degraded logic to it, but not any of the others. Breen, Darber, Jenni, none of them stood to gain from it, and none had shown an inclination towards cruelty before. And besides, how had they intercepted it from the post, preventing it from reaching the magazine? Trevelyan was baffled, drawing his knees up to his chest as the night crept about him.

Sounds came from downstairs.

At first, he thought it was the midnight rhythms of the house settling, but it wasn't. It had none of the languid spread of normal night noises, none of the unwinding ease of them. Instead, it was a hurried, tenser sound, a chittering that made him think of palsied teeth. It was lurid, feverish, growing louder, more urgent, filling the room and pressing the darkness down against him like old, damp sacking. He reached out and turned on his bedside lamp, but the wan electric light made no difference; the sound shivered around him.

Eventually, Trevelyan had to move; it was that or remain frozen in his bed all night, he told himself, nestled under his quilt like a child, and he would not do that. No. *No.* This was his house, his *home,* he had bought it, was paying for it still, had arranged things within it the way he wanted them. It bore his imprint, held his reflection, was *his* place, and he would not be trapped within any part of it by something as simple as sound. Taking hold of his irritation, his tiredness, his fear, Trevelyan rose from the bed and went to the door. Quickly, before his sense of anger faded, he opened the door.

The hallway was filled with a shifting darkness, the shadows flowing across the walls like oil on the surface of water. It was words, Trevelyan saw, words creating themselves out of nothing, flowing black lines expanding and forming, some collapsing down to unintelligible strings of shapes that could be letters but that were so tiny it was impossible to make out individual characteristics. They moved, worm-like and sinuous and impossible, their noise the frantic, dry scratching of branches against old glass.

The lines swirled now, funneling around the doorway but never quite crossing the edge of the light that fell out around him, remaining just beyond it. When they came close to the light's glimmer, the words and sentences and paragraphs reared away, rising from the floor like threatened insects, Devil's Coachmen showing their armored bellies or scorpions lifting claws that glinted half-seen and dull. He saw words form and disappear in the tangles, close enough now to read, *paltry* and *ill-thought* and once simply *NO* in heavy, rigid capitals. Trevelyan couldn't scream; the words seemed to have dwindled his voice and breath to little more than a failing wheeze. They clustered, closer and tighter, closer and tighter, until they were dancing near Trevelyan's feet, filling the whole of the hallway.

Very slowly, Trevelyan shut the door and stepped back into his room, into the cradling arms of the light from his bedside lamp. Lines of words, writing he knew, crept under the door before the light drove them away, *stupid* looping alongside *confused* and *pointless*. Now on his bed, he pulled the quilt up around his chest. Words continued emerging and vanishing under the door as, silently, he prayed for morning.

The sunlight, pale and weak and clean, came with summer's earliness, for which Trevelyan was grateful. The souring darkness that had trembled and bled under his door only retreated with its arrival, and was completely gone by the time he risked looking into the hallway. The walls were unmarked, the floors clear, and the noise had faded like the last static of a dying radio. Going downstairs, the house itself felt tired, exhausted after a long and aching battle, and the closer to his study he came, the greater this impression became. The room *throbbed*, the bitter center of an infection that had taken root during the night, and when he opened the door, it smelled sickened and dry and old.

The room was dark, but the darkness contracted as Trevelyan watched, swirling like ink flowing down a plug-hole until only a dense patch remained gathered around the envelope on his desk and then this too was gone. Weary, Trevelyan shook the papers out onto the desk without touching them; they were still covered with writing, different from the previous day, thicker and more layered, some of the words faded and others glaring and new. Using a pencil to lift each sheet, he flicked through the pages until he came to the last one. The longer comment had faded down to a dusty, wretched grey, and over it, written in large, black letters, was a single savage *NO*.

Campus was busy, buffeting Trevelyan as he walked. He was exhausted, and had the feeling that his world was shifting, bucking under him like the deck of a ship that he had not even known he was on. *All these people, have they got any idea?* he wondered, looking at the students around him, and thought that they didn't, *couldn't*. How could they? If he tried to talk to any of them, would they think him mad? Probably. Were it not for the packet of papers in his bag, he might have suspected that himself.

"Do you think it's funny?"

Trevelyan started, his reverie broken by Darber, who had stepped out in front of him, blocking his path. Darber looked different and for a moment, Trevelyan couldn't work out why, and then he realized: he was angry. His face, normally so smooth, was twisted into an ugly snarl Trevelyan couldn't remember Darber ever wearing before. He couldn't remember him showing any emotion, really, other than a kind of faintly amused disdain. The man wasn't just angry, he saw, but disheveled as well, his suit wrinkled, his shirt unbuttoned. He was tieless and was holding something, waving it at Trevelyan as he spoke.

"I don't appreciate this sort of thing. You and Grey may be upset, that's fine, but I couldn't have helped the man."

"I don't know what you're talking about," said Trevelyan, but he thought that perhaps he did. It was papers that Darber was holding and shaking that told him, a sheaf that rattled like snakeskin.

"Nonsense," said Darber, an attempt at composure showing on his face. He shook the papers again and Trevelyan caught sight of printed text covered with the now-familiar writing. "I mean, is it a joke? If so, it's not funny, it's just offensive. By all means criticize me to my face, but to attack my work like this, work that you clearly don't really understand? It's childish." Darber danced the papers under Trevelyan's nose again, and he smelled the sour, trapped odor of age, even though the sheets that Darber held were a new, bright white. Even upside down, he made out the words *You are a fool, man!*

"We didn't write those things," said Trevelyan, but Darber only grinned, his face grey and wretched.

"You and Grey have always hated me, I know that, but I thought you could be professional about it."

"We don't hate you," said Trevelyan. "We didn't write those things, I promise you. Look, I got one myself," and he reached in his bag and withdrew his article, holding it out for Darber to see. Darber knocked Trevelyan's outstretched hand down without looking at it.

"I don't give a fuck," said Darber. "Just stay away from me, you and that bitch too." And with that, he turned and strode away, not looking back even when Trevelyan called him.

Trevelyan made his way to the department common room, and as he went, he thought he could hear the insistent scratch of new words being created rising from his bag. He wondered what would happen when he opened it; would they burst out in a shower of ink, coating the room, or would he simply find the papers bloating obscenely, swollen with words that were not his? Would they have spread to the other books and papers in there? He looked around him and wondered about how far the writing would go, whether it would take over, eventually cover the world. Would everything he knew and valued and loved eventually vanish under a swirling, vehement black tide? He saw it then, saw himself staggering through a world where the shadows had become the lightest thing around him, paler than the ever-expanding blackness, saw himself climbing out of a window to escape it, or taking pills or slipping his head into a noose in an anonymous room and kicking away a stool, somehow finding a way to follow McTeague, and then he was angry again, and he opened his bag.

The envelope fell out onto the table in front of him. As he watched, it bulged and shook slightly, as though the papers within were breathing. He picked it up and upended it, shaking the contents loose. They fluttered out, falling to the table in scattered drifts. Trevelyan picked up the sheet nearest to him, seeing his own writing caged by new words. *Moron* caught his eye, as did *imbecile* and *poor* and, once, *dolt*. Dolt? he thought. *Who speaks like that? Who uses that as an insult?* Fully two-thirds of his own work had been literally blotted out; thick black lines now lay across his own writing, obscuring it completely, and over it were new words, new phrases.

New ideas.

"My God, where did you get a Rathbone from?" asked a voice from his side.

Severn was the oldest member of the department, if not the oldest member of the university staff. "That takes me back," he said, lowering himself into the chair next to Trevelyan without waiting for Trevelyan to reply. "May I see?" He was reaching, Trevelyan saw, for the papers, surprisingly fast for an old man, and before Trevelyan could move them out of reach, he had hold of them and they were gone. Trevelyan wanted to say something, a warning, but his voice had abandoned him. He waited for the writing to writhe, to flow around Severn's fingers, to create new words over the old. For the man to scream.

"He was a nasty piece of work, wasn't he? Where did you find this? One of the old filing cabinets, I suppose?" Severn looked expectantly at Trevelyan who, confused, nodded.

"We used to dread getting one of these, back when I started. All that criticism and never a positive thing to say about anything or anyone. I tell you, I don't miss seeing these in my pigeonhole."

Trevelyan thought that he was probably gaping; his mouth was definitely open and he shut it with an audible pop. His brain leapt, darting back over what Severn had said, trying to drag some sense from it. "You recognize it?" he managed to say. "The writing? You know it?"

"Of course," said Severn, looking more closely at Trevelyan. "Are you all right? You look pale."

"I didn't sleep well," replied Trevelyan. "Please, tell me about—" he tailed off, waving his hand at the paper. He still didn't know how to describe it—criticism? Abuse? Attack? All those and more.

"It was written by a man called Rathbone, David Robert Rathbone. Look, he signed this one *DRR*, but he sometimes used to put *DR Rathbone*, which used to make us laugh, only never so he could hear us. We used to joke that he hoped that people would read it as *Dr. Rathbone*. He wasn't a doctor, you see, only a lecturer, and not even a good one. He was a glorified administrator, really, good at pushing pencils and forms around but less good with the academic end of things. You know the sort." Trevelyan nodded again, terrified of interrupting Severn and slowing the flow of information. There were no answers yet, but Severn was finally giving him a framework for his questions.

"He was here when I started, and he was the strictest man I ever met. The department was run by Nixon, who was mostly old and senile, like me." Severn looked slyly at Trevelyan, waiting. Trevelyan merely returned his look, hoping his expression conveyed the message *Of course not, Severn, you're as sharp as ever* without needing to say it. He liked Severn well enough, but sometimes he could be difficult if he thought you weren't deferential enough to him.

"Rathbone was Deputy Head, but essentially, he ran the department. He was a tyrant, controlled everything. What's that modern phrase? Micromanaged, that's it! He *micromanaged* things. Everything had to go through him, every order for books or stationery, every change to timetables or the syllabus. He made us all show him our research papers, journal articles, book chapters, what have you, before we were allowed to send them out. He claimed it was to ensure that the department's reputation wasn't adversely affected by poor work, but really it was because he was a critical old woman who couldn't stand the thought of someone having ideas better than his own. I don't think he even wanted to take credit for the ideas, not really. I think he just wanted to stop anything coming out of the department that he hadn't made his own in some way, molded it the way he thought it ought to be."

Trevelyan watched, as Severn held the paper up before him, waiting for the lines of text to move. They remained still, their heavy black print visible through the paper like veins under skin. Severn was looking at the writing, making sad little laughing sounds as he read it. Finally, he lowered it and looked at Trevelyan and said, "Have you read this? It's terrible isn't it? That he could be so vicious, I mean, and no one challenged it."

"What happened?"

"To Rathbone? He retired in the end, and no one was sorry to see him go. The department was a miserable place under him, especially at the end."

"The end? Why?"

"Because of his book," said Severn simply. "Because of the reviews it received."

The volume wasn't hard to find; there were several in the library, one of which Trevelyan stole.

It was slim, a 1970s paperback, and it was dusty with lack of use. It smelled of old thought, of fustiness and abandoned shelves, and it left its marks across Trevelyan's fingers in grime like the powder from moths' wings. He flicked through its brittle, cheap pages, feeling the waft of air across his face and tasting the paper's shedding skin. Its pages, he noticed, were unmarked, which made him smile grimly. Its cover was a light blue, decorated with a line drawing of a quill and parchment. The picture was badly executed, or maybe badly reproduced, and it looked rough and cheap. On the rear cover was a grainy head and shoulders picture of an unsmiling man in a shirt and tie. Rathbone, in all his grim glory.

Trevelyan tried to see into the man's eyes, but they were lost in the poor print quality of the photograph, mere dark ovals hanging under a pale forehead and black-slash eyebrows. He ran his finger across the picture, not sure what to expect, but felt only the not-quite-smooth cover of a poorly bound and produced book. Where had such malevolence come from, he wondered? Where had that hate birthed?

How could it still be here now?

Even in print, Trevelyan thought he might have known that Rathbone was the author; the tone of the essays that formed each chapter of the book was dismissive, showing in the way in which he swept aside earlier ideas about the various works he was analyzing. Rathbone was a man of absolutes, leaving no space for discussion. The problem was, most of his ideas were at best unoriginal and, at worst, old and stale. They would have been dated at the time the book was published, thought Trevelyan. In his Introduction, Rathbone said they were "a summation of many years' teaching and thinking," but Trevelyan found little evidence in what he read of anything original or creative or progressive. If this was the pinnacle of Rathbone's career, it was a stunted, low thing and it left little legacy.

In his office, Trevelyan took his article from his bag and put it on the table beside the book. It was now almost entirely black with additional text, illegible marks covering illegible marks, and he felt a wave of helpless fury. Even now, as he watched, swirling lines of words were creeping out over the edge of paper. They looked like the shadows of distant airplanes as they slipped across the surface of the table, like the X-rays of broken limbs made fluid and animate. They slithered around the edges of Rathbone's book, gathering about it but not touching it, until the tabletop was black with them, was bucking like the surface of an ink sea.

All except Rathbone's book, which was an island of pallid serenity on the table, a blue square of stillness at the heart of pulsing, malignant motion. Trevelyan gazed at it, hating it, hating Rathbone, and not knowing what to do about it. He reached out, lifting the book from the table, letting the shifting words rush in to fill the space it left behind so that the desktop was entirely covered, and held it in front of his face, flicking through its pages again.

"What are you?" he murmured. "What are you, and what do you want from me?" There was no reply. He wanted to ask it again, but didn't; if he was to escape from Rathbone, from the criticism and the bullying and the impossibility if it all, he would have to find his own solutions.

Trevelyan placed the book back onto the table, watching as venomous words shifted out from under it, clearing it a space. He reached out, knocking the book farther away from him so that it slid across the tabletop and Rathbone's writing danced out of its way and flowed in behind it, always leaving it unmarked. Trevelyan tried to think; what had Severn said? That it was the book that made things bad? No, not just the book, but the book and the reviews, and as he remembered he thought that maybe, just maybe, he might have a chance.

Trevelyan listened as the department went to rest around him, as his colleagues locked their offices and called their good-byes and trailed out, their footsteps like the pock of rain on cold stone. The lights dimmed, turning the corridor beyond the frosted glass wall of his office into a shadowed thing, and the passing staff into edgeless, moving shapes. As he watched, Trevelyan wished that had could be on the other side of the glass, could be walking along the corridor with them, unaware of writing that created itself, of long-gone academics and their savage opinions.

One of the dark shapes stopped by his door. The edges of it rippled against the mottled glass, and for a moment Trevelyan thought it was some new aspect of Rathbone, writing that had plaited and formed itself into a figure, was coming for him on spindle, text legs. He tensed, and then the shape knocked on the door and opened it without waiting for a response.

"Hello," said Severn. "I saw the light and thought I'd pop my head in."

"Hello," said Trevelyan, his heart shuddering.

"I've been thinking about your Rathbone papers," said Severn. "I wondered what you had thought you might do with them? He might have been a terrible man, and I didn't like him, but he's still a part of this place's history." He waved a vague hand at the ceiling, somehow taking in not just the department but the building and the campus beyond. "History isn't always pleasant, is it? But we have to treasure it."

"I don't know," said Trevelyan, feeling a dreadful black humor bubbling in his throat. "Maybe the university library might want them, or I may give them to his estate. I haven't thought about it."

"Estate?" said Severn. "Oh, no, you misunderstand me. Rathbone retired years ago, but he isn't dead."

The room was dim but not dark, the light warm and diffuse. "This is very unusual," said the care assistant whose name Trevelyan could not remember. "Mr. Rathbone hasn't had a visitor for such a long time, and he's such a sweet old man."

"Sweet?" asked Trevelyan, startled.

"Yes," said the care assistant. "I mean, he doesn't speak much these days, but when does he's always polite and he's so kind. And generous! He helped Mary's son with his homework last year when he heard her talk about how he couldn't understand the book he was reading."

I'll bet he did, thought Trevelyan bitterly. *I'll just bet.* "Can I see him?" he asked.

"If he's awake," the young man replied. "It's late, but it'd be good for Mr. R to have a visitor."

Mr. R? thought Trevelyan as the care assistant went to the huddled shape in the chair on the far side of the room. After a moment, he turned and beckoned Trevelyan over. "Mr. R," he whispered as Trevelyan came close, "you have a guest. Someone's come all the way from the university to see you. Isn't that nice? Well, I'll leave you to talk. Not too long, now, we don't want you getting too tired, do we?" The care assistant shot Trevelyan a look as he went past, stern and sure and protective.

Trevelyan wasn't sure what he expected, but the grizzled, hunched figure in the chair wasn't it. All the way to the rest home, driving through streets that were filling with the night, he had imagined some unholy terror lurking in a room that smelled of candles and incense, but the man in front of him looked delicate to the point of frailty, shriveled, his skin sallow and thin. He didn't look frightening, simply pathetic, a hunched and decaying thing whose eyes, crusted and rimmed with the dry, raw touch of age, hadn't focused on him.

"Can you hear me?" Trevelyan asked, and was surprised to hear tenderness in his voice. This man had terrified him, *tortured* him, and yet Trevelyan felt the anger that had helped drive him here slip away in the face of this withered, pathetic thing.

"Hello?" he said, and withdrew the article from the envelope in his bag. The pages were creased now, and the ever-moving writing was clumped in the creases as though it had flowed there and was struggling to escape. "You wrote this," Trevelyan continued. "You keep writing it, and I need you to stop. It has to stop. *You* have to stop." Rathbone did not reply. The only indication that he had heard, that he knew Trevelyan was there at all, was a brief nod of his head, birdlike and fragile, when he saw the papers.

"Please," said Trevelyan. "This is my work, and you're destroying it. You're frightening people, frightening *me*. Someone I know has already killed himself because of what you're doing. I don't know how you're doing it, I don't know why, but please stop. *Please*." Rathbone still didn't respond and, frustrated, Trevelyan crouched by him, dropping the paper onto the man's legs, stick thin inside shiny, worn suit pants. At the sound of their dry rustle, Rathbone tilted his head down. A line of spittle slipped over his lower lip and trailed down to the edge of the uppermost sheet, glinting. One trembling hand came up and drifted across the sheets and then jerked violently, sending them wafting to the floor about his feet. He wore check carpet slippers, Trevelyan saw, and felt that black mirth roil again in him. *A demon who wears slippers*, he thought, and then, with surprising speed, Rathbone's hand darted forward and clasped around his wrist.

"It's not me," said the old man, in a voice like pages turning. "Not me."

"It is," said Trevelyan, trying to pull his wrist away but unable to, and surprised by the man's strength.

"No. Not me, not any more. I was that person, but no more." Rathbone coughed as though he wasn't used to speaking, swallowed, and carried on. "No one comes, no one visits. I'm alone, because of what I was. Was I so bad? Yes. Yes, I was, but no more. I try to be kind now, to not be the person I was. That . . ." and the hand finally let go of Trevelyan's wrist and waved at the paper on the floor, ". . . isn't me. Whoever it is, it isn't me."

"It is," said Trevelyan. "It's you. It's how you were."

"Yes," said the old man, and Trevelyan was horrified to see tears roll from his eyes. "I was him, but not now. I'm old and I'm so lonely here and I have so much time to think. I look back at him, and I don't recognize him even though I know who he was. I've tried to change, to be different. Tried to be the person I should have been all these years and I am, I do it, but it's not enough. I can feel it, every time that other me does what I used to do. It hurts. It hurts so much. I'm here, but I'm out there as well, and I don't want to be. I'm so tired.

"Please, can you stop him?"

"I don't know," said Trevelyan. "I was hoping you could."

"No," croaked Rathbone. "Not me. I can't. I haven't the strength. I've tried, tried to stop it but I can't. I'm too old, too weak. You have to. Promise me. Promise."

"I'll try," said Trevelyan.

"Promise," said Rathbone again, drool slipping once more from the side of his mouth and slicking across his chin. Trevelyan watched as tears gathered and spilled from the older man's eyes, their rheumy blue irises lost in sclera that were yellowed and exhausted. The room lights reflected on the trickling liquid as he spoke. "Promise," he murmured again. "Promise."

The door to McTeague's office was locked but the keys Trevelyan had taken from the departmental office allowed him to enter. Once inside, he shut the door and locked it again. He did not turn on the overhead light, instead flicking on the desk lamp. Its pale yellow light crept across the walls and ceiling, making the shadows huddle together in the corners. The office looked bigger now that it had been cleared out, the floor bare and the walls like old ivory. The bookshelves, free of their tottering masses of books and magazines, stood sentinel against the walls and the desk, its scarred surface bare, had been pushed back into the far corner. Dust had gathered across the surfaces and a smell of neglect and abandonment had gathered in the few days since Trevelyan had been here with Jenni.

Trevelyan dragged the desk back to its place in front of the window, deliberately not looking out at the courtyard below. Even in the darkness, the paved ground that had been McTeague's landing place glared up in mute appeal. He removed his article from his bag, shaking it out of the envelope and placing it on the desk. Most of the additional comments had faded down to grey slivers now, so that in the dim light his writing looked scarred and weary. A tight smile on his face, he took a pen from his pocket and then, very deliberately, crossed out one of the extra comments with a heavy black line. Underneath, he wrote the word *Nonsense* and then recapped his pen and put it back in his pocket. Sitting back in the chair, Trevelyan waited.

It did not take long. Around him, the air seemed to thicken. Shadows that had, only moments earlier, been light suddenly darkened to a gravid, opaque gloom. The temperature dropped, raising gooseflesh on his arms, and the lamp flickered, guttering like candlelight before catching again and returning to full strength, buzzing and humming as it did so. Trevelyan tried not to shiver, removing Rathbone's book from his bag and clutching it; its solidity was oddly reassuring. *This has to work*, he thought. *This has to work*. He repeated it silently, rolling the book tightly in his fist. The word he had written on the paper seemed to glow, gleaming blackly. He rolled the book tighter, twisting the cover and pages around into a dense tube, and then relaxed his grip and let it spring back into shape. It flapped as it did so, sending a breath of old paper across his hands. He rolled it again, released it. Rolled it; released it. Rolled it, and there was a noise, of fingers dragging across stone and of insects rattling their wings, and Rathbone stepped out of the far shadows and into the light.

It was the Rathbone of the cover's rear, an anonymous-looking middle-aged man in formal clothes with short, bristling hair, not the shrunken thing he had been earlier that evening. He wore a neat suit, in a somber grey that spoke of conformity and rigidity. His shoes shone, clean but not ostentatious, and his shirt collar clutched tightly at his wattle neck. His bearing was controlled, his hands held clenched in front of him, one gripping the other as though to stop it flying away like some bone-white bird of fury. He looked respectable, conservative, unobtrusive.

Except in his face.

Rathbone's pupils glinted out from the pooled shadows that hung below his brows, and in that glitter was fervent anger. His grave-worm lips were pressed together, tight and thin and sour, and his chin sloped away from them as if to escape their bitter attentions. The lamplight flashed across the lenses of his spectacles, glinting. His hair was swept back and thick, shiny with pomade, and the smell of it was cloying and sweet. He stepped forwards and Trevelyan saw that, at his very edges, Rathbone was blurring slightly as though he was continually being made, unmade, made again from the shadows around him. His feet made no sound as he stepped forward.

"You ignore my advice?" asked Rathbone, pointing at the paper on the desk. His voice was dry. He took another step forward, his hand trembling as he continued to point.

"Advice given freely, meant only to help, and yet you consider it 'nonsense'?" He came forward, leaning over the desk so that he was between the light and Trevelyan. He cast no shadow, Trevelyan saw, but the light falling through him onto the desk was hazy, splintered. This close, Rathbone's edge was impossible to define. Strands of him, of his substance, unknitted from his body and trailed away, growing thinner and indistinct the farther away from him it went. It gave him a greying corona like an aura gone desiccated and lifeless.

"You believe my advice to be flawed?" asked Rathbone, with dangerous politeness. "Incorrect in some way? Do you believe you know this subject better than I?"

Trevelyan didn't reply. Instead, he reached into his bag and pulled out the sheaf of photocopies and printouts, dropping them onto the desk in front of him. It had been a hard job to find them and copy them, and now he would see if it had been worth it or not. He leaned forward, ignoring how close he was to Rathbone, ignoring the way his skin prickled as though there was a source of electricity nearby, and chose one at random, picking a sentence and speaking it aloud.

"'A man with no valid ideas.'"

"What?" said Rathbone. Trevelyan felt a wash of cold, writhing fear jittering across his skin and into his belly. He pushed the paper aside and picked up a new one.

"'Empty of originality, dull and likely to illuminate no one.'" *I'm reading to something that's not even a real ghost*, he thought. *It's a fragment of one man, his vitriol, let loose and made independent.*

"I beg your pardon?" said Rathbone, and when Trevelyan risked looking up at him, he saw that he had backed away a step. His edges were blurring further, mutable and frenzied, and Trevelyan thought his expression had changed, shifting from anger to a kind of cold dismay.

"'Broad-brush arguments that never hit the mark,'" said Trevelyan, reading from another paper," and then "'a mystery why this work has been published'" from a fourth.

"They were fools!" hissed Rathbone, his edges dancing like the tips of ocean waves. "They didn't understand what I was saying!"

"Not nice when the tables are turned, is it?" said Trevelyan, leaning back in his seat. His heart yammered so that he felt sure Rathbone would see his shirt trembling above it. He felt brittle, dangling above a place both vast and desolate, with only one way forward and no way back.

"It's so easy to feel under attack, isn't it?" Trevelyan lifted another of the copied reviews from the desk, smiling as insolently as he could manage, and read, "'Feeble ideas buttressed by writing as dull and lifeless as day-old custard.' Now, that's harsh, isn't it?"

"*How dare you?*" shrieked Rathbone, his voice like flies battering against metal. "*How dare you?*" and he dashed forward, those eyes seeming to sweep up all the light in the room and draw it in until Trevelyan could focus on nothing else, not papers nor print nor walls nor the lamp at his side. There was simply Rathbone, gray and bristling.

"They were fools, all of them!" hissed Rathbone again, his voice dropping now to a sibilant whisper. "They know nothing. I spent my life at this university, reading and listening and understanding, and I know those texts better than those people ever could."

"Really?" Trevelyan managed to say. Rathbone's face was all, a vast cold moon hanging before him.

"Yes! And you, you choose to ignore my advice and yet you take that of your friends? Some of them not even in the English department. What understanding have they of the written word? Of art? Of literature? *Scientists!*"

He's not touched me, thought Trevelyan and his confidence suddenly, shockingly, felt genuine rather than a brittle carapace, *because I don't think he can! It's all words and written savagery, an intellectual violence not a physical one!* He grinned, leaning forward. Rathbone fell back as though they were in some stylized gavotte and Trevelyan grinned more widely. He let the book fall from his fist and reached for the last time into his bag. He continued looking at Rathbone, whose entire body was breaking apart and reforming now, only his face remaining constant, hanging above the shifting, dust-cloud shadows that swirled below his neck.

"It's your book, isn't it? Your creation? Your life's work? Only it's not very good, is it?" asked Trevelyan. He felt a rough edge under his fingers and clasped the last object he needed, lifting it from his bag. It rattled as he placed it on the desk by the book. His grin was painful now, stretching at the edges of his face and pulling at his muscles. He reached for the book, knowing that Rathbone was watching. The maddening *scritch* of new words being written came from his article again, now buried under other paper. He ignored it. Without looking down, keeping his gaze firmly on the figure ahead of him, Trevelyan lifted the book.

Rathbone's face was growing again, filling the room. It came towards Trevelyan, the crown of the head brushing against the ceiling and the chin grazing the surface of the desk, ruffling the papers. "You dare to stand against me?" Rathbone asked, and his voice boomed around the room like the rattle of closing doors and dropping lids.

"Yes," said Trevelyan simply, and tore a page from the book.

It felt good; no, it felt *wonderful*. The paper made a noise like a ragged exhalation as it came away from the binding, and Rathbone screamed, wordless and terrible. Trevelyan tore another page away, dropping the two into the metal bin by his feet. He tore another, then clamped his hand around a wedge of pages and yanked at them, feeling them tug loose from the cover like teeth from diseased gums. He dropped them, seeing them flutter like butterflies at the edges of his vision, and then Rathbone was over the desk, crashing back to a more normal size and shape—a stiff, weary man screeching helplessly, "No, no, no" over and over again as his hands waved around in a semaphore of anger and despair.

Trevelyan risked looking down, sweeping the papers off the surface of the desk and into the bin before dropping the remains of the book on top of them. He picked up the last object he had taken from his bag and shook it; the rattlesnake chatter of it sounded good in his ears. Pushing open the box, he removed a match.

When he struck it, the dancing light was somehow brighter than that of the lamp, a shimmering flame that filled the room. It washed across Rathbone, pushing him back even farther, scoring his face to a sickly orange and withering his body to little more than a smear in the glare. Trevelyan held the match for a second, twisting it so that the wooden stem was truly alight, and then dropped it into the bin with the paper.

The sheets ignited with slow, lazy grace. The flames moved along one page and then stepped across to another, pirouetting as they went to catch more in their grip. When they came to the book, they burned more brightly, as though fed by unseen fuel. First, the cover shriveled from blue to brown, curling, and then the pages within it caught and burned. Trevelyan heard Rathbone yowl, inhuman and thin, and then more loose pages were swallowed by the growing conflagration and the yowl turned into a scream of pure vitriol.

Rathbone was tearing apart. Pieces of him were ripping loose, spinning away to the corner of the room, leaving sooty trails behind them. They smelled, not the healthy scent of flame but the greasy stink of uncooked meat. His voice rose, staggering up through registers of sound until it became something stabbing and toneless—bitter—and Trevelyan had to cover his ears. The flames leapt at his legs and he moved away, watching as their frenetic jig encircled the rim of the bin and blackened the thin metal.

Still Rathbone sounded as pieces of him, smaller and smaller, whirled away to the walls, old grudges being released and the distant smell of rottenness filling the room. Trevelyan watched the sheets curl, blacken, disintegrate, ashy fragments detaching and swirling up, carried by the breath of the fire. They capered around the last of Rathbone as he broke apart and was dashed away, until only eyes and a mouth remained, and then only a mouth, dwindling, shrieking, the scream falling away to nothing and, at last, it was done.

The office smelled of burned wood, but there was nothing Trevelyan could do about that. At some point, the flames must have crawled over his hand; there was an ugly pink blister across his knuckles and the hair had been scorched from the skin. The flames had also blackened and charred one leg of the desk, and had buckled the bin into an irregular, ballooning shape like a frozen cloud. Of Rathbone, there was no trace except some darker streaks across the walls and a smell under the burning of something old and decayed.

One of the scraps of paper that had danced loose during the fire was from Trevelyan's article, and on it, he saw the printed words *the Monster's greatest purpose*. Above them, in Rathbone's tense writing, were the words *terrible fool*. Trevelyan crushed the damaged paper to nothing with his uninjured hand and then left the office. Exhausted, he went home.

He slept badly, and in the early hours Trevelyan rose from his bed and walked away from dreams in which flames licked at figures whose faces swelled and twisted. He went to his office and printed a new copy of the article, placing it in an envelope and addressing it, and then he made himself coffee and waited for sunrise. After it came, he showered and then checked on his article; it was unmarked. He sealed the envelope and wanted to feel happy, but didn't.

The drive was long, through heavy morning traffic, and he arrived later than he hoped. He was made to wait in the reception area before being shown through to the manager's office.

"Did you know Mr. Rathbone well?" the handsome black woman behind the desk asked.

"No, not really. We were acquaintances, I suppose you'd say. Can I see him, please? I have some news for him."

"Mr. Rathbone didn't have any family, as far as we know," the manager continued as though he hadn't spoken. "If you hadn't visited him yesterday, I wouldn't be telling you this, but really, I can't see the harm. Mr. Rathbone died in his sleep some time during the night."

"I see," said Trevelyan, not wanting to ask if Rathbone had gone peacefully, whether the smell of burning had filled the room. "Thank you for letting me know."

"He had some papers, and we think that his will leaves them to the university. May we call you to collect them once the formalities are complete?"

"No," said Trevelyan, rising. "Call the faculty office. Call anyone but me." He left the office and walked back across the foyer, wanting to be gone from there, to leave Rathbone and everything he had created behind. He wanted to go back to his house, to plan boring lectures, to mark essays, to read and think. To get his life back.

Behind him, Trevelyan's feet left dusted black marks on the floor.

The Church at Monte Saturno

ROBERT SILVERBERG

ROBERT SILVERBERG is a multiple winner of both the Hugo and Nebula
Awards, and he was named a Grand Master by the Science Fiction and
Fantasy Writers of America in 2004.

He began submitting stories to science fiction magazines in his early
teens, and his first published novel, a children's book entitled *Revolt on
Alpha C*, appeared 1955. He won his first Hugo Award the following year.

Always a prolific writer—for the first four years of his career he
reportedly wrote a million words a year—his numerous books include such
novels as *To Open the Sky*, *To Live Again*, *Dying Inside*, *Nightwings*, and *Lord
Valentine's Castle*. The last became the basis for his popular "Majipoor"
series, set on the eponymous alien planet, and he is currently putting
together *Tales of Majipoor*, a collection of related stories that he has written
over the past ten years.

About the following tale, Silverberg says, "I wrote it soon after
returning from a visit to Sicily, where nothing like this had happened
to me."

SERAFINA SAID, "You are English, no?"

"American, actually," Gardiner told her.

"I would say English. The studious look. The glasses. The bad
haircut. The way you dress. Like you have money but don't think it's
nice to spend it. Very English, I think."

True enough. Only he wasn't. And he had taken her at first glance for a simple Sicilian peasant girl, but obviously that was wrong also. There was nothing simple about her. Both of them, it seemed, had instantly invented imaginary identities for each other and were working their way backward now to the actual ones.

"I'm a professor. An associate professor, actually. History of art." Who had taught at three different universities in fourteen years, and still was only an associate professor. Who did not even have his doctorate. And now was roaming the edges of the classical world peering at Byzantine mosaics in the hope they would somehow rescue him. "Associate professors often tend to seem a little English. I dress like this because it's what I can afford. It's also very comfortable."

They were sitting under a gnarled old oak on a summer-parched brown hillside at the edge of the little town of Monte Saturno in central Sicily, looking southward into a steep gorge densely covered on both slopes with tough, leathery-looking grey-green shrubs. The sky was a hot iron dome, painted a pale blue. Even at this early hour of the day the air was stifling. Gardiner felt a little dizzy. This was a dizzying place, Sicily. The air, rich with lemon and herbs. The heat. The dark fissures of decay everywhere. The beauty. The taint of antiquity, the unfathomable mysteries lurking in every narrow alleyway, behind every crumbling façade.

He had arrived in town late the night before, driving down from Palermo, and had known her for less than half an hour. He was just finishing breakfast at the little *albergo* where he was staying when she came in to chat with the proprietor, her uncle. Gardiner had lured her out for a stroll: past the low lopsided cathedral, the scruffy and padlocked municipal museum, the ancient windowless building that was the post office. Almost at once they were in the open countryside, staring out into the island's immense empty hinterland. She was long and lean, nearly as tall as he was, with prominent cheekbones, a long sharp nose, dark penetrating eyes. She had been born in this village, she told him, but lived in Palermo and had spent considerable time in

Rome; she had come here a few days before to visit her grandfather, who was ninety. Gardiner found her attractive, and also oddly forward, flirtatious. But of course he knew better than to indulge in any fantasies. This was Sicily, after all.

"The history of art? You come to *Sicily* to study Italian art? There is some confusion here, I think. You should be in Florence, Venice, Rome."

"Not Italian art, especially. Byzantine. I'm writing a doctoral thesis on the transition from the Roman style of mosaic work to the Byzantine." How tidy that sounded! But he hardly wanted to tell her that he had come to Italy seeking something that he could not define, that his life, though satisfying in some ways, seemed fundamentally static and insubstantial: that he yearned for a *coup*, a grand achievement that would establish him before the world. Serafina sat leaning towards him, listening intently, with her long legs crossed, her hands outstretched on her knees. "You understand what that is, a doctoral thesis?" he asked.

"*Capisco, si.*" She was speaking mostly in English, which she handled well, though she dropped into Italian now and then for emphasis. Gardiner, fairly fluent in Italian, had begun the conversation in that language but something about her expression made him think that she found that condescending, and he had cut it out. She could be, he suspected, a prickly, difficult woman. "You write your thesis, they make you a *dottore della filosofia*, and then you become a real professor, that is how it works, no?"

"A *full* professor."

"Ah. *Si*. So you are here to see our mosaics. Already you have seen the mosaics in Palermo? The Capella Palatina, the church of La Martorana, the cathedral at Monreale?"

"All of them. Plus the one at Cefalu. They're all later than the ones I'm studying, really, but how could I pass them up?" Gardiner loved mosaics with a powerful passion. Not for the religious scenes they depicted, which had no real importance or significance to him beyond an esthetic one. He was in no way a religious man. The holy saints and martyrs of the Christian mosaics and the gods and goddesses of the older, pagan ones were simply just so much mythology for him, quaint, mildly amusing. But the mosaics themselves—their plasticity of design, their glinting surfaces, their inner light—that was what excited him. It was nearly impossible for him to put his feelings into words: an almost sexual yearning, focused on bits of colored tile glued to walls. He was possessed, and he knew it.

"And now?"

"Today I'll head down to Piazza Armerina, the Villa Romana, the palace of the Roman emperor. With absolutely wonderful mosaics."

"I have never been there," she said.

Never? That was odd. Piazza Armerina was, he calculated, no more than an hour's drive away. But New Yorkers never went to the Statue of Liberty or Parisians to the Eiffel Tower, either. Gardiner toyed with the idea of inviting Serafina to accompany him.

"From Piazza Armerina I'll continue on south to Agrigento for a look at the Greek temples, and then up along the coast to Trapani, where I can catch the ferry for Tunis. The Bardo Museum in Tunis has one of the finest collections of mosaics in the world." Into his mind now there sprang the wild notion of asking her to join him for the Tunisian expedition too, and he was startled by the sudden throbbing beneath his breastbone at the idea. On half an hour's acquaintance, though? At best she would laugh; she might spit in his face. The old days of impenetrably guarded chastity might be gone here, but at the outset she would want him at least to pretend that he thought of her as a respectable woman. He looked guiltily away, as if fearing that his intentions were visible on his face.

I should ask her now, he thought, about herself: where she went to school, what she does, how it happens that she speaks English so well. But he hesitated, momentarily unwilling to plod through the standard conversational gambits. A sharp silence fell between them. Gardiner heard the buzz and click of insects all around, and a peculiar ticking coming from a nearby tree, as though the heat were shrinking its bark. The sudden tension sharpened his senses, and he became aware of a tumult of Mediterranean scents assailing him on all sides, lavender, maybe, rosemary, the fragrance of prickly-pear blossoms and lemon leaves.

A hawk drifted diagonally across the sky. Gardiner, idly following its path with his eyes, watched it descend abruptly into the gorge as if diving to seize a rabbit. His gaze traveled downward with the plunging hawk and he noticed for the first time what appeared to be a small isolated building on the far side of the valley, all but hidden in the scrubby brush. Not much more than the curving arc of its low white dome was visible. Something about the shape of that dome aroused his attention. He had seen buildings like that before. But not in Sicily.

"What is that across the way?" he asked her, pointing.

She knew what he meant. "A ruin. Not important."

His guidebook had said nothing about ruins in Monte Saturno. So far as he knew there was nothing of that sort here, neither Greek, Roman, Byzantine, nor Norman, none of the multitudinous layers upon layers of superimposed realities out of which this island was built. He had stopped here last night simply because he had had a late start out of Palermo and decided *en route* not to risk driving on into Piazza Armerina after dark on this rough country road. It had been pure luck that the town's one *trattoria* maintained a few upstairs rooms for tourists passing through.

"A church of some sort, is it?"

"Of some sort, yes. Not Catholic. A Greek church, the Orthodox faith. Empty a long time. Not a holy place any more."

"Empty how long?"

A shrug. "A long time?"

"Five hundred years? A thousand?"

"Who knows? But a long time. It is very ruined. Nobody goes there except goats. And young *innamorati*. You know, lovers looking for a place to be alone."

Gardiner felt a slow stirring of excitement.

"A Greek church," he said slowly. "Byzantine, you mean?"

"That may be." Serafina laughed. "Ah, you think there are mosaics there? You think you have made a great artistic discovery? There is nothing. Dirt. Ghosts."

"Ghosts?"

"It is very haunted there. Yes."

She sounded almost serious. He had, for a moment, a sense that a door had opened into a dark place forever inaccessible to him and Serafina was standing on the far side of the threshold. He knew that many of the villagers here lived on the interface between modern civilization and that shadowy realm of antiquity that was beyond his understanding; but Serafina, he had thought, was entirely of his world. He saw now that he might have been wrong about that. But then she grinned and was a contemporary woman again.

He said, forcing a grin of his own, "I'd be interested in seeing it, haunted or not. Is there any way of getting to it?"

"A road. Very bad, very rough."

"Could you take me there? I very much would like to have a look at it."

Anger flashed like summer lightning in her eyes. "Ah, you are so subtle, you *inglesi!*"

"American," he said. And then, comprehending: "And you misunderstand me, if you think I'm trying in some roundabout fashion to engineer a rendezvous with you. *Lei capisce,* 'rendezvous'?" She nodded. "But as long as I'm here—a Byzantine church that isn't even in the guidebook—"

Another eyeflash, this one more mischievous. She still seemed angry, but in a different way now.

"Truly, *Professore,* you are interested only in the architecture of this dirty abandoned church? You take me to this rendezvous for lovers merely to see stone walls? Ah, I think I misjudge the kind of man you are. A beautiful woman means nothing to you, I think."

Gardiner sighed. He was caught in a no-win situation. Bluntness seemed the best tactic.

"They mean a great deal. And you are extremely beautiful. But I know better than to proposition a *Siciliana* five minutes after I've met her, and in any case there's a bed in my hotel room, if that's what I was after. I don't need to take you to an abandoned building full of goat shit and straw. But I would like to see the church. Honestly."

Serafina's expression softened. She looked merely amused now.

"You want to go?" she said. "Really? *Allora.* We go, then."

She snapped her fingers under his nose. "Come! Up! We get ready, we go, at once, *subito*!"

But of course they didn't go *subito*. Nothing ever happened *subito* in Sicily. They had to prepare themselves properly for the expedition, sturdy boots, jackets to ward off brambles, and wide-brimmed hats for the sun, plus a bottle of wine, some bread and cheese and salami and fruit, as if they were going on a long journey, not just down the side of one nearby hill and up another. The preparations mysteriously stretched on for hours. He had a suitable jacket and even a hat but no hiking boots, only sneakers, which Serafina glanced at with contempt. Her cousin Gino would lend him a pair of boots.

Cousin Gino was twenty-three or so, sullenly handsome, a swarthy, bull-necked bushy-haired man with enormous forearms and bright, fierce eyes, unexpectedly blue in this land of dark-eyed people. Though Gardiner was a big man himself, broad-shouldered and ruggedly athletic of build, who looked more like a football coach than an assistant professor of the history of art, it appeared likely to him that in any kind of fight Gino would twirl him around his wrist like spaghetti. And just now Gino was glowering at Gardiner with what looked very much like unconcealed hostility, bringing to mind all of Gardiner's stereotyped notions of the way the men of this island defended their women's chastity. Serafina said something to him in the transmogrified and deformed dialect of Italian, both clipped and slurred, that was

Sicilian—a patois which Gardiner found utterly opaque. Gino, replying with an equally unintelligible stream of brusque, sputtering words, gave them both a furious glare and went whirling away from them.

"What's bothering him?" Gardiner asked, still inventing Gino's proprietary rage, imagining dire warnings, threats of vendetta.

"He says your feet are too big, they will stretch his boots."

"That's all?" Gardiner felt something close to disappointment. "Well, tell him not to worry. If anything, his feet look bigger than mine."

"Maybe yes, maybe no. He will get the boots anyway, he said. As a special favor for me. We are very good friends, Gino and I."

The image came unbidden to Gardiner's mind of Serafina and her brutish cousin, over there across the gorge one languid summer night seven or eight years ago, lying naked in each other's arms, ferociously entwined in the incestuous embraces that he assumed were altogether customary among the rural adolescents of this backward country. He doubted that any such thing had ever happened between them; but if it had, no wonder Gino was pissed off over her taking this *straniero* to their special place, and in his own best boots, yet.

Gardiner smiled at his own foolishness. He was capable of engendering an ethnic cliché for any occasion. It was a habit, he told himself, that he needed to break.

Eventually Gino came back with a pair of huge clodhoppers dangling from one immense hand. To Gardiner's surprise, and apparently Gino's, the boots were a perfect fit.

It was a little before noon when they finally set out. The sun filled half the sky, blazing like a permanent atomic explosion, and the hot, shimmering air was full of madly dancing bugs that sang manic droning songs in his ears. There was a sort of a road at first, but it morphed into a narrow untidy trail after a few hundred yards and then, a little while later, became nothing more than a faint exiguous track through the dry stiff-branched chaparral.

Despite the heat and the difficulties of the route, long-legged Serafina set a brisk pace. Gardiner kept up with her without much effort, but he was marinating in his own sweat under the jacket that she had insisted he wear. At the bottom of the Monte Saturno side of the gorge they came to a campsite, a flat rock and a fire pit and enough discarded wine bottles to keep future archaeologists amused for centuries, and she said crisply, "We make the lunch here."

"*Va bene.*" He welcomed the break. The climb ahead looked formidable.

Serafina assembled sandwiches while he opened the wine. As they ate and drank she offered snippets of autobiography. She had lived here until she was sixteen, she told him, and then was taken away to Rome by her uncle, not the same one who owned the *trattoria*, to be educated. There was a bit of extra spin about the way she said "uncle" and "educated," and Gardiner flamboyantly hypothesized all manner of sinister iniquities, some wealthy waxed-mustachioed stranger buying the beautiful girl from her impoverished parents to be put to the most depraved uses in his elegant baroque apartment overlooking the Spanish Stairs. But she talked instead of learning English at a genteel Roman academy whose name meant nothing to Gardiner but sounded quite elite; then a stint in the Roman office of a big British investment bank; an affair, apparently, with a young British bond trader that brought her a transfer to the London office, a dizzying taste of the international high life, and, so she appeared to be saying, the inevitable accidental pregnancy and concomitant mess, letdown, and heartbreak. Her fair-haired bond trader operated out of Prague now and she, having had her fill of banking, worked at the Hertz Rent-a-Car office in Palermo. She was fluent in English, French, Spanish, and German, as well as Italian and the local dialect. So much for her being a simple peasant girl, he thought. He guessed that she was around twenty-nine. He was nine years older. In the thick afternoon warmth the aura of her lean, sleek Mediterranean attractiveness expanded into the hazy air around him, dazzling and mesmerizing him, enveloping him in an unexpected and astonishing explosion of impulsive speculation. How it would startle everyone at the college, Gardiner told himself, if he came back from his summer research trip not only with material for his thesis but with a beautiful and cosmopolitan Italian wife!

"*Andiamo*," she said, the moment the bottle was empty. "Now I show you the fabulous Byzantine church."

The hill on the southern side of the gorge was steep, all right, and the heat was unthinkable now, and Serafina moved with jackrabbit energy up the slope, as though deliberately testing his endurance; but, fortified by the good red wine of Monte Saturno and his own implacable curiosity about the ruin ahead and now, also, this absurd but amusing new bit of romantic fancy of his, he matched her step for step, a couple of yards behind her with his gaze fixed steadily on the taut, tantalizing seat of her jeans.

Suddenly they were in a little scraggly clearing, and the ruined church lay right in front of them.

"*Ecco*," she said. "Behold your heart's desire."

The building was a little one, no bigger than a garage and half concealed in tangles of brush, but it was pure late-Byzantine in form, a squared-off Greek cross of a structure with a squat dome perched atop its four blocky walls. He knew of no other building of this sort in Sicily. It reminded him of nothing so much as the 11th-century church at Daphni, outside Athens. But Daphni was world-famous for its luminous mosaics.

It was impossible, Gardiner thought, that mosaics like those of Daphni could have gone unnoticed all this time, even in this obscure hilltop village.

"Let's go in," he said hoarsely.

"*Si, si.*" She beckoned to him. "*Venga di qua.*"

The main entrance was sealed by a dense barrier of interwoven woody shrubs, but a smaller door stood slightly ajar on the northern side, a crudely made wooden one, cracked and crazed, that looked as though it had been tacked on about a hundred years ago by some farmer using this place as a barn. Serafina, with a surprising show of strength, levered it open just far enough to let them slip inside.

The church was rank, musty, dismal, a claustrophobe's nightmare. When Gardiner switched on his flashlight he saw that over the centuries enough sandy dirt had blown in through the narrow window-grates and through crevices in the walls to lift the floor level at least eight feet in most places, so that he was standing practically within arm's reach of the dome. Heaps of ancient mildewed straw were piled everywhere: a barn, yes. The pungent aroma of innumerable copulations hovered in the air. For how many generations had the passionate young of Monte Saturno committed sins of the flesh in this bedraggled former house of God?

He aimed his beam upward, praying that he would see the stark somber face of Christ the Pantocrator scowling down at him, as at Daphni and other Byzantine churches. No. The dome was bare. He had not really expected anything else. Probably this had been some simple chapel for wayfarers, in use for perhaps fifty years a thousand years ago, then abandoned, forgotten.

"You are satisfied?" Serafina asked.

"I suppose."

"I myself parted with my virtue here," she said, in a bold, cool, self-mocking tone. He looked at her, taken aback, angered and repelled by her unsolicited revelation. The idea that Serafina had ever engaged in any sexual event in this grim squalid place was sickening to him. She and some clumsy village Romeo sprawling on a scratchy tick-infested blanket, his shaggy eager body pressing down on hers, her splendid slender legs spraddled wide, toes pointed at the dome: the thrusts, the grunts, the gasps. "I was fifteen. We thought we were being very brave coming here, because of the ghosts. But every young couple in town is brave like that when the time comes. Some things are so urgent that even ghosts are unimportant. The ghosts must be defied."

Gardiner shook his head. "Ghosts?" he muttered, roaming the edges of the building, scuffing at the mounded straw. That door into the unknown opening again. This damned island, he thought: level after level of superstition, evil, and madness. You were forever toppling down through the detritus of all its many occupiers to the jolting incomprehensibilities beneath.

He was no good at dealing with such stuff. It forever amazed him when he came running up against some apparently rational person's firmly held belief in the irrational, the impossible, the altogether inexplicable. For Gardiner there was nothing inexplicable, only phenomena that had not yet been properly explained; anything that seemed to be truly and eternally inexplicable was, he suspected, something that had either been badly misinterpreted or had simply never in fact occurred.

He prodded and kicked at the ground along the perimeter of the building with the tip of Gino's boot. "Who was the lucky boy?" he asked, after a time, amazed at himself for keeping the distasteful subject open.

"Does it matter?" she said. "His name was Calogero. He is dead now."

"I'm sorry," said Gardiner automatically. He continued to kick and scuff. Then came a surprise. "Hold on. What's this?"

A forehead of glistening tile was showing along the wall, just at the debris line. He dropped to his knees and scrabbled at it, hurling handfuls of sand behind him. Other things came into view. Eyebrows. Eyes. A serene face, nearly complete; a halo. He trembled. There was a mosaic here after all.

"It is not easy to believe," she said, as they made their way wearily back to town at dusk after a long breathless afternoon of clearing away debris. "All those years, and those beautiful things on the wall, and no one ever thought to look under the dirt, until you."

Gardiner barely heard her. He was lost in a feverish dream of academic triumph. There would be articles in the journals; there would be a book; he would waltz to his doctorate. The mosaics were not of the first rank, hardly that, but they were undeniably late-Byzantine, a continuous band of them that circled the walls just below the surface of the intrusive fill, saints and pilgrims and Biblical figures in bright, intense reds and greens and golds and blacks. The tesserae, the bits of colored glass out of which the mosaic patterns were fashioned, were large and crude and not always perfectly fitted together—this was not Monreale or Cefalu, not Ravenna's San Vitale, not the Keriye Djami in Istanbul—and the figures were awkward and often poorly arranged; but there was a purity about them, an innocence, that made them very beautiful in their own less sophisticated manner.

Schemes, plans, were swiftly unfolding now. He would use his meager funds to hire workmen in town; he would clear out all the fill; he would photograph, he would analyze, he would compare and contrast, he would publish, he would publish, he would publish—

As he and Serafina entered the town's central *piazza* Gardiner saw that the entire population had turned out, making the nightly promenade, families moving in clustered groups, old men walking arm in arm, young couples holding hands. Some glanced at them, smiling. It seemed to him that everyone was remarking knowingly on their dusty, sweaty look, speculating vividly, lubriciously, on what they had been up to all afternoon in the church across the gorge. And not one with any idea of the truth.

Gardiner had been thinking of inviting her into the *trattoria* for a celebratory dinner, candles and a fine bottle of red Regeleali *riserva* with the meal, and then, perhaps, a night of glorious celebratory delights upstairs: all the way back, he had seen that as a natural and inevitable sequel to the day's triumphant events. But here in town he perceived instantly the impossibility of any such thing. Sweep her grandly into the inn with everybody watching, his carnal notions as manifest to all as if he had exposed himself in the street, and she not to be seen again until morning? Hardly. Whatever destiny awaited him with this woman, and Gardiner was convinced now that some sort of destiny did, it would not be consummated in this tiny and hermetic village. Not tonight, at any rate, virtually in public, as it were.

She appeared to have figured all that out long before him. "Well," she said, hardly pausing a moment outside the little inn before turning away, "I congratulate you on your good fortune. I am happy to have been of service." She touched the tips of her fingers to his, and then she was gone, walking in long strides across the *piazza* to greet a pair of hatchet-faced old women who were clad in the traditional somber costume of an earlier era.

There was no bath in his room, only a washbasin. Gardiner stripped, quickly splashed himself clean, lay down on the creaking bed to reflect on the day's achievement and perhaps enjoy a little repose. Instantly he was asleep. When he woke, with a start, it was past ten. He dressed hastily. As he descended the stairs, he met someone coming upward, a sturdy-looking, black-bearded, youngish man in a priest's black robe, who smiled and saluted him when they passed each other. So the *albergo* had acquired a new guest during the day. Two guests at once: a booming tourist season for them, Gardiner supposed.

The *padrona* was in the dining room, reading a newspaper. She seemed untroubled by his tardiness, and immediately went about putting together dinner for him, pasta with sardines, some roasted pork, a carafe of the red *vino di casa*. "It was a good day for you?" she asked.

"Fine. Splendid." His glow could leave no doubt.

"You stay here tomorrow?"

"Certainly. Even past tomorrow."

This time, when he settled down on his bed again after dinner, sleep was impossible for a long time. He stared up at the low fly-specked ceiling and saw mosaics on the screen of his wearied mind, stylized mosaic figures, angels, patriarchs, sheep, frolicking dogs. It was too good to be true: much too good. Perhaps he had imagined the whole thing. The heat, the wine, the enchanting proximity of Serafina—

No. No. No. No. They had really been there. His discovery, his mosaics. He had touched them with his own hands. Felt their smooth shining surfaces.

He slept, finally. It was a night of strange frightening dreams, masked figures dancing around him as he lay strapped to a smoldering pyre in the middle of the *piazza*.

At nine he awakened, breakfasted downstairs on cheese and figs and rolls, and peered out into the town square, which was utterly empty except for a couple of elderly dogs. He had no idea where Serafina was and felt uncomfortable about asking; and in any case he and she had made no arrangements for today. He equipped himself with his hat, his jacket, and Gino's ponderous boots, and tucked a bottle of wine from the display on the dining room table into his backpack, along with enough rolls and cheese and fruit to last him through lunch, and, armed with flashlight, notebook, camera, went capering off alone towards the ravine.

He dug all morning, using as his shovel a slab of grey slate that was lying in the clearing outside the church. As the layer of loose fill retreated, and he laid bare more and more of the band of mosaic ornament that rimmed the walls, Gardiner grew increasingly excited by his find. The work was on the crude side, yes, but it had a raw power that marked it as an important stylistic mode in its own right. The background in particular was an intense bluish white, giving the newly exposed parts of the wall a fierce brilliance that flamed wondrously as the sun came slanting occasionally in through the narrow windows and the cracks in the dome, fading when it moved along. Each moment of brightness was the occasion for a hasty flurry of photographs, and soon all his film was gone. It was a giddy, magical few hours.

He postulated some 10th or 11th-century craftsman traveling down from Palermo, perhaps to do a job of interior decoration at some baron's palazzo along the island's south shore, being inveigled *en route* into spending a few weeks touching up this little chapel. And really getting into it, seeing it as an opportunity to experiment with an individual style of work, perhaps slipping into a little romantic entanglement with one of the town girls that gave him motivation to linger a little while longer, now a real labor of love, so that months went by, maybe even a year or two of solitary toil, preparing the little colored cubes and painstakingly mortaring them into place, his own private masterpiece. All too soon to be forgotten, the building allowed to go derelict, a habitation for donkeys, the brilliant mosaics covered in time by an accretion of wind-blown rubble many feet deep.

There was more than a thesis to be had here. There was an entire scholarly reputation.

At midday, unable to move another molecule of dirt, Gardiner slipped outside into the stupefying heat for his wine and cheese. As soon as he had finished, sleep came over him, in an instant, as though a thick velvet curtain had been dropped on him.

Awakening just as instantly some ninety minutes later, he went back into the church and beheld something so bewildering that his mind could not at first encompass it, and he thought he might still be dreaming. But he knew that he had to be awake. The evidence of physical sensation was compelling. The heavy, shimmering, almost tangible air, the penetrating heat, the myriad musty pungent smells left behind by vanished centuries: all of that was too vividly real.

And the mosaics had undergone a bizarre transformation. The saints had grown leering faces with forked tongues, and their haloes glowed and pulsated with a neon fury. The peasants tending their flocks had been rearranged into obscene configurations, and looked back jeeringly over their shoulders at him while buggering bat-winged monstrosities. Placid sheep and bounding dogs had been replaced by grotesque reptilian horrors. Colors everywhere clashed garishly.

Impossible.

Impossible.

There was no conceivable explanation for this. Gardiner was shaken, stunned. He felt physically ill. A wild vertigo assailed him. Numbed, half dazed, his heart racing wildly, he backed out of the building, cautiously returned, looked again. Monsters, nightmares, abominations. Frightful sights, all. But what frightened him more than the ghastliness on the walls was the feeling of utter destabilization that whirled through him, the sense that his mind had lost its moorings. He had never experienced any kind of dislocation like this. Never.

He fought himself into calmness. It must be the heat, Gardiner told himself carefully. He had to be hallucinating. His photographs would show the truth.

With unsteady hands he lifted his camera, remembering only after the shutter's first click that he had used up all his film. He shrugged. For a long moment he stood staring at the hideous things on the walls.

All I need now, he thought, is for one of them to wink at me.

All I need—

Abruptly all his hard-won calmness dissolved and something close to panic overcame him.

Turning, he fled down the side of the gorge, ran with superhuman energy up the far side into town, arriving panting and dizzied, and found Serafina on the porch of her grandparents' decrepit old stone house behind the post office. "Come with me," he said. "The mosaics—I was just there, and they looked all *changed*. You've got to come and tell me it isn't so."

"Changed?"

"Into something horrible. Monsters and demons all over the wall. I couldn't believe it."

"Ah," she said, smiling amiably, a calm knowing smile as old as Zeus. "So the ghosts are at work."

Gardiner felt a shiver run along his back. The ghosts, again.

"It was the ghosts, yes," he said harshly. "Or the heat making me crazy. Or something I ate. Whatever it is, you've got to go back there with me. To check those mosaics out with your own eyes. I need to prove to myself that I didn't actually see what I saw. Will you come? Right now?"

She hesitated only a beat. "Yes," she said, still looking more amused than anything else. "Of course."

This time he led the way. It was the hottest part of the afternoon; but Gardiner was in the grip of a crazy adrenaline surge, and moved so quickly that Serafina was hard-pressed to match his speed.

He entered the church first and switched on his flashlight, bracing himself for the worst. But what he saw were the scenes he had uncovered that morning. Benign golden-haloed saints, looking back at him with gazes of sappy medieval sanctity. Smiling dull-eyed shepherds stood amidst their patient sheep. Innocent dogs performed mindless leaps. He was limp with relief.

Serafina, following him in, glanced around at the mosaics, and said, smiling, "Yes, well, so tell me: where are all these horrible things?"

Gardiner peered at the walls, baffled.

"I swear, Serafina, I was absolutely certain that they were there. A completely convincing hallucination, as real as—as real as these walls. The saints had turned into demons. The farm animals had become monsters. The colors—"

She gave him a queer look. "You drank a whole bottle of wine with your lunch, yes? And slept in the sun. And then you dreamed. Ah, yes, yes, *caro*, a very bad dream. Which the oh-so-devilish ghosts of this place playfully put into your sleeping mind to perplex you. Look, look, there are no monsters here. It would be a good story if there were, but there are not. They are very pretty, your mosaics, I think."

Yes. Yes, they were. Gentle scenes, lovely, innocuous.

Perplexed indeed, altogether lost in bewilderment, Gardiner said almost nothing while they trudged back to town. Already that panoply of monsters was becoming unreal to him. But what he could not put aside was his conviction that he had, at least for a moment, truly seen those things with his own sober eyes, though he knew, *knew* that it was impossible that he had.

As they came up the path into the *piazza* Serafina said, "You should take the Greek priest over to see the church. He will find it a very exciting surprise."

"Who?"

"Father Demetrios. He is Eastern Orthodox, of the Martorana church in Palermo. He is visiting here since yesterday."

Gardiner recalled, now, the other guest at the hotel, the black-bearded young priest of the night before.

An *Orthodox* priest, though? The Greek rite? All thoughts of ghosts and monsters, and of his own possibly wobbling sanity, fled from Gardiner at once. He was seized by sudden overmastering practical fear. The priest, if he found out about the mosaics, would surely claim the derelict church on behalf of his sect and take control of any scholarly use of the art within it. Gardiner would be shut out, his rights of discovery overridden by the assertion of the higher right of prior ownership.

"No," he said. "I'd rather not show the mosaics to anybody just yet. You haven't already told him about them, have you?"

"No," she said, "of course not."

Was she telling the truth? There was something almost petulant about that *of course*, and something ambivalent about the shake of the head.

The town square was deserted. The villagers were still enjoying their siesta, the whole town torpid in the late-day heat. Serafina accompanied him as far as the porch of his inn, and lingered there a moment, long enough for him to wonder whether he should invite her upstairs. But even now, with no one to spy on them, it felt somehow inappropriate, even sordid, to make such an overture to her out of the blue. Their frantic jog over to the ruin had hardly been a proper romantic prelude, and his strange hallucination, his babbling account of imagining that he had witnessed a demonic transformation of the mosaics, left him feeling abashed and demeaned now. He offered no invitation.

"Well, then, *ciao, amico.* I will be seeing you," she added formally, and turned away.

Was that a touch of disappointment in her tone? So it seemed to him, for a moment. But it was too late to call her back. Already, moving swiftly as always, she was halfway across the *piazza.*

Gardiner went to his room, rinsed himself perfunctorily, unloaded his camera and buried the roll of film deep in his suitcase. For a long time he sat by his fly-specked window, staring into the square below, pondering many strangenesses. It was half past seven, now; the day was cooling, the townsfolk were coming forth for their pre-dinner stroll.

Without warning, a desperate reckless desire to see the mosaics again, to confirm the reality of them, overcame him. He seized his camera and in a few minutes found himself once more laboring down the now-familiar path into the gorge.

In the greyness of early evening he saw what he took to be bats flitting about the little domed church. Brushing impatiently past them, Gardiner marched inside, grim-faced, and cast his flashlight beam on the walls.

The mosaics were in nightmare mode again. Everything was fangs, claws, tentacles, jutting swollen penises, jagged blurts of discordant color.

He felt like sobbing. Why did the damned things keep oscillating in this maddening way? Why couldn't they keep to one form or the other?

"*Serafina!*" he howled, as if expecting her to be able to hear him across the canyon. "It's happened again!"

This time he had had no wine. The day's heat had relented. He believed himself to be sane. What explanation could there be for this?

There was none. He was staring into the abyss of the incomprehensible.

Waves of nausea went sweeping through him. He was trembling, and his teeth were chattering, which was something he could not remember having experienced ever before, that convulsive spastic movement of his jaws, that terrible eerie clacking of his teeth. He steadied himself with an immense effort. This must be recorded, he thought. Yes. Yes. Aiming his camera at the ghastliest of the designs, Gardiner pressed and pressed again, but the flash attachment would not operate. He had no idea why. Fear gave way to rage. He spat, slapped the camera, pressed once more. Nothing. Fumblingly he took some photos by flashlight illumination alone, knowing they would never come out.

He gave the things on the wall one long last hard look. Then he turned and ran from the building, struggling at every step through the tangled knots of brambles that blocked the path and were so much harder to see, this late in the day. He moved like a machine, never pausing. A void had taken possession of his mind; it was empty now of all thought, all speculation. He dared not even try to think.

Darkness had fallen when he entered the town. His legs were aching mercilessly from the uphill run. His powerful thighs, of which he was so proud, the product of endless miles of dawn jogging, throbbed with pain. As he rounded the corner by the museum, a figure stepped out of the shadows and struck him a terrible blow in the stomach. His eyeglasses went flying. Astounded, Gardiner staggered back, doubling over, gagging and choking and reeling, though in some reflexive way he managed to put his fists up anyway to ward off another punch.

It was Gino, Serafina's cousin. He loomed over Gardiner, swollen with wrath, rocking from side to side as he prepared his next swing. His blue eyes were ablaze with rage. Gardiner slapped at the balled fist confronting him.

"Hey, hold it," he said. "I'll give you back your goddamn boots, if that's what you want."

"It is not the boots," said Gino venomously, speaking remarkably precise Italian now. He swung again. Gardiner pivoted so that he took the punch on the meaty part of his left arm instead of in the middle of his chest. It went through him like a bolt of electricity.

He could not remember when he had last been in a fistfight: not since he was twelve, most likely. But he was no weakling. He would fight back, if he had to. Automatically he dropped into a boxer's crouch and weave, and when Gino swung again he ducked and threw a punch of his own, which Serafina's cousin batted away with a contemptuous swipe, as though he were swatting at a mosquito. Gino's next punch caught Gardiner just below his right clavicle, landing with thunderbolt force and sending him sprawling to the ground.

Through a mist of pain and humiliation he became aware that Serafina had emerged from somewhere and was pounding her fists furiously against Gino's chest. "*Pazzo!*" she cried. "*Cretino! Imbecile!*"

"Tell him I'm finished with his precious boots," Gardiner muttered feebly.

"The boots are not the issue," she said, in English. "He is enraged because you have not slept with me. Because you have rejected me two nights twice."

Gardiner, still on the ground, gaped. "What the hell are you saying? I thought Sicilian men were supposed to *defend* the honor of their women, not to—"

"It is because he thinks you think you are too good for me. He wants you to take me to bed, and then he will make you marry me, and you will settle a fortune on the entire family, because you are American and Americans are rich. In his mind it is my job to seduce you. In this, he believes, I have failed, and so he is angered." Serafina extended her hand to Gardiner and pulled him to his feet. "Angered with you," she said, "not me. Of me he is afraid." She turned to Gino, standing to one side like a fettered ox, and unleashed on him a torrent of fiery Sicilian. Gardiner was unable to understand a word of it. When at last she fell silent, Gino went slinking wordlessly away into the night.

"Come," she said, picking up Gardiner's glasses and handing them to him. Still befogged, he put them in his shirt pocket. "Are you badly hurt?"

"Nothing broken. Only bent."

She led him into the *albergo*, pausing at the bar to pick up a bottle of grappa. Upstairs, in his room, she poured a drink for him, helped him get his backpack off, gently probed his chest and shoulders for damage. "You will live," she said, and measured out some grappa for herself.

"Gino is very stupid, but he means well. I apologize on his behalf."
Then, with a sly smile: "You are much more handsome without your
glasses, *Professore*. A strong face, like a Roman emperor, hard, virile.
All beveled planes and stony angles. The glasses destroy your face
completely, do you know?" She was wearing a thin green cardigan and
a flimsy purple skirt, and now she began to unbutton the cardigan.
"You do not have to marry me, only to be nice," she said. "You went to
the mosaics again tonight?"

"Yes."

"And?"

"What I saw—it makes no sense, Serafina. They'd gone all strange
again." He felt abashed even to say such a thing. "I'm sorry. That's how
they were."

"The ghosts have you in their grip," she said. "I am sorry for you
for that. But come. Lie down with me. You want to, don't you?" She
was narrow through the hips and small-bottomed, not at all Italian
that way, and her arms and shoulders were almost distressingly thin,
but her breasts were agreeably full. They stayed in his room for two
hours. The bed was too small for two, and creaked loudly enough to
be heard all over town, but they coped, and coped well. In the close
humid atmosphere of the little room Gardiner forgot entirely the pain
of Gino's punches and, in Serafina's arms, even for a time succeeded in
exorcising the nightmarish threat to his sense of his own sanity that his
most recent visit to the ruined church had awakened in him.

Afterward they went downstairs. The *padrone* and his wife appeared
to have gone to sleep, but Serafina went into the kitchen of the trattoria
and put together a dinner for the two of them out of whatever she could
find there, some leftover pasta with anchovies and a cold shoulder of
lamb and a platter of broiled tomatoes and garlicky mushrooms, along
with what was left in several open bottles of wine. When they had
eaten Gardiner asked her to go back up to his room with him again,
but this time she declined with a polite smile, explaining it would not

be wise for her to stay the night with him. "Until tomorrow," she said. "And you should not go to the church again alone. *Buona notte, caro.*" Blew him a fingertip kiss and was gone.

This has been a very weird day, Gardiner thought.

In the morning, as he was finishing breakfast, Serafina appeared at the *albergo* and said, "Let us make another visit to your mosaics. I still would like to see them, these horrors of yours."

"Most likely they'll have changed back overnight," Gardiner said, almost jauntily. "But let's go anyway." He realized that he was becoming obsessed by the improbability of all this: an encounter with the absurd, his very first. There was a certain charm to its very inexplicability, even. But behind the charm lay something truly scary that would not relinquish its hold on him: the terrifying possibility that the hinges of his mind had begun to loosen. It was either that or ghosts, and he had never been very successful at believing in ghosts.

He was stiff and sore, not only from Gino's onslaught but from all of yesterday's running to and fro, and Serafina had to pause several times to wait for him to catch up as they crossed the valley. But at last they were at the church. "Let me go in first," he said grandly, which brought the sly knowing smile from her once again. She waved him forward.

He expected everything to be normal again, that they would see nothing more than gentle pastoral scenes. But no—no, almost with gratitude he saw that the walls of the chapel this morning were still full of terrifying hideosities. But they were different ones from last night's. Today's carnival of abominations featured savage, carnivorous things with rows of red glaring eyes; extraterrestrial-looking, spindly headed satyrs in full spate; pious pilgrims with melting slimy faces. Hieronymus Bosch on acid. He was surprised at how little dismay he felt. He was becoming almost resigned to these metamorphoses, he thought. The trick was not to search for explanations. "Take a look," he called hoarsely to her. She came in and stood for a moment by his side as he shined his beam here and there and there. He heard her soft little gasp: plainly, she had not really expected to see the things that she was seeing here now. She slipped her arm through his and pressed close against him, shivering. When he attempted once more to take photographs, the flash attachment again refused to function.

"This is the work of demons," Serafina said, in a tone an octave deeper than normal. "*Andiamo! Fuori!*" They went swiftly outside. With a visibly shaky hand she crossed herself three times. All that ballsy cosmopolitan pizzazz had been stripped from her in an instant; she was a country girl again, and a terrified one. "You should tell Father Demetrios about this right away," she said. Her eyes were wide rigid disks.

"Why?"

"This church formerly belonged to his faith. It is his responsibility to drive these things away."

"To—drive them away—?"

She was talking about an exorcism, this very modern young Sicilian woman. Gardiner stared. Moment by moment he could feel himself being drawn backward into the opaque, inscrutable medieval past.

She said, as though explaining to a child, "You and I both saw saints and shepherds here yesterday afternoon, but in the morning and the evening, alone, you saw monsters. This morning, the monsters are still there, and now I see them too. So we are both hallucinating or else it is real, and I do not think we are hallucinating. It is easier for me to believe in demons than in shared hallucinations."

"I suppose."

"Look, strange things have occurred in this church for many years. Although not like this, not that I have ever heard. It is a serious thing, this deception in a place that once was holy. If nothing is done to cure it, who can say what harm might befall to others who come here?"

"Let me think about all this a little."

"What is there to think?"

The unreality of it all was overwhelming. But Gardiner struggled to keep things in a practical perspective. "I can't predict what might happen to the mosaics once Father Demetrios knows about them. Suppose he insists on destroying them? I found them, Serafina. They're important to me."

"This is my village, *caro*. It is important to me."

Gardiner had no answer for that. He had no answers for any of this.

They returned to town in silence. Serafina grew perceptibly less tense the farther they got from the ruined church, as though they were returning not from a searing glimpse into the pit but only from some spooky horror film, and by the time they entered the village she was her familiar lively self again, whistling, joking, walking with easy, free strides. "We will go to see Father Demetrios now, all right?" she said. "He will be at the cathedral, with Father Giuseppe, I think. They are great friends, Father Demetrios and Father Giuseppe. Father Demetrios comes here every few months to play chess with him, and to argue doctrinal matters, whether the Holy Spirit proceeds from the Father alone or from the Father and the Son, and matters like that which will never be settled if they argue about them for ten million years."

"Does that mean Father Giuseppe will have to be told about the mosaics too?" Gardiner asked.

"No. No. This matter is not the business of his church, only of the Greek Orthodox people. Let Father Demetrios handle it. If we tell Father Giuseppe, we will have the Pope here by next Tuesday, and the reporters and the television people, and everybody else. Look, here is Father Demetrios now." She pointed across the *piazza* towards the pathetic little cathedral, the only badly designed one Gardiner had ever seen, a shallow-vaulted asymmetrical structure fashioned from rough-hewn blocks of dark stone ineptly fitted together. "He is very sexy, I think, Father Demetrios," said Serafina slyly, giving Gardiner a playful nudge. "It is a great waste, a man like that in the priesthood. Come." He was swept along in her wake, unable to protest.

Father Demetrios was garbed in black from head to toe, even now in the blowtorch blast of midday heat: cylindrical flat-topped black hat, long high-collared black robe sweeping down to shining black shoes. A heavy golden cross lay on his breast, its upper half vanishing into the dense coils of his long, thick, square-cut beard. He was about thirty-five, a handsome man, stocky and deep-chested, youthfully vigorous, with glossy, intelligent eyes buried in networks of little precocious wrinkles.

"The building has a bad history," he said, speaking in passable English, over a cold bottle of white wine at the *trattoria*, when Gardiner had finished telling his tale. "I myself have never entered it. The mosaics, be they holy or otherwise, are a surprise to me. But the tradition is that a murder was done there, a priest struck down by a furious Norman knight. It was then deconsecrated. You will take me there now?"

"The road is very bad, father," Serafina said, indicating the priest's flowing robe, his gleaming shoes.

He grinned broadly. "No problem," he said, and winked. Sexy, yes. Gardiner could see that. "I will be right back." He went up to his room and returned quickly in khaki trousers, a light windbreaker over a T-shirt, and sturdy boots. All that remained of his clerical garb was the cross and the black cylindrical hat.

When they reached the church, Gardiner made as though to enter first, but Father Demetrios asked for the flashlight and waved him aside. Entering the building a step behind Father Demetrios, Gardiner saw that the mosaics had reverted to their original innocuous form: shepherds and patriarchs, Abraham and Isaac, the Nativity, the journey to Bethlehem.

"Quite remarkable," said Father Demetrios. "You have photographs of the other state?"

"I tried. The camera flash wouldn't go off."

"That is to be expected. Let us go outside and wait a little while."

For ten minutes they stood in the clearing; then the priest sent Gardiner into the church alone. This time the walls were covered with a wild conglomeration of diabolic filth: a gory massacre, a bestial orgy, a witches' Sabbath, and more. He ran to the doorway. "Father! *Father!*

Come and see!" The priest hurried in, followed by Serafina. When Gardiner turned to illuminate the mosaics again, they were as they had been before, pure, holy.

He felt his face flaming. "I swear to you, father—"

"Yes. I understand. They are great masters of roguery. We will wait once again." But, though they went in and out of the church several times over the next hour, the mosaics were unchanged. They would not revert to the hideous apocalyptic form. Gardiner found that maddening. He wanted to see the demons again, with the priest as witness. He *needed* to see the demons again.

But the demons would not appear, and finally they gave up. On the way back to town Gardiner studied the priest carefully, wondering if the man suspected him of being some kind of lunatic. But Serafina had seen the distorted mosaics too. Thank God for that, he thought. He would be just about ready to sign up with a shrink by now, otherwise.

"I must think profoundly about this," said Father Demetrios, and went to his room. Serafina said she had to go to her grandmother: she told Gardiner she would join him for dinner. Gardiner stood by himself in the empty *piazza*, watching solid-looking heat-shimmers go spiraling upward. This was the hottest day yet. The town was like an oven.

In late afternoon, unable to bear any of this any longer, Gardiner went back across to the church yet again, and found its walls once more bright with capering loathsomenesses. They no longer frightened him; they simply made him sad. He could weep with the sadness of it all. He had found such lovely sweet mosaics in this unexpected place, such marvels of naïve medieval art. Why wouldn't they stay that way? Why did they have to assail him like this, striking at the foundations of his sanity? For a long time he stood swaying in the midst of this den of horrors, looking with distaste and disbelief from scene to scene. The chapel seemed airless in the pounding heat, as though every atom of oxygen had fled from it into the sky.

The figures appeared to be moving. That was a new phenomenon, and an awful one. He blinked at them. His hand quivered as he moved the flashlight beam from place to place. The leering dancers—the unthinkable shapes—

Somehow the flashlight fell from his hand, and went out as it hit the ground. Gardiner knelt, groping for it in the stifling darkness. He was unable to find it, nor did he have the strength to make his way out of the church. He simply crouched where he was, kneeling, head downward, wearily resting both his palms on the sandy soil.

He felt a hand on his shoulder. A calm voice: "Let us go outside, my friend." Father Demetrios.

"I fell asleep, I guess," said Gardiner.

"No," said the priest. "Not really."

Father Demetrios had a flashlight of his own, a dim one. Gardiner pointed at the walls. They were still covered with monsters.

"Do you see them?" Gardiner asked raggedly.

"I see them, yes. You wanted to find mosaics here, and you found them, eh? But I think you wanted it a little too hard. This is what happens, when they know you want something too hard."

"When *they* know? What *they*? Who?"

"Come," the priest said. "Outside."

Father Demetrios led him from the building and sat him down in the clearing. Dusk had come. Serafina was not there. Gardiner noticed that the priest had placed a number of lighted candles on the ground all about the building. He was taking things from a backpack: a crucifix, a couple of small silver chalices, a Bible.

"Are you going to do an exorcism?" Gardiner asked.

"A reconsecration," said Father Demetrios. "I have not the authority to do exorcisms. The effect will be the same, though. You will please say nothing of this to anyone, yes? There is some irregularity in my proceeding on my own this way." He was going about the building now, anointing it with oil from one of the chalices. "This is all to be our little secret, do we agree?"

Gardiner's head was swimming. He heard the priest chanting in Greek and saw him raising and lowering candles and making the sign of the cross on the walls with the holy oil. It went on and on. Then he knelt a long time in prayer. "We are done," Father Demetrios said at last. "Let us go back to the village, now."

"Shall we look inside the church, first?" Gardiner asked.

"I think not. Let us simply go."

"No. I have to see," said Gardiner. He took one of the candles out of the ground and used it to light his way.

The walls were as blank as if Father Demetrios had whitewashed them. After a moment's hesitation he put out his forefinger and rubbed. A rough stucco surface; no hint of the smoothness of mosaic tile anywhere. Even in this asphyxiating heat, Gardiner felt a chill spreading over him. This was the last straw, this newest mutation. He knew he had to flee, not just the church but the town itself. There was nothing solid here, only abysses beneath abysses.

He went stumbling out. "There's nothing there, father. An hour ago there were mosaics all over those walls!"

"There were?" Father Demetrios said.

Serafina met him at the hotel and said, "Will we have dinner together tonight?"

"I think not," Gardiner said. "I'm going to leave."

"Leave? Now? But it is already dark, and you have not eaten!"

"That's all right. I think I should go."

"Ah. Do you?"

"This is no place for me. You've got too many different kinds of reality here, I think. A little retreating is in order, a little regrouping. There are other places, other mosaics, elsewhere, you know. Best to try my luck at one of those. A place without any ghosts."

She considered that for a moment. "Yes. Maybe you're right." She gave him a sad smile. "Do you blame me for this, what happened here?"

"You? Why should I blame *you*?"

"Good," she said. "I would like you to have at least one happy memory of my village."

He thought he saw an unstated appeal in her eyes. "Will I see you again somewhere?" he asked. "In Palermo, maybe? If I ask for you at the Hertz office?"

"You could do that, yes," she said. "Yes. Please do."

They stood a little while together, neither of them speaking. Then she leaned forward and kissed him lightly, a quick brush against his lips, and took his hand and squeezed it, and smiled, not so sadly this time; and then she was gone.

Gardiner went to his room and packed, and found the *padrone* and settled his bill, and started off down the road, southward into the sultry night, heading for the coast, not daring to look back at dwindling Monte Saturno in his mirror, as though fearing that he would see some titanic winged figure standing with folded arms above the town, grinning at his departure. Was there any place on this island, he wondered, that had no ghosts? Maybe not. But he knew that he needed a change of air. Different ghosts. Less volatile, less mischievous. Relicts of an older, cooler realm, one where reason had held sway at least for a little while. Monte Saturno's mysteries had been too much for him—immense, unanswerable.

He reached Agrigento on the southern shore just before dawn. The ancient Agrigentum, it was, where the clear-minded, logic-loving old Greeks had built a dozen elegant temples whose austere remains still could be seen. It was cooler, here. A fresh breeze was blowing from the sea. Gardiner felt a measure of steadiness returning. Amidst the clean, stark, tranquil ruins of the calm and rational classical era he watched, with tears of happiness and relief streaming down his face, the sun come up over the shattered columns of the Temple of Olympian Zeus.

The Hidden Chamber

NEIL GAIMAN

NEIL GAIMAN is the author of many works, most recently a *Doctor Who* TV episode called "The Doctor's Wife."

He is the first author to win both the Carnegie and the Newbery Medals for the same work, *The Graveyard Book*. His other books include *Good Omens* (with Terry Pratchett); *Neverwhere*; *Stardust*; the Hugo, Nebula, and Bram Stoker Award–winning *American Gods*; *Coraline*; the British Fantasy Award–winning *Anansi Boys*; *Interworld* (with Michael Reeves); and *Odd and the Frost Giants*.

Gaiman's short fiction is collected in *Angels and Visitations: A Miscellany, Smoke and Mirrors: Short Fictions and Illusions, Adventures in the Dream Trade, Fragile Things: Short Fictions & Wonders, M is for Magic,* and *The Book of Cthulhu* (with Laird Barron and Caitlín R. Kiernan).

Gaiman has also co-edited *Ghastly Beyond Belief* (with Kim Newman), *Now We Are Sick: An Anthology of Nasty Verse* (with Stephen Jones), and *Stories* (with Al Sarrantonio), while *Prince of Stories: The Many Worlds of Neil Gaiman* is a nonfiction study by Hank Wagner, Christopher Golden, and Stephen R. Bissette.

He is not certain what he will do next.

"I wrote 'The Hidden Chamber' in a big empty house in Ireland in mid-winter," Gaiman recalls, "the day I found a butterfly in the house, woken by me turning on the central heating a few days earlier. It wanted to get out into the world outside, where it would die.

"I thought about that, and about Bluebeard, and Neal Adams covers of early 1970s comics with beautiful women running away from dark mansions (one light is always on, in the attic), and I wrote this."

DO NOT FEAR the ghosts in this house; they are the least of your
     worries.
Personally I find the noises they make reassuring,
The creaks and footsteps in the night,
their little tricks of hiding things, or moving them, I find
endearing, not upsetting. It makes the place feel so much more like
     home.
Inhabited.
Apart from ghosts nothing lives here for long. No cats
no mice, no flies, no dreams, no bats. Two days ago
I saw a butterfly,
a monarch I believe, which danced from room to room
and perched on walls and waited near to me.
There are no flowers in this empty place,
and, scared the butterfly would starve, I forced a window wide,
cupped my two hands around her fluttering self,
feeling her wings kiss my palms so gentle,
and put her out, and watched her fly away.

I've little patience with the seasons here, but
your arrival eased this winter's chill.
Please, wander round. Explore it all you wish.
I've broken with tradition on some points. If there is
one locked room here, you'll never know. You'll not find
in the cellar's fireplace old bones or hair. You'll find no blood.
Regard:
just tools, a washing machine, a drier, a water heater, and a chain of
     keys.
Nothing that can alarm you. Nothing dark.

I may be grim, perhaps, but only just as grim
as any man who suffered such affairs. Misfortune,
carelessness or pain, what matters is the loss. You'll see

the heartbreak linger in my eyes, and dream
of making me forget what came before you walked
into the hallway of this house. Bringing a little summer
in your glance, and with your smile.

While you are here, of course, you will hear the ghosts, always a room
    away,
and you may wake beside me in the night,
knowing that there's a space without a door
knowing that there's a place that's locked but isn't there. Hearing
them scuffle, echo, thump and pound.

If you are wise you'll run into the night, fluttering away into the cold
wearing perhaps the laciest of shifts. The lane's hard flints
will cut your feet all bloody as you run,
so, if I wished, I could just follow you,
tasting the blood and oceans of your tears. I'll wait instead,
here in my private place, and soon I'll put
a candle
in the window, love, to light your way back home.
The world flutters like insects. I think this is how I shall remember you,
my head between the white swell of your breasts,
listening to the chambers of your heart.

Good Grief

ROBERT SHEARMAN

ROBERT SHEARMAN is an award-winning writer for stage, television, and radio. He was resident playwright at the Northcott Theatre in Exeter, UK, and a regular writer for Alan Ayckbourn at the Stephen Joseph Theatre in Scarborough. He is the winner of the Sunday Times Playwriting Award, the Sophie Winter Memorial Trust Award, and the Guinness Award for Ingenuity in association with the Royal National Theatre. Many of his plays are collected in *Caustic Comedies*, published by Big Finish Productions.

For BBC Radio, he is a regular contributor to the *Afternoon Play* slot, produced by Martin Jarvis, and his series *The Chain Gang* has won two Sony Awards. However, he is probably best known for his work on *Doctor Who*. He helped bring the Daleks back to the screen with the BAFTA-winning first series of the revival, in an episode nominated for a Hugo Award.

Shearman's first collection of short stories, *Tiny Deaths*, was published by Comma Press in 2007; it won the World Fantasy Award for Best Collection, and was short-listed for the Edge Hill Short Story Prize and nominated for the Frank O'Connor International Short Story Prize. His second collection, *Love Songs for the Shy and Cynical*, published by Big Finish, won the British Fantasy Award and the Edge Hill Readers' Prize. A third collection, *Everyone's Just So So Special*, appeared in 2011, again published by Big Finish.

"I think sometimes we write stories in order to ward the horrors off," says Shearman. "The darker the stuff I write, the more I believe that some karma will come into place—if I make my characters suffer, maybe I'll have a series of terribly happy days of giddy sunshine and laughter in contrast. I'm superstitious.

"So, when my wife one day in bed began talking (quite cheerfully, for she is nothing if not morbid) about what we should do if either of us were to die suddenly—what to do with funerals and coffins and catering and things—I felt the need to counteract this as soon as possible, and to write a tale which starts with a couple doing that exact same thing. Just so whatever happens to poor David and Janet *never ever happens to me*.

"If karma is listening, please note—with this story, I've already paid. Thank you."

ONCE IN A WHILE, for a joke, they'd talk about what they'd do if the other died.

They'd be lying in bed together, dozing, cuddling, they might even just have made love—and it was so warm in there, and death seemed so very far away.

Janet would say, "I'm going to get you to scatter my ashes, somewhere really obscure," and he'd ask her how obscure, and she'd laugh, and say, "I don't know, the top of Mount Everest."

And David would say, "I'm going to leave you everything in my will, but only on condition you stay the night in a haunted house," and she'd ask where he might find this haunted house, and he'd tell her he'd Google one on the Internet—don't you worry, missy, you're not getting out of it that easily!

She'd tell him that if he died she'd never marry again—and she'd keep his head in a box, or on display on the mantelpiece, to ward off potential suitors. And he told her that he *would* marry again, in unseemly haste that would shock the in-laws, someone young and pretty, and bring her to his wife's own funeral. She kicked him for that. And then they'd doze some more, or cuddle some more—or maybe even make love again, there was plenty of lovemaking to be had back then.

What actually happened, when he found out his wife was dead, was that he went quite numb. He felt sorry for the policewoman who brought him the bad news; she was so upset; she was so young; she probably hadn't done this much before.

But only *vaguely* sorry, he wasn't sure how to express himself. And when he thanked her for her time and wished her a nice day, he hoped it had come out right.

And it was while numb that he accepted condolences, opened greetings cards telling him, "Sorry for your loss," received flowers. That he phoned Janet's parents, first to tell them their daughter was dead—the words slipped out more easily than he expected, too easily—and then on each night thereafter to see how they were, how they were holding up, whether they were doing okay, and he heard their numbness too, the way that the voices became ever softer, their words large and round and bland. And he thought, I'm doing this to them, I'm infecting them with numbness.

It was while numbed that he had to take his sister's phone calls, because she'd phone him every night too, "to see how you are, how you're holding up, are you okay"—and *she* was crying, sometimes she'd be unable to speak through the tears, "Oh, God, I've lost a sister, I always wanted a proper sister of my own," and he felt annoyed at that, that her grief was better than his. Especially when she hadn't even known Janet that well, she had never once given a Christmas present Janet had wanted, Janet had never liked his sister much.

He prepared the funeral numbed, was numbed as he organized flowers and arranged a nice buffet for the wake; he was really quite spectacularly numb as he wrote a eulogy to Janet. He wanted to tell the world how he felt now she'd gone forever, but he didn't know how he felt, that was what he was still trying to work out; "I'm in shock," he said, to reassure himself, "it has to be expected, I'm in shock," but it had been *days* now. How long could you be "in shock" for?

The words of his eulogy did the right things on the page, all sad and regretful, but even as he plucked them out of his brain (from God knows which part) they didn't seem much to do with him, or with Janet, or their seven-year-old marriage, or their however-many-years-long marriage that they ought to have had.

I'm a fraud, he thought. Friends said he shouldn't deliver the eulogy himself, he'd be too upset, let the minister do it. And the minister was a nice old man, and he talked a lot about God, and he had a kind face and kind eyes and a white beard, he was pretty much what David thought God looked like, maybe he *was* God—except David didn't believe in God, and neither had Janet, so wasn't this all a bit pointless?

Wasn't it pointless? With her there in the coffin (and the coffin was so expensive, and they were only going to use it the once!), and he couldn't even see Janet inside, it might have been stuffed with old newspaper. And David looked at Janet's parents, and they were crying now, their numbness had broken, they'd snapped right out of it, "Why not me?" I'm a fraud, I feel nothing, shout it out, dare you, maybe I never loved her enough to feel, I'm a fraud.

The minister read the eulogy, and he got the emphasis wrong, he made all the funny bits too serious, and all the serious bits, the bits about loss and pain and whatever else David had managed to dredge up, all the serious bits just sounded trivial. And David thought, it should have been me after all. And he supposed that meant, I should have been the one who read the eulogy, but now the thought was in his head, he thought, I should have been the one in the car crash. It should have been me. It should have been me.

But not hysterical, not upset. No. Numb.

The collision had been head on. Both drivers were killed. The other woman had been drinking. They told him Janet wouldn't have known anything about it, she'd have died instantly. David supposed that was better, right? To die in ignorance.

She hadn't left a will, and so hadn't put any funny conditions in it.

He didn't know where to scatter her ashes. He did it in the park. It wasn't especially obscure, but, so.

At the wake he was told, by a series of well-meaning but irritating people, that he should see the doctor and get himself some sleeping pills. "Why?" So he could sleep, of course! But sleeping really hadn't been a problem, there was so much to do, so much to plan (so many well-meaning people to navigate), that he'd fall asleep the moment his head hit the pillow.

He didn't have nightmares. He didn't have dreams, actually, when he slept he was (*ho-ho!*) dead to the world. In fact, David was only ever going to have two more dreams, and only the first he thought of as a nightmare.

It happened just a couple of days after the funeral was done and there wasn't anything to plan any more—and David welcomed it, he'd been expecting *something*, this would be a release—and annoyed too, because it turned out to be entirely the wrong *sort* of nightmare altogether. No dead wife. No car crash. Nothing like grief at all, no grief in which his unconscious state could relax in, and kick back, and say, yes, this, *this*, is what I've been waiting for.

This is what he dreamed.

He couldn't close his eyes.

It wasn't even interesting at first, and hardly distressing, and it took him quite a while to work out anything was wrong at all. He was— somewhere, anywhere. He was—standing, sitting, it didn't matter. Nothing was going on. There was nothing to be concerned about. He was just himself, his ordinary self, who else might he be, and he was content, and a little bored perhaps, waiting for the action to start.

It occurred to him that he hadn't blinked for a while. That was just how engaging this dream was—it gave him time to count his blinks.

And now he registered it, of course, he decided he *wanted* to blink. That would feel good. Just a little blink, thank you, he deserved one of those. And he wasn't able to.

This was silly. The brain wasn't sending the right message to the eyes. He sent a message to his brain, from another part of his brain, telling it to pull its socks up. The brain told the eyes to close. To do one of those blink things they were so expert at. David felt the muscles at the sides of his eyes squeeze—just a little, complacently, this wasn't a problem, the eyes knew they could do this (*ho-ho!* again) in their sleep.

And then, when that didn't work out, the muscles putting a little more effort in, straining.

Nothing. The eyes stared open, resolutely fixed.

David was quite surprised by this. So much so that he raised his eyebrows, and the brows pulled the eyelids ever upwards. David couldn't relax his face from that surprise. He now found he couldn't even lower the eyelids back to where they'd been before, back to where this whole stupid non-blinking problem had started.

"It's all right," he told himself, but it wasn't all right, it was a nightmare, and his eyes were stuck, and he'd forever look like an idiot, some stupid boggle-eyed staring idiot. And where the hell was Janet, shouldn't she be showing up soon, wouldn't dealing with that particular trauma be a bit more *useful*?

Now he thought of blinking, naturally enough, there was nothing he more wanted to do. His body was screaming at him to blink. It was like thinking of an itch, and then in the thought of it needing to scratch. Except, no, don't think of itching, keep away from that.

Too late. Because now David was beginning to panic. And panic over such a ridiculous thing—and he felt that itch now, his *eyes* were itching. They were tingling, God, he'd have to scratch them, he'd have to reach up his hand, reach out his nails, and *scratch* them, hard, scratch away that itch, scratch until the eyeballs were shreds.

And he knew the eyelids wouldn't even shut down, the little bits of protection those fragile flaps of skin could offer wouldn't be there. Because the eyelids only moved *upwards* now, didn't they? And at that, oops, he raised them further, he opened his eyes as wide as they would go, and they locked tight into that position. Fixed, bulging, and so very, very ticklish.

David knew he was asleep. And because of that he knew that in real life his eyes must be *closed*. He wanted to wake up, get out of the dream. Before he did something terrible, before the fingernails did their work. But he couldn't. He felt himself hit out at the bed, he was struggling, he was crying out. This other self of his, the one he could detect faintly in the waking world, he was *useless*, wasn't he? If only he could get his eyes opened for *real*, he could shut the ones in his fantasy. But neither eyes were willing to help. Staying right where we are, said the dream eyes. So are we, said the ones sleeping in David's bed. And he thought for one merciful moment, it'll be okay, with all this commotion I'll wake Janet, and she'll wake me, she'll look after me, I'll be safe—but, oh, shit—and he could feel he was really screaming out now, no one beside him could have slept through that, but there was no one beside him to hear.

He tried to remember what blinking was supposed to achieve. It was to moisturize the eyeball, wasn't it? Give it a little spray of water.

Why would the eye need that? Why would we need to blink so often, did we need that water so very urgently? He thought perhaps we did. He thought perhaps it was essential. And they were *raging* with itches now, his eyes were blazing raw in their sockets—give us some water, we're parched!—and his brain was sending down messages to the fingernails, go to it, lads, scratch away, scratch hard until the eyeballs pop, but (thank God) it seemed the fingernails weren't listening, they stayed right were they were, it seemed no one was taking orders from brain tonight.

David's eyes were so large now, so wide-open, he could feel the pressure on his forehead. And they were hardening too, all the water was gone, they were tightening up like old mud, and then the cracks would appear, and the cracks would break into bigger fissures, and his eyeballs would *splinter*, wouldn't they, they'd shatter all over his stupid stupefied stupid face.

And he was sweating with fear, and he suspected this was both in the dream and out of it, and maybe that'd be good, all that sweat might run into his eyes and give them the liquid refreshment they needed—except, wait—wouldn't it be very salty? That'd sting, that'd *burn*, and he was screaming different messages at his eyes, no wonder they were getting confused—"Open up!" "Shut down!" —and no one was obeying him, someone else was in control, someone else giving instructions to both eyes inner and outer, someone wanted him to *hurt*.

He threw himself out of bed. His eyes snapped open in shock. He fought off the duvet, still wrapped around him, and yes, he had been sweating, the duvet was *drenched*.

In his panic he thought that even in real life he wouldn't be able to close his eyes, that he'd be trapped forever looking at this poor empty bedroom that ought to have had two people in it and now only had one—but no, they closed, and again, and again, and again.

He went to the bathroom. Stared in the mirror. Already he was calming down, it was all right, he was all right. He saw reflected back at him not the terrified man of the dream, but someone who was tired, and confused, and so sad, and slumping back into the numbness. But he watched himself blink some thirty or forty times, one blink after the other. Deliberately, enjoying it. Enjoying the sweet sensation of it, and the freedom that he could do as he wished. Enjoying himself, so it seemed, for the first time since Janet had died.

His lips felt a bit thick. He'd probably hurt them when he fell out of bed, maybe he'd bitten them or something. He prodded at them, but they stayed rubbery to the touch. It took him going downstairs and making himself a hot cup of coffee before he got any proper feeling back.

Pretty soon, David realized, people were getting bored with him. This struck him as rather unfair. He wasn't the one who kept on talking about the death, he mentioned it as little as possible. Everyone was sympathetic, but sympathy was so *tiring*.

He'd gone back to work, but the boss soon called him into his office. "I don't think you should be here yet," he said. "I think you should take all the time you need."

"I want to be busy," said David.

"And you can be busy at home, I'm sure. Don't you worry, we can survive without you!" And then the boss looked embarrassed, looked away; people kept doing that.

So by the time the man from the gas company knocked on the door,

David hadn't seen a living soul for three days. "Suspected gas leak," he said. "I've come to check your meter."

"Oh, all right," said David.

"I'm not disturbing you, then?"

David thought that maybe he was still in his pajamas, sometimes he didn't get out of his pajamas all day, it depended on whether he'd remembered to get dressed. He looked down, and saw that he was actually pretty smart today, presentable. "No, no."

"I'll come in then."

David showed the man where the meter was.

"Nice house," said the meter reader.

"Thank you."

"Big."

"Yes."

"You live with someone else, a wife, perhaps, or . . .?"

"No, no, it's just me."

"Pretty big, just for you on your own."

"Yes," said David. He watched the man take the meter reading. He showed him out.

About half an hour later, the phone rang. David answered it. On the other end he heard someone in tears.

"Hello?" he said. "Hello, who is this? Are you all right?"

"I'm sorry," said the voice. It was a man's voice. He didn't recognize it.

"Who is this?"

"I didn't need to read your meter. I just wanted to see you."

"Hello?" said David. He didn't know why, it just seemed as if the conversation might make more sense started from scratch.

"I'm so sorry for your loss," said the voice. It stuttered in between the sobs. "You must hate me. I'm sorry. It was. My wife, she. She was the one in the car. In the crash."

"Oh," said David. "I don't . . ."

"I'm sorry."

"Yes."

"I just had to . . . oh, shit, can't . . . The words won't. Sorry. See you. See you were okay."

"I'm okay."

"See what I'd done."

"That's okay," said David. "Really."

"Could we meet?"

"What, you mean, come here? I . . ."

And the voice sounded shocked, angry. "To your house? I wouldn't *presume*. That I should . . . I wouldn't deserve it. No."

"Okay."

"But in a pub? I'm in a phone box. Just down the road from you. There's a pub opposite, do you know it?"

"Well, yes, but . . ."

"The King's Arms."

"Yes, I know."

"I'll be there. Thank you. You've no idea how much this means to me." And the man hung up.

Had David still been in pajamas, he might not have bothered going out. But all he had to do was put on a pair of shoes, a coat. They're such easy things, shoes and coats.

He'd never been inside the pub before, though he passed it most days on his way to work. There wasn't much of an afternoon trade, and the woman behind the bar raised her head to him in dulled acknowledgement.

The man in the gas company uniform wasn't crying any more; he sat on his own, nursing a pint of thick dark beer, and when he saw David he smiled as if recognizing an old friend. He stood up to greet him, and it struck David how short he was, all bullish and tightly squeezed into those blue overalls. "Can I get you a pint?" he said.

"Well, it's a bit early."

"Please, a pint, it's the least I can do."

He bought David a pint, as thick and dark as his own.

"I'm sorry about that stunt with the meter," said the man.

"It's okay."

"Bit of a mad thing to do."

"It's okay." There was a pause. The man wouldn't look at David, stared at his pint instead. David said, "So, what do you really do? You know, for a living?"

"I work for the gas company. I read meters."

"Oh, right. I thought that . . ."

"You thought I was in *disguise*? That I'd, what, rent a costume as a meter reader, and come to your house under false pretences?" And for a moment David thought the man was angry, but he wasn't, he was just appalled at the idea; he laughed at the absurdity of it. "Disguise," he chuckled. "That's a good one. That really would make me mad, wouldn't it? How's the drink?"

"Okay." David sipped at it. It was too hoppy for his taste. He hadn't had beer in years. He and Janet had never bothered with pubs, their perfect evening would be a bottle of nice wine in front of the telly.

"Good. Well, there's more where that came from. I owe you. I don't drink much either. Just so you know. I mean, under the circumstances. Inappropriate. But we couldn't just sit in the pub together without a pint. That'd be gay."

David supposed that it would.

"How are you feeling? How are you holding up?" The man looked him directly in the face, and it was the first time he had. David tried to frame the usual bland reply, but the man continued. "Bet you get a lot of that. I do. Gets pretty annoying, doesn't it?"

"Yes," said David.

"They should mind their own fucking business."

"Yes," said David, with feeling. "They should."

"God knows how I feel," said the man. "I keep crying. In front of strangers. I mean, it's bad enough Tracey's dead. But knowing she took someone with her, that's what makes it hard. You're lucky. You've no idea how lucky. I mean, not that lucky, of course, sorry."

"Well, no," said David.

"D'you bury or cremate her?"

"Oh," said David. "Cremate."

"Tracey didn't want to go with cremate," said the man. "She didn't like getting burned. And besides, she'd say, what if they found a cure? Afterwards we could just dig her up. Couldn't be brought back if she were just ashes. Mind you, I don't suppose they'll ever find a cure for car crashes, but you know, it's what she wanted."

"I never knew what Janet really wanted," said David.

"She drank a lot, Mr. Reynolds. I won't tell a lie. I used to ask her to stop. And over the years, I just gave up. And I think, if I hadn't, maybe she'd be alive today. Maybe you'd still have your Janet. Maybe she wouldn't have suffered."

"They say that she died instantly, she wouldn't have felt a thing."

"Yeah, they always say that. But how do they know, eh? I mean, when Janet's head smashed through that sheet of glass. At forty miles-an-hour. And, what, her skull got pulped. How could they know?"

"Well," said David. "I ought to be going."

"Let me get you another pint."

"I haven't finished this one."

"Tracey didn't drink in the beginning," said the man. "So I wonder. Did I drive her to it? Was it something about me? Because I loved her, you know, I really did. But maybe my love wasn't enough? Or too much? I drove her to suicide, because that's what it was, wasn't it? It's my fault. And murder, I killed your wife, it was down to me."

"Not murder," said David. "If anything, manslaughter."

"Yeah," said the man, "I manslaughtered Janet. I'm sorry." He took a long pull at his beer, and David thought this pause in the conversation might give him a second chance to flee, but no, too late, he was off again. "I'm a bad man. I think I was better with Tracey, you know, in spite of everything, we were a *unit*. Do you know what I mean? Together, we made *sense*."

"I do know what you mean," said David.

"And now I've lost her. And I've lost myself too, because she was the best part of me. I don't have any friends. Can you forgive me?"

"I forgive you," said David.

"Can you find it in your heart to forgive me?"

"I do forgive you," said David.

"I won't ask you to be a friend. I don't deserve your friendship. Just your forgiveness."

"I do, I forgive you," said David.

"Thank you," said the man. "Thank you. I feel. Whew. I feel at peace." He smiled, stuck out his hand. It was big and meaty, at odds with how small his body was. David took it. "I'm Alex," said the man.

"David," said David.

"I know."

The numbness kept returning to his lips, and David didn't know what he should do about that. He'd wake in the morning and feel them with his fingers and they didn't seem to belong to him; he had to smack them together for a couple of minutes just to get some life back into them.

When he ate his breakfast cereal the spoon would feel strange in his mouth, the flakes would feel strange, the strangeness made him a bit nauseous. One breakfast they felt so thick and swollen it was as if he'd been anaesthetized at a dentist's. It made him drool. He'd bite his tongue.

David didn't want to go to a doctor, and nearly cancelled the appointment at the last minute. The doctor didn't even want to examine the lips, which was annoying. Was David diabetic? David said that he wasn't. Had he an allergy to shellfish? David assured the doctor he'd been nowhere near a shellfish. Sometimes numb lips, the doctor said, were the first symptoms of migraine headaches, had he had any migraines? No. "Hmm," said the doctor. Then he asked the clincher. He asked if there'd been any trauma in his life recently, any reason he might feel depressed. David admitted his wife had just been killed. "Aha!" said the doctor, and he actually looked pleased. He told David that numb lips were a classic form of stress, of panic attack, of something psychosomatic—he had really nothing to worry about, it'd all come out in the wash when he cheered up. David asked if from now on every single little ailment he ever felt was in some way going to be related to the death of his wife, and the doctor just sort of blinked. "Watch and see if it spreads to other parts of your face," the doctor said. "If it does, I'll put you down for a CAT scan."

One night the numbness of his lips woke David up. He'd been woken by pain before—never by the opposite of it, by pure lack of sensation. He lay there. He ran his tongue over the lips and felt nothing. Smacked them together, nothing.

But no, not nothing.

He felt himself lean forward, just a little—he twitched the lips, he puckered. And there it was. Right next to them. And it was soft and yielding. It was fleshy. It was another pair of lips.

At this he started; he jolted forward in alarm, and thought suddenly that by doing so he'd head-bang whoever was kissing him, and he cried out in expectation of the pain. But there wasn't any, and there was no head to collide with—and his own head kept on rocketing forward at great speed and there was nothing there to stop it, until his own spine yanked it back like a seat belt—and he was breathing fast, panicked, and he slowed that breath down, swallowed, lay his head back upon the pillow. Relaxed. Relaxed . . . Twitched those lips forward again.

He was kissed for his effort.

It was very gentle, very sweet, and there was just the faint taste of lipstick.

"Janet?" he whispered, and wished he hadn't, because he'd chased her away, the spell was broken.

He spent the next hour or so trying to chase those lips, puckering out at the darkened room to no avail. He must have fallen asleep at some point.

The next morning his lips were numb again, but this time he didn't much try to get the feeling back. So he'd drool during breakfast, so what? And during the day he'd keep prodding at the lips, pressing down on them with his fingers hard—staring at them in the mirror and flexing them slowly. He'd close his eyes and make little moues towards a lover who wasn't there.

He went to bed early that night. "Janet," he said to the darkness. He didn't know how to summon her. He didn't know how to let her know he was ready.

Beneath the sheets his hands balled up into tight fists of frustration.

He dozed, slept in fits and starts. And she came to him at last; he woke and she was *there*, he could feel her, her breath against his mouth, she was so very very close—and he wasn't going to say a word, he'd learned his lesson, he wasn't going to move a muscle. Or not just any muscle, he'd choose the muscle carefully—and he pressed his lips forward. Pressed them onto hers. And he couldn't be sure at first, but there, there was that taste of lipstick, a little bit of something sweet and slippery—and Janet had never been much of one for make-up, but he was glad of it now, just so he could taste something and be sure he wasn't pretending.

He extended his tongue—very slowly, carefully. And it went into a place that was warmer and wetter. Pushed it out as far as it would go—it quivered in the hot breath of his dead lover.

She stayed all night. Sometimes he'd sleep, just for a while— and he'd wake with a start, with the certainty that she'd have crept away, that he'd have lost her once more. But she was always there, that softness, that tickle close to his skin, that body heat, those lips, those lips.

The next morning he found the numbness had spread. It was no longer just his lips, the chin had no feeling, his cheeks felt odd and tingling. He called the doctor for an appointment. This time he *did* cancel at the last minute.

Because he realized she didn't come to him at all—no, she never left—she was always there, she was always just a few delicate millimeters away from his face. He could smell her, and taste, and touch, and *feel*, God, and all it required was concentration and just a little bit of forward momentum. And he went to bed with her. He'd cuddle the pillow and pretend his arms were around her body, and he'd make love to her, and he'd make love to himself.

It took three days of this sort of thing before he began to think that this might be unhealthy. And he determined he had to get out of the house, interact with the living again. Alex had left four messages on the answering machine, asking him to call. So he did.

"I'm glad you came," said Alex. "I wasn't sure you would. But this means that we're friends now, right? We're proper friends."

He'd bought them both a glass of house red. "Because I could tell you weren't really enjoying the beer, I'm not entirely insensitive!" The pub was quiet; nothing but Alex's voice and the occasional burp from the fruit machine. Alex wasn't dressed in uniform now, and he'd lost any authority it might have given him; he just looked like a small sad man with a paunch.

"How are you holding up?" he asked.

"I'm doing okay. I think I'm doing better," said David. "I think I'm adjusting."

"Adjusting. Yeah. Good for you. Yeah, we should all be adjusting, yeah."

Alex finished his drink. David offered to buy him another. There was still time for one more round before they had to get to the cinema.

"No, no," said Alex. "I'm not letting you put your hand in your pocket. All the drinks are on me. I owe you, remember?"

David hadn't been out to see a movie in years. The last time had been with Janet in Marbella. It had been a fantastic holiday, they'd laughed so much. And the weather had been mostly glorious. But the sudden downpour had taken them by surprise, and they had taken refuge in the cinema. They arrived in the middle of an action movie in which Bruce Willis killed lots of people, his wisecracks were dubbed into Spanish. They could just about follow the plot, it wasn't too difficult, and David would whisper to Janet his own suggestions for what an English translation of the dialogue might be, and sometimes they were very funny, and even when they weren't Janet would laugh.

Alex insisted on paying for the tickets. It was for some romcom, David hadn't thought it'd be to Alex's taste. Alex said, "Do you want some popcorn?", and David didn't. "You've got to have popcorn!" said Alex, "my treat!", and bought David a big tub overflowing with the stuff. David picked at it through the trailers, but it didn't taste of anything. "You probably need more salt," said Alan, "here, we'll swap." He gave David his popcorn. But it didn't make any difference, David still couldn't taste a thing.

The movie had lots of jokes, but they weren't necessarily very good jokes. Alex would lean across to David and tell him his own punchlines. He'd lean in very close, and David could smell the hot breath on his face—but for all that, he still wouldn't whisper quietly enough. People kept on glaring at Alex and shushing him. He ignored them.

After the movie Alex suggested they should go off for another drink; David said he was tired; Alex wouldn't hear of it.

The pub was much busier now, and Alex had to shout for David to hear him over the noise. Alex brought to the table an entire bottle of wine, and poured glasses for himself and his friend. It wasn't an especially nice wine, normally it'd have been too acidic for David, he preferred something smooth. But he drank it anyway, and he could barely taste it.

"That stuff you were saying," shouted Alex, "about adjusting. Yeah. I can see the value in it. Because, what do they say? Because life goes on. They do say that, don't they?"

"Cheers," said David.

"It's funny how things work out," shouted Alex. "Because we wouldn't even be friends. If our wives hadn't killed each other. But you're a great friend. I think you're the best friend I've ever had!"

"Thanks," said David.

"It wasn't such a tragedy. If it brought us together."

"No."

"And with no blame on either side! And why should there be? Just a, just an accident of circumstance. My wife killed your wife. But then again, your wife killed my wife, didn't she?"

"Wait a moment," said David.

"I'm just saying. There had to be a car for Tracey to hit. And your wife was the one driving it. And yeah, my wife is a little more to blame than your wife. I don't dispute that. But accident of circumstance, yeah? That day, my wife was the one who happened to be drink-driving. The next day, it might have been *yours* drink-driving. Let's not get too fussed about blame."

"My wife didn't ever go drink-driving," said David.

"No, I know, hey, I'm just saying. What I'm saying is, we're the same. Right? Right!" He clinked his glass against David's, frowned. "No need to get nasty about it."

"Sorry."

"Is this seat taken?" said one girl, and "Is it taken?" said her prettier friend. "Do you mind if we join you?" The pub was heaving now, there were no spare tables.

"No, that's fine," said David.

"Fine," said Alex.

The girls' presence seemed to throw Alex off his stride; they chattered together for a minute or so, and then he said, "We went to the cinema."

"Oh . . . yes?" ventured a girl.

"We saw this movie. It wasn't very good."

"It was all right," said David.

"Oh, you say it's all right now, but you were sighing and humphing all the way through it," said Alex.

"Goodness," said a girl. And, "What was it?" said the other.

David told them.

"It hasn't had very good reviews," said the uglier girl to David. "And it's a shame, because I think she was very funny when she was in *Friends*, I just don't know whether she's choosing the right projects, and of course she's getting older now, so maybe she's not getting the offers she once had . . ."

"He is taken, you know," said Alex.

"Sorry?"

"My friend. He is *taken*."

"I didn't mean to . . ."

"Oh, we're not *gay*," sneered Alex. "I bet you think we are. But we were married to *women*. They're dead now. But we still keep them in our hearts, we'll never betray them. We'd do anything for them! Show us some fucking respect, we're fucking mourning!"

By now Alex was on his feet, and the girls were backing into the crowd, and David was dragging his friend out of the pub.

"Get your hands off me, David, I swear to God, I'll fucking *glass* them, what do they think, they think we can't find wives as good as ours?"

"Now calm down," said David. "Come on."

Alex threw him off; David flinched. And Alex looked at him in surprise. "I'd never hurt you," he said. "I'm hurt you think I would."

"All right," said David. "Just breathe."

Alex took a couple of gulps of night air, and began to sob. Dry sobs, they made his little fat body heave with the effort. "I've ruined the evening," he said. "And we were having a brilliant evening. It's the drink. I shouldn't, for her sake, I mean, when you bear in mind. What she. But I've been so down, mate. I miss her. I miss her really bad."

"I know," said David.

"I don't want to be out with *you*. I don't know *you*. I want to be with *her*."

"I understand," said David.

And a look of relief washed over Alex's face, and his eyes lit up, and even his tongue came out for a second, he looked like a little puppy dog so eager to please. "Next time I won't drink. Promise. Just fizzy water. Yeah?" David didn't say anything. Alex's face creased up. "I *need* her," he said. "And you understand."

And his breath was all over David again, and it made him think of Janet, and how close her breath could be, that he wanted to be home with her right now. And he didn't agree to see Alex again, but he nodded, and that was enough.

The trick, David soon realized, was not to think about it too much.

Someone had told him once—it may have been a medical student, someone he met in the university bar—about the way the brain can screen out unwanted objects it doesn't want us to see. The nose is the best example. We all see the nose—he told David, and David thought he was very drunk, and wondered why he was bothering him—we all see the nose *all* the time. It's a big pointy thing sticking straight out the center of our face, of course we can see it. And if we think about it too much, this permanent obstruction getting in the way of what we want to look at, always there in our peripheral vision, it'd make us feel claustrophobic. It'd drive us nuts. So the brain refuses to acknowledge it. Ignores it, tries to make us look *through* it, makes it seem transparent.

David assumed he was a medical student, but he supposed that was just because he was talking about brains and noses and body parts, he supposed he could have been anyone really. And he really wished the student had shut up, he hadn't wanted to think about such things, now he'd been alerted to it he couldn't stop seeing his own nose for days.

And David now had to play the same game with Janet. Because it was obvious to him now—she wasn't just in front of his face, she was *growing herself onto his face*. She was there all the time, always in his peripheral vision, just like a nose—but now there was another nose to contend with, and much more besides. Staring out at her as she stared back at him. He could feel the bristles on his chin flattened against her chin. Her hair tickling his cheeks. Her lipsticked lips. When he breathed, he did so first through his mouth and then through her mouth and then out through the back of her head. Sometimes, when he tried to focus upon any specific object, when he really had to sharpen his eyes and concentrate, he fancied he was having to do so by peering through her forehead, her skull, her very brain. But, like the nose, he tried not to think about it, he *didn't* think about it; like the nose, he found a way of keeping the obstruction in the corner of his eye. Or else, he knew, he really *would* go nuts.

He wondered why she was there. He wondered why he was so special. And then he wondered whether maybe he wasn't special at all—maybe this is what happened to all the poor widowers, maybe they all ended up haunted by a dead wife's face. Maybe they just chose never to talk about it.

Her company made him happy, most of the time. Sometimes the claustrophobia would be too much. Her head right against his head, no room, no space of his own, a wife always there bearing down on him, he couldn't breathe. That's when she would help him. She'd suck in big lungfuls of air, then blow them back into his mouth. She'd give him what he needed. She'd take care of him. She'd breathe for both of them.

It did occur to him that those lungfuls of air she was sucking must have been his air to begin with. But that made him feel a little churlish.

Her mouth would move against his perfectly; when he yawned, she yawned in unison; when he chewed, she chewed; when he forced his mouth into a scowl, a grimace, an artificial grin, just to see, just to test her, yes, she'd do it too. He'd say, "I love you," when he went to sleep at night, and her lips would whisper back the same words to him, in an instant, he didn't even have to wait.

Having her this way was better than nothing.

He didn't like to eat much. He didn't like the way it looked, the concentration he needed to change the way it looked: he had to take his fork and push the food through the back of her head, past her tongue, past her teeth, past her lips, before it could reach his own. Everything he ate seemed now second-hand. She'd sucked all the taste out of it all. Sometimes the food was merely stale. Sometimes it seemed like dirt. Like earth.

All he could really taste properly was that lipstick, her lipstick, creamy and gloopy and clamping down on him hard.

One night, as he was brushing his teeth, he felt something wriggling in his mouth. He assumed it was Janet's tongue, it often found its way in there. But out with the gobbet of soil-mint toothpaste he also spat out a worm. It wasn't a very big worm, to be fair, but seeing it there in the sink was still alarming. David stared at it. He gave it a jab with the end of his toothbrush, and it writhed at the touch. "But what are you doing there?" he said. And, "But she was *cremated*!" The worm looked at him, or so David thought, it was frankly rather hard to tell; it twitched, and that might have been a shrug—hey, I'm a worm, what would I know? And then it slid itself down the plug-hole.

He dreamed of Janet at last. And it was the last dream he ever had, or, at least, the last dream that was truly his.

She was wearing her favorite summer dress, the one she'd wear even when it was cold and raining because she'd say it made her feel better.

"I've been waiting for you," he said, "and for such a long time!" And she kissed him, but as her face leaned in to his she changed direction, she avoided the lips altogether and plumped for the cheek. And what was the good of that, he couldn't taste it at all?

"Should we eat?" she said, and they took their places in the restaurant. It was the same restaurant at which they'd had their first date. Where he'd first dared use the "love" word on her. Where he'd proposed. And it was odd, because they had all been different restaurants.

"How have you been?" she asked. "How have you been holding up?"

"I miss you," he said.

It took a couple of hours for the waiter to take their order, but that didn't matter, and they swapped stories of old adventures together, two lives well led. And after a while David realized he was the only one doing the talking, and Janet was just sitting there, listening, smiling, drinking his memories in, drinking in his happiness.

The food arrived, and it wasn't what David had ordered; he'd thought they were somewhere Italian, but now it was all Chinese. And he didn't expect he'd be able to taste his meal, but it was good, it was so good, that sweet and sour sauce was simply to die for, he cried at how good it was.

They ate their fill. Once in a while David would have to turn his head away, spit out a few worms here and there. And Janet would *tut* amiably, and say, "David, I thought *I* was the one who's dead!" They'd laugh a lot about that.

It was the same restaurant in their honeymoon hotel. It was the restaurant of every birthday and anniversary. It was the restaurant to which he'd take her to say sorry after they'd had a fight, and where, by accepting the invitation, she was assuring him it was all right, everything was all right, she still loved him.

"I didn't know where to scatter your ashes," he said.

"That's okay."

"I scattered them in the park. I'm sorry."

"But it's a nice park," she said.

"I can't remember," he said. "I keep trying to remember. What the last thing I ever said to you was. Do you know? Can you tell me? Tell me it was something nice. Tell me I said I loved you. Please. I loved you."

It was the restaurant where she'd told him she was pregnant. It was the restaurant to which he'd taken her once she lost the child, because they couldn't face being at home, they didn't want to eat at all.

"Why do you haunt my face?" he asked her. She looked a bit hurt at that.

"You need to move on," said Janet, at last.

"I can't move on."

She paused. "I've moved on."

He took this in.

"Are you breaking up with me?" he asked.

"I'm sorry."

"Is it something I've done?"

"No," she said. "No. It was just. An accident of circumstance. Oh, baby, please. Please don't cry."

"But I love you," he said, and the tears were flowing now, why was he crying now and ruining the date, why now when he'd all those weeks of numbness to get through? "I love you," he said, as if that solved a blind thing, as if that did even the slightest bit of good.

"I know," she said. And she took his hand. And she squeezed it. And she let it go.

It was the restaurant in which he had the dream his dead wife didn't want him any more.

They talked a bit more after that. Other adventures they'd had, some of them just the same adventures as before, he repeated his anecdotes a little.

"Save me," David said, but it was so quiet he didn't think she heard.

The waiter brought them the bill. "I've got this," said Janet, "it's on me." She took money from her purse, lots of money, and gave the waiter a generous tip. He bowed his thanks.

"Well," she said.

"Well," said David.

"Well," she said, "this has been fun. We should do it again some time."

"Yes," said David, and he knew they wouldn't. And he got up from the table to get her chair, and she thanked him, and let him give her a peck goodbye.

When he woke up he wasn't crying, his face was still dry, he'd wanted to cry, but only in the dream, just the bloody dream. And he thought that he'd lost her, he patted at his face, to tried to find some trace of her, and part of him wanted her gone—wanted that freedom, his face back to normal—and another part was terrified she'd kept her promise and had gone for good, and then what would he do, who would he even be? And she was still there—she was still there—she hadn't deserted him—still the numbness—still numb. And he laughed and she laughed in unison, and he gulped for air and she gulped too, and he went back to sleep wrapping his arms around himself in a tight hug.

"Look, fizzy water!" said Alex, as he opened the front door, and he laughed, and he waved the bottle about like it was some sort of trophy. He showed David into the house. It was quite a small house; David still felt his own was conspicuously designed for two people, and rattling about there on his own was awkward and embarrassing—but it was hard to believe that Alex had shared this house with his wife, there surely wasn't the space to keep her anywhere. "Nice place, isn't it?" asked Alex, and David agreed. Alex was in a good mood. He seemed very proud of whatever he was concocting in the kitchen, he kept on winking and going back in there to stir it and telling David it'd be a surprise. And, "It's just so nice to have you here, mate," he said. "It's just so nice to have company."

They settled down in the sitting room together for a little while— Alex told David that this stage of the cooking could take care of itself. There wasn't much room, David and Alex sat close, side by side on the sofa. "So," said Alex, "how are you holding up?"

"I'm not sure," said David, honestly.

Alex nodded at that, as if it were the wisest thing he had ever heard. "Not still adjusting, then?"

"What?"

"You said you were 'adjusting.'"

"Oh. Yes. Yes, I don't know."

Alex nodded again. "As for me, I took your advice. Knocked the booze on the head. Thanks. Thank you for looking out for me." He waggled the bottle of water again. "Refill?"

"Why not?" said David.

"It's helped me to clear my head a bit. Know where I stand with this whole death thing. The drink, it was keeping me away from those important decisions. But now I know what's going on. What we both need to do."

"Oh?"

"But there's time enough for that," said Alex, as a timer went in the kitchen. "And I think dinner is served!"

"I hope you like this," said Alex, as he brought over to the table a steaming saucepan. "Tracey's the real cook. Well. But I've been practicing. Got a book and everything." He tipped onto David's plate a pile of spaghetti Bolognese. "Enjoy!"

Each time David lifted his fork he saw worms wriggle on the end of it. Each time he lifted the fork near his mouth, he at first had to pass it through the back of Janet's skull, and he didn't know why, he thought that as the worms brushed against her brain they *became* her brain somehow, that her brain was unraveling into these flapping tendrils, that in death the brain was finally rotting to these thin white ribbons. In his mouth the brain tasted of soil, and he was used to that, but it was a squirming soil, if he didn't gulp it down quickly it'd try to escape back into Janet's head, and he couldn't have that, you couldn't go home again.

So he sucked in those earthworms, and those strands of his dead wife's mind too, he stuffed them in his mouth, he swallowed, swallowed hard so they couldn't come up again and beat a path to freedom; he did it again, the same mechanical exercise, gulping down, trying to gulp all the food away. It took him a minute or two to realize that Alex was looking at him, hard.

"You're not enjoying that, are you?"

"It's fine."

"Fucking typical. Well, then." And Alex got up, and he took David's plate away, and he slammed it into the sink.

David said weakly, "I don't like pasta very much."

"Right," said Alex. "Of course not. You know, I don't think you're putting much effort into this relationship. I'm the one who's doing all the running. Aren't I? I buy the drinks, the cinema tickets, it's me that cooks dinner. You didn't even bring any wine, did you?"

"You told me you weren't drinking."

"Always some excuse with you. Is this what you were like with Janet? Christ. No wonder she drank. No wonder the poor bitch killed herself."

David started to explain that Janet hadn't killed herself. Had she? She'd been happy with him. Wasn't that the case? It'd been an accident, a tragic accident of circumstance.

"Upstairs," said Alex.

"What? No."

"Upstairs, to the bedroom."

"No way."

"Upstairs," said Alex, picking up a knife. "Or I'll fucking *cut* you. I will. I'll *cut* you, you bastard. Upstairs. Now."

So they went upstairs.

"The problem with you," said Alex. "Is you don't know what love is." And he opened the bedroom door, pushed David inside.

It was like a shrine. The walls were covered with hundreds of photographs, and all of the same woman. Some were posed for, some caught unawares. But either way, whether ready for the camera or not, in each picture she had the same expression, the same smile, and that struck David as odd, how could she always make her face the same, so fixed and unmoving?

She wasn't a pretty woman, her head was too round—but she wasn't ugly, had you seen a single picture of her you wouldn't have given her a second glance. But the whole array of these pictures, this presentation of her entire facial repertoire—and she had *one* smile, just *one*—and it made David feel suddenly sick, as if he were looking upon something that wasn't quite human, just something slightly off, something that his brain would normally have consigned to his peripheral vision. Her nostrils always flared, her eyes so wide and unblinking, and that mouth in each picture contorted into an identical smile, the smile so big and broad and covered with thick gloopy lipstick.

"I've had a bad time," said Alex. "I've had a very bad time. But do you see? Do you see how much I love her?"

"Yes, I see," croaked David through the nausea.

"No, really. Look. *Look.*" And Alex grabbed David's hair, and dragged him to the wall, and forced his face hard against a patch of photos—and all David could think of was what this would do to his invisible wife, he'll squash Janet over all the pictures, he'll squash my wife all over *his* wife, how's that going to look?

Close up, of course, with Tracey's face against his, David couldn't make out any identifying features at all.

"I went to your house," said Alex. "I looked for photos. Just some evidence that you were missing your wife the way I missed mine. But there's nothing, is there? I thought maybe you'd done what I did, put all her things in one room so you could see them better. I *believed* that of you. But you haven't."

"No," said David.

"She gave you all that love. And you gave none back. You can't even *feel* anything now she's dead. Can you? You're a fraud. Aren't you?"

"I'm a fraud," said David.

"Your problem is," repeated Alex, "you don't know what love is. It's not a little thing. It's life and death. You don't give someone your heart one day, make them the center of your life. Become a unit. And then *adjust* when they die. Well, I'm better than you. I'm not going to adjust. I'll never adjust. You'll see."

And he gave David the knife. David stared down at it, blankly. As ever, numb.

"You've always had such contempt for me," said Alex, gentler somehow. "Right from the start. Do you think I'm that stupid? Do you think I couldn't see? But ask yourself. You kept coming back to me. Why did you do that?"

"I honestly don't know," said David.

"I know," said Alex. "Because you have a job to do." He got on to his knees. "Kill me," he said.

David slowly registered what Alex had said. Looked down at the knife again, then across to Alex, waiting, unafraid, even smiling— smiling like his dead wife in all the pictures about them, it was as if he were trying to parrot her.

"I can't," said David, but his hand was grasping on to that knife, it was getting the feel for it.

"And I can't go on without her. And if you had any fucking balls, you'd feel the same way about your wife. But now. Now. Your wife killed my wife. And now you kill me. It's fitting. It's simple."

And it was simple, David could see that, any fool could see that. The hand was stroking the knife, it *liked* this knife. The brain didn't like it, told the hand to stop, but no one listened to David's brain any more. He couldn't even feel the blade against his fingers, he was oh so numb.

He bent down to Alex. Lifted the knife, right up to his face, right up to his eyes. And Alex flinched in spite of himself.

"No," David breathed on him, and his breath was hot, but it wasn't his breath, it was hers, it was hers.

"Why not?" said Alex, and he looked like a child, a sad spent little child.

"Because I don't care. I don't care." He dropped the knife to the carpet. Got to his feet. And smiled such a broad smile, and blew him a little kiss. "And I never did."

David left the room, left the house, left Alex weeping on his bedroom floor.

David went home.

He went to every desk drawer, every cupboard. He took from them all the photographs of Janet. He couldn't even remember why he had done that now. He couldn't remember why he wouldn't want to see her face. He looked at that face now. He looked at every single one of those photographs, and studied her face each time. He found her diary, and it wasn't a diary, really, just a notebook of birthdays and doctor's appointments, but nevertheless he read it from cover to cover.

Then he went upstairs to her wardrobe, and pulled out all of Janet's clothes. He didn't smell many, he didn't stroke them—well, maybe one or two. He pulled out her favorite summer dress.

He put all her belongings into a big heap on the sitting room floor. Like a funeral pyre, waiting for a light.

And then he said goodbye to his wife. And he cried. Without sound, but it was real, and it was long, and it hurt.

He hurt. And he grieved. And he let Janet go. He let every trace of her go.

He went to the bathroom mirror to wash his face. He knew now it wouldn't be his face looking back at him. He knew, too, that it wouldn't be his wife's. And he was so tired, so very tired.

He looked at her. He tried to look away. Tried to blink, even—but he wasn't able to blink, he wasn't able to close his eyes, and they opened wide and large and sore.

She wouldn't let him close his eyes. She wanted him to see her at last. She wouldn't let him *not* see.

He felt his eyes harden from lack of moisture. Felt little cracks appear in them. There was no water in his head left, he'd wasted it all, he'd wept it all away. She'd taken Janet's life, and now she was taking his, and she didn't care, she didn't care, she never had, and he *wanted* his eyes to crack, let them fissure, let them pop. But they didn't, they didn't.

"And now," he said, and he smiled, and the smile was big and broad and sticky. "Now, let's have some fun."

Blue Lady, Come Back

KARL EDWARD WAGNER

KARL EDWARD WAGNER (1945-94) died at the ridiculously young age of forty-eight years old. He is remembered as the insightful editor of fifteen volumes of *The Year's Best Horror Stories* series from DAW Books (1980-94) and as an author of superior horror and fantasy fiction.

While attending medical school, Wagner set about creating his own character, Kane, the Mystic Swordsman. After the first book in the series, *Darkness Weaves with Many Shades*, was published in 1970, Wagner relinquished his chance to become a doctor and turned to writing full time. *Death Angel's Shadow*, a collection of three original Kane novellas, was followed by the novels *Bloodstone* and *Dark Crusade,* and the collections *Night Winds* and *The Book of Kane*. These books were later reissued in the omnibus volumes *Gods in Darkness* and *Midnight Sun* from Night Shade Books.

Wagner's horror fiction appeared in a variety of magazines and anthologies, and was collected in *In a Lonely Place, Why Not You and I?, Author's Choice Monthly Issue 2: Unthreatened by the Morning Light,* and the posthumous *Exorcisms and Ecstasies*. More recently, all of the author's weird and supernatural fiction has been collected together by Centipede Press as part of its Masters of the Weird Tale series.

"There are various approaches to writing a story," explained Wagner. "One is to write 'idea stories'—get an idea for a story, plot it out, write it down. On the other hand, I usually write to create a certain mood—often as a response to having experienced that mood. I'm more interested in atmosphere than action, both in what I read and what I write. If a story achieves the moment that I want, then I'm satisfied."

I

THIS ONE STARTS with a blazing bright day and a trim split-level house looking woodsy against the pines.

"Wind shrieked a howling toscin as John Chance slewed his Duesenberg Torpedo down the streaming mountain road. A sudden burst of lightning picked out the sinister silhouette of legend-haunted Corrington Manor, hunched starkly against the storm-swept Adirondacks. John Chance's square jaw was grim-set as he scowled at the Georgian mansion just ahead. Why had lovely Gayle Corrington's hysterical phone call been broken off in the midst of her plea for help? Could even John Chance thwart the horror of the Corrington Curse from striking terror on the eve of Gayle and young Hartley's wedding?"

"Humph," was the sour comment of Curtiss Stryker, who four decades previous had thrilled thousands of pulp readers with his yarns of John Chance, psychic detective. He stretched his bony legs from the cramped interior of his friend's brand-new Jensen Interceptor and stood scowling through the blacktop's heat.

"Well, seems like that's the way a haunted house *ought* to be approached," Mandarin went on, joining him on the sticky asphalt driveway.

Stryker twitched a grin. Sixty years had left his tall, spare frame gristled and knobby, like an old pine on a rocky slope. His face was tanned and seamed, setting off the bristling white mustache and close-cut hair that had once been blond. Mandarin always thought he looked like an old sea captain—and recalled that Stryker had sailed on a Norwegian whaler in his youth.

"Yeah, and here comes the snarling mastiff," Stryker obliged him.

A curious border collie peered out from around the Corvette in the carport, wondered if it ought to bark. Russ whistled, and the dog wagged over to be petted.

The yard was just mowed, and someone had put a lot of care into the rose beds that bordered the flagstone walk. That and the pine woods gave the place a cool, inviting atmosphere—more like a mountain cabin than a house only minutes outside Knoxville's sooty reach. The house had an expensive feel about it. Someone had hired an architect—and a good one—to do the design. Mountain stone and untreated redwood on the outside walls; cedar shakes on the roof; copper flashings; long areas of glass. Its split-level design, adapted to the gentle hillside, seemed to curl around the grey outcroppings of limestone.

"Nice place to haunt," Mandarin reflected.

"I hope you're going to keep a straight face once we get inside," his friend admonished gruffly. "Mrs. Corrington was a little reluctant to have us come here at all. Doesn't want folks laughing, calling her a kook. People from all over descending on her to investigate her haunted house. You know what it'd be like."

"I'll maintain my best professional decorum."

Styker grunted. He could trust Russ, or he wouldn't have invited him along. A psychiatrist at least knew how to listen, ask questions without making his informant shut up in embarrassment. And Russ's opinion of Gayle Corrington's emotional stability would be valuable—Stryker had wasted too many interviews with cranks and would-be psychics whose hauntings derived from their own troubled minds. Besides, he knew Mandarin was interested in this sort of thing and would welcome a diversion from his own difficulties.

"Well, let's go inside before we boil over," Stryker decided.

Russ straightened from petting the dog, carelessly wiped his long-fingered hands on his lightweight sport coat. About half the writer's age, he was shorter by a couple inches, heavier by forty pounds. He wore his bright-black hair fashionably long for the time, and occasionally trimmed his long mustache. Piercing blue eyes beneath a prominent brow dominated his thin face. Movie-minded patients had told him variously that he reminded them of Terence Stamp or Bruce Dern, and Russ asked them how they felt about that.

On the flagstone walk the heady scent of warm roses washed out the taint of the asphalt. Russ thought he heard the murmur of a heat pump around back. It would be cool inside, then—earlier he had envied Stryker for his open-collar sport shirt.

The paneled door had a bell push, but Stryker crisply struck the brass knocker. The door quickly swung open, and Russ guessed their hostess had been politely waiting for their knock.

Cool air and a faint perfume swirled from within. "Please come in," Mrs. Corrington invited.

She was blond and freckled, had stayed away from the sun enough so that her skin still looked fresh at the shadow of forty. Enough of her figure was displayed by the backless hostess ensemble she wore to prove she had taken care of herself in other respects as well. It made both men remember that she was divorced.

"Mrs. Corrington? I'm Curtiss Stryker."

"Please call me Gayle. I've read enough of your books to feel like an old friend."

Stryker beamed and bent low over her hand in the continental mannerisms Russ always wished he was old enough to pull off. "Then make it Curt, Gayle. And this is Dr. Mandarin."

"Russ," said Mandarin, shaking her hand.

"Dr. Mandarin is interested in this sort of thing, too," Stryker explained. "I wanted him to come along so a man of science could add his thoughts to what you have to tell us."

"Oh, are you with the University Center here, Dr. Mandarin?"

"Please—Russ. No, not any longer." He kept the bitterness from his voice. "I'm in private practice in the University area."

"Your practice is . . .?"

"I'm a psychiatrist."

Her green eyes widened, then grew wary—the usual response—but she recovered easily. "Can I fix something for you gentlemen? Or is it too early in the afternoon for drinks? I've got iced tea."

"Sun's past the yardarm," Stryker told her quickly. "Gin and tonic for me."

"Scotch for you, Russ?" she asked.

"Bourbon and ice, if you have it."

"Well, you must be a southern psychiatrist."

"Russ is from way out west," Stryker filled in smoothly. "But he's lived around here a good long while. I met him when he was doing an internship at the Center here, and I had an appendix that had waited fifty years to go bad. Found out he was an old fan—even had a bunch of my old pulp yarns on his shelves alongside my later books. Showed me a fan letter one magazine had published: he'd written it when he was about twelve, asking that they print more of my John Chance stories. Kept tabs on each other ever since."

She handed them their drinks, poured a bourbon and ginger ale for herself.

"Well, of course I've only read your serious stuff. The mysteries you've had in paperback, and the two books on the occult."

"Do you like to read up on the occult?" Russ asked, mentally correcting her—*three* books on the occult.

"Well, I never have . . . you know . . . believed in ghosts and like that. But when all this started, I began to wonder—so I checked out a few books. I'd always liked Mr. Stryker's mystery novels, so I was especially interested to read what he had to say on the subject of hauntings. Then, when I found out that he was a local author, and that he was looking for material for a new book—well, I got up my courage and wrote to him. I hope you didn't think I was some sort of nut."

"Not at all!" Stryker assured her. "But suppose we sit down and have you tell us about it. From your letter and our conversation on the phone, I gather this is mostly poltergeist-like phenomena."

Gayle Corrington's flair-legged gown brushed against the varnished hardwood floor as she led them to her living room. A stone fireplace with a raised hearth of used brick made up one wall. Odd bits of antique ironware were arranged along the hearth; above the mantelpiece hung an engraved double-barreled shotgun. Walnut paneling enclosed the remainder of the room—paneling, not plywood, Russ noted. Chairs and a sofa were arranged informally about the Couristan carpet. Russ dropped onto a cream leather couch and looked for a place to set his drink.

Stryker was digging a handful of salted nuts from the wooden bowl on the low table beside his chair. "Suppose you start with the history of the house?" he suggested.

Sipping nervously from her glass, Gayle settled cross-legged next to the hearth. Opposite her, a large area of sliding glass panels opened onto the sun-bright backyard. A multitude of birds and two fat squirrels worked at the feeders positioned beneath the pines. The dogs sat on the patio expectantly, staring back at them through the glass door.

Gayle drew up her freckled shoulders and began. "Well, the house was put up about ten years back by two career girls."

"Must have had some money," Russ interposed.

"They were sort of in your line of work—they were medical secretaries at the psychiatric unit. And they had, well, a relationship together."

"How do you mean that?" Stryker asked, opening his notepad.

Mrs. Corrington blushed. "They were lesbians."

This was heavy going for a southern belle, and she glanced at their composed expressions, then continued. "So they built this place under peculiar conditions—sort of man and wife, if you follow. No legal agreement as to what belonged to whom. That became important afterward.

"Listen, this is, well, personal information. Will it be okay for me to use just first names?"

"I promise you this will be completely confidential," Stryker told her gravely.

"I was worried about your using this in your new book on haunted houses of the South."

"If I can't preserve your confidence, then I promise you I won't use it at all."

"All right then. The two women were Libby and Cass."

Mandarin made a mental note.

"They lived together here for about three years. Then Libby died. She was only about thirty."

"Do you know what she died of?" Russ asked.

"I found out after I got interested in this. How's the song go—'too much pills and liquor.'"

"Seems awfully young."

"She hadn't been taking care of herself. One night she passed out after tying one on, and she died in the hospital emergency room."

"Did the hauntings start then?"

"Well, there's no way to be sure. The house stood empty for a couple of years afterward. Legal problems. Libby's father hadn't cared for her lifestyle, and when she died he saw to it that Cass couldn't buy Libby's share of the house and property. That made Cass angry, so she wouldn't sell out her share. Finally they agreed on selling the house and land, lock, stock, and barrel, and dividing the payment. That's when I bought it."

"No one else has ever lived here, then?"

Gayle hesitated a moment. "No—except for a third girl they had here once, a nurse. They rented a third bedroom to her. But that didn't work out, and she left after a few months. Otherwise, I'm the only other person to live here."

"It seems a little large for one person," Stryker observed.

"Not really. I have a son in college now who stays here over breaks. And now and then a niece comes to visit. So the spare rooms are handy."

"Well, what happened after you moved in?"

She wrinkled her forehead. "Just . . . well, a series of things. Just strange things . . .

"Lights wouldn't stay on or off. I used to think I was just getting absentminded, but then I began to pay careful attention. Like I'd go off to a movie, then come back and find the carport light off—when the switch was inside. It really scared me. There's other houses closer now, but this is a rural area pretty much. Prissy's company, but I don't know if she could fight off a prowler. I keep a gun."

"Has an electrician ever checked your wiring?"

"No. It was OK'd originally, of course."

"Can anyone break in without your having realized it?"

"No. You see, I'm worried about break-ins, as I say. I've got double locks on all the doors, and the windows have special locks. Someone would have to break the glass, or pry open the woodwork around the doors—leave marks. That's never happened.

"And other things seem to turn on and off. My electric toothbrush, for instance. I told my son and he laughed—then one night the light beside his bed flashed off."

"Presumably you could trace all this to electrical disturbances," Russ pointed out.

Gayle gestured towards the corner of the living room. "All right. See that wind-up Victrola? No electricity. Yet the damn thing turns itself on. Several times at night I've heard it playing—that old song, you know . . ."

She sang a line or two: "Come back, blue lady, come back. Don't be blue anymore . . ."

Stryker quickly moved to the machine. It was an old Victrola walnut-veneer console model, with speaker and record storage in the lower cabinet. He lifted the hinged lid. It was heavy. Inside, the huge tonearm was swung back on its pivot.

"Do you keep a record on the turntable normally?"

"Yes. I like to show the thing off. But I'm certain I haven't left 'Blue Skirt Waltz' on every time."

"It's on now."

"Yes, I leave it there now."

"Why not get rid of the record as an experiment?"

"What could I think if I found it back again?"

Stryker grinned. He moved the starting lever with his finger. The turntable began to spin.

"You keep this thing wound?" Russ asked.

"Yes," Gayle answered uneasily.

Curtiss swung the hinged tonearm down, rested the thick steel needle on the shellac disc.

I dream of that night with you
Darling, when first we met . . .

"Turn it off again—please!"

II

Stryker hastily complied. "Just wanted to see what was involved in turning it on."

"Sorry," Gayle apologized. "The thing has gotten on my nerves, I guess. How about refills all around?"

"Fine," Stryker agreed, taking a final chew on his lime twist.

When their hostess had disappeared into the kitchen with their glasses, he murmured aside to Mandarin, "What do you think?"

Russ shrugged. "What can I say from a few minutes talking, listening to her? There's no blatant elevation of her porcelain titer, if that's what you mean."

"What's that mean?" the writer asked, annoyed.

"She doesn't come on as an outright crock."

Stryker's mustache twitched. "Think I'll write that down."

He did.

"Useful for rounds," Russ explained in apology.

"What about the occult angle? So far I'm betting on screwy electrical wiring and vibrations from passing trucks or something."

Stryker started to reply, but then Gayle Corrington rustled back, three glasses and a wedge of cheese on a tray.

"I've been told most of this can be explained by wiring problems or vibrations," she was saying. "Like when the house settles on its foundation."

Russ accepted his drink with aplomb—wondering if she had overheard.

"But I asked the real estate man about that," she went on, "and he told me the house rests on bedrock. You've seen the limestone outcroppings in the yard. They even had to use dynamite putting down the foundation footings."

"Is there a cellar?"

"No. Not even a crawl space. But I have storage in the carport and in the spare rooms. There's a gardening shed out back, you'll notice—by the crepe myrtle. Libby liked to garden. All these roses were her doing. I pay a man from the nursery to keep them up for me. Seems like Libby would be sad if I just let them go to pot."

"Do you feel like Libby is still here?" Russ asked casually.

She hadn't missed the implication, and Russ wished again Curtiss hadn't introduced him as a psychiatrist. "Well, yes," she answered cautiously. "I hope that doesn't sound neurotic."

"Has anything happened that you feel can't be explained—well, by the usual explanations?" Curtiss asked, steering the interview towards safer waters.

"Poltergeist phenomena, you mean? Well, I've only touched on that. One night the phone cord started swinging back and forth. All by itself—nothing near it. I was sitting out here reading when I saw that happen. Then my maid was here one afternoon when all the paper cups dropped out of the dispenser and started rolling up and down the kitchen counter. Another night that brass table lamp there started rocking back and forth on its base—just like someone had struck it. Of course, I was the only one here. Christ, I felt like yelling, 'Libby! Cut it out!'"

"Is there much truck traffic on the highway out front?" Stryker asked. "Stone transmits vibrations a long way, and if the house rests on bedrock . . ."

"No truck traffic to speak of—not since the interstates were completed through Knoxville. Maybe a pickup or that sort of thing drives by. I've thought of that angle, too.

"But, darn it—there's too many other things." Her face seemed defiant. She's thought a lot about this, Russ surmised—and now that she's decided to tell someone else about it, she doesn't want to be taken for a credulous fool.

"Like my television." She pointed to the color portable resting on one end of the long raised hearth. "If you've ever tried to lug one of these things around, you know how portable they really are. I keep it here because I can watch it either from that chair or when I'm out sunning on the patio. Twice, though, I've come back and found it's somehow slid down the hearth a foot or so. I noticed because the picture was blocked by the edge of that end table when I tried to watch from my lounge chair on the patio. And I know the other furniture wasn't out of place, because I line the set up with that cracked brick there—so I know I can see it from the patio, in case I've moved it around someplace else. Both times it was several inches past that brick."

Russ examined the set, a recent portable model. One edge of its simulated walnut chassis was lined up one row of bricks down from where a crack caused by heat expansion crossed the hearth. He pushed at the set experimentally. It wouldn't slide.

"Tell me truck vibrations were responsible for *this*," Gayle challenged.

"Your cleaning maid . . ."

"Had not been in either time. Nor had anyone else in the time between when I noticed it and when I'd last watched it from outside."

"No one else that you knew of."

"No one at all. I could have told if there'd been a break-in. Besides, a burglar would have stolen the darn thing."

Russ smoothed his mustache thoughtfully. Stryker was scribbling energetically on his notepad.

Gayle pressed home her advantage. "I asked Cass about it once. She looked at me funny and said they used to keep their TV on the hearth, too—only over a foot or so, because the furniture was arranged differently."

Stryker's grey eyes seemed to glow beneath his shaggy eyebrows. Russ knew the signs—Curtiss was on the scent.

Trying to control his own interest, Russ asked: "Cass is still in Knoxville, then?"

Gayle appeared annoyed with herself. "Yes, that's why I wanted to keep this confidential. She and another girl have set up together in an old farmhouse they've redone—out towards Norris."

"There's no need for me to mention names or details of personal life," Curtiss reassured her. "But I take it you've said something to Cass about these happenings?"

"Well, yes. She had a few things stored out in the garden shed that she finally came over to pick up. Most of the furnishings were jointly owned—I bought them with the house—but there was some personal property, items I didn't want." She said the last with a nervous grimace.

"So I came flat out and said to her: 'Cass, did you ever think this house was haunted?' and she looked at me and said quite seriously: 'Libby?'"

"She didn't seem incredulous?"

"No. Just like that, She said: 'Libby?' Didn't sound surprised—a little shaken maybe. I told her about some of the things here, and she just shrugged. I didn't need her to think I was out of my mind, so I left off. But that's when I started to think about Libby's spirit lingering on here."

"She seemed to take it rather matter-of-factly." Russ suggested.

"I think she and Libby liked to dabble in the occult. There were a few books of that sort that Cass picked up—a Ouija board, tarot deck, black candles, a few other things like that. And I believe there was something said about Libby's dying on April the 30th—that's Walpurgis Night, I learned from my reading."

Witches' Sabbath, Russ reflected. So he was going to find his Gothic trappings after all.

It must have showed on his face. "Nothing sinister about her death," Gayle told him quickly. "Sordid maybe, but thoroughly prosaic. She was dead by the time they got her to the emergency room, and a check of her bloodstream showed toxic levels of alcohol and barbs. Took a little prying to get the facts on that. Family likes the version where she died of a heart attack or something while the doctors worked over her.

"But let me freshen those ice cubes for you. This show-and-tell session is murder on the throat."

Stryker hopped out of his chair. "Here, we'll carry our own glasses."

Smiling, she led them into the kitchen. Russ lagged behind to work at the cheese. He hadn't taken time for lunch, and he thought he'd better put something in his stomach besides bourbon.

"There's another thing," Gayle was saying when he joined them. "The antique clocks."

Russ followed her gesture. The ornate dial of a pendulum wall clock stared back at him from the dining room wall. He remembered the huge walnut grandfather's clock striking solemnly in the corner of the living room.

"Came back one night and found both cabinets wide open. And you have to turn a key to open the cabinets."

"Like this?" Stryker demonstrated on the wall clock.

"Yes. I keep the keys in the locks because I need to reset the pendulum weights. But as you see, it takes a sharp twist to turn the lock. Explain that one for me."

Russ sipped his drink. She must have poured him a good double. "Have you ever thought that someone might have a duplicate key to one of the doors?" he asked.

"Yes," Gayle answered, following his train of thought. "That occurred to me some time ago—though God knows what reason there might be to pull stunts like these. But I had every lock in the house changed—that was after I had come back and found lights on or off that had been left off or on one time too many to call it absentmindedness. It made no difference, and both the TV and the clock incidents took place since then."

"You know, this is really intriguing!" Curtiss exclaimed, beaming over his notepad.

Gayle smiled back, seemed to be fully at ease for the first time.

"Well, I'll tell you it had me baffled. Here, let me show you the rest of the house."

A hallway led off from the open space between living room and dining area. There was a study off one side, another room beyond, and two bedrooms opposite. A rather large tile bath with sunken tub opened at the far end.

"The study's a mess, I'm afraid," she apologized, closing the door on an agreeably unkempt room that seemed chiefly cluttered with fashion magazines and bits of dress material. "And the spare bedroom I only use for storage." She indicated the adjoining room, but did not offer to open it. "My son sleeps here when he's home."

"You keep it locked?" Russ asked, noting the outdoor-type lock.

"No." Gayle hastily turned the knob for them, opened the door on a room cluttered with far more of the same as her study. There was a chain lock inside, another door on the outside wall. "As you see, this room has a private entrance. This is the room they rented out."

"Their boarder must have felt threatened," Russ remarked. He received a frown that made him regret his levity.

"These are the bedrooms." She turned to the hallway opposite. "This was Cass's." A rather masculine room with knotty pine paneling, a large brass bed, cherry furnishings, and an oriental throw rug on the hardwood floor. "And this was Libby's." Blue walls, white ceiling, white deep-pile carpet, queen-sized bed with a blue quilted spread touching the floor on three sides. In both rooms, sliding glass doors opened onto the backyard.

"Where do you sleep?" Russ wanted to know.

"In the other bedroom. I find this one a bit too frilly."

"Have you ever, well, seen anything—any sort of, say, spiritual manifestations?" Stryker asked.

"Myself, no," Gayle told them. "Though there are a few things. My niece was staying with me one night not long after I'd moved in—sleeping in Libby's room. Next morning she said to me, 'Gayle, that room is haunted. All night I kept waking up thinking someone else was there with me.' I laughed, but she was serious."

"Is that when you started thinking in terms of ghosts?"

"Well, there had been a few things before that," she admitted. "But I suppose that was when I really started noticing things."

Russ chalked up a point for his side.

"But another time a friend of mine dropped by to visit. I was out of town, so no one answered her ring. Anyway, she heard voices and figured I was in back watching TV, with the set drowning out the doorbell. So she walked around back. I wasn't here, of course. No one was here. And when she looked inside from the patio, she could see that my set was turned off. She was rather puzzled when she told me about it. I told her a radio was left on—only that wasn't true."

"The dog ever act strangely?" Stryker asked.

"Not really. A few times she seems a little nervous is all. She's a good watchdog though—barks at strangers. That's one reason why I don't suspect prowlers. Prissy lets me know when something's going on that she doesn't like.

"Aside from that, the only other thing I can think of is one night when my son was here alone. I got back late and he was sitting in the living room awake. Said he'd seen a sort of blue mist taking shape in the darkness of his bedroom—like a naked woman. Well, the only mist was the smoke you could still smell from the pot party he and his friends had had here earlier. We had a long talk about that little matter."

Stryker studied his notepad. "I'd like to suggest a minor experiment of sorts, if you don't mind. I'd like for Russ and myself to take a turn just sitting alone in Libby's room for a few minutes. See what impressions we have—if any."

"I'll take first watch," Russ decided, at their hostess's expression of consent.

Curtiss shot him a warning glance and returned with Gayle to the living room.

Waiting until they were around the corner, Mandarin stepped into the room now occupied by Gayle Corrington. Cass's room. There was a scent of perfume and such, a soft aura of femininity that he hadn't noticed from the hallway. It softened the masculine feel of the room somewhat, gave it sort of a ski lodge atmosphere. The bedroom had the look of having been recently straightened for company's inspection. As was the case. There were crescent scratches about three feet up on the corner paneling next to the head of the bed, and Russ guessed that the pump shotgun did not usually hang from brackets on the bedroom wall as it did now.

The bathroom was out of Nero's mountain retreat. Big enough to play tennis in, with synthetic fur rugs scattered on the slate-tiled floor, and with a dressing table and elaborate toilet fixtures that matched the tiles and included a bidet. A cross between a boudoir and the Roman baths. The sunken tub was a round affair and like an indoor pool. Russ wondered if the mirror on the ceiling fogged up when things got hot.

Swallowing the rest of his drink, he stepped into the guest room. Libby's room. This would, of course, be the Blue Room in one of those sprawling mansions where pulp mysteries had a habit of placing their murders. Come to think of it, hadn't he seen an old '30s movie called something like *The Secret of the Blue Room?*

Sitting on the edge of the bed, he crunched an ice cube and studied the room about him. Very feminine—though the brightness of the patio outside kept it from becoming cloying. It had a comfortable feel about it, he decided—not the disused sensation that generally hangs over a guest room. There was just a hint of perfume still lingering— probably Gayle kept clothes in the closet here.

Russ resisted the temptation to lie down. Glancing outside, he reflected that, when drawn, the blue curtains would fill the room with blue light. Might be a point worth bringing up to Curtiss, in case the old fellow got too excited over ectoplasm and the like. Aside from that, Russ decided that the room was as thoroughly unhaunted as any bedroom he'd ever sat in.

Giving it up at length, he ambled back to the living room.

Stryker was just closing his notepad. Either he'd got another drink, or else he'd been too interested to do more than sip his gin and tonic. At Mandarin's entry, he excused himself and strode off for the bedroom.

Gayle's face was a trifle flushed, her manner somewhat nervous. Russ wondered whether it was the liquor, or if he'd broken in on something. She had that familiar edgy look of a patient after an hour of soul-bearing on the analyst's couch. As he thought about it, Russ agreed that this interview must be a similar strain for her.

"You've eaten your ice cubes," she observed. "Shall I get you another?"

Russ swallowed a mouthful of salted nuts. "Thank you—but I've got to drive."

She made a wry face. "You look big enough to hold another few. A light one, then?"

"Hell, why not. A light one, please." Probably she would feel more at ease if she supposed his psychiatric powers were disarmed by bourbon.

He paced about the living room while she saw to his glass. Coming to the fireplace, he studied the beautifully engraved shotgun that hung there. It was a Parker. Russ started to touch it.

"That's loaded."

He jerked back his hand like a scolded kid. "Sorry. Just wanted to get the feel of an engraved Parker double-barrel. That's some gun you have to decorate your fireplace with."

"Thank you. I know." She handed him his drink.

"Don't you worry about keeping a loaded shotgun in your living room?" The drink was at least equal to its predecessors.

"I'd worry more with an empty one. I'm alone here at night, and there aren't many neighbors. Besides, there aren't any kids around who might get in trouble with it."

"I'd think a woman would prefer something easier to handle than a shotgun."

"Come out on the skeet range with me sometime, and I'll show you something."

Mandarin must have looked properly chastened. With a quick grin

Gayle drew down the weapon, opened the breech, and extracted two red shells. "Here." She handed the shotgun to him.

"Double ought," Russ observed, closing the breech.

"It's not for shooting starlings."

He sighted along the barrel a few times, gave it back. Briskly she replaced the shells and returned it to its mounting.

"Might I ask what you do, Mrs. Corrington?"

"Gayle. I assume you mean for a living. I own and manage a mixed bag of fashion stores—two here in Knoxville, plus a resort-wear shop in Gatlinburg, and a boutique on the Strip by the University. So you see, Doctor, not all working girls fall into the nurse or secretary system of things."

"Russ. No, of course not. Some of them make excellent psychiatrists."

She softened again. "Sorry for coming on strong for women's lib. Just that you find yourself a little defensive after being questioned for an hour."

"Sorry about that." Russ decided not to remind her that this was at her own invitation. "But this has been extremely interesting, and Curtiss is like a bloodhound on a fresh trail.

"But how do you feel about this, Gayle? Do you believe a poltergeist or some sort of spirit has attached itself to the house?"

She gave him a freckled frown and shrugged her shoulders. No, Russ concluded, she wasn't wearing some sort of backless bra beneath her gown—not that she needed one.

"Well, I can't really say. I mean, there's just been so many things happening that I can't explain. No, I don't believe in witches and vampires and ghosts all draped in bedsheets, if that's what you mean. But some of the books I've read explain poltergeists on an ESP basis— telekinesis or something on that order."

"Do you believe in ESP?"

"Yes, to an extent."

"Do you consider yourself psychic?"

She did the thing with her shoulders again. "A little maybe. I've had a few experiences that are what the books put down as psychic phenomena. I guess most of us have. But now it's my turn. What do you think, Russ? Do you believe in ghosts?"

"Well, not the chain-rattling kind anyway."

"Then ESP?"

"Yes, I'll have to admit to a weakness towards ESP."

"Then here's to ESP."

They clinked glasses and drank.

"I'll second that," announced Stryker, rejoining them.

III

"Jesus!" Stryker swore. "Slow down, Russ!" He braced himself with one hand against the dash, almost slung out of his bucket seat as the Jensen took a curve at 70.

"Use the seat belt," advised Mandarin, slowing down somewhat. After all, he *was* a little high to be pushing the car this hard.

"Don't like them," Curtiss grunted. "The harnesses make me claustrophobic."

"They say they're someday going to pass a law making it compulsory to wear them."

"Like to see them try—we're not to 1984 yet! Why don't the prying bastards work to prevent accidents instead of putting all their bright ideas into ways of letting the damn fools who cause them live through it. And speaking of prevention, how about slowing this sports car down to legal velocities. The cops would sure like to nail you on a drunk driving charge."

"Who's drunk?" Russ slowed to 65, the legal limit for non-interstate highways.

"Son, you had a few before you picked me up this noon—and Gayle Corrington wasn't running up her water bill on those drinks she poured for us."

Russ veered from the ragged shoulder of the old two-lane blacktop.

"If she starts the day customarily with drinks like she was pouring for me, I think I know where her poltergeist comes from."

"You weren't impressed?" Stryker sounded amused. "But you'll admit natural explanations get a little forced and tenuous after a while."

A stop sign bobbed over the crest of a hill, and Russ hit the brakes hard. Four disc brakes brought the Jensen up almost in its length. Stryker uncovered his eyes.

"Yeah," Russ went on. "There were a number of damned things she said that sounded like telling points in favor of a poltergeist. But you have to bear in mind that all this is by her unsupported evidence. Hell, we can't be sure she isn't hallucinating this stuff, or even just making the whole thing up to string you along. Women do get bored at forty-ish—to say nothing of what the thought of starting over the hill does to their libidos."

"She didn't look bored—and certainly not headed over the hill. Another few years, my friend, and you'll stop thinking of womanhood withering at thirty. Hell, it's just starting to bloom. But do you think she's unreliable? Seemed to be just the opposite. A level-headed woman who was frankly baffled and a little embarrassed with the entire affair."

Russ grunted, unwilling to agree offhand—though these were his own impressions as well. "I'm just saying you need to keep everything in perspective. I've gotten fooled by too many patients with a smooth façade—even when I was expecting things to be different beneath the surface."

"But you'll hazard an opinion that Mrs. Corrington is playing straight with us, so far as signs indicate?" Stryker persisted.

"Yeah," Mandarin conceded. "But that's one tough woman lurking beneath all that sweet southern-belle charm she knows how to turn on. Watch out."

He turned onto the interstate leading into Knoxville's downtown. In deference to Curtiss's uneasiness with high speed, he held the needle at 80, safely just over the 75 limit of the time.

"What's your opinion of it all, then?" the author prodded.

"Well, I'll maintain scientific neutrality. While I consider poltergeists improbable, I'll accept the improbable when the probable explanations have all been eliminated."

"Nicely phrased, Holmes," Stryker chuckled. "And taking a position that will have you coming out sounding correct no matter what."

"The secret of medical training."

"I knew you'd come in handy for something."

"Well, then, what's your opinion?"

The author decided it was safe to release the dashboard and light his pipe. "Well, I guess I've used the supernatural too often in my fiction to accept it as willingly as I might otherwise. Seems every time I start gathering the facts on something like this, I find myself studying it as a fiction plot. You know—like those yarns I used to crank out for pulps like *Dime Mystery Stories*, where when you get to the end you learn that the Phantom of Ghastly Manor was really Cousin Rodney dressed up in a monster suit so he could murder Uncle Ethelred and claim the inheritance before the will was changed. Something like that. I start putting facts together like I was plotting a murder thriller, you know. Kind of spoils the effect for me. This thing, for instance . . ."

Russ cursed and braked viciously to avoid the traffic stopped ahead at Malfunction Junction. Knoxville's infamous rush hour tangle had the interstate blocked solid ahead of them. Swerving onto the shoulder, he darted for the upcoming exit and turned towards the University section. Curtiss seemed about to bite his pipe in two.

"Stop off at the Yardarm? I don't want to fight this traffic."

Stryker thought he could use a drink.

Safely seated in a back booth, stein of draft in hand, Curtiss regained his color. It was a favorite bar—just off the Strip section of the University area. When Stryker had first come to the area years back, it had been a traditional Rathskeller college bar. Styles had changed, and so had students. Long hair had replaced crew cuts, Zen and revolution had shoved fraternities and football from conversational standards, and there was a faint hint of marijuana discernible through the beer smell. Someone had once suggested changing the name of the Yardarm to the Electric Foreskin or some such, and had been tossed out for his own good.

Stryker didn't care. He'd been coming here for years—sometimes having a round with his creative writing students. Now—well, if they wanted to talk football, he'd played some; if they wanted to talk revolution, he'd fought in some. The beer was good, and the atmosphere not too frantic for conversation.

His office was a block or two away—an upstairs room in a ramshackle office building only slightly less disreputable in appearance than the dilapidated Edwardian mansion turned community clinic where Russ worked. This was several blocks in the other direction, so the bar made a convenient meeting place for them. Afternoons often found the pair talking over a pitcher of beer (Knoxville bars could not serve liquor at the time), and the bartender—a huge red-bearded Viking named Blackie—knew them both by name.

"You were saying that your faith in the supernatural was fraught with skepticism," Mandarin reminded, wiping foam from his mustache.

"No. I said it was tempered with rationality," Stryker hedged. "That doesn't mean I don't believe in the supernatural. It means I examine facts with several of those famous grains of salt before I offer them to my readers."

"I take it then you're going to use this business today in your new book."

Stryker nodded enthusiastically. "It's worth a chapter, I'm certain."

"Well, that's your judgement, of course," commented Mandarin, glancing at his watch. "Personally, I didn't read any irrefutable evidence of the supernatural into all this."

"Science scoffing under the shadow of truths inadmissible to its system of logic." Stryker snorted. "You're as blind in your beliefs as the old-guard priesthood holding the bastions of disease-by-wrath-of-God against the germ-theory heretics."

"I suppose," Russ admitted around a belch.

"But then, I forgot that you were back in Libby's room while I was finishing up the interview with Gayle Corrington," Stryker said suddenly. "Hell, you missed out on what I considered the most significant and intriguing part of her story. Let me read this off to you." He fumbled for his notepad.

Mandarin had had enough of hauntings for the day. "Let me have you fill me in later," he begged off. "I've got an evening clinic tonight, and I'd like to run back to the house beforehand and get packed."

"Going out of town?"

"I need to see my high-priced lawyers in New York tomorrow."

"That's right. How's that look?"

Russ frowned, said with more confidence than he felt: "I think we'll make our case. Police just can't burglarize a physician's confidential files in order to get evidence for a drug bust."

"Well, I wish you luck," Stryker allowed. "There's a few angles I want to check out on this business first, anyway. I'll probably have the chapter roughed out by the time you're back in town. Why don't I give you a carbon then, and let you comment?"

"Fine." Russ stood up and downed his beer. "Can I give you a lift somewhere?"

"Thanks—but I've got my car parked just down the block. You take it easy driving back though."

Russ grinned. "Sure. Take it easy yourself."

Two nights later Mandarin's phone woke him up. Stryker hadn't taken it easy.

IV

Disheveled and coatless in the misty rain, Mandarin stood glumly beside the broken guardrail. It was past 3:00 a.m. His clothes looked slept in, which they were. He'd continued the cocktail hour that began on his evening flight from New York once he got home. Sometime towards the end of the network movie that he wasn't really watching, he fell asleep on the couch. The set was blank and hissing when he stumbled awake to answer the phone.

"Hello, Russ," greeted Saunders, puffing up the steep bank from the black lakeshore. His face was grim. "Thought you ought to be called. You're about as close to him as anyone Stryker had here."

Mandarin swallowed and nodded thanks. With the back of his hand he wiped the beads of mist and sweat from his face. Below them the wrecker crew and police diver worked to secure cables to the big maroon Buick submerged there. Spotlights, red taillights burning through the mist. Yellow beacon on the wrecker, blue flashers on the two patrol cars. It washed the brush-grown lakeshore with a flickering nightmarish glow. Contorted shadows wavered around objects made grotesque, unreal. It was like a Dalíesque landscape.

"What happened, Ed?" he managed to say.

The police lieutenant wiped mud from his hands. "Nobody saw it. No houses along this stretch, not a lot of traffic this hour of night."

An ambulance drove up slowly, siren off. Static outbursts of the two-way radios echoed like sick thunder in the silence.

"Couple of kids parked on a side road down by the lake. Thought they heard brakes squeal, then a sort of crashing noise. Not loud enough to make them stop what they were doing, and they'd been hearing cars drive by fast off and on all night. But they remembered it a little later when they drove past here and saw the gap in the guardrail."

He indicated the snapped-off stumps of the old-style wood post and cable guardrail. "Saw where the brush was smashed down along the bank and called it in. Investigating officer's flashlight picked out the rear end plain enough to make out the license number. I was on hand when owner's identification came in; had you called."

Russ muttered something. He'd met Saunders a few years before when the lieutenant was taking Styker's evening class in creative writing. The detective had remained a casual friend despite Mandarin's recent confrontations with the department.

"Any chance Curtiss might have made it?"

Saunders shook his head. "Been better than a couple hours since it happened. If he'd gotten out, he'd have hiked it to a house down the road, flagged down a motorist. We'd have heard."

Someone called out from the shore below, and the wrecker's winch began to rattle. Russ shivered.

"Rained a little earlier tonight," Saunders went on. "Enough to make this old blacktop slick as greased glass. Likely, Curtiss had been visiting some friends. Had maybe a few drinks more than he should have—you know how he liked gin in hot weather. Misjudged his speed on these slippery curves and piled on over into the lake."

"Hell, Curtiss could hold his liquor," Mandarin mumbled. "And he hardly ever pushed that big Buick over 35."

"Sometimes that's fast enough."

The Buick's back end broke through the lake's black surface like a monster in a Japanese horror flick. With an obscene gurgle, the rest of the car followed. Lake water gushed from the car body and from the open door on the passenger side.

"Okay! Hold it!" someone yelled.

The maroon sedan halted, drowned and streaming, on the brush-covered shore. Workers grouped around it. Two attendants unlimbered a stretcher from the ambulance. Russ wanted to vomit.

"Not inside!" a patrolman called up to them.

The diver pushed back his face mask. "Didn't see him in there before we started hauling either."

"Take another look around where he went in," Saunders advised. "Someone call in and have the Rescue Squad ready to start dragging at daylight."

"He never would wear his seat belt," Russ muttered.

Saunders's beefy frame shrugged heavily. "Don't guess it would have helped this time. Lake's deep here along the bluff. May have to wait till the body floats up somewhere." He set his jaw so tight his teeth grated. "Goddamn it to hell."

"We don't know he's dead for sure." Russ's voice held faint hope.

Sloshing and clanking, the Buick floundered up the lakeshore and onto the narrow blacktop. The door was sprung open, evidently by the impact. The front end was badly mauled—grille smashed and hood buckled—from collision with the guardrail and underbrush. Several branches were jammed into the mangled wreckage. A spiderweb spread in an ominous pattern across the windshield on the driver's side.

Russ glowered at the sodden wreck, silently damning it for murdering its driver. Curtiss had always sworn by Buicks—had driven them all his life. Trusted the car. And the wallowing juggernaut had plunged into Fort Loundon Lake like a chrome-trimmed coffin.

Saunders tried the door on the driver's side. It was jammed. Deep gouges scored the sheet metal on that side.

"What's the white paint?" Mandarin pointed to the crumpled side panels.

"From the guardrail. He glanced along that post there as he tore through. Goddamn it! Why can't they put up modern guardrails along these back roads! This didn't have to happen!"

Death is like that, Russ thought. It never had to happen the way it did. You could always go back over the chain of circumstances leading up to an accident, find so many places where things could have turned out okay. Seemed like the odds were tremendous against everything falling in place for the worst.

"Maybe he got out," he whispered.

Saunders started to reply, looked at his face, kept silent.

V

It missed the morning papers, but the afternoon *News-Sentinel* carried Stryker's book-jacket portrait and a few paragraphs on page one, a photograph of the wreck and a short continuation of the story on the back page of the first section. And there was a long notice on the obituary page.

Russ grinned crookedly and swallowed the rest of his drink. Mechanically he groped for the Jack Daniel's bottle and poured another over the remains of his ice cubes. God. Half-a-dozen errors in the obituary. A man gives his whole life to writing, and the day of his death they can't even get their information straight on his major books.

The phone was ringing again. Expressionlessly Mandarin caught up the receiver. The first score or so times he'd still hoped he'd hear Curtiss's voice—probably growling something like: "The rumors of my death have been greatly exaggerated." Eventually he'd quit hoping.

"Yes. Dr Mandarin speaking."

(Curtiss had always ribbed him. "Hell, don't tell them who you are until they tell you who's calling.")

"No. They haven't found him yet."

("Hot as it is, he'll bob up before long," one of the workers had commented. Saunders had had to keep Russ off the bastard.)

"Yeah. It's a damn dirty shame. I know how you feel, Mrs. Hollister."

(You always called him a hack behind his back, you bloated bitch.)

"No I can't say what funeral arrangements will be made."

(Got to have a body for a funeral, you stupid bitch.)

"I'm sure someone will decide something."

(Don't want to be left out of the social event of the season, do you?)

"Well, we all have to bear up somehow, I'm sure."

(Try cutting your wrists.)

"Uh-huh. Goodbye, Mrs. Hollister."

Jesus! Mandarin pushed the phone aside and downed his drink with a shudder. No more of this!

He groped his way out of his office. That morning he'd canceled all his appointments; his section of the makeshift clinic was deserted. Faces from the downstairs rooms glanced at him uneasily as he swept down the stairs. Yes, he must look pretty bad.

Summer twilight was cooling the grey pavement furnace of the University section. Russ tugged off his wrinkled necktie, stuffed it into his hip pocket. With the determined stride of someone in a hurry to get someplace, he plodded down the cracked sidewalk. Sweat quickly sheened his blue-black stubbled jaw, beaded his forehead and eyebrows. Damp hair clung to his neck and ears. Dimly he regretted that the crew cut of his college days was no longer fashionable.

Despite his unswerving stride, he had no destination in mind. The ramshackle front of the Yardarm suddenly loomed before him, made him aware of his surroundings. Mandarin paused a moment by the doorway. Subconsciously he'd been thinking how good a cold beer would taste, and his feet had carried him over the familiar route. With a grimace, he turned away. Too many memories haunted the Yardarm.

He walked on. He was on the Strip now. Student bars, bookshops, drugstores, clothing shops, and other student-oriented businesses. Garish head shops and boutiques poured out echoes of incense and rock music. Gayle Corrington owned a boutique along here, he recalled—he dully wondered which one.

Summer students and others of the University crowd passed along the sidewalks, lounged in doorways. Occasionally someone recognized him and called a greeting. Russ returned a dumb nod, not wavering in his mechanical stride. He didn't see their faces.

Then someone had hold of his arm.

"Russ! Russ, for God's sake! Hold up!"

Scowling, he spun around. The smooth-skinned hand anchored to his elbow belonged to Royce Blaine. Mandarin made his face polite as he recognized him. Dr. Blaine had been on the medicine house staff during Mandarin's psychiatric residency. Their acquaintance had not died out completely since those days.

"Hello, Royce."

The internist's solemn eyes searched his face. "Sorry to bother you at a time like now, Russ," he apologized. "Just wanted to tell you we were sad to hear about your friend Stryker. Know how good a friend of yours he was."

Mandarin mumbled something appropriate.

"Funeral arrangements made yet, or are they still looking?"

"Haven't found him yet."

His face must have slipped its polite mask. Blaine winced.

"Yeah? Well, just wanted to let you know we were all sorry. He was working on a new one, wasn't he?"

"Right. Another book on the occult."

"Always thought it was tragic when an author left his last book unfinished. Was it as good as his others?"

"I hadn't seen any of it. I believe all he had were notes and a few chapters rough."

"Really a damn shame. Say, Russ—Tina says for me to ask you how about dropping out our way for dinner some night. We don't see much of you these days—not since you and Alicia used to come out for fish fries."

"I'll take you up on that some night," Russ temporized.

"This week maybe?" Blaine persisted. "How about Friday?"

"Sure. That'd be fine."

"Friday, then. 6:30, say. Time for a happy hour."

Mandarin nodded and smiled thinly. Blaine squeezed his shoulder, gave him a sympathetic face, and scurried off down the sidewalk. Mandarin resumed his walk.

The hot afternoon sun was in decline, throwing long shadows past the mismatched storefronts and deteriorating houses. Russ was dimly aware that his feet were carrying him along the familiar path to Stryker's office. Did he want to walk past there? Probably not—but he felt too apathetic to redirect his course.

The sun was behind the old drugstore whose second floor housed a number of small businesses, and the dirty windows of Stryker's office lay in shadow. Behind their uncurtained panes, a light was burning.

Mandarin frowned uncertainly. Curtiss never left his lights on. He had an obsession about wasting electricity.

Leaning heavily on the weathered railing, Russ climbed the outside stairway that gave access to the second floor. Above, a dusty hallway led down the center of the building. Several doorways opened off either side. A tailor, a leather shop, several student-owned businesses—which might or might not reopen with the fall term. Only Frank the Tailor was open for the summer, and he took Mondays off.

Dust and silence and the stale smell of disused rooms. Stryker's office was one of the two which fronted the street. It was silent as the rest of the hallway of locked doors, but light leaked through the not-quite-closed doorway.

Mandarin started to knock, then noticed the scars on the doorjamb where the lock had been forced. His descending fist shoved the door open.

Curtiss's chair was empty. No one sat behind the scarred desk with its battered typewriter.

Russ glanced around the barren room with its cracked plaster and book-laden, mismatched furniture. Anger drove a curse to his lips.

Stryker's office had always been in total disorder; now it looked like it had been stirred with a stick. Whoever had ransacked the office had done a thorough job.

VI

Through the Yardarm jukebox Johnny Cash was singing "Ring of Fire" for maybe the tenth time that evening. Some of those patrons who had hung around since nightfall were beginning to notice.

Ed Saunders hauled his hairy arms out of the sleeves of his ill-fitting suit coat, slung the damp garment over the vacant chair beside him. He leaned over the beer-smeared table, truculently intent, like a linebacker in a defensive huddle.

"It still looks completely routine to me, Russ," he concluded.

Mandarin poked a finger through the pile of cold, greasy pizza crusts, singing an almost inaudible chorus of "down, down, down, in a burnin' ring of far . . ." A belch broke off his monotone, and he mechanically fumbled through the litter of green Rolling Rock bottles for one that had a swallow left. Blackie the bartender was off tonight, and his stand-in had no conception of how to heat a frozen pizza. Mandarin's throat still tasted sour, and he felt certain a bad case of heartburn was building up.

The bottles all seemed empty. He waved for two more, still not replying to Saunders's assertion. A wavy-haired girl, braless in a tank top, carried the beers over to them—glanced suspiciously at Saunders while she made change. Mandarin slid the coins across the rough boards and eyed the jukebox speculatively.

The city detective sighed. "Look, Russ—why don't you let Johnny Cash catch his breath, what do you say?"

Russ grinned crookedly and turned to his beer. "But it wasn't routine," he pronounced, tipping back the bottle. His eyes were suddenly clear.

Saunders made an exasperated gesture. "You know, Russ, we got God knows how many break-ins a week in this neighborhood. I talked to the investigating officer before I came down. He handled it okay."

"Handled it like a routine break-in—which it wasn't," Mandarin doggedly pointed out.

The lieutenant pursed his lips and reached for the other beer—his second against Mandarin's tenth. Maybe, he mused, it was pointless to trot down here in response to Mandarin's insistent phone call. But he liked the psychiatrist, understood the hell of his mood. Both of them had known Curtiss Stryker as a friend.

He began again. "By our records, two of the other shops on that floor have been broken into since spring. It goes on all the time around here—I don't have to tell you about this neighborhood. You got a black slum just a few blocks away, winos and bums squatting in all these empty houses here that ought to be torn down. Then there's all these other old dumps, rented out full of hippies and junkies and God knows what. Hell, Russ—you know how bad it is. That clinic of yours—we have to just about keep a patrol car parked in front all night to keep the junkies from busting in, and then the men have to watch sharp or they'll lose their hubcaps just sitting there."

Mandarin reflected that the cessation of break-ins was more likely due to the all-night talking point now run by university volunteers at the community clinic—and that the patrol car seemed more interested in observing callers for potential dope busts than in discouraging prowlers. Instead, he said: "That's my point, Ed. Routine break-ins follow a routine pattern. Rip off a TV, stereo, small stuff that can easily be converted into cash. Maybe booze or drugs, if any's around. Petty theft.

"Doesn't hold for whoever hit Stryker's office. Hell, he never kept anything around there to attract a burglar."

"So the burglar made a mistake. After all, he couldn't know what was there until he looked."

Russ shook his head. "Then he would have taken the typewriter—beat up as it is—or finished the half bottle of Gallo sherry Curtiss had on the shelf. Doubt if he would have recognized any of his books as worth stealing, but at least he would have taken something for his trouble."

"Probably knew the stuff wasn't worth the risk of carrying off," the detective pointed out. "Left it to try somewhere else. Looked like the door on the leather shop was jimmied, though we haven't contacted the guy who leases it. It's a standard pattern, Russ. Thief works down a hallway room by room until he gets enough or someone scares him off. Probably started at Stryker's office, gave it up and was working on another door when he got scared off."

"Ed, I know Curtiss's office as well as I know my own. Every book in that place had been picked up and set down again. Someone must have spent an hour at it. Everything had been gone through."

"Well, I've been up in his office before, too," Saunders recalled, "and I'd be surprised if anyone could remember what kind of order he kept his stuff in—if there *was* any order I don't know—maybe the thief was up on his rare books. Say he was scanning title pages for first editions or something."

"Then he passed up a nice copy of Lovecraft's *The Outsider* that would have brought him a couple hundred bucks."

"Did he? I never heard of it. I meant stuff like Hemingway and all—things you'd likely know were valuable. Or maybe he was just checking for money. Lot of people keep maybe ten or twenty dollars lying around the office for emergencies—stuck back in a drawer, behind a picture, inside a book or something."

Mandarin snorted and finished his beer. He signaled for two more despite the other's protest.

"Look, Russ," Saunders argued gently, "why are you making such a big thing out of this? So far as we can tell, nothing was taken. Just a simple case of break and enter—thief looks the place over a bit, then gives up and moves on. It's routine."

"No, it isn't." Mandarin's thin face was stubborn. "And something was missing. The place was too neat, that's the conclusion. Usually Curtiss had the place littered with notes, pieces of clippings, pages of manuscript, wadded-up rough drafts—you've seen how it is. Now his desk is clean, stuff's been picked up off the floor and shelves. All of it gone—even his wastebaskets!"

"Do you want to report a stolen wastebasket, Russ?" Saunders asked tiredly.

"Goddamn it all, can't you put it together? Somebody broke into Curtiss's office, spent a good deal of time gathering up all of his notes and pages of manuscript—all of it, even the scrap paper—then piled it into the wastebasket and walked out. Who'd stop a man who was walking down the alley with a wastebasket full of paper?"

Saunders decided he'd have that third beer—if for no better reason than to keep the psychiatrist from downing it. "Russ, it seems to me you're ignoring the obvious. Look, you've been gone for a few days, right? Now isn't it pretty likely that Curtiss just decided to tidy the place up? So he goes through all his stuff, reorganizes things, dumps all his scrap paper and old notes into the wastebasket, sets the wastebasket out to be picked up, and takes the stuff he's working on for the moment on home with him."

"That place hasn't been straightened out in years—since the fire inspectors got on his ass."

"So he figured it was high time. Then later some punk breaks in, sees there's nothing there for him, moves on. Why not, Russ?"

Mandarin seemed to subside. "Just doesn't feel right to me, is all," he muttered.

"So why would somebody steal Curtiss's scrap paper, can you tell me?"

Mandarin scowled at his beer.

"Morbid souvenir hunters? Spies trying to intercept secret information? Maybe it was ghosts trying to recover forbidden secrets? Hell, Russ—you've been reading too many of Stryker's old thrillers."

"Look, I don't know the motives or the logic involved," Russ admitted grandiosely. "That's why I say it *isn't* routine."

The detective rolled his eyes and gave it up. "All right, Russ. I can't go along with your half-assed logic, but I'll make sure the department checks into this to the best of our ability. Good enough?"

"Good enough."

Saunders grunted and glanced at his watch. "Look, Russ. I got to make a phone call before I forget. What do you say you wait around and after I get through I'll run you on back to your place?"

"My car's just over at the clinic."

"Are you sure . . .?"

"Hell, I can drive. Few beers don't amount to anything."

"Well, wait here a minute for me," urged Saunders, deciding to argue it later. He lifted his sweaty bulk from the chair's sticky vinyl and made for the pay phone in the rear of the bar.

Mandarin swore sourly and began to stuff the rinds of pizza crust into one of the empty bottles. Heartburn, for sure. He supposed he ought to get headed home.

"Well, well, well. Dr. Mandarin, I presume. This is a coincidence. Holding office hours here now, Doctor?"

Russ glowered upward. A grinning face leaned over the table. Russ continued to glower.

Natty in double-knit slacks and sport shirt, Brooke Hamilton dropped onto Saunders's vacated chair. "Rather thought I'd find you here, actually," he confided. "Believe you and the old man used to drop by here regularly, right?"

Hamilton was drinking beer in a frosted mug. It made an icy puddle on the cigarette-scarred tabletop. Mandarin had a private opinion of people who drank beer in frosted mugs.

"Really a shock hearing about old Stryker," Hamilton went on. "Really too bad—though I'm sure a man like Stryker never would have wanted to die in bed. A man of action, old Curtiss. A living legend now passed on to the realm of legends. Yes, we're all going to miss the old man. Not many of the old pulp greats left around. Well, *sic transit.*" He made a toast.

Mandarin did not join him. He had met Hamilton at various cocktail parties and writers' symposiums around the University. He was quite popular in some circles—taught creative writing, edited several "little magazines" and writers' projects, was prominent at gatherings of regional writers and camp followers. His own writing consisted of several startlingly bad novels published by various local presses—often after Hamilton had cornered their editors at some cocktail affair.

Stryker had loathed him—calling him at one such gathering an ingratiating, self-serving, conceited phony. Hamilton had been within earshot, but chose not to hear. Their admiration was mutual. Since Hamilton was in the habit of referring to Stryker as an over-the-hill pulp hack, Mandarin was not moved by the man's show of grief.

"Where's the funeral, Dr. Mandarin—or do you know?"

Mandarin shook his head, measuring the distance to the other man's Kirk Douglas chin. "No body found yet," he said.

"Well, I suppose they'll have some sort of memorial service before long, whatever. Give the writers' community opportunity to pay our last respects to the old man. Professor Kettering has asked me to act as spokesman for the University. A little tribute for the school paper, and I suppose I'll say a few words at the memorial service. Old Stryker is going to be missed by those of us who carry on."

"I'm sure."

"Thought I might get you to fill me in on a few details of his career, if you don't mind. After all, you saw a lot of the old man here in his last years." Hamilton glanced pointedly at the litter of beer bottles. "But I can catch you another time."

Mandarin grunted noncommittally.

"One thing I did want to ask though. Has old Stryker finished that last book he was working on?"

"No, he was still working on it last time I saw him."

"Oh, you don't think he did. Christ, isn't it tragic to think of all the unfinished work his pen will never take up again. And just when Stryker was as popular with readers as he ever was in the golden age of the pulps."

"Damn shame."

Hamilton nodded gravely. "Yes, it is a shame. You know, I was over at the Frostfire Press this morning, talking with Morris Sheldon about it. Christ, they're all so down about it over there. But we got to talking, and Morris suddenly came out and said: 'Brooke, how'd you like to edit a memorial volume for old Stryker?' You know, sort of an anthology of his best stuff, and I'd write the introduction—a short biography and criticism of his work. Well, I told him I'd be honored to do it for old Stryker, maybe even edit a few of his last, unfinished works for publication.

"Well, this started Morris thinking still further, and all of a sudden he came out and said: 'Brooke, there's no reason Stryker's public has to be deprived of these last few masterworks. He always made extensive notes, and you were always close to him as a writer and friend . . .'"

"You son of a bitch."

"How's that?"

"You ass-kissing, cocksucking son of a bitch." Mandarin's voice was thick with rage.

Hamilton drew himself up. "Now hold it there, Mandarin." In his egotism it had not occurred to him that Mandarin might resent his assumption of role as Stryker's literary heir. But he was confident of his ability to destroy the other man in any verbal duel—his wit, termed variously "acid" or "rapier," had dazzled his fans at many a social function.

Heads were turning, as both men came to their feet in an angry crouch.

"You ass-licking fake! You couldn't write your name and phone number on a shit house wall! And after all the snotty condescension you had for Stryker, you're stealing his name and his work before his grave's even been spaded!"

"I don't have to take that—even from a drunk!" Hamilton snarled. "Although I understand I'm not likely to ever find you sober."

The distance to his movie-star chin had already been noted. Mandarin reached across the table, put a fist there.

Hamilton sat down, hard. The rickety chair cracked under him. Arms flailing, he hit the floor in a tangle of splintered wood. The beer stein smashed against the dirty concrete.

Anger burned the dazed look from his eyes. Accustomed to urbane exchanges of insults at cocktail parties and catfights, Hamilton had not expected the manners of a barroom brawl. "You goddamn drunk!" he spat, struggling to rise.

Mandarin, who before medical school had spent a lot of Saturday nights in Montana saloons, was not a gentleman. He waited until Hamilton had risen halfway from the wreckage of his chair, then put another straight right to his chin. Hamilton went down again.

The writer shook the stars from his head and came up frothing mad. He was only five years or so older than Mandarin and of approximate physical size. Regular workouts at the faculty health club had hardened his body into the finely tuned fighting machine of the heroes of his novels. Now he discarded his initial intent of dispatching his drunken opponent with a few precisely devastating karate blows.

The beer stein had shattered with a jagged chunk still attached to its handle. Hamilton rolled to his feet, gripping the handle in his fist like a pair of brass knuckles.

Mandarin, unhappy that he had not had more on his punches, cleared the end of the table with no apparent intention of helping the other man to his feet. Hamilton's fist with its jagged knuckle-duster slashed at his face.

Rolling under the punch, Russ blocked Hamilton's arm aside and threw a shoulder into his chest. They smashed to the floor, Mandarin on top with a knee planted in the other man's belly.

Breath whooshed from the writer's lips as his head cracked against the floor. Mandarin took the broken stein away from him, grinned down at his pinned opponent. Hamilton gave a hoarse bleat of fear.

"Jesus H. Christ! Russ, stop it!"

Saunders shouldered through the crowd, caught Russ's arm in a shovel fist, hauled the two men apart. His interference was booed.

Groggily, Hamilton came to his feet, his face astonishingly pale. He glared at Mandarin, struggling to break away from the burly detective, decided not to risk a punch against him.

"Call the police!" he said shakily. "This man attacked me!"

"I'm a policeman, buddy!" Saunders growled. "What I saw was this man disarming you after you tried to jam a busted bottle in his face! Want to take out a warrant?"

The writer composed himself, massaging his bruised chin. "A policeman? Yes, I believe I recognize you now. One of the late Curtiss Stryker's night-school protégés, I recall. No doubt you learned more effective ways of writing parking tickets, officer—although it's always encouraging to see one of your sort trying to improve his mind."

"Ask him if he's stolen any good wastebaskets lately," Mandarin suggested, wriggling out of the detective's grasp.

"Very clever, aren't we," Hamilton sneered. "I wonder what the state medical association will say about an alcoholic psychiatrist who gets into barroom brawls?"

"I wonder what the English department will say about faggot faculty members who try to chop a man's face up with a busted beer stein?" Saunders wondered.

Hamilton brushed himself off, his smile supercilious. "Well, I can see there's no point taking out a warrant when the arresting officer is a personal friend of the guilty party."

He turned to the onlookers. "You see the kind of police protection our community enjoys. I leave you to judge!"

"Hit him again, Doc!" Someone yelled from across the bar. "We'll keep the pig from pulling you off before you're finished!"

Hamilton's face turned pale again.

"I think you'd better get going," Saunders warned. "Russ, get back here!"

"We shall, of course, take this up again when we aren't immersed in the rabble," Hamilton promised, moving for the door.

"Oh, to be sure!" Mandarin mimicked.

The writer swept out the door to a chorus of catcalls.

"Okay, what started that!" Saunders demanded, picking up his coat.

The wavy-haired barmaid had brought Mandarin another beer. He was toasting her with a pleased expression on his stubbled face. Despite his annoyance, Saunders reflected that it was the first smile he'd seen from the psychiatrist since the accident.

"That son of a bitch Hamilton, " Mandarin informed him, "that piece of shit—he's talked Stryker's publisher here into letting him edit Curtiss's last work—do a memorial volume and shit like that! Hell, you know how he and Curtiss felt about each other. Ed, get your fingerprint men up to Stryker's office. You'll find Hamilton's sticky little fingers were all over the place."

"Let's not get started on that one again," Saunders told him wearily.

"Bet you dollars to dog shit, and you can hold the stakes in your mouth."

"Come on, Russ. I'll drop you off."

Protesting, Mandarin let himself be led away.

VII

"What's the matter?"

Mandarin had paused with his hand on the door of Saunders's Ford. He stared out across the parking lot. "Somebody's following us. Just saw his shadow duck behind that old VW van. If it's that son of a bitch Hamilton looking for more trouble . . ."

Saunders followed Mandarin's gaze, saw nothing. "Oh hell, get in, Russ! Jesus, you're starting to sound paranoid!"

"There's somebody there," Russ insisted. "Follow us from the Yardarm."

"Some damn hippie afraid of a bust," Saunders scoffed. "Will you just get in!"

His expression wounded, Mandarin complied.

Backing the Ford out of the parking place, Saunders turned down Forest Avenue. Mandarin took a last swig from the Rolling Rock he had carried with him from the bar, then struck his arm out and fired the green bottle in the general direction of his imagined skulker. From the darkness came the rattle of breaking glass.

"Ka-pow!" echoed Russ.

Saunders winced and drove on in silence.

"Hey, you went past the clinic," Russ protested several blocks later.

"Look, I'll run you back down in the morning."

"I can drive okay."

"Will you let me do this as a favor?" Saunders asked, not making it clear whose favor he meant it to be.

Mandarin sighed and shrugged. "Home, James."

Pressing his lips tightly, the detective turned onto Kingston Pike.

After a while he said: "You know, Russ, there's several on the force who'd really like to put your ass in a sling. Drunken driving is a really tough charge."

When Mandarin started to argue, Saunders shouted him down. "Look, Russ. I know this is rough on you. It is on all of us who knew Curtiss. But damn it, this isn't going to make it any better for you. I thought you finally learned that for yourself after Alicia . . ."

"Goddamn it, Ed! Don't *you* start lecturing me now!"

"Okay, Russ," his friend subsided, remembering the hell Mandarin had gone through three years before. "Just wanted to remind you that you'd tried this blind alley once before."

"Ed, I drink only socially these days." He waited for the other to say something, finally added: "Except for an occasional binge, maybe."

"Just trying to make a friendly suggestion."

"Well, I can do without friendly suggestions."

"Okay, Russ."

They drove the rest of the way in silence. Saunders expected the psychiatrist to drop off, but the other sat rigidly upright all the way. Too much adrenaline, Saunders decided.

He pulled into the long driveway of Mandarin's Cherokee Hills estate. It was a rambling Tudor-style house of the 1920s, constructed when this had been the snob residential section of Knoxville. Although most of the new money had now moved into the suburbs, Cherokee Hills had resisted urban decay with stately aloofness.

"I'll give you a ring in the morning," Saunders promised.

"It's all right; I'll call a cab," muttered Russ.

Saunders shrugged. "Good night, Russ."

He climbed out of the car. "Sure."

Saunders waited until he was in the front door before driving off.

The phone started to ring while Russ was dropping Alka-Seltzers into a highball glass. Holding the frothing glass carefully, he picked up the receiver.

"Hello." He wondered if he could finish the conversation before the tablets finished their dancing disintegration.

"Dr. Mandarin?"

"Speaking." He didn't recognize the voice.

"This is Morris Sheldon from the Frostfire Press. Been trying to get in touch with you this evening."

"Yeah? Well, what can I do for you, Morris old buddy?"

"Well, I know you were close to poor Curtiss Stryker. I believe he mentioned to me that you were giving him some medical opinions relative to the research he was doing on this last book."

"I was," Russ acknowledged, taking time for a swallow of Alka-Seltzer.

"Do you know how far along he'd gotten before the accident?"

"Well now, you probably know better than I. All I'd seen were several of the early chapters."

"I'd wondered if you perhaps had seen the rough draft of the chapters you were involved in."

"The poltergeist house? No, didn't know he'd had time to put that in rough draft yet."

"Yes, he had. At least he said so in our last conversation."

"Well, that's news to me. I was out of town the last couple days." Mandarin downed the last of the seltzer. "Why do you ask?"

Sheldon paused. "Well, frankly I'd hoped Curtiss might have passed a carbon of it on to you. He didn't send me the typescript. And we're rather afraid it was with his papers when the accident occurred. If so, I'm afraid his last chapter has been lost forever."

"Probably so," Russ agreed, his voice carefully civil. "But why are you concerned?"

"Well, as a friend of Curtiss you'll be glad to know that Frostfire Press had decided not to let his last book go unfinished. We've approached his close friend and colleague, Brooke Hamilton . . ."

"Oh," said Mandarin, revelation dawning in his voice. "Hey, you mean his confidant and bosom pal, Brooke Hamilton, hopes to use Stryker's notes and all for a posthumous collaboration?"

"That's right," Sheldon agreed. "And naturally we want to locate as much of Stryker's material as we can."

"Well, then you're in luck, Morris old buddy. Stryker's dear friend, that critically acclaimed writer and all around *bon vivant*, Brooke Hamilton, was so overcome with grief at his mentor's death that he wasted no time in breaking into Stryker's office and stealing every shred of Stryker's unpublished writing. Just give him time to sort through the wastebasket, and dear old Brooke will keep you in posthumous collaborations for the next ten years."

"Now wait, Dr. Mandarin! You mean you're accusing Brooke Hamilton of . . ."

"Of following his natural talents. And may the pair of you be buggered in Hell by ghouls! Good night, Morris old buddy."

He slammed the receiver over Sheldon's rejoinder, and swore for a while.

Returning to the sink, he carefully rinsed his glass, then added a few ice cubes. There was bourbon in the decanter.

Sipping his drink, he collapsed on the den couch and glared at the silent television screen. He didn't feel like watching the idiot tube tonight. Nor did he care to go to bed, despite extended lack of sleep. His belly felt sour, his head ached. He was too damn mad and disgusted to relax.

Ghouls. All of them. Gathering for the feast. *More Haunted Houses of the South*, by Curtiss Stryker and Brooke Hamilton. Probably they'd already approached Stryker's agent, set up a contract. Stryker would spin in his grave. If he ever reached his grave.

Mandarin wondered if he ought to phone Stryker's agent and protest—then remembered that he had no idea who his agent had been. No, make that *was*, not *had been*. As a literary property, Curtiss Stryker was suddenly more alive than before.

Sheldon would know who the agent was. Maybe he should phone and ask. Russ discarded the idea. Who was he to protest, anyway? Just another obnoxious "friend of the deceased."

His thoughts turned to Stryker's unfinished book, to the missing last chapter. Curtiss had promised to give him the carbon. Probably Hamilton had made off with that along with his other tomb spoils.

Maybe not.

Stryker kept a file of all his more recent manuscripts. A big filing cabinet in his study at home. Sometimes he worked there at night—when he was pushed by a deadline, or really caught up in something.

Russ hauled himself to his feet. A picture was taking shape. Stryker, due at a friend's home for dinner, knowing he wouldn't be back until late. But too interested in his new chapter to leave the material in his office. Instead he brings his notes home and works on the manuscript until time to leave. Had anyone thought to check his study?

Someone would soon—if they hadn't already. Climbing the stairs to his bedroom, Russ fumbled through his dresser. There it was—in a box crammed mostly with cuff links, tie tacks, and spare keys. The key to his house that Stryker had given him once when the author left for several months' knocking about Mexico.

A look of angry resolve on his black-stubbled jaw, Mandarin snatched up the key and stalked to the garage. The battery was low in the old GTO that he'd kept because it had been Alicia's favorite car, but the engine caught at the last moment. With an echo of throaty exhaust, he backed out of the garage.

His plans were only half-formulated, as he carefully steered the rumbling Pontiac through the downtown streets. He meant to check Stryker's study immediately, however. If the chapter manuscripts were there, he'd take it to read, and Brooke Hamilton could go to hell. And if he didn't find the manuscript—maybe that would be because somebody had already broken into the house. A horrid grin twisted Mandarin's face. He'd like for that to be the case. Like to show the evidence to Saunders, place charges against Brooke Hamilton for stealing from a dead man.

It was past 11:00, and traffic was thinning out—for which Russ was grateful. With far more caution than was his custom, he overcame his impatience and made the short drive out Lyons View Pike without mishap.

He turned into the empty drive and cut his lights. Stryker's house, an old brick farmhouse laid out in a T, hunched dark beneath huge white pines. The windows were black against the brick from the front; the remainder of the house was shadowed by the looming pines from what little moonlight the clouds hadn't kept.

Mandarin remembered a flashlight in the glove compartment and dug it out. The beam was yellow and weak, but enough to see by. Suspiciously, he played the light across the front of the house. Seeing nothing untoward, he started around back.

The front of the house was two stories and contained living quarters. Like the stem of a T, the rear section came out perpendicularly from the rest—a single-story wing that housed kitchen and storage. A side porch came off from one side of the kitchen wing, where Stryker and Russ had spent many a summer evening, slouched in wooden rockers and with something cold to drink.

Having seen nothing out of the ordinary, Russ crossed the unscreened porch to the kitchen door, jabbed his key at the lock. As he fumbled for the knob, the door nudged open.

Mandarin brought up his flashlight. The old-fashioned latch had been forced.

He breathed a silent curse. Stealthily he pushed open the door, stepped inside.

Thunder spat flame from across the room. Russ pitched backward onto the porch, and the flame burst across his skull.

VIII

She was the most beautiful, and at the same time the most frightening, woman Mandarin had ever seen. She danced in a whirl of blue, how could his heart forget? Blue were the skies, and blue were her eyes, just like the blue skirt she wore . . .

And she whispered to him as she waltzed, and the things she whispered to him were beautiful, and Mandarin wanted to hear more, even though her whispers terrified him.

And the more she danced and whispered and sang, the worse his vertigo became, and he was dizzy and falling, and he was clutching at her blue skirt to keep from falling, and she kept dancing away from him, and he cried out to her to come back . . .

He didn't understand . . .

But he *had* to understand . . .

"Come back!" he screamed. His voice was a tortured rasp.

The blue light became a lance of blue flame, searing his brain. And her hands of coldest ice pierced through him and seized upon his soul, and the blue lady was drawing him away, pulling him through the darkness . . .

Dimly, through the haze of throbbing pain, Mandarin became aware of the man bending over him.

Gritting his teeth, he forced his eyes to focus. It was hard. A bright beam of light bored into his face.

"Christ! He's coming around, Sid!"

The light swept away.

Mandarin struggled to rise—groaned and fell back. Bright flashes of pain rippled from the numbing ache of his skull.

"Just stay put, buddy. Jesus! We thought you were . . ."

Russ's vision was clearing. Blotchy green afterimages swam across his eyes. But he saw the patrolman's uniform, and the rising wave of panic subsided.

"Neighbor says she knows who he is, Hardin." The other voice drifted from farther away. "He's a friend of the guy who owned this place. Drops by every week or so."

Russ dully recognized the floor of Stryker's side porch spread out around him. It was damp and sticky. He could hear a woman's voice speaking from the kitchen, though he couldn't follow her words.

"I think the bullet must've just grazed the top his forehead," the first man called out. "There's blood all over the back of his head, but it looks like he just busted his scalp open falling back against the post here. You're one lucky hard-headed bastard, buddy."

His partner was examining Russ's billfold. "Name's Dr. Russell Mandarin. He's that shrink friend of Lieutenant Saunders, I think. Hope that's the ambulance I hear coming. He's been out a damn long time."

"I'm all right," protested Mandarin without conviction. He tried again to rise, made it to his knees. The porch seemed to whirl and pitch. He shut his eyes hard and waited.

An arm steadied his shoulder. "Maybe you better stay down, buddy. You got blood leaking all across the back of your head."

Doggedly Mandarin got his feet under him, lurched onto a porch rocker. The chair almost tipped, then steadied. With careful fingers he touched his forehead, found pain there. His hair was clotted with blood. Squinting across the narrow porch, Russ saw the support post opposite the back door. He remembered a gunshot, and falling backward. He must have bashed his head against the oak pillar.

"Dr. Mandarin? Are you all right?"

Russ recognized Mrs. Lieberman, Stryker's closest neighbor. Russ had often kidded Stryker that the widow had designs on him, and Stryker would always reply that only a cad tells.

"I heard that loud old car of yours turn into Mr. Stryker's driveway," she was saying. "And then I heard a shot. I thought it must be a gang of burglars, and so I called the police."

"And it's good you did, ma'am. They might have finished the job on your friend here otherwise."

The one called Hardin looked down the driveway. "Here's the ambulance—and our backup, now that we don't need it."

"I think I heard them miss the turnoff twice," his partner replied.

"What's happening?" Mandarin asked, recovering enough to become aware of his situation.

"You been shot, Doc, but you're going to be all right now."

"Shot?"

"Reckon you busted in on whoever it was that'd broke into the house. Can't see that anything's taken, but the place is sure a mess."

IX

Saunders was waiting for him when Mandarin got out of x-ray. Russ had insisted on viewing the films himself, after making enough of a scene that the radiologist seemed a little disappointed to find no evidence of fracture or subdural. Russ let them wheel him back down to the ER, where a nervous resident began to patch him up.

"I am goddamn glad to see you here," was Saunders's first comment.

"Same to you, sideways," Russ said. "Did you know those two clowns of yours had radioed me in as DOA? Damn lucky I didn't bleed out waiting."

"Damn lucky you got a thick skull and a hippie haircut. Somebody bounced a bullet off your head, and if they'd aimed an inch or so lower, it would've gone between your eyes instead of parting your hair. I hear you busted loose a porch rail banging it with your head afterward."

"Nothing much hurt but my good looks," Russ allowed. "They want to keep me overnight for observation, but I'm heading home from here. I can damn well observe myself—no point in being a doctor if you can't change your own oil. And don't tell me the one about '. . . has a fool for a physician.'"

Saunders was serious now. Too serious.

"Russ, I'm going to tell you that the only reason you're not headed from here to the station is because you were lying there DOA on Stryker's porch at the same time Brooke Hamilton was being murdered."

Mandarin decided he was still suffering the effects of his concussion. "What's that about Hamilton?"

Saunders was looking for a cigarette, then remembered he couldn't smoke here. "Just came from his place. A boyfriend let himself in around midnight, found Hamilton tied to a chair, throat had just been cut. And he'd been cut up pretty good elsewhere before he got his second smile. After that business this afternoon, I was afraid it was you I'd be bringing in. I was at your house when word came in that you were dead at the time of the murder. Reckon we'll hold his boyfriend now instead."

"Jesus!" Russ muttered. It was all coming too fast for him.

"These queers do some weird shit when they have their love spats," Saunders informed him. "Likely high on pot and LSD."

"I didn't know Hamilton was gay."

"No? Well, he looked queer. I can spot them. Anyway, if you hadn't been busy getting shot in the head at Curtiss's house at the time Hamilton was last seen alive, you'd be in worse trouble now."

"I think I want to go home."

"I'll see that you get there," Saunders said. "Only this time you stay put."

"Scout's honor." Russ held up three fingers.

Saunders watched him without amusement. "And when you get there, you can help fill out a report. Tell us if anything's missing."

"Missing?"

"Somebody'd broke into your house right before we got there."

X

Mandarin had a bottle of Percodan tablets for pain—contraindicated, of course, in the presence of recent head injury—and he prescribed himself a couple and washed them down with a medicinal glass of Jack Daniel's. He supposed he should sue himself for malpractice. After all, he'd only been permitted to leave the hospital after signing an "against medical advice" form. A fool for a physician.

Was it possible for a head to ache any worse than his did? He had a gash above his forehead where the bullet had grazed his scalp, a lump across the back of his skull from his fall, and a terminal hangover.

Russ almost wished his assailant had aimed lower. Saunders's people hadn't turned up any brass, and Saunders was of the opinion that Russ's attacker had got off a lucky shot with a junk .22 revolver—probably one of his hippie dope-fiend patients. Typical of the times, Saunders judged, and with our boys dying in Vietnam while scum like this dodged the draft.

Three break-ins in one night—not to mention the burglary of Stryker's office the day before—hardly seemed random, Mandarin had argued. Saunders had pointed out that these were only a few of the dozens of break-ins that took place each night, and that it was all due to drugs, and that if certain psychiatrists would stick to shrinking heads and let the police go about their business, a lot of this sort of thing would be stopped.

Russ promised to go to bed.

But neither the Percodan nor the bourbon could ease the pain in his skull. And the thoughts kept running through his brain. And every time he closed his eyes, she was there.

I dream of that night with you,

Darling, when first we met . . .

Mandarin realized that his eyes weren't closed. She was there. In his room. And she whispered to him . . .

Mandarin screamed and sat up. His drink, balanced on the back of the couch, fell over and spilled melted ice cubes onto his lap.

The dancing image faded.

Never, thought Mandarin, *never* mix Percodan and alcohol. He was shaking badly, and his feet seemed to float above the floor as he stumbled into the kitchen for another drink. Maybe he ought to take a couple Valiums. Christ, he was in worse shape now than when Alicia died.

Could a poltergeist direct a bullet?

Russ noticed that he was pouring bourbon over the top of his glass. He gulped down a mouthful, not tasting it. His hands were steadier.

Could a poltergeist direct a bullet?

Either he was succumbing to paranoid fantasies and alcoholic hallucinations, or maybe he *should* have stayed in the hospital for observation. Was he going over the edge? What the hell—he hadn't been worth shooting since Alicia died.

Someone thought he was worth shooting.

Could a poltergeist direct a bullet?

Was *he* haunted?

It wasn't random; Saunders was wrong. There was a pattern, and it had all started that afternoon when Gayle Corrington told them about her poltergeist. A ghostly lesbian who dabbled in the occult and who liked blue. The stuff of one of Stryker's pulp thrillers, but now there were two people dead, and someone—or something—had broken into the homes of everyone involved and scattered things about like a vengeful whirlwind.

Mandarin decided that a walk in the early dawn would do him good. He just might be sober by the time he reached the clinic and his car.

Could a poltergeist *deflect* a bullet?

XI

This one ends on a bright summer morning, and a fresh dew on the roses that perfume the dawn.

Russ Mandarin eased his Jensen Interceptor into the driveway and killed the engine. All at once it seemed absurdly dramatic to him. He really should have phoned Gayle Corrington before driving over to her house at this hour.

Or maybe he shouldn't have.

He closed the door quietly and walked up to the carport. The white Corvette was parked there as before, only before there hadn't been a scraping of maroon paint along its scored right front fender. Fiberglass is a bitch to touch up.

Russ tried the doorbell long enough to decide that Gayle Corrington wasn't going to answer. Either not at home (her car was still there) or a sound sleeper. Russ pounded loudly against the door. After a time his knuckles began to hurt. He stopped and thought about it.

Nothing made sense. Mandarin wished he had a drink—that was always a good answer to any crisis.

He ought to call Saunders, tell him about the maroon paint on Gayle Corrington's white Corvette. Maybe just a fender-bender, but it might match up with the crease on the left side of Stryker's Buick. And so what if it did? Curtiss was a terrible driver—he might well have paid Gayle a second visit, scraped up against her car in parking.

Nothing made sense.

Just this: Gayle Corrington had told Stryker *something* in the course of the interview—while Mandarin had been out of the room. Stryker had been excited about it, had written it into his account of the haunting. And someone had gone to a lot of trouble to make certain that whatever Stryker had discovered would never be published.

Only Gayle Corrington had freely asked Stryker to investigate her haunted house.

Nothing made sense.

Mandarin thought he heard a television set going. Maybe Gayle was around back, catching some early morning sun, and couldn't hear his knock. Worth trying.

Russ headed towards the rear of the house. As he reached the patio, he saw Prissy lying beside a holly bush. At first he thought the little border collie was asleep.

Not random. A pattern.

The sliding glass door from the patio was curtained and at first glance appeared to be closed. Russ saw that the catch had been forced, and he cautiously slid the glass panel open, stepped inside.

Gayle Corrington was wearing dark slacks and a black sweatshirt. She was hog-tied with her wrists bound back to her ankles, her body arched like a bow upon the couch. Her lips were taped with adhesive, but the cord knotted tightly into her neck would assure that she would never cry out.

Russ stared at her dumbly. He knew there was no point in searching for a pulse.

"Hello, Russ," said Stryker. "Come on in."

Russ did as he was told.

Curtiss Stryker was straightening out from where he worked over the brick hearth. The hearth had been lifted away, revealing an opening beneath the floor.

"Used brick hearth on a mountain stone fireplace. Should have tipped me off from the first—an obvious lapse in taste." Stryker was holding a Colt Woodsman. It was pointed at Mandarin's heart.

"Rumors of my death have been greatly exaggerated," said Stryker.

"You son of a bitch," said Mandarin.

"Probably. But you just stand still where you are."

Russ nodded towards Gayle's body. "Your work?"

"Yes. While you were ringing. Just not quite in the nick of time, Doctor. But don't waste any tears on our Mrs. Corrington. She tried to kill both of us, after all—and I gather she was certain that you, at least, were most decidedly dead. This is her gun, and she would be disappointed to learn that her aim was not as infallible as she imagined."

"I don't get it," Russ said. "What are you doing?"

Stryker glanced towards the opened hearth. "Just getting a little social security. Maybe you can understand."

"I don't understand a goddamned thing! I came here to ask Gayle what it was that she told you while I was out of the room that day. Seems that a lot of people are interested."

"You might as well know," Stryker decided. "She wanted me to perform an exorcism."

"An exorcism?"

"Or something to that effect. She'd read my books on the occult, decided I was a better ghost chaser than a priest would be. Maybe she'd already tried a priest."

"I don't follow."

"Then I'll make it short and snappy."

"Is this the point in your story where the villain always explains everything to the hero before he shoots him?"

"It is. I'm afraid this story won't have a happy ending, though. After all, an author has his privileges."

"I wept for you."

"I know. I'll weep for you."

Stryker kept the Colt Woodsman steady in the direction of Mandarin's chest. Russ recalled that Curtiss had always bragged about his marksmanship.

"Our Mrs. Corrington changed a few details, and she changed a few names. She played the part of Cass in the highly revised account she gave us of this house. She and her Libby were medical secretaries. They had access to patients' records, and they knew various prominent citizens who had certain sexual quirks. Knowing their particular weaknesses, it was simple enough to lure them out here for an odd orgy or two—black magic, S&M, any sort of kink their secret selves desired. Then there were the hidden mikes and camera, the two-way mirrors. Made for some lovely footage. Here's a respected publisher who likes to dress up in women's clothing and be whipped; here's a noted doctor who prefers to give enemas to submissive girls. Maybe just a Baptist preacher who can't get a blow job from his wife. They knew about them, and preyed on them.

"But they needed another girl—another feminine one for their fantasies-delivered orgies. So they brought in a third girl—and that was a crowd. Cass—Gayle—liked her better than Libby, and Libby got jealous. She was going to blow the whistle on the entire operation unless the other girl was sent away. But that was too dangerous, and Gayle was growing tired of Libby. They had a special Black Sabbath orgy that night, and when it was over they gave Libby an injection of insulin. Your friend, Dr. Royce Blaine, didn't give any trouble over signing the death certificate; after all, he was in the photos. Later, when

Gayle grew tired of Tina, she married Dr. Blaine—probably saved her life; his too, maybe."

"But why did Mrs. Corrington call you in on this?" Russ wondered if he could jump the older man.

"Because she really did think she was being haunted. Nothing more than a nuisance, but it preyed on her nerves. So she made up this plausible story, and she reckoned I'd perform some magical miracle, just like the heroes in my stories. But she didn't reckon on how good a researcher I was. I got suspicious—you know: 'Doctor, I have this friend . . .' and it didn't take long to dig out the facts. It happened while you were off in New York."

"So then?"

"Well, I wrote down my findings, made a carbon for you, then set out for another talk with Gayle Corrington. Of course, then I didn't know about the blackmail angle—I just wanted to confront Gayle with the fact that I knew her part in the story was more than just an innocent bystander.

"She followed me after I left her house, ran me off the road into the lake. By then I knew about the blackmail—she was too upset with me to lie convincingly that night—so I thought I'd just lie doggo for a few days and see what happened. I destroyed my notes, but that little bastard Brooke Hamilton beat me to my office and stole your carbon of the chapter rough. I caught up with him last night, made him tell me where he'd hidden everything, then destroyed it all—and that little shit. In the meantime, Gayle knew of my carbons, so she was checking out my house, and afterward yours. You walked in on her at my house, and she thought she'd killed you. That's two mistakes. You should have seen her expression when she walked in here afterward. Thought she'd seen a real ghost this time."

"Just Uncle Dudley in a monster suit."

"Just like one of my old thrillers. No ghosts. Just greed. And a guilty conscience that made ghosts out of chance phenomena."

"Now what?"

"I take over the racket, that's all. After a little persuasion, Gayle told me what I already knew—that the films and tapes were all hidden in a little safe here beneath the raised hearth. I've got enough on some of our city's finest and wealthiest to retire in style. I'll just make an appearance later on today, say I was knocked for a loop by my accident, took a day or two wandering around the lakeside to remember who I was."

"What about me?"

"Now that does bother me, Russ. I hadn't counted on your dropping in like this. I think you'll be the drugged-out killer in the story—the one who conveniently takes his life when he realizes what he's done."

"Saunders won't buy that."

"Sure he will. You've been walking around town with a screw loose ever since your wife died—before that maybe. You were the one who blew her diagnosis when she complained of chronic headaches."

"I was your friend, Curtiss."

"Writers don't have friends. Only deadlines. And cheating publishers. And meddling editors. And carping reviewers. And checks that never come when they're supposed to come, and are always short when they do come. I've scraped along for a living at this damn trade for over forty years, and I'm still living hand-to-mouth, and I'm just an old hack to my fellow writers. This is my chance to make someone else pay—pay big."

Stryker steadied the pistol. "Sorry, Russ. I'll miss you. Hope you can understand."

The Victrola behind them made a rattle and whir. There was an audible *clunk* as the heavy tonearm descended.

Stryker looked towards it for an instant. Russ started to go for him. Stryker nailed him through the upper left shoulder with his first shot. Russ collapsed.

I dream of that night with you . . .

"Going to be a tough job of suicide now," Mandarin whispered.

"I'll figure something," Stryker assured him.

Blue were the skies

And blue were your eyes

Stryker leveled his pistol again. "Very interesting."

Come back, blue lady, come back

"There are too many dead!" Russ managed. "She's grown too strong."

"I never really believed in ghosts," said Stryker, lining up on Russ's heart.

Don't be blue anymore.

There was a sudden scraping at the fireplace behind them.

From its brackets, the Parker shotgun swung away from the stone wall. It seemed to hesitate an instant, then slowly fell to the hearth, stock downward.

Stryker turned to stare at it, open-mouthed in wonder. He was still gaping into its double barrels, looking down into the blackness within, when both shells fired at once.

The Naughty Step

MICHAEL MARSHALL SMITH

MICHAEL MARSHALL SMITH is a novelist and screenwriter. He has published seventy short stories and three novels: *Only Forward*, *Spares*, and *One of Us*, winning the Philip K. Dick Award, International Horror Guild Award, August Derleth Award and the Prix Bob Morane in France. He has won the British Fantasy Award for Best Short Fiction four times, more than any other author.

Writing as "Michael Marshall," he has published five international best-selling thrillers, including *The Straw Men*, *The Intruders*, *Bad Things* and, most recently, *Killer Move*. *The Intruders* is under series development with BBC Television.

Smith is currently involved in several screenwriting projects, including a television pilot set in New York and an animated horror movie for children. He currently lives in North London with his wife, son, and two cats.

"I've always found something a little spooky and disconcerting about the three words in the title of this story," confesses Smith. "I'd originally intended it to be about five thousand words long, but then suddenly realized that it might be better coming in low and fast . . ."

WHEN I AM BAD my daddy makes me sit on the naughty step. It is a funny name for a step because it is not naughty, just the step where I have to sit. It is a step near the bottom of the stairs that go from the bottom of our house up to the next floor. Because of the way our house is made, the bottom of our house is actually a bit below the street outside. But the next floor up is a little bit above the street, and so when you leave the house through the front door you have to go down a few stone steps to get to the path. I don't know why they would make a house like that, but they did, and that is where we live.

When I am on the naughty step I can see into the family room. It used to be the kitchen but someone who lived here turned the other room into the kitchen and now the kitchen is the family room. There are windows in there and I can see them through the doorway. One of the windows is brighter than the others now, and more interesting things happen through it. So when I am on the naughty step I watch that one if I can.

I am on the naughty step a lot.

At first my daddy used to only put me on it once in a while. But he says that I got naughtier and naughtier, and so I ended up sitting on here more. I think it is true that I got more naughty, but I think also he got cross more too.

The last time I was bad my daddy got so cross, much more cross than I have ever seen before. I had been very, very naughty, it is true. I had deliberately broken something that belonged to my mummy and then I hit her on the arm, but it was not hard. I was just grumpy because they would not listen to me.

But Daddy was very mad at me anyway and he looked like he was going to hit me, which he is not allowed to do, which is why we have the naughty step. He shouted and his face was red and Mummy was telling him not to shout, which was strange because she had been shouting too and just as cross as he was, but then she stopped looking cross and started to look afraid. My daddy was so angry he did not look like himself.

I don't think he hit me, but I do not remember. I am on the naughty step, so I think he must not have done.

I have to stay here until Daddy comes and tells me I can leave. Sometimes he looks sad when he comes to tell me that, and says he is sorry, but I do not believe he will do that this time. He was very, very cross.

Sometimes another boy comes to sit with me, when his daddy is mad with him, which is not very often. The boy sits right next to me. Once he sat exactly where I do but he did not like it there and moved along. I tried to talk to him but he would not answer. You are not supposed to talk when you are on the naughty step, so maybe that was it. It made me sad because it would have been nice to talk to someone. But he would not talk, so I just sit there and look through into the family room and at the window where all the different things happen.

I think you can change what you see through the bright window in the family room, but I do not know how. So I just watch whatever I can see through it.

After a while they always let the boy off the step, and he goes into the room with his mummy and daddy and they watch the window together, and soon everyone stops being cross and they laugh at what they see. I wish I could go in there with them, but I am not allowed off the naughty step and so I do not.

I cannot leave the step until my Daddy says I can.

It has been a long time now.

About the Editor

STEPHEN JONES lives in London, England. He is the winner of three World Fantasy Awards, four Horror Writers Association Bram Stoker Awards and three International Horror Guild Awards as well as being a twenty-one time recipient of the British Fantasy Award and a Hugo Award nominee. A former television producer/director and genre movie publicist and consultant (the first three *Hellraiser* movies, *Nightbreed*, *Split Second* etc.), he has written and edited more than 110 books, including *Visitants: Stories of Fallen Angels & Heavenly Hosts*, *The Dead That Walk: Zombie Stories*, *Coraline: A Visual Companion*, *The Essential Monster Movie Guide*, *Horror: 100 Best Books* and *Horror: Another 100 Best Books* (both with Kim Newman), and the *Dark Terrors*, *Dark Voices* and *The Mammoth Book of Best New Horror* series. A Guest of Honor at the 2002 World Fantasy Convention in Minneapolis, Minnesota, and the 2004 World Horror Convention in Phoenix, Arizona, he has been a guest lecturer at UCLA in California and London's Kingston University and St. Mary's University College. You can visit his web site at: *www.stephenjoneseditor.com*